Don't Believe Everything You See

by
D.A. Richardson

Don't Believe Everything You See, will take you on a roller coaster ride of love, lies and deception from an all-inclusive resort near Puerto Vallarta Mexico, to a funeral home in Denver, Colorado, and back again; when star crossed lovers are re-united only to be separated by death ... A shark attack ... or was it?

With an unexpected turn of events; a multitude of fascinating, complex characters ... each with their own motive, this mystery will leave you thinking ... and yearning for more!

Acknowledgements

I believe my best work comes from good research ... for without research ... I would have nothing to write about!

My thanks and sincere appreciation to the following:

- *Oscar Gonzalez, Angelina de la Esprillea, Abel Medina Garcia, Janet Rodgeguz and the staff of the Decameron All-Inclusive Hotels & Resorts in Bucerias, Mexico, for giving me the opportunity to go behind the scene and witness first-hand the team effort involved in successfully running a resort of this size.*

- *To Vallarta Adventures in Nuevo Vallarta, Mexico, and the tour guides who helped make my research not only informative, but a lot of fun. A special thanks to dive instructor, Jens Faustmann, for putting up with my inability to swim!*

- *Ernie Hagel, Kathy Cloutier, Leanne Macdonald, Brent Wilson, Stephanie Hulshof and the staff of McInnis and Holloway Funeral Homes in Calgary, Alberta, for showing me that funeral directors do have a sense of humor and allowing me to witness how their kindness and compassion comforts the families they serve.*

- *Glenda Stansbury and Doug Manning of Insite Books, Oklahome City, Oklahoma, for teaching me the value of a funeral celebrant.*

- *Todd Van Beck for his wonderful stories.*

- *Angel Edwin Leal Burgos for helping with my Spanish.*

1

"MS. GRANGER, WOULD YOU like another glass of champagne?"

Alex smiled up at the attractive young woman standing over her and nodded her head. "Yes, thank you. That would be great."

Alex had thought of being a stewardess once. She was twenty when she filled out an application for Trans Jet Airlines and was invited for an interview. It went well; the personnel manager offered her a job, and she was thrilled. She signed the contract, shook Bob's hand, and thanked him for the opportunity he was offering her. As she was leaving his office on her way to a uniform fitting; a handsome, blonde haired, blue eyed, six-foot pilot strolled through the door like a proud peacock. His bright, white-capped smile lit up the entire room.

"Cameron, I'd like you to meet Alex Granger," Trans Jet's personnel manager announced. "She's just joined our flight crew."

Cameron casually strolled to Alex's side and took her hand in his. He held it just a little too long while eyeing her tall, lean frame. "Welcome aboard, Alex." Cameron stepped back and made a circular motion with his finger. "Turn around, sweetheart. I want to get a good look at you." He licked his lips and grinned like a coyote in a hen house. "Oh yes, you'll fit quite nicely into our roster!"

"I hope so," Alex blushed. "I've wanted to be a stewardess since I was twelve and flew for the first time!"

Cameron took Alex by the arm and escorted her to the hunter green leather sofa. "Sit down." He sat down beside her and rested his right hand on her knee. "I'm sure Bob's told you all about the services you'll be providing." Cameron looked at the personnel manager and winked; Bob winked back.

"Oh, yes!" Alex beamed. "I'll be looking after the passengers' needs. I'll be serving them meals and offering complimentary beverages. I'll be getting them magazines and blankets and lighting their cigarettes. Basically, I'll be doing everything I can to ensure that their flight is as comfortable as possible!"

"Did Bob tell you that sometimes we get three-day layovers in rather exotic places?"

"Yes! Yes he did." The excitement rose in Alex's voice. "I can't wait! I haven't done much traveling. I grew up on a farm, but I've always wanted to travel. I love looking after people, so this job will let me do both!"

The pilot tightened his grip on Alex's knee. "Well, you know darlin', when we're on layovers, the stewardesses get a chance to service the pilots."

"Oh, I don't mind getting you beverages while you're lying by the pool!" Alex beamed.

Cameron couldn't help but laugh at the girl's innocence. "You really are from the farm, aren't you kid!" He raised a devious brow. "Sweetheart, you'll be doing more than getting us beverages. When I say you'll be servicing the pilots, I mean ... you'll be *servicing the pilots!*"

Alex cringed as Cameron's hand traveled up her leg and rested beneath the hem of her short-blue skirt. This was getting uncomfortable. Was he talking about what she thought he was talking about? What did he mean, *servicing the pilots*? She glared at the personnel manager. "What's he talking about?"

"You know, kid," Bob thrust his loins back and forth, "servicing the pilots. All our girls do it!"

Alex took a deep breath, pulled Cameron's hand from under her skirt, and abruptly stood up. "If you'll excuse me, I have to leave." She threw back her shoulders, stuck out her chest, and marched across the office. "Other girls may provide sexual favors to arrogant pilots," she announced, "but I don't!" She snatched her employment contract off Bob's desk ripped it in half, and handed it to him. "Good day gentlemen."

A slam of the door ended Alex's airline career.

***

"Your champagne, Ms. Granger."

Alex looked up at the flight attendant and smiled. "Please, call me Alex. We've been together on this plane for so long, I feel like I've known you for years!"

The young woman offered a tired sigh. "Yes. It's been a very, very long day." A passenger yelled from behind the curtain that divided first class from coach and the flight attendant glanced over her shoulder. "Unfortunately, it's not over yet. If you'll excuse me, duty calls."

Watching the young woman walk away, Alex couldn't help but wonder if flight attendants were still expected to service the pilots. Service them or not, right now, she wouldn't have wanted this girl's job for all the tea in China. Their flight from Denver to Puerto Vallarta was scheduled to land three hours ago. Five minutes from the airport, the tower called them off because of fog. The flight was rerouted to Guadalajara, where they sat on the tarmac; for what seemed an eternity, waiting to be squeezed into the line of aircraft waiting to take off. The natives were getting restless.

Several times in the past hour, Alex had heard the flight crew apologizing to the passengers in coach: "I'm terribly sorry that we're cutting into your tanning time, but unfortunately the airline has no control over the weather. No, I'm afraid that we won't be putting you up in a hotel in Guadalajara overnight, sir. I do apologize, madam, but the tower can't just delay the other traffic. We do have to wait our turn."

Alex was positive the crew would be thankful when Flight 346 came to a conclusion. When she traveled, she lived by two rules: she'd rather eat at MacDonald's than stay in a dump, and she refused to fly coach.

Reaching into her carry-on bag, Alex pulled out the travel brochure her daughter had given her at the airport and stared down at it. The Mexican vacation had been Sarah's idea: "Mom, we'll celebrate your fiftieth birthday on the beach!"

Some birthday celebration this is going to be, Alex thought. She was spending it alone. An hour before the family was leaving for the airport, her husband suddenly had a business emergency and her daughter was called back to the hospital. Alex suggested they postpone her birthday bash, but Sarah and Brian both insisted she go: "Mom, when's the last time you took time for yourself? You've been working like a dog around here lately and you need a break. Dad and I can take care of each other, and Ted can take care of everything else." After a great deal of protesting on her part and a great deal of persuasion on the part of her daughter, and her husband, Alex finally gave in and agreed to take the one-week Mexican vacation, solo.

Glancing through the brochure, Alex had to admit that *Las Tropicales* looked beautiful. There were white, sandy beaches and a turquoise blue sea. Lush vegetation was spread throughout the Mexican architecture of the property. Sarah had stayed there twice, and assured her that the all-inclusive resort was first class: "Mom, they have seven restaurants and the food is fabulous! Wait till you see the desserts! All you can eat! You have to try Picollo ... the Italian is to die for, but make reservations, first thing in the morning is usually best. Oh, and there's a Japanese restaurant too! If you eat there, which I'm sure you will, ask for Fernando. He'll take good care of you. The resort has a disco, and theme dinners, and a different show every night. The activity staff doubles as the evening entertainment. They put on a great show! There are three pools, and six bars. You can play tennis, or beach volleyball."

Sarah also suggested Alex take one of the Adventure Tours offered by the hotel. She could swim with the dolphins, go whale watching, take a sunset boat cruise, or go on a jeep tour. If she was really ambitious she could experience the canopy adventure. It looked interesting, but Alex was positive she was too old to go swinging through the trees like Tarzan, ninety feet above the forest floor.

Maybe she'd break down and use the new diving gear Brian had given her for her birthday. Alex found the gift a rather strange present. She hadn't been diving in years, not since experiencing a near drowning for the second time in her life.

The first happened when she was eight and her cousin convinced her that the entire pool was only four-feet deep. It was thirty years before Alex was convinced to get back in the water, but Brian assured her that she would love diving, and he'd been right. Diving was much easier than swimming had been and it wasn't long before Alex was spending three days a month on a dive excursion. She loved the sport and she was thrilled when Brian took her on a dive to the Great Barrier Reef for their twenty-first wedding anniversary. It was the best dive she'd ever been on. It was also her last!

Brian and Alex were down thirty feet when Alex ran out of air. She tugged at Brian's arm and gave him the signal that her tank was empty. He shook his head, pointed to his watch, and held up ten fingers. Yes, she knew she should have ten minutes of air, but her lungs told her differently. She panicked and grabbed at her husband's regulator. He pushed her away and held her down by the shoulders. The look Alex saw in his eyes told her she was going to die. When she came to, they were back on the boat. The subject of diving hadn't come up since.

Alex was sure the new diving gear was a peace offering, rather than a birthday present. When she discovered that Brian was sleeping with one of the legal assistants from her lawyer's office, it was the last straw. She told him she wanted a divorce. He begged her to forgive him, and then blamed the whole thing on the young woman: "When she came on to me, what could I do?" he'd told her with pleading eyes. "She was

talking about committing suicide. Please, Alex, give me another chance. Haven't I been good lately?"

Alex had to admit, other than Brian's most recent sexual
adventure, he had been making an attempt to change his life-
style. He'd quit drinking, at least around her. He hadn't been
to the track in months and by the looks of their joint bank
account, his cocaine habit had subsided, but she still didn't
love him. When they married, she hadn't even taken his last
name.

Brian was never attentive towards Alex, unless he wanted something, and she attributed it to the fact that he'd been
forced into wedlock. She was pregnant and the child needed
a father.

"May I take your glass, Ms. Granger?" a voice asked.

Alex looked up at the flight attendant and smiled. "I hope
you get a few days off after we land?"

"I'm afraid not," the woman frowned. "We unload, they
clean the plane, we reload, and then it's back to Denver. This
will be an eighteen-hour day by the time it's finished." She
pointed to Alex's waist. "You better fasten your seat belt. We'll
be landing any minute."

"You're sure this time?" Alex chuckled.

"Yes. This time, we will definitely be landing. Thank
God!"

Alex put away her brochure, and buckled in. As the lights
of Puerto Vallarta grew brighter in the distance, she couldn't
help but wonder how Sarah was making out. *Sarah, it seems
so funny to call her that,* Alex thought. She'd been calling
her daughter Sam from the day she was born, but the name
change had been at her daughter's request: "Mom, I'm twenty-five now, and a doctor. Maybe, I should start using my giv-
en name. Don't you think Doctor Sarah, sounds better then
Doctor Sam?"

A male voice interrupted Alex's thoughts. "Ladies and
gentlemen, this is Captain Donaldson speaking. Welcome to
Puerto Vallarta." The passengers broke into a cheer as the

wheels of the aircraft bounced on the runway. "Once again, we apologize for the delay. Unfortunately, we can't do much about the weather. We appreciate your patience and realize that most of you have probably been up since early yesterday morning and you're all tired, but please be considerate of the other passengers as you leave the aircraft.

"The buses on the tarmac will take you to the terminal. Once you've passed through customs, please pick up your luggage from the main carousel and make your way to the security counter. When you've been cleared, proceed through the terminal to the east exit. There, you'll find representatives from each of the different tour companies. They'll tell you which bus to take to get to the resort you're staying at. Enjoy your vacation, and thank you for flying with American Airlines."

Inside the terminal building, Alex approached the customs officer and handed him her passport. He scanned the document. "This is you? This doesn't look like you, *Señora*." The officer held the passport to Alex's face. He was right, it didn't. The photo was taken after she'd let a girlfriend talk her into a platinum blonde Billy Idol haircut: "Come on Alex, it will make you look younger." Younger! It made her look like an idiot.

Alex smiled politely at the customs officer and dropped her carry-on bag at her feet. "*Si, Señor, si*. It's me." She took off her glasses and pulled her hair up off her shoulders. "It's me, honest!" The guard stared at the passport and then at Alex. Without taking his eyes from her face, he stamped her tourist card and handed back the travel documents. Alex gave him a thankful smile, put her passport back in her waist pouch and made a quick exit. She found her luggage and waited in line with the other passengers to go through the security check. It took thirty minutes.

Stepping from the cool of the terminal, the heat and humidity in the air wrapped itself around Alex like an electric blanket. She took a moment to catch her breath. Already beads of perspiration were forming on her skin and she promised herself that no matter what time she got to the hotel, the first thing she'd do was have a shower.

"*Buenos dias, Señora, bienvenido,*" an attractive Latino man said with a smile as he approached her. "Where are you staying?"

"*Las Tropicales.*"

"*Si*, this is your bus. Please, your luggage. You board the bus now. We take very good care of you."

Alex gave him a tired smile and slipped him a crisp American five dollar bill.

"*Gracias*, he nodded."

"How long before we get to the hotel?" she asked.

"Forty-five minutes, *Señora*. We have other stops to make along the way. You rest. I will wake you when we arrive"

Alex found a vacant spot at the back of the travel coach, slid into the seat, and made herself comfortable. While waiting for the remaining passengers to board, she stared out the window at the lone car sitting in the middle of the empty parking lot, sleeping like most people were at this time of the morning.

"I'm over here," a female voice called out. The words were followed by a high-pitch whistle and a black Mercedes suddenly came to life. The engine turned over and the headlights flashed on. The tires screeched as the vehicle lunged forward and quickly made its way across the parking lot, pulling into the empty stall beside the bus.

Alex watched with interest when the driver's door opened and a tall, grey haired gentleman stepped out. He appeared to be in his mid-fifties. She couldn't see his face, but there was an air of sophistication in the way he moved. Her eyes followed him as he rounded the front of the vehicle and moved through the beam of the headlights. He was well turned out in taupe dress slacks and a navy blue blazer. A woman ran into his arms and they embraced. He ushered her to the passenger door, opened it, and helped her inside.

When he closed the car door and turned, Alex caught a glimpse of his face and her breath caught in her throat. "It can't be," she whispered. She pressed her face against the glass. "Sam Bennett, he looks just like Sam Bennett!" Her heart beat faster as she watched the man move around the car to the driver's door. He was tall like Sam, built like Sam, he even walked like Sam. But it couldn't be Sam ... Sam was ... dead.

A shiver ran up her spine and she gave her head a shake. It had been a very long day and now she knew she was tired ... she was seeing things. "Maybe I needed this vacation more than I realized." She checked her watch as the last passengers boarded the bus. It was five in the morning. She'd been up for almost twenty-four hours.

The driver told her the trip to *Las Tropicales* would take forty-five minutes. Maybe she'd take a *siesta*. Alex closed her eyes and rested her head on the seat. As she drifted off to sleep, visions of her first meeting with Sam Bennett filled her dreams.

***

When Alex drove through the wrought iron gates of Sundance Farms, she couldn't help but stop to admire the surrounding beauty. Massive weeping willow trees lined the winding driveway. As far as the eye could see, white-railed fences divided the rolling hills like a checkerboard, each square separating mares, from foals, and yearlings from two-year-olds. She hit the power window button and stuck her head through the opening as the pane of glass disappeared into the door panel.

A long deep breath filled her nostrils with the aroma of freshly cut hay. The sound of summer played in her ears like a symphony. Birds twittered their cheerful tunes, while cattle from her father's nearby ranch provided the horn section. In the distance, there was the faint echo of a stallion calling out to his mare.

With one more deep breath, Alex put the truck in gear and continued on her journey. Cresting the final hill of the long winding driveway, the Sandersons' impressive Georgian mansion came into view for the first time. Her eyes widened at the sight that looked as if it had just been plucked from the pages of *Better Homes and Gardens*. Proudly displayed; in the middle of the circular driveway, stood a life-size bronze statue of a jockey and his mount. The foals she had seen earlier would someday stand as proudly in the winners' circle.

Surrounding the statue, tenderly-cared-for rose bushes had been pruned into the shape of a horseshoe. Now in full bloom, they burst forth with the farm's colors of yellow and white. Fifty-feet behind, a magnificent 10,000 square foot, red brick mansion erupted in its entire splendor. Erect white pillars guarded the home's front door. There were green shutters on each window and in the middle of the second floor, a quaint Romeo-and-Juliet-style balcony built for lovers and moonlit nights.

Alex followed the driveway to the five-car garage and pulled in beside a silver grey Jaguar. She turned off the engine and reached across the seat for the Kentucky Fried Chicken she promised her brother she'd deliver at noon. Stepping from the truck, she took a moment to examine her reflection in the West Coast mirror. "I look like shit!" she proclaimed.

There were specks of dirt on her face from wrestling with a yearling stud colt that almost got the best of her. Straw hung from the ends of her long, blonde ponytail. She hadn't bothered to take her make-up off last night and it was now creating dark circles under her emerald green eyes. Looking down, she realized that her torn jeans and T-shirt were filthy. *Maybe I should have changed,* she thought. *Nah, I'm not here to impress anyone.*

Alex marched across the driveway, climbed the four steps leading to the huge front door, and rang the bell. The elderly gentleman who answered wasn't tall in actual height, but very stately in appearance. He wore a black tailcoat and grey pinstriped trousers. From the collar of his crisply pressed white shirt hung a black and grey striped tie. His full head of white hair was parted neatly to one side. His moustache was trimmed to perfection and showed a slight trace of yellow, indicating that he smoked a pipe. Alex's suspicions were confirmed when she leaned forward and caught the faint aroma of pipe tobacco.

"May I help you, miss?" he asked in a staunch British accent. After explaining the reason for her visit, the butler pointed Alex toward the side of the house and promptly shut the door in her face.

Having been dismissed, she walked down the cobblestone footpath that ran beside the fourteen-foot hedge. When she found the gate the butler had mentioned, she pushed down on the latch, swung it open and stepped through.

The wall of shrubbery gave way to the most magnificent backyard Alex had ever seen. There were two tennis courts, a shuffleboard court and a putting green. Strategically placed around the oversized kidney-shaped swimming pool were intimate groupings of wrought iron and glass patio furniture with white and green seat cushions and matching umbrellas, now positioned to block the noonday sun.

On the opposite side of the pool, a large brick fire pit separated two built-in stainless steel gas barbecues. Bright yellow mums, blossoming with fragrance, sprang up from the raised cedar flower boxes that ran the entire length of the back fence. To compliment their color and add balance to the yard, striped yellow and white canvas awnings protruded above each window and doorway at the back of the house.

When Alex reached the spot where Michael had set up his table saw, she stood behind her brother and watched while he diligently ran a piece of plywood through the blade. "Did someone order KFC," she asked when the buzzing stopped and silence returned to the air.

Michael spun around to face his baby sister. "It's about time you got here! We're starving!"

Alex raised a questioning brow. "Are you feeding an army?" "There's a fifteen-piece bucket of chicken, a family-size order of fries, large gravy, a loaf of bread and three large salads."

"No," Michael replied. "Just me and Sam."

"Who's Sam?"

"Believe it or not, he's an old buddy of mine from college."

"What's he doing here?" she asked.

"His dad's a friend of old man Sanderson's," Michael told her. "He's staying here for a week, checking out the livestock. He wants to buy a racehorse. He came over to have coffee with me this morning and when those two clowns who work for me didn't show up, Sam offered to help. He's pretty handy with a hammer. Maybe I should see if he wants to stick around and help me finish this pool house!"

Alex stared at the food in her arms. "You mean to tell me that the two of you are going to eat all this food?"

"Well, we may throw you a bone," Michael winked. "Come on. I'll introduce you to him. Follow me."

Michael grabbed a bag of chicken to free up one of Alex's arms, and enthusiastically pulled her through the maze of lumber and cords until they reached the shell of the Sandersons' new pool house. At the framed doorway, they were greeted by the intense pounding of a hammer. "Sam ... Sam, this is my kid sister, Alex."

The hammering stopped and Alex watched in silence as the man's head traveled upwards. When their eyes met for the first time, she felt the air rush from her lungs and her legs quivered. When he rose to his full height of six-foot-two, he became larger than life. His head was covered with thick, dark brown hair. Set between high cheekbones were eyes the color of a Caribbean sea. His jaw was firm and square. Powerful arms were attached to strong, broad shoulders and she felt her face flush imagining what they would feel like wrapped around her.

When he turned to put down the hammer, Alex couldn't help but notice how well he filled out the pockets of his Wrangler jeans. He turned to face her and tipped his head slightly. A shy smile curled up the corners of his mouth and in a deep-sexy voice he said, "Hello."

Alex's hand shook as she extended it to meet his. When their fingers touched, a surge of electricity raced through her entire body and caused an explosion in the very depths of her soul. For a brief moment, the world as she knew it stopped. No one else mattered; nothing else mattered, except the vision standing in front of her.

***

"*Por favor, Señora, despierte.*" The bus driver poked Alex again and repeated the sentence in English. "Please, lady, wake up."

She opened her eyes and smiled warmly at the figure standing over her. "Sam, it's so nice to meet you."

"No, *Señora*, my name is Pedro."

Alex shifted uncomfortably in her seat. She wasn't at the Sandersons' estate meeting Sam for the first time. She was on a bus, somewhere in Mexico. Her body was soaked with perspiration. Embarrassed, she reached to the corner of her mouth and delicately wiped away the moisture that had accumulated there. "I'm sorry," she apologized. "I must have dozed off." The driver offered his hand and helped her from her seat. "*Gracias, Señor,*" she smiled.

"No," he corrected. "Me, no *Señor,*"

"I don't know very much Spanish," Alex confessed as she followed him down the aisle, "but I'm sure my daughter told me that a man was a *Señor.*"

"Si, *Señora*, if he is a married man. I am not married." The driver stepped from the coach and helped Alex onto the cobblestone street in front of the hotel lobby. "You will have a good time here. It is the best resort," he smiled. "I have many friends who work at *Las Tropicales*. You ask for my *Amiga,* Angel, she will take good care of you. *Adios.*"

When Alex entered the open-air lobby of the resort, she found it as inviting as Sarah had described. Large wooden ceiling fans were suspended from the trusses of the thatched roof twenty feet above. Exotic birds sang from the rafters. The floor was covered in ceramic tiles and brightly painted cement walls of orange, yellow and terracotta displayed beautiful Mexican art. Beyond the lobby, there were palm trees and bright flowered hibiscus bushes and pathways illuminated by lanterns. Alex couldn't see the ocean, but she could hear it rolling onto the beach.

"*Hola* ladies and gentlemen. *Bievenidos* to *Las Tropicales*." A beautiful woman with long dark hair, mysterious dark eyes, and a shapely figure, stepped from behind the check-in desk. She was wearing taupe slacks and a navy blue blazer, similar to the one Alex had seen on the man at the airport ... the man she thought looked like Sam.

"My name is Angelina Rodriguez," she smiled. "I am the *subgerente*, the assistant manager for the resort." Her English was perfect and her Spanish accent as intriguing as her beauty. "We realize it's been several hours since you left home, and I'm sure you must be hungry, so please, help yourself to the light snack we have provided for you." She pointed towards a table of finger sandwiches, cheeses, tropical fruit and pastries set up on the far side of the lobby. "Coffee and tea are also available. For those of you who may want to wait for breakfast, our main restaurant opens at six-thirty. She glanced at her watch. "That's thirty minutes from now, if you'd like to set your watches to the correct time.

"Once you have checked in, please wait for a porter to take you, and your luggage, to your room. If there is anything you need during your stay, anything at all, please don't hesitate to ask. The staff is here to look after your every need. Tomorrow in the disco, at eleven o'clock in the morning, there will be an orientation. We recommend that you attend. It will tell you all about our resort and the activities, as well as tours in and around the area. Enjoy your stay."

While the majority of the crowd made its way towards the food, Alex opted for the check-in desk. She was exhausted and right now, she needed a shower and sleep more than she needed to fill the hollow spot in her stomach that told her she hadn't eaten in hours. She smiled at the uniformed man behind the desk. "Hello."

"*Hola, Señora, como esta usted?*" Alex shook her head. "How are you?" he repeated in English.

"Tired," she answered.

"May I have your name, please?"

"Granger, Alex Granger."

"*Si, Señora.*" The clerk examined the box of information envelopes until he found the one with Alex's name and pulled it from its alphabetical spot. "Here you are. There are three in your party, correct? I have Alex Granger, and Sarah and Brian Williams."

Alex let out a disappointed sigh. "I'm afraid not. My daughter and my husband couldn't make it, so I'm alone."

"Ah, *Señora,* a beautiful lady like you won't be alone for long." Alex blushed at the compliment. "May I see *eh,* your travel voucher, please?" The clerk pointed to the travel folder Alex was holding. "In there, *Señora.* It should be inside, with your airline ticket."

Alex handed him the folder and he searched through the documentation until he found the voucher. "Here it is." He removed it from the ticket jacket and handed the folder back to Alex. Next, he pulled out a map of the resort, a list of the restaurants and beach activities, a *Basic Guide to Spanish* handbook, three plastic wristbands, and three room keys. He unclipped one of the identification wristbands. "May I see your arm, please?" Alex held out her left arm and the young man attached a gold-colored plastic bracelet around her wrist. "Don't lose this," he winked, "it tells us that you are a guest at the resort. You are in room 4211. That is building four, on the second floor of our Gold Club section. I'm confident that you'll enjoy the room," he proudly beamed. "You are in, the building closest to the beach. There, you have a beautiful view of the ocean."

He opened the diagram of the property and circled the building that would be Alex's home for the next seven days. "Here, Ms. Granger. We are here, in the lobby. Go back out there," he pointed over Alex's shoulder, "turn right and follow the path until it divides at the big palm tree, then turn left. That is your building. There is a safe in your room and you can set your own combination."

"Do you charge for the safe, like most resorts?" Alex asked.

"No, *Señora*. We do not charge for using the safe. The instructions are on the front of the door." He pointed to the bellman at his side. "Miguel will escort you to your room, Ms. Granger. We will tag your scuba gear and store it for you in our dive shop." He handed Alex a ticket. "With this, you can get your diving gear when you need it. Please enjoy your stay at *Las Tropicales*."

2

SAM BENNETT, OWNER OF *Las Tropicales*, stared at his computer screen and shook his head in disbelief. "It can't be." He quickly picked up the telephone and dialed the front desk.

"*Hola*," a pleasant voice answered.

"*Hola,* this is Sam. Who was on the desk when the flight from Denver checked in?"

"Carlos," the voice answered.

"Is he in?"

"Yes. Would you like me to get him for you?"

"*Si, por favor.*" Sam tapped his fingers impatiently on the desk while he waited.

"*Si, Señor* Bennett. This is Carlos."

"Carlos, you checked in the flight from Denver this morning, right?"

"*Si.*"

"Did you check in an Alex Granger?"

"*Si, Señor*, I did."

"Was Alex a man," Sam paused, "or a woman?"

"A woman, *Señor*. A beautiful woman. Would you like her room number?"

"No, *gracias*, I have it."

Sam hung up the phone and ran his hands through his thick, grey hair. Of all the gin joints; in all the towns, in the entire world, Alex had to end up at his. It had been twenty years since he'd seen her and now she was staying at his resort. He was bound to run into her and if he did, what would he say?

How would he explain that he was still alive? He doubted, at this point, that the truth would work.

If he hadn't been blackmailed into going through with his marriage to Grace Sanderson all those years ago, today things would be different. Today, he'd be married to Alex, instead of trying to figure out a way to avoid her.

***

Prominent New York lawyer, Sam Bennett, was scheduled to be married in a month and he was getting cold feet. He loved Grace Sanderson, but something deep in his gut told him that marrying her would be a terrible mistake. Grace grew up with a silver spoon in her mouth. Whatever she wanted, she got. When she wanted to learn French, her father bought her a villa in the south of France and hired a private tutor. To keep her occupied ... when the French lessons got boring, her father bought her a sixty-foot yacht complete with captain and crew. When Grace wanted Sam Bennett, her father did everything he could to ensure that his little girl got her wish.

Sam first met Grace at Sundance Farms, her father's thoroughbred racing stable. They were re-introduced two years later at the Kentucky Derby. When they started dating, Sam found Grace to be a breath of fresh air. She was an attractive, intelligent, sophisticated woman. They traveled in the same circles, socialized with the same people and her father, Moe Sanderson, had been instrumental in getting him his current legal position.

Unfortunately, the more time Sam spent with Grace, the more he began questioning his marriage proposal. Twice, he'd walked in on her while she was doing lines of cocaine: "Oh, I'm not addicted to it, darling," Grace reassured him. "This is just to calm my nerves until after the wedding. Then I'll stop. Not to worry."

When Sam's best friend, Michael Granger, invited him on a ten-day fishing trip to Campbell River on Vancouver Island in British Columbia, Canada, he jumped at the chance. He needed time away to think about his future, this trip would give him the opportunity.

"Sam, you remember my baby sister, Alex, don't you?" Michael asked.

"No, I'm afraid I don't." With the sun in his eyes, Sam couldn't see the woman's face, but the confidence in her stride intrigued him.

"Hi, big brother," Alex smiled. "I made it at last!"

Michael kissed his sister on the cheek and turned her to face Sam. "You remember, Sam Bennett, don't you?"

"Yes. Hi, Sam," Alex extended her hand. "It's nice to see you again."

When their fingers touched, Sam's breath caught in his throat. "Your brother tells me we've met, but I'm sure I wouldn't forget such a pretty face." The color rose in Alex's cheeks at the compliment.

"You've met her!" Michael gave Sam a friendly shove. "Quit trying to dazzle my baby sister with the 'old Bennett charm'."

"Are you sure we've met before?" Sam asked her again.

"Yes," Alex smiled, "but it was a long time ago. You probably don't remember."

"Here, maybe this will help you out." Michael took off his baseball cap and dropped it onto his sister's head. "Recognize her now?"

Sam stared for only a moment. "The ball cap! Of course, I remember you. I was helping Michael build a pool house at Grace's dad's place. What was that, about five years ago? You brought us lunch. Your brother told me that you were quite a cowgirl."

"She still is," Michael proudly announced.

Sam shook his head. "I remember, when I saw you that day, I couldn't help but wonder if you'd been wrestling with the livestock."

"Actually, I had been," Alex laughed.

Letting go of her hand, Sam stepped back to take a better look. The tomboy had blossomed into a beautiful woman. She was tall and lean, and her tight fitting turtleneck sweater and snug Wrangler jeans accentuated every curve of her body. "Little Alex Granger, I can't believe it. You've certainly changed!"

"She cleans up pretty good doesn't she, Sam?" Michael gave his sister a wink and snatched his cap from her head. "Are we ready?'

"Where are Dad and Uncle Charlie?" Alex asked.

"They'll meet us there."

On the ferry ride from Horseshoe Bay in Vancouver to Nanaimo on Vancouver Island, Sam and Alex stood outside on deck and shared each others' life stories. Sam told Alex that he lived in New York and worked in a law firm. He didn't tell her he was engaged. He told her he had two sisters, both older. One was a doctor, the other a housewife and mother of three. Sam told Alex he loved being an uncle and wanted to be a father some day.

He played football in high school, which earned him a college scholarship but a knee injury forced him to give up the game. He loved to ski and he'd been to every major resort in Canada, Europe and the United States. Baseball was his favorite sport and although he lived in the home of the Yankees, his favorite team was the Toronto Blue Jays.

Sam learned that Alex had spent time in Boston getting her business degree. After graduation, she went back to her parents' ranch and started a quarter horse breeding operation. She currently had three stallions standing at stud; two quarter horses and a thoroughbred her father won in a poker game. Sam chuckled to himself when he learned the thoroughbred had come from Grace's father's racing stable, Sundance Farms.

Sam discovered that Alex liked the opera and the ballet, and occasionally took in the symphony. She'd been to New York once, and vowed never to go back. In her opinion, there were far too many people. She'd never been scuba diving, but she knew that some day she'd like to try. She'd been to Barbados, and the Bahamas, but she'd always wanted to go to Tahiti. She hated shopping and women who were afraid to get their hands dirty. She could change a tire, or the oil in her truck, but she couldn't bake a pie if her life depended on it.

Alex had a sense of humor that made Sam laugh, and a childlike innocence that made him want to protect her. By the third day of the ten-day trip, he was hooked; addicted to her like a junky was addicted to his needle. In the days that followed, Sam spent little time thinking of Grace, or his pending nuptials. He still hadn't told Alex he was engaged but he knew he had to. In three days, she'd be going back to Denver and he'd be going back to Grace.

"It's beautiful here, isn't it?" Alex casually remarked as she stared out at the ocean. "It's like being on the other side of the world." She inhaled a deep breath of sea air and savored it for a moment before exhaling. "Right out there," she pointed, "is Japan."

Sam furrowed his brow. "All I see out there ... is a storm brewing!" The sky was turning a nasty shade of grey and a cold wind had come up. "Maybe we should head back to the jeep?"

"Come on, I want to show you something." Alex grabbed Sam's hand and together they ran down the beach towards the tall-jagged rocks rising up from the sand. "How are you at climbing?" she asked.

"Why?"

Alex pointed up. "See those rock formations? At high tide, they look like miniature islands. But right now, before the tide comes in you can maneuver around them."

"I'm game, if you are," he smiled.

"Let's do it!"

Sam followed Alex upward, glad now that he'd worn his hiking boots. They made their way from stone to stone, climb-

ing up and down, until they were on the rock formation closest to the sea. "Have a seat," she smiled.

For half an hour the two of them sat in silence. Not an
uncomfortable silence between two people who didn't have a
thing to say to each other, but the type of silence that was only
experienced by good friends, and old married couples. Sam
wondered if he would ever feel this comfortable with Grace.
He was sure he wouldn't. He took a deep breath, and turned
to the beauty beside him. "I want you to know how much fun
I've had since we've been here, Alex"

"Me too," she smiled. "I really like you, Sam. My brother
was right, you're fun people."

"I'm glad Michael invited me along. I needed to get away
for awhile."

"Away from business ... or for personal reasons?"

"A little of both, I guess." Sam's heart sunk as he turned
and stared at the ocean. How could he tell Alex that he was going to be married in a month? She'd hate him, and he was sure
she was having the same feelings he was. Last night, while she
was making hot chocolate, he'd walked up behind her and
wrapped his arms around her like a golf instructor. She hadn't
pushed him away. Sam could feel her heart beat faster when
he pulled her closer. The scent of her perfume made him light-
headed and lingered in his nostrils.

Alex had given him a kiss on the cheek before she turned
in, but then, she'd kissed her father, her uncle, and her brother too. On his cheek, Sam was sure she'd lingered just a little
longer. He was falling head over heels in love with her and
there was no way to stop it. A loud clap of thunder exploded
in the sky, and it was as if God himself was telling Sam to quit
being such a fool. He couldn't fall for this beauty ... he was
already spoken for.

Alex suddenly jumped to her feet and grabbed at Sam's
arm. "We have to get out of here, right now!"

"Why? What's wrong?" he asked.

"That's what's wrong!"

Sam's eyes followed Alex's finger as she pointed down the jagged rocks towards the sand below. The tide was coming in fast and angry. "How long have we been sitting here?" she asked. "I completely lost track of the time. I must have been mesmerized by the ocean."

And I was mesmerized by you, Sam told himself. Another crack of thunder ripped open the sky and it started to pour. He took Alex by the hand and they picked their way back through the rock formations, careful not to slip. If they fell in, the waves would slam their bodies into the rocks and rip their flesh from the bone before the anger of the sea took them under.

When they reached the jeep, they were soaked to the skin. Sam quickly opened the door and helped Alex inside. Watching her fasten the seat belt, he couldn't help but notice the way her wet, white cotton T-shirt clung to her firm round breasts. He felt his face flush and reached behind the seat for his jacket. "Here, you better put this on before you freeze." Sam climbed into the driver's seat, put the vehicle into gear and pulled back onto the highway. They drove in silence for twenty minutes.

When they reached the cabin, it was raining harder then it had been when they left the beach. "Will this let up?" Sam asked, "Or should we sit it out for awhile?"

"We already look like drowned rats!" Alex laughed. "We might as well make a run for it!"

"Okay, if you say so."

Alex jumped from the jeep and raced for the cabin with Sam hot on her heels. She pushed open the front door and they stepped over the threshold to be greeted by a welcoming fire. She dropped Sam's jacket on the floor and rushed to the hearth. "I'm frozen!"

I could warm you, Sam told himself as he watched her run her hands up and down her shivering body. Last night, he'd dreamt that Alex came to his room. She dropped her silk robe on the floor and walked towards the bed. Moonlight glistened off the sensuous curves of her naked body. "Do you want me, Sam?" she asked in a soft seductive voice. "Yes," he said. "I've wanted you since I first saw you at the airport." Alex told him to take her then, and he had, with a passion he'd never experienced. There was a seductive heat between them that melted their bodies together as one. Again and again they reached plateaus Sam never thought possible. Afterward, Alex fell asleep in his arms.

Before leaving the fishing lodge, Sam's dream of being with Alex became a reality. They made love in a sleeping bag under the stars and his feelings for her were overwhelming. Not considering the consequences, Sam asked Alex to be his wife and she accepted.

One week later, while Sam was waiting at the airport to catch a flight to Bermuda, where he would meet Alex and they would be married on the beach, his plans took an abrupt about face. "Excuse me. Are you Sam Bennett?"

Sam looked up from his magazine. Two uniformed customs agents hovered over him. "Yes, I'm Sam Bennett," he answered. "What can I help you with?"

The taller of the men grabbed his arm. "Please come with us, Mr. Bennett."

"Is there a problem, gentleman?" He glanced at his watch. "I'm about to board my flight."

"Please, sir," the agent insisted.

Sam was escorted through the airport terminal to a tiny office in the baggage department. His luggage was open on the table; two pounds of cocaine lay beside it. "You've got to be kidding, right?"

The smaller of the two agents stepped forward. "Mr. Bennett, smuggling cocaine is a very serious criminal offense."

"But that's not mine!"

"Then what was it doing in your suitcase," the agent asked.

"I couldn't tell you." Sam gave the man a cocky grin. "For all I know," he leaned closer to read the identification tag clipped to the customs agent's pocket, "Bernie, you put it there yourself." It was the wrong answer; Bernie's partner grabbed Sam by the arm and slammed him into the wall.

"Let's see what's in your briefcase, shall we?" Bernie Peck opened the case and dumped the contents on the floor. He reached into his pocket, pulled out a Swiss army knife and slashed at the lining. "Let's see what you've got hiding in here, shall we?" He stuck his chubby fingers inside the opening and pulled out four small plastic bags. "Are you going to tell me that these don't belong to you either, Mr. Bennett?" Bernie ripped open a bag and the powder floated down like snow. He ran his finger through the white dust, then stuck it in his mouth and smacked his lips. "Yup, it's coke all right!"

After being placed in custody, Sam was allowed one phone call. There was no need to use it when Grace's father showed up. "Sam, what's this all about," Moe Sanderson asked. "I never figured you to be involved in drugs. You know, it wouldn't look good if your face was plastered on the front page of every newspaper in this city tomorrow, you being a lawyer and all, and your father ... a United States senator."

Moe reached into his pocket, pulled out a fifty-dollar Cuban cigar and clipped off the tip. "Now, I can take care of this little cocaine matter for you, Sam," he smiled, "if you'll take care of something for me." He stuffed the cigar in his mouth and lit it, puffing until smoke rose in the air above his head, then blew out the match and flipped it into the ashtray. "You love my daughter, don't you, Sam?" Moe didn't give his future son-in-law the opportunity to answer. "Of course, you do. Well, Sam, my little girl has been crying her eyes out since this morning. She tells me that you've called off the wedding." Moe took a long drag from his cigar and blew the smoke at Sam in displeasure. "That doesn't make me very happy. Your news has upset my baby. Anything that upsets my little Gracie, well, it's only natural that it would upset me. Don't you agree? After all, I am her father. Some day you'll have kids of your own, and then you'll understand."

Sanderson ground his Cuban into the ashtray. "I'm a reasonable man, Sam, so here's what we're going to do. You're going to marry my daughter, but not next month as planned. You're going to marry her tomorrow." He motioned to the ape-of-a-man guarding the door of the interrogation room. "Bruno, here, is going to take you back to the brownstone. Grace is waiting there. The two of you will have a nice, romantic candlelight dinner. You'll apologize to her and tell her that you just had a case of cold feet. Then, Bruno is going to bring you back to the airport and my private jet is going to take you to Bermuda." Moe reached into his pocket and pulled out a piece of paper. "Where was it you were staying? Here it is ... the bridal suite at that ritzy joint in Hamilton. What's it called? Oh, it doesn't matter." He crumpled the paper and tossed it on the desk. "What matters is, tomorrow Grace's mother and I will fly down with your family and you will marry my daughter on the beach, just like you'd planned. If you don't," he leaned over and picked up a bag of cocaine. "I'll not only ruin you, Sam, I'll ruin your father. Oh, and Sam, there's just one more thing. You will forget about Alex Granger, won't you? After all, we wouldn't want anything happening to her, would we?"

***

That day, was the beginning of the end of Sam Bennett's life. Not a day had passed since, when he hadn't thought about Alex and how his life could have been so different. Grace was gone now, dead from a cocaine overdose.

A knock at the door interrupted his thoughts. "Hi boss, looks like we're overbooked again." Angelina Rodriguez announced as she bounded into the room. She plopped herself down in a chair and fanned her face with the clipboard she was carrying. "Wow, it's a hot one out there today! I brought you the list of room numbers we're going to ask to relocate. I really hate doing this but, that tour company from Canada overbooked again." She gave her boss a cocky grin. "Pretty soon, this will be an all-inclusive *Canadian* destination!"

Since opening its doors, *Las Tropicales* had become a favorite vacation spot of sun-worshipers from around the globe. So much so, that Sam was adding a new building to the complex. When it opened, the property would house 1400 guests.

The little Mexican hideaway had always done well, but since Angelina took over as assistant manager a year ago, the Canadian market had risen to the top of their list. At any given time, seventy per cent of the hotel guests were from Canada, fifteen per cent came from the United States and the balance of guests were from Germany, Mexico, Europe and Asia.

It wasn't uncommon for the resort to be sold out of their 509 rooms, and it bothered the hell out of Sam that guests were being asked to relocate for a few days. After complaining about it to Angelina, she and Carmen Sanchez, the guest services manager, put their heads together and came up with a great solution. The women created a three-day excursion package to Puerto Vallarta that included first class ocean view accommodations at a spa resort owned by a friend of Carmen's. Evening passes to Carlos O'Brian's, the hottest spot on the *Malecon*, and a tour of the city that took in a visit to the Church of *Lady Guadalupe*, the flea market, and the home that was once owned by Liz Taylor and Richard Burton.

"It looks like we'll be ten rooms short for the flight coming in from Montreal tomorrow." Angelina frowned. "Do you want to check the list?"

Sam shook his head. "No, you handle it. That's why I pay you the Big Bucks!"

"My pleasure," she smiled. "I'm already getting the packages together for the guests we're asking to transfer to Puerto Vallarta. By the number of people who indicated on their questionnaire that they wanted to go to the city, we should be okay. We just have one small problem."

"What's that?" Sam asked.

"The Lawrences', David and Pat, are back again to celebrate their wedding anniversary. Somehow, their arrival information got misplaced and the front desk accidentally gave
out their room to an," Angelina pulled a piece of paper from
her pocket, "to an Alex Granger. We'll have to see if he'd be
willing to go into PV for a few days."

"It's not a he," Sam mumbled. "It's a she."

"Excuse me?"

"Alex Granger isn't a man, she's a woman and you won't
find her another room." Sam pushed himself back from his
desk. "Don't move the Granger party. Give the Lawrences another room."

"But we don't have another room! We're completely sold
out!"

"Then give them the private suite."

The color drained from Angelina's face. "But Sam, no one
has been in that room for ... well ... since your wife died there
... last year."

"Don't argue with me, Angelina. Just have Maria air it out,
and give it to the Lawrences." He stood up and yanked his
navy blue blazer from the back of his chair. "I'm going for a
drive."

3

OTHER THEN BUMPING OFF his wife, Brian Williams had no idea where he was going to come up with the remaining ninety grand ... of the one hundred and ten he owed his bookie. He'd thought about dipping into his and Alex's joint savings account but she was so tight with money, you couldn't pound a two-by-four up her ass with a sledgehammer! She'd notice the fluctuation in funds immediately and think he was snorting coke again. He was, but this time he'd done a much better job of keeping his habit from his wife.

Brian had managed to get his hands on five grand when he sold a vial of semen from Alex's prize winning thoroughbred racehorse stallion. He told the purchaser that it was worth five times that, but beggars couldn't be choosers. His daughter hadn't missed the gold Rolex her grandfather had given her, but what he got for that was a far cry from the coin he still needed to cover his gambling debt. A month ago, he'd almost given up hope of getting his hands on that kind of cash until his daughter reminded him about the diamond and sapphire necklace: "Dad, I think it would be great if Mom wore Grandmother's necklace at your wedding anniversary dinner."

Brian had heard about the necklace, but he'd never had the privilege of seeing it. The Granger family heirloom was given to Alex on their wedding day. She'd worn it under her wedding dress. Immediately following the ceremony, the necklace was whisked back to the safety of the bank under the protection of armored guards.

Brian's plan was simple. He'd get the necklace from the bank, pawn it and turn the cash over to his bookie. He had a guaranteed tip on an upcoming race. When his horse won, he'd buy back the necklace, return it to the safety deposit box and no one would be the wiser.

The morning Brian arrived at the bank there was a new spring in his step. Soon his current money problems would be solved. "Good morning, Alicia." He smiled down at the attractive thirty-something brunette sitting behind the reception desk. "It's a beautiful day, isn't it?" Brian took her hand and bent to greet it with his lips. In doing so, he slipped a note from his palm to hers and whispered. "I'll see you at nine. Here's the address."

Their conversation was interrupted by Bank Manager Donald Barkwell. "Brian, it's so good to see you!" The lanky gentleman extended his hand. "What can we do for you today?"

"I need to get into the safety deposit box."

"Of course Brian. Anything you like." Donald fumbled through the pockets of his navy blue suit until he found the vault keys. He opened the gate beside the desk and motioned for Brian to step through. "If you'll just give me a minute, I'll be more than happy to personally escort you downstairs."

"That's not necessary, Don." Brian turned and smiled down at the receptionist. If Alicia took him to the vault ... he'd be getting into more than just the safety deposit box!

"Oh, I insist. Please, wait here. I'll just be a minute."

When Don was out of earshot, Alicia reached up and tugged at Brian's coat. "You know what the old fool did yesterday? When he got up to go for lunch, he hit the silent alarm button under his desk. He was just walking out the front door when the SWAT team showed up! The poor man damn near had a heart attack!"

Brian had to agree that Donald Barkwell wasn't the sharpest tool in the shed. Once, during a dinner party, he dropped a deep-fried shrimp on the top of Alex's hand while trying to pass it to her from the fondue pot. The hot seafood left his wife with a nasty horseshoe shaped scar. Brian often wondered why Alex's uncle Charlie had ever hired this clown to run the bank, but whatever the reason, it didn't matter. Alex was Barkwell's best client and because of it, Don Barkwell treated Brian like a king.

The two men made their way to the basement, through the metal detector, and into the vault. Don put his key in box number 2354 and asked Brian to do the same. When the lock clicked, Don opened the door and pulled out the metal box. He led Brian to a small privacy room and set the box on the table. "I'll be right outside. Just tap on the door when you're finished."

Brian closed the door, locked it, and sat down. His hands shook as he pulled the safety deposit box towards him. Soon, his problems would be over, at least temporarily. He held his breath, and slowly opened the lid. Much to his surprise, the box was empty. His heart started racing. Tiny beads of sweat broke out over his brow. "That fucking bitch! What the hell has she done with the goddamn necklace?" In frustration, Brian slammed his fist on the desk. The safety deposit box flew across the room and crashed onto the floor.

"Are you okay?" Barkwell asked from the hall.

"Yeah, it's nothing," Brian answered. "I just knocked over the chair when I took my coat off. Everything's fine."

Brian stood up and paced the tiny room. Everything wasn't fine! He was in deep shit! His bookie had given him a week to pay off his gambling debt. If he didn't, he'd be taking a long-dirt nap. "Sarah must know where it is," he mumbled under his breath as he punched out the phone number of the hospital.

"Good morning, Mercy Hospital," a pleasant voice answered.

"Doctor Sarah Granger Williams, please." Brian drummed his fingers nervously on the table while he waited for his daughter to answer.

"This is Doctor Williams."

"Hi, it's Dad."

"Hi, Pops, what's up?"

"I'm here at the bank. After our conversation the other night, I thought I'd pick up your grandmother's necklace and take it to the jewelers to have it cleaned. It's not here. You don't happen to know where it might be. Do you?"

"No I don't," Sarah replied. "Maybe Mom had the same idea about wearing the necklace. Perhaps she took it to the jewelers. Check it out. I have to go Dad. I'm being called to emergency. I'm staying at the hospital tonight to cover a shift, so I won't be home. I'll see you in the morning. Goodbye."

"Goodbye." Brian hung up the phone, closed the safety deposit box and opened the door. He followed Don Barkwell back to the vault and placed the metal box back in its pigeon hole, then immediately left the bank.

Brian ran the three blocks to Heintz Jewelers. When he pushed his way through the front door, he was out of breath. He hurried through the showroom to the customer service desk at the back of the store and asked to see the owner.

"I'm afraid Mr. Heintz isn't in," the security guard told him. "Can someone else help you?"

"What about his wife, Hilda. Is she here?"

"Yes. She is here." The guard motioned to the leather sofa. "Please, have a seat. May I tell her who is calling?"

"Williams, Brian Williams."

While Brian waited, he watched a young couple enthusiastically examine an array of diamond engagement rings. Judging by their attire, he was positive they couldn't afford anything on the tray, but his father always said you shouldn't judge a book by its cover. He looked like a million bucks and he didn't have a pot to piss in.

A portly German woman, wearing a motherly smile and a floral print dress, waddled out from the back room. "Auch, Brian. Stand up, let me give you a big hug, jah?" When he obliged, the jolly woman threw her arms around him, and squeezed. "What brings you to us today, Brian?"

"Did Alex bring her diamond and sapphire necklace in to be cleaned?"

"Yah," Hilda smiled, "she dropped it off last week."

"I'm here to pick it up. Would you get it for me, please?"

"Is Alex going to wear it on her birthday?" Hilda asked.

Brian shook his head. "No. Alex will be in Mexico on her birthday, but I thought it might be nice if she wore it for our anniversary dinner next month."

"Very good," Hilda smiled. "I'll just go get it for you. I'll be right back." Hilda was gone for five minutes and returned empty handed. "I'm sorry, Brian, the necklace is not here. I have looked everywhere. Alex must have picked it up."

Panic filled Brian's voice. "What do you mean, it isn't here?"

"I remember Alex bringing it in, but I can't find the tag that says she picked it up. Let me check with Carl."

Again Hilda disappeared into the back room. When she returned this time, she had promising news. "Carl gave the necklace back to Alex two days ago. He remembers because when he gave it to her, he told her how beautiful it was and he hoped she kept it in the bank. Alex told him she was taking it home."

The forty-five-minute drive from downtown Denver to the Granger ranch took Brian twenty-five minutes. He raced upstairs to Alex's bedroom, confident that he would find the necklace in her jewelry case. When he looked there, the box was empty. For hours Brian ripped the house apart ... room by room. He looked in every closet, and through every drawer. He searched under mattresses, and behind furniture. He was frantic by the time he found the wall safe hidden behind the family portrait in the library.

Brian couldn't help but wonder how long the safe had been there or why Alex installed it in the first place, but right now that didn't matter. All that mattered was that he found it and he was sure that's where he'd find the necklace. He tried every number combination he could think of: Sarah's birthday, his birthday, and Alex's birthday. He'd even tried their wedding anniversary, but nothing worked.

As a last resort, he decided to call Alex's lawyer, but hung up while he was waiting on hold. Even if Peter Bailey did have the combination ... which Brian was sure he did, he'd never divulge it. Since getting caught screwing Peter's legal assistant, the lawyer hardly gave him the time of day. Brian stared at his watch. It was cocktail hour at the Legal Eagle, a well-known hangout for Denver lawyers and their staff. Surely, someone there would know who Peter Bailey's new assistant was. He had a quick shower, changed his clothes and headed to town.

When Brian arrived at the Legal Eagle, the joint was jumping. He strolled around the bar with one ear on the conversation and one eye on the door. All the broads from Bailey and Associates hung out at the Eagle on Fridays; surely he'd recognize one of them. On his second pass through the premises, he hit pay dirt. Four women, all looking as if they'd just stepped from the pages of Vogue, were hoisting their glasses in the air.

"Here's to our employer, Bailey and Associates," one of them said.

"Yeah, and to Peter Bailey becoming fair game!" the brunette among them added.

This is perfect, Brian thought, *I'll chat them up and pump them for info.* He straightened his tie and ran his hand through his thick-wavy hair, then popped a breath mint in his mouth and turned on the charm. "Good evening, ladies," he smiled as he approached their table. "I'll bet you girls all work at Bailey and Associates?"

"Why, yes," the brunette answered. "How can you tell?"

Brian took the woman's hand, raised it to his lips and gently kissed her fingers. "Because," he grinned, "you all look like models."

The brunett gave him a strange look. "Excuse me?"

Brian let go of her hand and took a step back. "Well, word on the street is that ladies from Bailey and Associates could all grace the cover of a glamour magazine. I'd say you four are living proof!"

The redhead leaned across the table and extended a graceful hand in his direction. "I'm afraid you have us at a disadvantage, Mr. ...?"

"I'm sorry," he stuck out his hand to meet hers. "My name's Brian and you are?"

"I'm Brook." She pointed to the women sitting with her. "This is Monica, Carol and Donna."

"It's nice to meet you, ladies. May I buy you a drink? How about a bottle of champagne? You look like you're celebrating something. Did one of you get a big promotion?"

"Yes. As a matter-of-fact, one of us did," Brook told him, "and here she comes now." The woman pointed over Brian's shoulder.

This will be a piece of cake, Brian told himself. He put on his best smile, confident that he was about to meet another beauty. When he turned around, the vision was almost frightening. Her business suit was well tailored and her eye make-up not as outrageous, but the woman standing in front of him now, reminded him of Mimi from the Drew Carey show ... they were both the same size.

"This is Doris," Brook announced.

Brian swallowed the lump in his throat. "Pleased to meet you, Doris, I'm Brian." He took her hand and kissed it and the overweight woman blushed. "Allow me." He pulled out a vacant chair and offered it to Doris. When she was seated, Brian gave her his best used-car-salesman smile. "So, Doris, I understand that you just got a promotion."

"Yeah, lucky bitch," Monica moaned. "She's going to be working for Peter Bailey."

Peter Bailey, Brian thought. *This has to be some type of a joke.* He looked back at Monica. "Did I hear you right? Did you say that Doris will be working for Peter Bailey?"

"That's right," the rotund woman smiled. "I'm Peter Bailey's new legal assistant."

Great, Brian thought. Sleeping with Bridget Regal was like going to Disneyland! This would be like going to hell! But, if screwing this fat cow was what it took to get the combination to Alex's wall safe, then that's exactly what he'd do. He drank with the women for three hours before offering to drive Doris Watson home.

Doris hadn't been a bad piece of ass for someone her size, but the whole time he was doing her, all Brian kept thinking about was a joke a friend told him years ago:

> "Brian, do you know the difference between a one-bagger, a two-bagger, a three-bagger and coyote ugly? A one-bagger is so ugly you put a bag over her head. A two-bagger is so ugly you put a bag over her head, and one over your head, in case hers falls off. A three-bagger is so ugly you put a bag over her head, a bag over your head, and one at the door in case you get company, and coyote ugly is so ugly, that you'd rather chew your arm off than disturb her!"

When it was all said and done, Doris had given him exactly what he'd come for; the combination to Alex's private safe.

Brian raced back to the ranch and went directly to the library. He pulled the family portrait off the wall and set in on the sofa, then reached into his shirt pocket and took out the small piece of paper that held the combination. He spun the dial left, then right, and then left again. When the tumblers clicked into place, he held his breath and pulled open the steel door.

Brian's fingers first made contact with a five-by-seven envelope. He pulled it from the safe, looked at it briefly and tossed it onto the sofa. On his second trip into the steel unit, he found the velvet box. Wrapping his hand around it, a tingle raced through his body like an electrical current. He pulled the case from its hiding place and flipped open the lid. The sight of the diamond and sapphire necklace took his breath away.

"Holy shit," Brian exclaimed as he flopped onto the sofa. He took the necklace from the velvet box and clenched the cold gems in his hand. This little bobble would more than cover his gambling debt. He'd even have enough money left over to take a junket to Paradise Islands in the Bahamas while Alex was in Mexico, and perhaps double what was left in the casino. He tossed the necklace back in the case, snapped the lid shut, and ran the velvet box under his nose like a fine Cuban cigar. "Ah," he grinned, "how sweet it is!"

Brian leaned back on the sofa and contemplated the past twenty-five years. In his mind, his marriage to Alex had been a complete waste. He'd been forced into the nuptials when they found out that she was pregnant. He still couldn't believe the condom broke. How stupid could he have been, using one he'd had in the glove compartment of his Porsche for months? He should have used the new one in his wallet, but Alex was hot to trot that night and he wasn't about to turn her down. Brian now considered that decision to be the biggest mistake of his life.

"You'll give up the stupid idea of driving race cars, get a decent job and marry that girl," his father had ordered. "Frankly, Son, as far as I'm concerned, you're the male version of a slut! I'm embarrassed to say we're even related. You've cost me a fortune over the years paying off those tramps you go out with. At least, Alex is a decent girl who comes from a decent family.

"I'm cutting you off, Brian. No more monthly allowance. I'm sure you're spending the money on drugs anyway. I've cut off all your credit cards and access to the company jet. There'll be no trips to the Caribbean. No more women. No more getting you out of legal jams. My lawyers are paid to look after my affairs, not yours. There will be nothing, Brian. You're on

your own. Your cock got you into this mess and I'm not getting
you out of it."

And so, for Brian Williams, the good times came to an end.
He was trapped; twenty-five with a wife and kid to support.
After Sarah was born, Alex's father offered him a job and he
had no choice but to take it. He worked his ass off delivering
horse trailers, manufactured by Alex's father, to racing stables
and tracks across the country. He was being paid well; a sal-
ary, plus mileage and all of his expenses. Best of all, he didn't
have to spend any time with the cold fish he'd married or a
screaming kid.

Hanging around the track brought out Brian's urge to
gamble and it wasn't long before he was spending more than
he was making. On one trip to Kentucky, he lost a year's wages betting on a sure thing. When he couldn't come up with
the cash, three boys at the racetrack put the boots to him and
threatened his life if he didn't pay up.

Brian was positive he was up shit-creek until he discovered ... while on a trip to Florida, that Alex's father was having an affair. The Grangers were church-going people and well
respected in the community. This type of scandal would dev-
astate Alex's mother and Brian was sure his wife wouldn't let
that happen. When he returned home, he broke the news of
the affair to Alex and threatened to blow the whistle unless
she started supporting him in the style he'd been accustomed
to before they were married.

Today, ten years later, Brian was the president of Alex's
quarter horse breeding operation and the title paid him
$350,000 a year. He had a Porsche, a Mercedes, and the use
of his father's company jet. He was a pillar of the community
Things couldn't have been better ... right up until the point
where he was stupid enough to get caught screwing around
with Alex's lawyer's legal assistant

Alex limited his access to their joint bank account, cancelled most of his credit cards, and threatened to take away
his company signing authority. Then, she put him on an allow-

ance of three grand a month. *Three grand!* That was bullshit. Some days, he snorted more than that up his nose.

In the past month alone, Brian had spent the money he got for the Granger family necklace and gone through all but ten grand of the cash he had stashed in an off-shore bank account. His financial situation was getting desperate and in his mind, there was only one way to handle it. The plan was brilliant and soon his money problems would be solved.

Brian's face broke into a devious grin. He reached across the night table and pulled a cigarette from the package of Winston's.

"I guess we're pretty lucky that your wife didn't walk in on us, huh?" a female voice called out from the bathroom.

"My wife is in Mexico," Brian casually replied, "but you need to get out of here. My daughter will be home soon."

"I want my money," the redheaded prostitute announced as she stepped from the bathroom and waddled across the room.

"I don't have your money."

The prostitute walked to the foot of the bed "Are you trying to fuck me for free again, Brian? I told you before, I gotta earn a living too!"

"I'll get your money, Trixie"

"And how are you gonna do that? Word on the street says you owe Benny Beans big time and I understand your wife has thrown you off the *sugar train express*."

"Well, the *sugar train express* is about to gather some steam." Brian stuck the cigarette between his lips and lit it. A single tear rolled down his cheek when smoke got trapped beneath his contact lens. "Must be, crocodile tears," he chuckled wiping the moisture from his face.

"What?"

"Crocodile tears, baby! You know. The tears crocodiles shed just before they devour their prey!"

Trixie flashed Brian a seductive grin and pulled her black spandex skirt up to her waist. "I think you've already devoured your prey baby!"

"Want to go again?" Brian asked.

"I can't stay. I've got another appointment." She straightened her skirt and waddled to the door. "I want my money."

"You'll have your money in two weeks. I promise," Brian told her.

"Yeah, and in two weeks, I'll be the Queen of England!"

"Trust me, Trixie, you'll get your cash."

"Are you planning on winning the power ball?" she sarcastically asked.

"No," Brian grinned. "I'm planning on inheriting the family farm!"

4

WHEN ALEX AWOKE, THE room was black, except for a small ray of light breaking in from under the heavy navy blue drapes that covered the French doors leading to the balcony. She rolled over and looked at the clock radio. The red glowing numbers read: 5:56 p.m. "That's impossible. I didn't lie down till six!"

Alex rubbed her eyes and studied the clock. It suddenly dawned on her that she'd been sleeping for almost twelve hours. "Oh my God! Sarah!" She shot up like a bullet, turned on the bedside lamp and dialed the hotel operator. She was lucky enough to get through to the States on the first try.

"*Hola*. This is the Mexican operator. I have a person-to-person call for *Señorita* Sarah Granger Williams."

"Yes, this is she."

"Go ahead, *Señora*."

"Sarah! It's Mom."

"Well, it's about time you called," Sarah scolded. "Dad and I have been worried sick about you!"

"I'm really sorry, dear," Alex apologized. "My flight was late getting in, and I was so exhausted, that ..."

"What do you think of the place?" Sarah voice filled with excitement. "Isn't it great? Have you met the owner yet? He's a babe, Mom!"

"I'm sure he is, dear."

"I think he's single!"

"Well, I'm not."

"Yeah, but there's no harm in looking, is there?" Sarah laughed.

Alex let out a gasp. "I'm shocked, young lady!"

"Come on, Mom. Dad looks at every pretty girl that walks by. That doesn't mean he handles the merchandise."

If you only knew, Alex thought. "No, Sarah, I haven't really seen any of the resort. I've been sleeping since I got here ... twelve hours ago." The rumble in her stomach reminded her that it had also been hours since she'd eaten. "I should go darling. I'll give you a call later on in the week. I just wanted to let you know that I'd arrived safely."

"Hang on, Mom. Dad wants to talk to you."

"Hey, Babe."

"Hello, Brian."

"How was your flight?"

"Long," Alex replied with a yawn.

"You sound tired."

"I am."

"Have you booked your dive yet?" Brian asked.

"No."

"Well, you should call the dive company as soon as possible. They may be really busy this time of the year."

"Brian, I don't think I'm going to go div..."

"Alex, you promised me you'd use the gear," he interrupted.

"Yes, Brian, I know but, I ..."

"You used to love to dive," Brian reminded her. "Remember the good times we had together when we were diving? I just wish I could be there, to go with you."

"Well, maybe I'll just wait, and we can go diving when I get back."

"Alex, you know I'm too busy. That's why I couldn't go with you to Mexico. May I remind you, dear," Brian's voice dropped to a whisper, "since you cut me off, I've actually had to work for a living." There was a moment of silence before he added: "Why waste an opportunity like this? You took the gear with you," his tone turned to annoyance, "the gear ... I might remind you ... was a birthday present from me. The least you can do is use it!"

Hearing the anger in her husband's voice, Alex couldn't help but wonder if he'd been drinking. Brian's tone was usually the first clue he'd been in the sauce; the second, when they started to quarrel. The last thing she needed right now was to have an argument with her husband. If all it took to shut him up was to say yes, then she would. "Okay, Brian, I promise. I'll use the gear."

"Good. I wrote a phone number on the back of the brochure. Call it, and ask for Carlos. He promised me he'd take care of you."

"Fine, Brian, I'll call this Carlos person, and make arrangements to go on a dive."

"Do it tomorrow."

"Yes, Brian, I'll do it tomorrow."

"Here, I'll let you say goodbye to your daughter."

"My daughter? Since when have you ever referred to Sarah as *my daughter*?"

"Well, she is, isn't she?"

The tone of Brian's voice made Alex feel sick. *He couldn't have found my diary*, she reassured herself. It was locked in a safe that Brian knew nothing about. The only person who had the combination was her lawyer.

"Alex, are you still there?" Brian asked.

"Yes, Brian, I'm here."

"Don't hang up, Sarah wants to say goodbye. Have a good dive and I'll see you when you get back."

"Hi, Mom. Bye, Mom. I have to go too. Dad's dropping me off at the hospital on his way to the airport."

"The airport?"

"Yeah, he said he's going out of town on business. Do you want to talk to him again?"

"No, it's okay."

"Mom, call me during the week. Oh, and listen to Dad, go for a dive, I've heard it's great down there! Got to run, love ya."

When the line went dead, Alex hung up the phone and scanned the room for her purse. She dug out her address book and looked up Peter Bailey's private number. She'd call him and make sure that he hadn't given the safe combination to Brian. Alex repeated the long distance telephone process with the hotel operator and waited patiently while Peter's phone rang.

"Hello," a deep male voice answered.

"Go ahead, *Señora*," the operator told her.

"Peter ... it's Alex."

"Alex, what are you doing calling me? You're supposed to be on vacation!"

"I know. I just have a quick question for you."

"Can't this wait till you get back?"

"No, Peter, it can't. I need to know if anyone but you and I have the combination to my wall safe."

"My legal assistant has it. In case, God forbid, something should ever happen to the both of us."

"She wouldn't give the combination to Brian, would she?"

"Brian? She doesn't even know Brian. Besides, Doris is as dependable as Duke."

"Duke?"

"Yeah, Duke, on the 'Bushes Baked Bean' commercials!"

"Isn't that the dog who's always trying to give away the family secret? Your assistants usually look like Vogue models and we both know how much Brian likes to read! Look what happened with Bridget Regal."

"You don't have to worry, Alex, Doris isn't Brian's type. She weighs in at 300 pounds!"

"Since when did you start lowering your standards in legal assistants, Mr. Bailey?"

"Since I realized that the unattractive ones were more interested in doing my work, than trying to do me! Don't worry,"

Peter reassured her, "no one but you, and I, know your family secret. Now, go and enjoy your vacation."

"Yes, I guess you're right," Alex sighed. "It's bad enough that I have to spend my birthday alone, I'm not going to make it worse by worrying about stuff that I shouldn't."

"I thought the whole family was going with you on this trip?"

"They were, but Sarah got called back to the hospital to cover shifts, and Brian had some sort of meeting he had to go to, so I'm here by myself."

"Speaking of Brian, did he actually remember your birthday this year?" Peter asked.

"Yes, he did and you're not going to believe this," Alex chuckled, "but he gave me diving gear."

"Diving gear? I didn't know that you were a diver."

"Brian and I did a lot of diving years ago."

"I hope you took it along?"

"Yes, I did, but I probably won't use it."

"Alex, there's some great diving not far from your resort. You should really take advantage of it and book a trip"

"Brian actually booked a dive for me."

"He did?" Peter grunted. "He must really be trying to win brownie points. What did you do, tell him that you were finally getting a divorce?"

"I mentioned it to him, but he wined and dined me and begged for forgiveness. I'm sure he thinks I've put the whole thing out of my mind, but he's in for a big surprise when I get back. Have you drawn up the papers?"

"Yes. They're in my desk at the office. All you have to do is sign them when you get home. So, don't worry about divorce papers, take your gear and go diving."

"I don't think so."

"Why not, I hear diving is good for the soul."

Alex let out a grunt. "I thought it was confession that was good for the soul."

"Listen, I have to run. Don't worry about anything. Your secret's safe with me. Have a good time, go diving, and I'll see you when you get back."

When Alex hung up the phone, she told herself to quit being so paranoid. Peter was right. Brian didn't have the combination to her wall safe and soon, he wouldn't have her money either. She shook the thought from her mind and headed to the shower.

Passing the front door of her suite, Alex noticed a piece of paper lying on the ceramic tile floor. She picked it up and read:

DEAR GUEST: WE HOPE YOU ARE ENJOY-
ING YOUR STAY AND WOULD APPRECIATE
IT IF YOU WOULD COME TO THE FRONT
DESK, BETWEEN THE HOURS OF 10 A.M.
AND 6 P.M. TODAY. THERE IS NO PROB-
LEM AND WE DO NOT WANT TO SELL YOU
ANYTHING. THE MANAGEMENT.

"I'll handle this later." Alex dropped the note on the desk and peeled off her clothes as she headed to the bathroom. She was thrilled with the size of the shower and even happier with the water pressure. There was nothing she loved more than a shower that pelted her body with the power of Jacuzzi jets. She adjusted the temperature until it was as hot as she could stand and stepped inside to let the water relieve her tired, aching muscles. Alex thought of going back to bed, but when she turned off the taps and her ears were greeted by the sound of a mariachi band, she changed her mind.

Emerging from the steamy bathroom, Alex felt refreshed and wide-awake. She wrapped herself in the fluffy-white bathrobe provided by the hotel and walked to the French doors with a new spring in her step. She pulled back the drapes and looked out. The front desk clerk had been right; the view from her room was fantastic!

Three hundred feet from the balcony was one of the resort's three pools. The deck was vacant now, except for the white-cushioned lounge chairs that had been placed neatly around the water's edge. Palm trees swayed softly in the evening breeze. There was a beautiful full moon and its glistening rays turned the ocean's waves orange as they rolled onto the beach. For the first time since getting on the plane in Denver, Alex was excited about her vacation. She'd been working like a dog lately setting up the farm's new breeding program and she deserved a rest. But first, she needed something to eat. She quickly dried her hair, put on her make-up, got dressed and left her room.

In the main lobby at *Las Tropicales*, hotel guests were congregating at the tour desk making reservations for their next outing. Others were lined up at the bar refreshing their new favorite cocktail. Some guests were playing backgammon and chess. Others were dancing to the mariachi band Alex heard when she stepped from the shower. Everywhere, people were enjoying themselves and she decided it was time she did the same.

The loud eruption of laughter drew Alex's attention to the group of firefighters she'd been sitting with in first class on the flight from Denver. Lorne Mills, the bald, blue eyed, six-foot-two firefighter, nicknamed Shrek, stood up and waved at her. "Alex. Come and join us."

She made her way to their table and accepted the chair that had been pulled out for her. "Well, good evening, gentlemen." Alex gave them a radiant smile. "How are you enjoying your vacation so far?"

"This place is great," Firefighter Blain Beck announced.

"Yeah, that's just 'cause you left Sarah at home," Lorne laughed.

"Is Sarah your girlfriend?" Alex asked.

"She's my wife," Blain smiled proudly. "We'll be married a year at Christmas."

"My daughter's name is Sarah," Alex told him," but we've been calling her Sam, for years."

"Sam?"

"Her name is Sarah Alexandra Marie. It was a nice abbreviation."

"Hey, boys what's up?" Harry Baker, the arrogant one of the group asked as he sat to join the table. "This place is great! I haven't seen this much skin since I dropped a crispy off at the burn unit last week!"

Lorne punched Harry in the shoulder. "Oh, man, that's gross! Have a little respect, will you, there's a lady present!" The other firefighters at the table nodded their heads in agreement.

"You boys are looking rather dapper this evening," Alex grinned. "You must have hot dates."

"Not tonight," Lorne told her. "Tonight, we check them out to see how well they can hold their liquor!"

"Speaking of which," Harry interrupted. "I hear they have a drink down here called a tequila popper."

Alex shook her head. "Yes, I've heard of them. They're made with tequila, Seven-Up and just a touch of grenadine. It's a shooter, actually. You put your hand over the glass, slam it on the bar until it fizzes, then down it. The alcohol doesn't go through your bloodstream; it gets absorbed through the palate and goes directly to the brain. You get loaded a lot faster. They say it only takes three of them, and most grown men fall off their chair."

"I don't think so," Harry laughed. "That wouldn't happen to me."

"Apparently, it happens to everyone," Alex advised.

"Well, I'm not everyone."

Alex didn't like Harry Baker. As far as she was concerned, he was an arrogant ass. He'd been rude and obnoxious on the flight to Mexico and his know-it-all attitude was getting on her nerves. Maybe it was time to teach him a lesson. She leaned across the table. "Harry, are you a betting man?"

"I've been known to lay down my cash a time or two. Why do you ask?"

"I'll bet I can go shot-for-shot with you."

Harry burst into laughter. "You're kidding right?"

"No, Harry, I'm not kidding. I'm dead serious."

"Look, Ms. Granger. No offence or nothing, but first of all, you're a woman. It's a proven fact, that a man can out drink a woman. Second of all, I probably weigh a 150 pounds more than you."

Alex raised her eyebrows. "Actually, Harry, I just read something not too long ago, and I believe it said that men were three times more likely to lose their inhibitions when given the same amount of alcohol as women."

"What were you reading," Harry grunted, "a comic book?"

"I believe it was the New York Times," Alex smiled.

"Well, wherever you read it, it's a crock of shit! I think your chances of drinking me under the table are pretty slim."

Alex raised a sarcastic brow. "And don't forget, that I'm at least fifteen years older than you are, too!"

"Well, there you go, three out of three in my favor!" Harry arrogantly folded his arms behind his head and leaned back in his chair. "Those are pretty lousy odds if you ask me."

"In that case," Alex winked, "you won't have to worry about losing, will you?"

"That's a given, Ms. Granger. Like I said, I'm twice your size. There's no way you could drink me under the table."

Alex flashed him a sexy grin. "You know what they say, Harry?"

"And what's that?" he asked.

"Don't believe everything you see!" she winked.

"Yeah ... whatever."

Harry waved off Alex's comment and focused his attention on the attractive blonde strolling past the table. If there was one thing Alex hated more than rudeness, it was being dismissed in the middle of a conversation. This cocky little bastard needed an old-fashioned, farm-type ass kicking, and she was just the one to give it to him. She reached across the table and poked him in the arm. "Harry, if you won't take a bet from me, what about a challenge? I've heard that firefighters are always up to a challenge."

"You've got that right," Harry replied as his eyes followed the blonde. "I'm up to that challenge for sure!"

When Harry stood up, Lorne pulled back into his seat. "God, I can't believe how rude you are, man."

"What?" Harry shrugged his shoulders. "I'm just checking out the action."

"Alex was talking to you," Lorne frowned. "Don't be such a dink."

Harry rolled his eyes and turned back to Alex. "Yeah, so, you were saying?"

"I challenge you to a private drinking contest, Harry. Just you ... me ... and a bottle of tequila."

"That's no contest," Harry laughed. "You'd be falling off your bar stool after the fourth shot."

Alex felt her anger build. "Would you like to bet on that, Harry?"

"Sure, why not." Harry tipped his head and gave her a cocky grin. "What do I get when I win?"

"What kind of a vehicle do you have?" Alex asked.

"I've got a jeep. Why do you ask?"

"If you could have a sports car, what would it be?"

"A Jag ... man." Harry puffed out his chest like a proud peacock. "I'd look pretty hot in a Jag!"

Alex reached into her handbag, pulled out a business card and passed it across the table to Harry. "This is my lawyer. If you win, call him when you get home and you'll have a brand new Jag ... of your choice, in your driveway within a week."

"Yeah, right," Harry belched. "I'm going to drink you under the table, and you're going to buy me a sports car?"

"That's the wager," Alex smiled.

"You must have a shit load of cash, lady."

Alex's voice took on a seductive charm. "Harry, darlin', I have more money than you will see in your entire lifetime."

"Well, if you want to give it away," Harry threw his arms up in the air, "who am I to argue?"

"And what do you get from Harry, if you win, Alex?" Lorne asked.

"Like that's going to happen," Harry laughed.

Alex stood up and glared down at Firefighter Harry Baker. "If I win," she smiled, "I get the satisfaction of knowing that tomorrow instead of trolling the beach for innocent victims; you'll be flat on your ass with a head the size of Texas!" She glanced at her watch. "We'll meet back here, at, say, ten?"

Alex excused herself and left the table. Walking to the lobby, she couldn't help but wonder what she was getting herself into. There was a time in her life when she could drink most grown men under the table, but that was ages ago. These days, she hardly drank at all; Brian did enough of that for the both of them.

The front desk clerk greeted Alex warmly as she approached. "*Buenas noches, Señora,*" the young man smiled. "What can we do for you this evening?" She handed him the note that had been slipped under her door. He examined the white piece of paper and opened the guest register. Beside room 4211, there was a bright red star with a notation in the margin:

A FRIEND OF THE BOSS NOT TO BE ASKED
TO RELOCATE. SEE THAT SHE'S TAKEN
CARE OF.

The desk clerk looked up at Alex and smiled. "There is no problem, *Señora.* The note must have been given to you by mistake." Alex thanked him and he called to her as she turned to walk away. "*Señora,* have you eaten yet?"

"No, I haven't," Alex smiled, "but I was just about to." She pointed down the pathway leading from the lobby. "Is that the way to the main restaurant?"

"Please, *Señora*," the young man handed her a small white ticket. "This is a reservation for our Japanese restaurant. It is *eh* for our last sitting at eight-thirty. If you wish, you may have it."

"Thank you," Alex smiled in appreciation. "My daughter tells me the food is great!"

"Your daughter has been here before, *Señora*?"

"Yes, a few times."

"Well, she is right." he smiled proudly. "Do you know how to find the restaurant?" he asked.

"No, I don't."

The clerk pulled a map from under the counter and opened it for Alex to look at. "Here are the directions to the restaurant. Enjoy your meal."

Alex took the information and left the lobby. On the pathway in front of the beach, she spotted a uniformed guard patrolling the shoreline. It gave her a sense of security. Last month, friends of hers were robbed at gunpoint while vacationing in Cancun.

At the restaurant, Alex was impressed with the décor. Colorful oriental rice paper lanterns hung from the ceiling. Beautiful Mexican women dressed in brightly colored silk kimonos scurried about the dining room carrying food, and beverages, and empty trays of dishes. The pleasant aroma wafting from the grill made her stomach growl and she was suddenly famished.

"*Buenas noches, Señora.*"

"Good evening," Alex replied with a smile.

"May I see your reservation, please?" Alex handed the young woman her ticket. "We are just clearing out the first dinner seating. Please," she pointed towards the brick walkway that circled the largest of the resort's pools. "Have a walk around, *Cinco minutos*." The woman held up five fingers. "Five minutes. Then you come back."

Alex admired the gardens and the scent of the tropical flowers filled her nostrils as she made her way around the pool. The water was turquoise blue. Looking at it now, she couldn't help but wonder about the dive adventure Brian had booked for her. She hadn't had scuba gear on in four years, but then she'd always told her niece, Eleanor: "The biggest fear is fear itself. If you get dumped, you better get back in the saddle." Alex needed to get back in the water and overcome her fear. She'd check the brochure again when she got back to her room and call Carlos in the morning.

Returning to the restaurant, Alex was taken to a table setting for four, where she joined the couple already seated. They appeared to be her age. "Hi," the redheaded gentleman smiled. "I'm David Lawrence and this is my charming wife, Pat."

"I'm pleased to meet you both." Alex shook their hands and sat down.

"May I get everyone a cocktail?" the waiter asked.

David ordered Scotch and water. Pat ordered rum and Coke, Alex ordered a martini. "Vodka martini please, straight up, shaken not stirred, three olives and really, really cold."

David screwed up his face. "I never could drink those things. My dad drank martinis. Tasted one once, it tasted like turpentine!"

"To me," Alex grinned, "a well-made vodka martini tastes just like a cold refreshing glass of water."

While they waited for their beverages to arrive, David told Alex that he owned an advertising agency in Chicago and Pat was a retired English professor. The couple had been coming to *Las Tropicales* to celebrate their wedding anniversary since they first met here, eight years ago. David had never been married. Pat had two daughters from a previous marriage; twenty-three and twenty-eight. The youngest was a fashion model for a garment manufacturer. The oldest was married to a doctor and expecting her first child. Pat and David were thrilled at the concept of becoming grandparents.

When the waiter returned with their drinks, the three raised their glasses in a toast. "Here's to new friends," David announced.

"To new friends," Alex replied.

"Well, how is it?" Pat asked when Alex set her martini glass on the table.

"Perfect!" Alex smiled.

"Are you married, Alex?"

"Yes I am."

"How long?"

"It will be twenty-five years next month."

"That's just wonderful," Pat beamed. "Is your husband here with you?"

"No, I'm afraid not."

"Oh, that's too bad, dear. Are you here alone?"

Alex nodded her head. "Actually, my daughter was supposed to come with me, but she was called back to the hospital at the eleventh hour.

"Is your daughter a nurse?"

"No, she's a doctor."

"Just like our son-in-law," Pat proudly announced. "You and her father must be so proud."

"We are proud of her," Alex beamed. "She passed with honors, in a class of thirty-two."

"What's her specialty?" David asked.

"She's interning in emergency at the moment. I don't think she's made up her mind yet."

"Is she married?" Pat inquired.

"No."

"Probably just as well." David replied. "Our son-in-law is a doctor. We know all too well how long the hours can be."

When Pat reached across the table towards the plate of sushi, Alex couldn't help but notice the turquoise inlay bracelet clasped around the woman's wrist. "What a beautiful bracelet."

"Oh, thank you, Pat gushed. "David got it from a shop in downtown Puerto Vallarta. It's my anniversary present!"

"When's your anniversary?" Alex asked.

"In two days," Pat smiled, "and the past seven years have been heaven." She turned and gave her husband a loving smile. "When I found David, I found the love of my life."

Alex thought she too had found the love of her life in Sam Bennett, twenty-five years ago. They'd fallen head over heels. He'd asked her to marry him. She believed him when he said he would never leave her. She was devastated when he didn't show up in Bermuda, and crushed when she discovered a week later that he'd married Grace Sanderson. Alex tried to forget Sam, to put him out of her mind like a bad dream, but nine months later she knew it would be impossible. Every time she looked at her daughter, she saw the man who'd helped create her.

"David and I come here every year to celebrate our anniversary." Pat blushed. "We usually stay in the same room, but this year they made a mistake with the reservation."

"I'm sure you must be disappointed," Alex frowned.

"Oh, no! The room we're in is fabulous! There's a living room and a bedroom and two balconies. The bathroom has a telephone, a double shower, and a jetted tub. The entire suite is decorated beautifully! But the best thing about it," Pat turned and smiled lovingly at her husband, "the music from the evening show and the disco doesn't keep David awake when he wants to go to bed early."

"Speaking of the evening show," David piped up, "if you're not doing anything after dinner, we'd love to have you join us. The entertainment starts at ten o'clock. I think tonight's performance is their International Show. The dance numbers are great, especially the *Jazz Hot* number from that movie Victor Victoria, with Julie Andrews and James Garner. Juanita, the choreographer, does the number herself, and boy," David swiped his hand across his brow, "she's *Jazz Hot*, baby!"

Alex was about to explain that she had a previous commitment when Angelina Rodriguez, the thirty-something beauty who'd welcomed her flight, appeared at the table.

"*Buenas noches, Señor y Señoras,*" Angelina smiled. "How are you enjoying yourselves so far?"

David pushed his large, muscular frame back from the table. "We're just about to chow down! Do you have a wheelbarrow handy to take me back to my room after I've pigged out?"

Angelina shook her head. "I'm afraid not *Señor,* but perhaps a golf cart." She gave David and Pat a warm friendly smile. "Mr. and Mrs. Lawrence, on behalf of the management, please accept our apologies for the problem with your room. I'm afraid there was a slight mix-up at our reservation desk."

"Oh, Angelina, don't apologize." Pat exclaimed. "The room we're in is fabulous! I've never seen anything like it."

"*Gracias Señora.* On behalf of Mr. B., please enjoy it."

"Speaking of the management," David scanned the restaurant. "Where is the boss? I haven't seen him all day."

"Neither have I." There was a loud crash from the direction of the kitchen. "If you will excuse me," Angelina frowned. "I'm afraid I need to take care of that."

5

ANGELINA RODRIGUEZ WAS BORN in Cuba. Her mother died when she was four. Brought up by her grandmother and aunt, she was a gifted child whom, by age six, could sing like a canary. At seven, Angelina expressed an interest in gymnastics. At ten, her grandmother enrolled her in the International School of Havana where she learned to dance. At twelve, her aunt married a man from Canada and moved to Montreal. To Angelina, it was like losing her mother all over again.

At age fourteen, Angelina's grandmother died and she was forced to move to Canada to live with her aunt and uncle. Her aunt promised that she would love Montreal. She promised her she would make new friends and start a new life. In Angelina's mind, her aunt lied. The winters in Canada weren't like Cuba. They were cold and damp and it snowed. In the summer, she didn't swim in the ocean, she swam in a pool.

Angelina was enrolled in a Catholic girls' school and she hated it. Her classmates were mean and cruel and made fun of the way she spoke. It wasn't long before she withdrew from everything except her dancing. Each day after class, Angelina rushed to Madame Prud'homme's dance studio where she practiced for hours in hopes of one day joining the ballet.

When she turned eighteen, Angelina moved back to Cuba and took a job as a dancer at a resort in Havana. There, she met Juan Montera and fell in love. When she turned twenty-one, her aunt and uncle purchased a villa in Puerto Vallarta, Mexico, and invited her to move in with them. They would get a visa for her and she would be free of a country darkened under a cloud of dictatorship. There was only one catch;

she had to leave Juan behind and marry a Mexican friend of her uncle's. At first, Angelina balked at the idea, but when her aunt told her that she could file for a divorce after one year and bring Juan to Mexico to join her, she changed her mind.

Two days after arriving in Mexico, there was a small wedding ceremony and *Señorita Rodriguez* became a *Señora*. The following week, Angelina auditioned for a position with the entertainment staff at a new vacation resort thirty minutes from the city. And so, began her career at *Las Tropicales*.

Angelina loved her job and worked very hard at it. By eight each morning, she had finished breakfast and was working on the daily activity schedule for guests at the resort. From eight-thirty until nine she practiced dance numbers with cast members. From nine-thirty until ten, she gave tennis lessons. From ten until ten forty-five, she helped teach Spanish. From eleven until noon, Angelina and the other members of the activity staff entertained hotel guests with beach volleyball, ping-pong tournaments, dance lessons and water aerobics.

From noon until one o'clock Angelina rested and refueled. Afterwards, she and the cast rehearsed the entire evening show from start to finish. From four p.m. until six, Angelina took care of the *Kids Club* at the resort so Rosa, a friend and fellow cast member, could pick her son up from school and make him dinner. At seven o'clock, she helped entertain guests at the bar with games of *'Name That Tune'* and *'Trivial Pursuit'*. At nine o'clock she went to the theater and began preparing for the evening show. At midnight, she went home and fell into bed.

During her first three months at *Las Tropicales*, Angelina wrote to Juan whenever she had a free moment. She told him about the people she'd met from around the world. She told him how much she enjoyed her job and all about the new friends she'd made. Most of all, Angelina told Juan how much she missed him and that she couldn't wait until they were together again.

By the end of Angelina's sixth month at *Las Tropicales*, Juan and the memories of their time together in Cuba had long been forgotten. She had a new interest. She'd taken up scuba diving and spent all of her free time in the ocean. When Angelina was diving, she forgot about the world on the surface and got immersed in the world below. She'd been to Las Marietas and Las Caletas. She'd gone diving in Corbetena where she'd seen mantas, schools of fish, turtles, dolphins and sharks. But her favorite dives were the twilight ones she took to *Los Arcos* once a month with Hans Zimmerman, the PADI dive instructor at the resort.

After living in Mexico for one year, Angelina was granted a divorce. A week later, her aunt surprised her with the news that she'd found a job for Juan in Puerto Vallarta, and was bringing him to Mexico. Angelina was furious. How dare her aunt make such a bold move without consulting her first! They quarreled, but in the end Angelina convinced her aunt that being single was the best thing. Her hours were long and she would have no time to entertain a husband; besides, there was a new love interest in her life.

For Angelina, life in Mexico was perfect until one afternoon, during a rehearsal; her dance partner lost his balance and dropped her. The fall broke her hip and the doctor told her she would never dance again. Angelina was terrified that she'd lose her job, but Sam Bennett was a wonderful boss who treated his staff like family. He assured her that she would always have a job, no matter what.

When Angelina was able to work again, she was transferred to housekeeping. She hated picking up after guests, but from a very young age, her grandmother taught her that only she could turn a bad situation into a good one. It was only after Angelina decided to leave her own personal touch in each room, that her job took on new meaning.

After scrubbing the shower, the sink, the toilet, making the beds, washing the ceramic tiled floor and dusting every piece of furniture, she folded the face cloths on the marble bathroom counter into a perfect square, then folded back the left corner and tucked a bright pink hibiscus flower inside. She molded two of the fresh white bath towels into the shape of swans and placed them on the end of the bed. Fresh flowers were left on the bedside tables, an extra bottle of water on the bureau, and the air conditioner adjusted so the temperature would be perfect when the occupants returned from their day on the beach. Soon, hotel guests were complimenting the management and Angelina's housekeeping skills became standard practice throughout the resort

Allowed to keep her tips, Angelina often took home an extra fifty American dollars a week. Some guests preferred leaving small gifts. During her six-month stint in housekeeping, she'd received nylons, hair combs, earrings, necklaces, perfume, fragrant soaps, bracelets and candles. She'd even collected enough make-up to open her own cosmetics' shop. She kept the cash, but once a month took the trinkets, put them in a box, and delivered them to a nearby orphanage.

From housekeeping, Angelina transferred to the food and beverage department and enjoyed waiting on hotel guests, most of the time. Once, when filling in as hostess at the Kyoto restaurant, a couple from Nebraska refused to be seated at a table of French-Canadians. The man told her that he'd been sitting beside the same people on the beach all day and found them rude and obnoxious. Angelina suggested a table for four, where they could join a charming elderly couple from Germany. The American refused: "I'm not sitting with any Krauts! And you can forget about the Nips too. Those bastards bombed Pearl Harbor! I'll sit with someone from the good old U. S. of A., or I won't eat here!"

Long forgotten were Angelina's dreams of the ballet and while working in the food and beverage department, she decided to make tourism her career. She took it upon herself to learn everything she could about the resort and requested postings in every restaurant, on every shift. Some mornings she arrived in the kitchen at four a.m. to begin preparations for breakfast. Some nights, she was still washing dishes at two in the morning.

In her next position at *Las Tropicales*, Angelina acted as an assistant to the guest services manager. She welcomed tour groups, handled complaints and took care of any special food requirements. Her most important task was reviewing the questionnaires given to each guest when they checked out. It was the typical *'How did you like our service'* and *'How can we make it better'* survey, but the information helped management with improvements.

The resort installed hairdryers in every room when female guests complained about having to borrow one from the front desk. They added more food selections to their midnight buffet, installed towel racks on every balcony, and placed a small writing desk in each room. Sam even fired two bartenders when Angelina reported that she'd received numerous complaints about their service.

Angelina's next assignment was her most challenging. Who would have thought that being Grace Sanderson Bennett's personal assistant would send her home each night physically and mentally drained. Grace was a demanding, snobbish, stuck-up *rich bitch* and for the life of her she couldn't understand how a kind, caring, considerate man like Sam Bennett could end up married to such a woman.

Each morning, except Sunday, Angelina's first duty was to serve Mrs. Bennett breakfast in bed. If the woman's omelet wasn't hot enough, or there was more than just a dusting of butter on her lightly-browned white toast, Mrs. Bennett threw the tray across the room. After drawing a bubble bath and laying out Grace's clothes for the day, Angelina cleared the suite of empty booze bottles, overflowing ashtrays, and remnants of the cocaine that had been snorted the night before. Once, she walked in while Grace was doing lines of cocaine. Angelina begged the woman to stop and told her the drugs would kill her, but Grace Bennett wouldn't listen. Instead, she threatened to have Angelina fired if she ever breathed a word of the drug activity to Sam.

Two months later, while carrying a tray of dirty dishes from Grace's bedroom, Angelina slipped on the wet ceramic floor, fell and broke her knee cap. When the doctor ordered her off work for eight weeks, Grace Bennett demanded that she be fired, but Sam wouldn't hear of it. Instead, he moved Angelina into an apartment behind the resort and dropped in on her three times a day to make sure she was okay. He took her to her doctor's appointments, and picked up her medications and personal items. Twice, he'd even stayed for dinner.

Over the course of her recovery, Angelina learned all about Sam's childhood and his summer vacations in Martha's Vineyard, Massachusetts. Compared to her childhood in Cuba, she couldn't even imagine living in such a place. Occasionally, he talked about his marriage and once, when she asked him why he'd stayed with Grace if his life had been so miserable Sam told her he had no choice. Angelina could only assume it meant that Sam Bennett believed in his wedding vows ... *for better or worse ... until death do us part.*

***

Having dealt with the tray disaster in the kitchen, Angelina continued searching the resort for Sam. It was like he'd vanished into thin air. No one had seen him all day. She'd tried his cell phone a dozen times, but there was no answer. When she called his apartment, she got his machine. She'd checked the spa, the tennis court, and even a nearby golf course all places where she could usually find him when he told her he was going for a drive. When Sam didn't show up for their three o'clock scuba date, she started to worry. He was missing in action; that wasn't like him.

After taking one more sweep of the property, Angelina decided to go back to Sam's office. There, she found him pacing the floor like a caged animal. "Where have you been?" she scolded. "I've been worried sick. You missed our dive date at three and you were noticeably absent from the managers' dinner meeting. Is something wrong?"

There was something wrong, all right, and her name was Alex Granger! For a moment, Sam thought about spilling his guts and telling Angelina how he and Alex met twenty-five years ago and had fallen head over heels in love. He thought about telling Angelina that he planned on marrying Alex until he was stopped at the airport by Grace's father ... and several grams of cocaine. He even thought about telling her how he'd staged his own death to prevent Grace from harming Alex's child.

Sam closed his eyes and Grace's threat from years earlier flashed before him like a bad movie: "What the hell is this?" she demanded, waving the photograph in his face. "Look at this, you and that slut you were going to run off with before we got married. Who's the kid, Sam? Is she your kid? She sure looks like you! I should have let Daddy take care of that bitch like he wanted to, but oh no, I told him that once we were married you'd forget all about her. Don't fuck with me Sam. I swear to God, if you go anywhere near that *slut* again, I'll kill the kid!" The hatred Sam saw in his wife's eyes that day ... told him she meant it.

"Did you hear me?" Angelina asked.

The sweet voice brought Sam back to reality. "I'm sorry, did you say something?"

"I asked you if anything was wrong."

"Nothing's wrong." Sam rubbed his stomach. "It's just a little indigestion from the burrito I ate at the airport this morning, that's all."

Angelina rushed to his side. "That was hours ago! You shouldn't still have indigestion. I told you there was something wrong with your stomach. Sit down. I'll get you an Alka-Seltzer."

Watching her walk to the mini-bar, Sam was reminded of what a good friend she'd become since Grace's death. At the funeral, he'd been standing alone at the casket when she approached him to offer her condolences. Angelina was a valued employee and he was touched that she'd attended the service especially after the way Grace had treated her. She told him how sorry she was for his loss and apologized for causing it.

When Sam asked what she meant, Angelina told him she knew that Grace had purchased the cocaine. She'd thought about coming to him with the information but he was the boss, she was just an employee. Angelina told him she begged and pleaded with his wife not to take the drug. She reminded Grace how well she was doing with her drug rehab, but Grace wouldn't listen. As a last resort, Angelina had gone to her friend, the priest, and taken him to the suite. By the time they arrived it was too late ...Grace was dead.

In Sam's mind, Grace's overdose had been a blessing in disguise. The Sandersons had been an albatross around his neck since he married into the family. For years, Moe used Sam's legal license for crooked horse deals and Grace's cocaine habit had nearly cost him his business and her drinking ... his reputation.

When Grace was drunk, she picked up male hotel guests and invited them back to her private little pleasure palace. Sam was sure every staff member at the resort knew about it, and thought him a fool for turning a blind eye, but at least her extra curricular sexual activities kept her out of his hair.

When Grace was stoned, she turned into a monster. Once, at a dinner party he was hosting for the governor of the State of Nayarit Mexico, she showed up high on the substance of the week. When the waiter tried to take her wrap, Grace accused him of making a pass at her: "How dare you touch me!" she'd shouted. "Don't you know who I am? I am Mrs. Samuel Bennett. I'm the daughter-in-law of a United States senator and the wife of the owner of this resort. You better learn some manners young man, or I'll have your ass fired." Grace protested even louder when Sam firmly took her by the arm and tried to remove her from the room. "He grabbed me Sam. He made a pass at me. Something you never do anymore!"

Sam ignored her comment and apologized to the new employee. "Please, forgive my wife. She hasn't been feeling well."

"You're goddamn right I haven't been feeling well," Grace spat, "but I'm sure I'd feel a whole lot better if you'd fuck me once in awhile." She spun around and glared at Angelina. "I'm sure Angelina feels great, Sam. You're fucking her, aren't you?"

Sam couldn't deny that the thought had crossed his mind a time or two, Angelina was a beautiful woman, but he knew better than to dip his pen in the company inkwell.

To make up for Grace's abusive behavior, two months after the funeral, Sam promoted Angelina to assistant manager. She took pride in her work and handled her duties with prompt efficiency. She knew every staff member by name and always pitched in when tables needed to be bussed, or rooms needed to be cleaned.

Angelina had an eye for decorating and she'd done a great job with the resort's recent room renovations. The only room Sam wouldn't let her touch was the luxuriously decorated private suite where Grace had entertained many a male hotel guest. Sam wanted the room left as is to remind him of the hell he'd gone through while his wife was alive.

"Here, drink this." Angelina handed Sam the fizzy beverage. "When you're finished, we'll go for a walk along the beach. The exercise will make your stomach feel better."

"*Si Señorita*." Sam downed the Alka-Seltzer in three gulps and handed back the glass. "Happy now?"

"*Si*." Angelina looked into Sam's blue eyes. "Where were you today?"

"No place special," he answered. "I just had some things I needed to do." Sam had spent the afternoon at his favorite secluded beach reading through his journal. On every other page, there was something about Alex. It was usually a comparison to Grace.

Seeing the vacant expression on Sam's face, Angelina reached out and touched him on the shoulder. "Is there anything you'd like to share with me, Sam?"

"Like what?" he asked.

"I know you said you have indigestion, but I'm beginning to think that your current state involves more than food. I think there's something else on your mind. Would you like to talk about it?"

Sam shook his head. "Talk about what?"

"Talk about why you were pacing around here like a cat in a cage when I walked in, and don't tell me that it has anything to do with a burrito. I don't believe that for a minute. I think what's bothering you, has more to do with Grace's death, than food."

The remark took Sam by surprise. "What do you mean?"

"You can stand there and pretend all you want, that you've forgotten what day Thursday is, but I know you better than that. In fact, I know you better than your own wife did."

Sam shrugged his shoulders. "What are you talking about?"

"Thursday is the one-year anniversary of Grace's death. You can't tell me you've forgotten."

Actually, he had. In fact, Sam hadn't thought about Grace since he buried her. Not until this morning, when he saw Alex's name in the guest register.

"Sam, talk to me. What's bothering you? Is it Grace?"

Sam turned away from Angelina then and told her a bald-faced lie. "Yes. Grace's death has been on my mind."

"Why didn't you come and talk to me about it? You didn't have to leave the property. We could have still gone diving. It would have taken your mind off things."

Sam turned back to face her. "Angelina, you know I love you, but I am a big boy. Sometimes I need to take care of things myself, okay?"

Offended by his remark, Angelina took a step back. "I'm sorry, Sam," she apologized, "it's just that I care about you. I want to be there for you."

"You are there for me." He gave her a boyish grin. "You always have been. Don't apologize. I know I'm not always the easiest person to get along with. Sometimes, I'm a complete asshole."

"You can say that again," Angelina grinned.

"Well, I'm about to make it up to you." Sam picked up a blue file folder from his desk. "When's the last time you had a vacation?" he asked.

"We both know that getting a vacation in this business is like pulling teeth. Besides," she smiled, "working here is like taking a vacation everyday."

"I'm serious. When's the last time you had a vacation?"

"I don't remember. Why?"

Sam held up the folder. "I'm thinking of buying this property in the Dominican Republic. I'd like you to fly down and check it out. If you like it, it's yours."

"What do you mean, *it's mine*?"

"If you like it, I'll buy it, and you can run the place."

"Oh, my God!" Angelina's face broke into an excited smile. "It's what I've been waiting for. It's what I've worked so hard for!"

She threw herself into Sam's arms and he was taken aback when she kissed him on the lips. When she buried her face in his chest, he couldn't help but recognize a familiar fragrance. It was the one Alex had been wearing the last time he held her in his arms. He closed his eyes and inhaled the enticing aroma. The Clinique Aromatics Elixir lingered in his nostrils and he got lost in the scent. For a moment ... Alex was back in his arms.

Without thinking, Sam pulled the warm body closer. As the soft curves melted into his, he could think of nothing but making love to Alex. He readied his mouth for a passionate kiss. Only inches from the hot breath, Sam opened his eyes and his body shuddered when he saw Angelina's lips waiting to greet his. He took a quick step backward; forcing her to release her arms from around his neck.

Sam had almost made a terrible mistake. This wasn't Alex, it was Angelina. Thank God he'd stopped himself in time! Angelina was a trusted employee and a valued friend. He would never do anything to screw that up. They'd grown closer since Grace's death and Sam found himself confiding in her more and more about his business and personal life. There was, however, one thing he'd never told Angelina. He'd never told her about Alex, just like he'd never told Alex about Grace. If he had, today things would be different.

It was then, when Sam made a decision. He had to find Alex and tell her the truth. "Listen, Angelina, would you mind if we called it a night?"

"But, Sam, I thought we were going to go for a moonlit walk?"

Hearing the disappointment in Angelina's voice, Sam gave her an apologetic smile. "I know doll, but the Alka-Seltzer seems to have worked. There's something really important that I need to take care of. Can I get a rain check?"

Angelina lowered her head. "Well, yes, I suppose so."

"Good." Sam put his arm around her shoulder and escorted her to the door. "Why don't you go home and decide what you're going to take on your trip. We'll have breakfast together in the morning."

6

WHEN ANGELINA WAS GONE, Sam picked up the telephone and called the front desk. "*Hola*," a pleasant voice answered. "This is Jonathan."

"Hi, Jonathan. It's Sam."

"What can I do for you this evening, sir?"

"Could you please check the dinner reservations and see where the party from room 4211 is dining tonight." Sam drummed his fingers nervously on his desk while he waited. He'd find out which restaurant Alex was in and hide in the shadows where he could watch her undetected.

"There were no dinner reservations made for room 4211 this evening." Jonathan told him.

"You're sure?"

"Yes, I've checked the reservation lists for all of the restaurants."

"And there's no Alex Granger on any of them?"

"Alex Granger!" Jonathan's voice suddenly lit up. "Why didn't you say so? I remember her. What a beautiful woman! She was here at the desk about an hour ago. Tomas gave her a ticket to the last seating at Kyoto."

Sam checked his watch. It was nine-thirty, the dinner guests would be finishing soon. "Jonathan, do you know what table she was seated at?"

"No, but if you'll hold on a minute, I'll call the restaurant."

Sam's heart beat faster knowing that in five minutes he would be looking at the face of an angel ... he would be looking at Alex.

"Here it is, sir. Ms. Granger is at table twenty-three with David and Pat Lawrence."

"Great," Sam mumbled under his breath. Pat Lawrence was a charming woman, but she could put a gossip columnist at the National Enquirer to shame. Yesterday while he was having lunch with the Lawrences, Pat filled him in on the comings and goings of several hotel guests. The couple sharing room 1918 wasn't married, and the couple in room 2120 were gay. Pat told Sam that there was a group of college girls she was sure were trying out for Hooters waitresses; the way they were flashing their boobs! She told Sam about a woman who'd spent the first two days of her vacation on the telephone fighting with her husband, and she pointed out the gentleman who was threatening to sue the resort.

Sam had met the middle-aged man Pat spoke of. The hotel guest had slipped and fallen down the five steps leading from the bar to the beach. He demanded that he be taken to the hospital by ambulance. The resort's doctor reassured him that an ambulance wouldn't be necessary; there were no broken bones, only a mild sprain. The guest wasn't satisfied. He demanded a wheelchair and a direct line to his lawyer's office in the States.

Sam smiled to himself, remembering now how well Angelina had handled the situation. Two minutes into her conversation with the disgruntled guest, she had him hook, line, and sinker with her seductive charm. Yes, Angelina was quite a woman and he was sure she'd make a great manager.

"Did you hear me, sir?" Jonathan asked.

"Yes," Sam quickly answered. "Ms. Granger is at table twenty-three with the Lawrences. Thanks."

Sam knew he would recognize Alex instantly. Her face was etched in his brain; the curves of her body burned in his soul. When he arrived at the Kyoto restaurant, the majority of dinner guests were leaving their tables and making their way to the theater for the evening show. He spotted the Lawrences, but Alex wasn't with them.

For five minutes, Sam waited impatiently in the shadows. When Alex didn't return, he went to the table to investigate. "Good evening. Did you enjoy your dinner?"

"It was great as always," David patted his full round stomach, "but once again, I ate too much!"

"Everybody does!" Sam turned to Pat. "How do you like your suite?"

"Oh, it's just perfect," Pat gushed. "In fact, I was telling the lady who was sitting with us that I've never been in a more beautiful room in my life." She turned to her husband. "What was her name, dear?"

"Granger, Alex Granger." David gave Sam a nudge and a wink. "She's quite a looker, Sam. Her husband is a lucky man."

"I'm sure he is," Sam casually remarked as he scanned the room. "Where is this breath of fresh air?"

"I'm not sure," David replied. "We invited her to come to the show with us tonight, but she mentioned something about having a date with a firefighter."

Sam had no reason to be, but as he listened to David talk about Alex and her date, he found himself growing jealous. It had been twenty years since he'd seen Alex; twenty-five since he'd made love to her with a passion he'd never felt with any other woman. Now that fate had brought her back into his life; nothing, and no one, was going to take her away, ever again. "Will you please excuse me? There's something I need to take care of." Sam left the table with the intent of seeking Alex out ... but decided against it. Instead, he'd go back to the office and write her a note.

Walking through the lobby, the echo of laughter turned his attention toward the bar. It was then, when Sam spotted Alex for the first time and the sight of her took his breath away. Her skin held a deep-radiant tan, accented by the white sundress she wore. He wanted to rush to her, take her in his arms, and tell her that he still loved her; that he'd always loved her.

Instead, Sam spent the next thirty minutes watching from the cover of a hibiscus bush. Alex was sitting with four muscular, good-looking men. Sam estimated them to range from age twenty-five to thirty-five. There was a bottle of tequila and two shot glasses in the middle of the table. Alex picked up the bottle, filled each glass, and passed one to the man across from her. She said something to him and they each drank. *Way to go Alex,* Sam chuckled to himself.

Alex set her glass on the table and began chatting with the other men in the group. They laughed and joked and one of them poured two more shots. Again, Alex and the man across from her drank. When they were finished, they stood up and touched the end of their nose with the index finger of their right hand, then their left, then their right again. Next, they walked across the bar, turned and walked back to the table.

"Shall we go again?" Sam heard the man say before he poured two more shots and pushed one of them across the table.

Alex motioned for the waiter. She whispered something to him and he left the table. When he returned he was carrying two glasses, a jug of water and a pitcher of beer. Alex poured a glass of water, took two sips, then stood up and excused herself from the table. Sam watched with interest as she gracefully glided across the ceramic floor on her way to the ladies' room. When she was out of sight, he turned his attention back to the table.

The man Alex had been drinking with poured himself a glass of beer and finished it in four big gulps. "Talking to Ralph on the great-white telephone already?" he asked when Alex returned to the table. "You've only had two tequilas, Ms. Granger. I told you I could drink you under the table, so you might as well call your lawyer right now!"

Alex poured another glass of water and sipped at it casually before returning to her conversation with the other men in the group. Growing impatient, her drinking partner filled his mug with beer and took two big gulps. He set the mug on the table and wiped his mouth with the back of his hand. "Are we going to do this, or what?" Alex nodded her head, picked up a shot glass of tequila and poured it down her throat. The man across from her did the same.

Watching the action, it took Sam about five minutes to figure out what Alex was doing and a proud smile danced across his face. "Way to go, Alex. You're a genius!" he chuckled. She was using an old drinking trick Sam had learned in college and tried himself a time or two. After each tequila shot, Alex started a conversation with the occupants of the table. Next, she picked up her glass of water and savored three small sips. Growing impatient, her opponent picked up his beer and did the same. Before long, Alex had the man chasing each shot of tequila with a *cerveza*.

After the fourth and sixth shot, the drinking contestants repeated their motor-skills test. Sam was impressed that Alex could still walk. Her opponent was beginning to weave. It was no wonder; he'd consumed twice as much alcohol. After the tenth shot, Alex rose to her feet. "Are you going to the *baño* again?" the man asked.

"No," Alex answered. "I'm ready to test my motor skills. Aren't you?" Her opponent pushed his chair back from the table. When he attempted to stand, he collapsed onto the floor. "I guess not," she laughed.

The men sitting with her stood and cheered: "You did it Alex! You got Harry good! I can't believe someone your size could drink him under the table. He weighs over 200 pounds!"

Alex grabbed the chair for support and slowly sat down. She gave the firefighter ... nick-named Shrek, a high-five and the three men dragged their buddy from the bar. Sam was tossing around the idea of approaching Alex when David Lawrence approached him.

"Did you see that?" David asked. "That's the lady who was sitting with us at dinner. Did you see her drink that big smart-ass under the table? Come on, I'll introduce you to her."

Sam didn't need an introduction and now probably wasn't the time to be popping back into Alex's life. "You know, I'd love to, David, but Miguel needs me to take care of something for him. How about I meet her tomorrow?"

"Suit yourself." David gave Sam a friendly slap on the shoulder. "See you at breakfast."

"*Buenas noches.*" Sam smiled. "I'll see you in the morning." He watched as David walked to Alex's table, bent over, and whispered something in her ear. When Alex turned to look in Sam direction, she slid off her chair.

7

WHEN ALEX OPENED HER eyes, her head was pounding like a drum and for a moment she didn't know where she was. Then it dawned on her ... she was on vacation. She held her hands to her head and forced her pickled brain to recall the chain of events that had led her to this current state.

After dinner with the Lawrences, she'd taken a tour of the resort. She remembered stopping near the main lobby, where people were gathering around the stage on the patio by the main pool. The Cuban beat of the four-piece band had hotel guests of all ages swaying their hips in time to the rhythm. At the microphone stood a six-foot-two gorgeous Antonio Banderas look-alike; with slick black hair, beautiful dark skin and inviting bedroom eyes. He was speaking to the band in Spanish and the words rolled off his tongue like a musical tune. He turned to the audience: "Ladies and gentlemen, tonight we are going to show you the Latin rhythm!" He swiveled his hips. "Please, *Señoras y Señoritas*, who will be the first to come to the stage and dance with me?"

At his invitation, women stood and raced across the patio. Two of them practically trampled Alex as they scurried past. To her left, a mother and daughter were having a heated discussion about the attractive MC standing center stage. "You're making a complete fool of yourself," the mother said. "He's too old for you, so quit following him around like a puppy dog."

The young woman pulled free from her mother's grasp. "He's not too old for me. He's twenty-eight and I'm twenty." She planted her hands firmly on her hips. "You can't forbid me to do anything, Mother! You don't own me. I can do whatever I want. Roberto loves me, he told me so."

"He doesn't love you," the mother laughed, "he just wants to get into your pants!"

"Just like you want to get into his?" the girl spat back in retaliation.

Alex quickly distanced herself from the squabbling women and strolled through the courtyard where vendors had set up their tables. There were turquoise and sterling silver bracelets for both ankle and wrist; rings for fingers and toes, money clips and sterling silver pot pipes. There were tables selling brightly colored Mexican blankets and sequin covered *sombreros*. Other tables featured everything from clay masks and wood carvings to oil paintings and straw drawings.

A gathering crowd on the far side of the courtyard peaked Alex's interest and she went to investigate. For his canvas, the artist used a ten-by-ten piece of ceramic tile. His paint brushes were the index and middle fingers of his right hand, and the one-inch fingernail that grew from the end of his pinky. First, he covered the tile with white paint then blended a mixture of blue and black, followed by brown, green and yellow. Before her eyes, the blank tile was transformed into a Mexican village at sunset. Alex remembered now that she ordered three of the artist's creations; one for her daughter, one for her niece, and one for herself.

From the courtyard, she'd gone to the bar to meet Harry Baker. He'd give her a T-shirt that read: *One tequila, two tequila, three tequila, floor*. Through her pounding headache, Alex remembered now that Harry's gift had pissed her off and she was determined to drink him under the table. She couldn't remember how many shots of tequila she'd had, but she did remember seeing Shrek and the other firefighters drag Harry from the bar.

Alex remembered talking to David Lawrence; he wanted to introduce her to the hotel manager. After that, her evening was a complete blank; except for the dream she'd had. Sam was in it. He'd swept her up in his arms and carried her down a moonlit beach. She could hear waves washing onto the shore and Sam was whispering in her ear: "I love you, Alex. I've always loved you."

A gentle tapping at the door brought Alex back to reality. When she sat up her head exploded into the worst hangover she'd had in years. "Hello," she croaked.

"*Buenos dias, Señora*, this is housekeeping. We come back later."

"Thank you."

Alex pushed back the covers, rolled out of bed and slowly stood up. Her head felt too heavy for her body. Carefully placing one foot in front of the other, she willed her legs to carry her across the room. Reaching the bathroom, Alex was positive the only thing that would make her feel better was a coffin. She closed the lid of the porcelain toilet and sat down to contemplate her next move. Go back to bed, or get something to eat. Deciding that a bagel and coffee couldn't hurt, she had a shower and got dressed.

It was only eight in the morning and already hotel guests were fanning out from their rooms and heading to the beach, and the pools, to claim their spot for the day. Alex made her way to the lobby and stopped at the internet café to check her e-mail. There was a birthday wish from Sarah, one from her brother, and a message from Brian reminding her about the dive trip he'd booked. Staring at the message, Alex knew she couldn't run from her fears forever. Maybe taking a lesson would be a good place to start.

She followed the signs through the resort until she found the dive shop. There was a notice hanging on the door that read: GIVING A LESSON, BACK IN AN HOUR. Alex looked around and spotted a hotel employee. "Excuse me. Could you please tell me where they give the diving lessons?"

"Pool number one, *Señora*. You follow the path past, *eh*, the bar and the restaurant," he pointed.

"Gracias."

At the pool, the PADI dive instructor was standing with a beautiful young blonde. Closer examination told Alex it was the same young woman who'd been fighting with her mother the night before. She pulled a lounge chair closer to the water's edge and sat to listen as the instructor coached his student.

"Water has weight and weight results in pressure," the instructor told the young woman. "The deeper you go, the more pressure there is. Pressure, on the other hand, has no affect on water. Our body is mostly water." He held up a diagram showing three balloons. "The water-filled balloon represents your body. See," he pointed at the picture in his flip chart, "the balloon is the same size on top of the water as it is under the water, because water pressure doesn't affect the water inside the balloon. Is this making sense?" he asked.

The blonde shook her head. "Yes, I think so."

"Air spaces on the other hand," the instructor continued, "are affected by water. When you go diving, you have four air spaces in your body. You have your ears, your sinus, your face mask and your lungs. Each of them is affected by pressure. The deeper you go, the more water pressure you have. Which means the volume of your air space becomes less. Why? Because ... the air inside your air space will be compressed. So, when you dive, you need to equalize your air space."

"Why," the blonde asked.

"Because it's not really healthy for your body if you don't. Have you ever been on a plane and felt pressure in your ears?"

"Yes."

"Well, it's basically the same thing when you dive." He gave his student an encouraging smile. "Now, how do we equalize our air pressure?" He flipped over the first page of the chart. "When we descend, we add air. When we ascend, we release air. Make sense?" The girl nodded her head. "Okay," he continued, "to equalize your ears and your sinus when you descend, you pinch your nose and blow gently." The instructor demonstrated. "You pinch your nose and blow through it every meter as you go down until your ears pop." Instructor and student practiced the exercise.

"To equalize the air space in your mask while you descend, blow through your nose into your mask as soon as you feel the mask press on your face." Again, he demonstrated. "If at any time during your descent you feel uncomfortable you stop, ascend one or two meters, so there's less pressure, and try to equalize again. How do we equalize?" he asked.

"I plug my nose and blow to equalize my ears and sinus," the girl answered. "To equalize my mask, I blow through my nose."

"Great, you're getting the hang of it. Now, our most important air space is of course our lungs. All you do, to equalize your lungs, is breathe. The most important rule in diving is to keep breathing. Never hold your breath. Holding your breath traps air in your lungs. The trapped air expands on ascent and your lungs stretch. Overstretched lungs, is a serious injury. Okay, let's get started." He tossed the diving gear into the pool and jumped in behind it, splashing two beauties sunbathing nearby.

"Hans Zimmerman, what are you doing?" one of them giggled. She sat up and stuck out her chest. "You're getting us all wet!"

The attractive thirty-something, well-built German dive instructor gave the women a devious grin. "Come on ladies, it's only water." Using the heel of his hand, he splashed them again.

"What was that?" one of them asked.

Hans held his arms in front of him and moved them a shoulder width apart. Next, he made a fist with his right hand and pounded it into the palm of his left. Then, he held the thumb of his right hand to his forehead and pointed his fingers straight ahead. The woman shook her head in confusion.

"What are you doing?" the other inquired.

"I'm just seeing if you understand diving lingo!"

"What do you mean, *diving lingo*?"

"It's a shark," Hans laughed. "A big ... fucking ... shark!" He let out a mischievous chuckle, and repeated his actions. Annoyed, his student cleared her throat to get his attention. "I'm sorry," he apologized. "Where were we? Oh yah, I was going to tell you some of the rules of diving."

"Rules?"

"Yes," Hans replied. "The best part of diving is seeing the aquatic life. So, we have a few rules. Not only to protect you, but to protect the sea creatures. Most of them don't sting or bite ... until they're provoked, so never tease or harass them. The other thing we ask when you dive, is to watch what you're doing and where you're putting your feet and hands. It doesn't take much to break off a piece of coral with your fins. And finally, never take anything out of the ocean. It would be like me coming into your home and taking a CD. Do you understand?" His student nodded her head.

"Okay, the other thing we have to learn when we go diving is how to communicate under water. In order to do that, we have a lot of hand signals we use when we dive. Let me show you the most important ones." Hans touched the tip of his thumb to his index finger. "This is my question, is everything okay? If everything is okay, you answer with the same hand signal. If there's something wrong, you indicate it by holding your hand in front of you, palm down and wave your hand from side to side. If I need, or want, to stop you for any reason, I will hold my hand up in front of you. Thumb up means to ascend. Thumb down means to descend.

"If I want to slow you down, I hold my hands, palm down, in front of me and move them up and down. If I want to check your air gauge, I will point to my air gauge. In response, you will show me your air gauge. Now, can you give me the signals?"

The student held her thumb to her forefinger. "This means that everything is okay." Next, she held her hand up in the air; palm facing her instructor. "This means stop." She made a fist and pointed upward with her thumb. "Go up." She flipped her wrist. "Go down."

"Good," Hans smiled. "If you want to slow down, or take it easy, you hold your hand out in front of you, palm down and move it up and down in the water. If you're having problems with your ears, just point to your ear. We will stop, and you can pressurize again." Hans held his hand palm down in front of his throat and waved it from left to right. "This means I'm out of air." He gave his student a reassuring smile, "but don't worry, I'll check your gauge often enough to make sure you don't run out of air. For the future, when you get certified, if this ever happens, give your diving buddy the signal so he knows what's happening with you, okay?"

Running out of air, Alex thought. The last time she dove, she'd almost drowned because she ran out of air. Perhaps she should have checked her own tank and not left it up to Brian.

"Excuse me, Ms. Granger?"

Alex looked up and blocked the sun with her hand. The attractive MC, she'd seen on the stage last night, was smiling down at her.

"*Buenos dias.* My name is Roberto Gomez."

The words were no more than out of his mouth when the young girl taking a diving lesson called out to him. "Good morning, Roberto. Am I going to see you tonight?"

"I don't know," he replied over his shoulder

"I need to know," she told him. "I have something special planned."

A devious grin curled Roberto's lips and he stared down at Alex. "I am so popular with the women," he winked. "They all want me! Will you excuse me, please?" He turned on his heels, took two steps towards the pool then stopped and turned back to Alex. "I almost forgot. This is for you." He handed her an ivory-colored envelope.

"What's this?" she asked.

"It's an invitation to the manager's cocktail party at six this evening. Mr. B. was very specific about making sure that you said yes."

"Mr. B.?"

"*Si*. He is the owner of the resort. Roberto gave Alex a seductive grin. "Will we see you at the cocktail party this evening, Ms. Granger?"

"Yes, of course," Alex smiled. "It's not everyday that I get invited to meet the owner of a resort. You can tell Mr. B. I'll be there."

8

FROM THE TIME SAM crawled into bed at two in the morning all he could think about was Alex and how unbelievable it was that she was here ... at his resort. He was impressed with the amount of booze she'd consumed during her little drinking contest. He'd carried her to her room just before midnight. Now hours later, he could still feel her arms wrapped around his neck and her soft breath against his shoulder.

Lucky for him, Angelina had come along when she did or he might have done something he would have regretted. She helped Sam open the door to Alex's room, then undressed her and put her to bed. Afterwards, she'd come to his office to ask about the woman. He told Angelina the woman was no one special.

Sam tossed and turned for hours thinking of what he would say to Alex when she saw him for the first time. He was sure she wouldn't remember last night and he couldn't keep avoiding her. They were bound to run into each other sooner or later.

He had no more then fallen asleep when the phone woke him up. Security had managed to separate the two brawling hotel guests, but now, one of the men was standing on a third-floor balcony threatening to jump.

It took Sam an hour to convince the man to come down from the balcony. When he did, he was handcuffed by the Mexican police and carted off to jail. Sam ran a tight ship. If a guest got out of line, they were asked to behave themselves. If they didn't, they were asked to leave.

It was four-thirty in the morning before things settled down. By then, Sam had given up on sleep altogether, so he headed to the main kitchen to help the morning crew with the breakfast prep. At the large stainless-steel sink, he took a box of fresh mangos and dumped them into a bath of soapy water. The fruit would rest there for twenty minutes before it was transferred to a bath of water and chlorine, where it rested for another ten minutes. Next, the fruit was placed in cool, purified water for half an hour. Every fruit and vegetable that came off the delivery truck was treated to the same disinfectant process, and Sam was very proud of the resort's health and safety program.

At six a.m. Sam left the kitchen and went to the *Tropical* lobby to greet a group of travelers arriving from Toronto, Canada. When the guests had checked in; their bracelets secured, and the bellmen were escorting them to their rooms, he went back to his apartment and had a shower.

At seven-thirty, Sam was sitting at the manager's table in the Royal restaurant. It was here where every morning, except Sunday, he met his management team for a breakfast meeting. With the food and beverage manager, he discussed suppliers and new items for the menu. With the controller Sam discussed finance. With human resources, Sam talked about his staff.

Las Tropicales paid its employees better than most resorts in the area. Each staff member was given twenty-five American dollars, or 250 *pesos* a day. In exchange, they worked eight hours, six days a week. Their uniforms were supplied, as were their meals. On the last Friday of every month, the accumulated tips collected from the restaurants were divided amongst the employees.

Sam looked up from his notes towards the entrance of the restaurant and his heart skipped a beat. Alex was standing in the doorway, looking in his direction. He panicked and sprang from his chair. "If you will all excuse me, there's something I need to take care of." The words were no more than out of his mouth when he turned on his heels and disappeared into the kitchen.

Angelina raced after him. "Sam," she called out. "Will you wait a moment, *por favor*." She caught up to him and grabbed his arm. "What is wrong with you? The meeting isn't finished yet. Carmen needs to give you her report about the people we moved last night after the fight."

"You handle it."

Without further explanation, Sam left the restaurant and hurried back to his office. It was time Alex knew the truth. He sat down at his desk, took a writing pad from the drawer and began to write:

> *Dear Alex, I need you to know that I am still alive and I still love you.*

Sam scribbled across the page and started again.

> *Dear Alex, Surprise, I'm not dead!*

When that didn't work, he scrunched the paper into a ball and threw it in the trash can and started again.

> *My dearest Alex, I know this is going to come as a shock to you, but I am still alive. I had my reasons for doing what I did twenty years ago after we had rekindled the spark. So please, you must forgive me for deceiving you.*
>
> *Please believe me when I say, if it could have been any different, it would have been. My heart aches every time I think about it. We were together again, and once more ripped from each others' arms.*

*I love you Alex, like I have never loved an-
other woman. Please, we need to talk. Now
that I've found you, I refuse to lose you again.*

*I have a V.I.P. visiting from a resort in the
Mayan Riviera, so I may not get a chance to
talk to you at the cocktail party, but please
wait for me. I've made arrangements for us to
have a private dinner in my suite.*

Forever, Sam

He folded the paper in half and placed it into an ivory-
colored envelope displaying the resort's logo and address. On
the front he wrote Alex's name and room number, then picked
up the telephone and called the front desk.

"*Hola.*"

"*Hola.* It's Sam. There's an envelope on my desk. I'd like
you to deliver it. I'll be off site until four."

9

ALEX LEFT THE POOL and found her way back to the restaurant where she'd had dinner the night before. It looked much different in the daylight; the oriental influence was gone. She made her way to an empty table and sat down. Within seconds, a young man named Armando was standing at her side. He was a tall, handsome Mexican smartly dressed in crisp-white trousers and a red, short-sleeved shirt. He had dark hair, dark brown eyes, and a brilliant smile. "*Buenas dias Señora*. Would you like coffee?"

"*Si*," Alex smiled.

Armando filled her cup and held up a white carafe. "Would you like *Leche?*" he asked.

"No milk. Thank you."

"*Habla usted Espanol?*" When Alex shook her head, Armando repeated the question in English. "Do you speak Spanish?"

Alex touched the tip of her thumb and index finger together. "*Pequeno*. Just a small bit," she smiled, "but I do know the two most important words and phrases! *baño* and *dos cerveza por favor.*"

Armando let out a hearty chuckle. "*Si Amiga*. It is very good that one knows where is the bathroom, and how to get more beer! Let me tell you first this morning about the buffet." Armando pointed to the display in the middle of the restaurant. "There is the buffet with the fresh tropical fruits and the cheeses and cold meats. There is also, the cold cereals and the yogurt. Or," he smiled, "if the *Señora* wishes, you can choose items from the hot buffet. We have the hash browns, quesadillas, refried beans and meat called *guisado*. You also got *huevo*, eggs, like *eh* the omelet, and how you say?" Armando turned his hand from palm up, to palm down.

"Over easy?" Alex smiled.

"*Si. Huevo* over easy. Also, there is the pancakes." Armando pointed to the grill. "Just over there to the grill. You wait in line. Margarita will make for you whatever you like."

"Thank you," Alex smiled. "I think the coffee will be good for now."

When Armando was gone, Alex watched the girl behind the grill flipping pancakes. *She'd be great at the Calgary Stampede*, Alex thought, where flipping flapjacks was an everyday occurrence during the ten-day rodeo. Alex had been to the Stampede once, with her father, twenty years ago. It was the first time she'd seen Sam, after he left her standing at the altar.

"Do you mind if I join you?"

Alex looked up. David Lawrence was standing over her. "Please, be my guest," she smiled. "Where's Pat?"

"I let her sleep in this morning. It was pretty late last night before things quieted down."

"Was the music from the disco too loud?" Alex asked.

"Hell no!" David exclaimed. "It was more exciting than that. Some young jackass got all drunk up and tried to jump off a balcony." David leaned closer to Alex. "Speaking of drinking, you sure tied one on last night." He gave her a friendly slap on the back. "I tell yah, it surprised the hell out of me that a little lady like you could drink that big bugger under the table!"

"Please don't remind me," Alex groaned.

"I see the boss got you back to your room okay."

"The boss?"

"Yeah," David chuckled. "You passed out just after the guys you were sitting with took their buddy away. The owner of the resort took you back to your room."

Alex was suddenly reminded of the dream she'd had last night; the one where Sam had carried her down the beach.

Had the manager carried her down the beach? Not likely. She was about to ask the name of her knight in shining armor when Pat Lawrence appeared at the table.

"Isn't it a beautiful day? I just love it here." Pat beamed.

"I thought you were going to sleep in?"

Pat kissed the top of David's head. "I was, but today is orientation day." She sat down and turned to Alex. "They always have an orientation the day after new guests arrive. David and I really don't need to go, because we come here every year, but its fun. Why don't you come with us?"

"Why not," Alex smiled, "I should get my bearings. Although," she grinned, "I did manage to find the dive instructor's shack this morning."

"Do you dive, Alex?" Pat asked.

"I used to, but I had a bit of a mishap that put me off the sport."

Concern filled Pat's face. "What happened?"

"I ran out of air when I was down thirty feet." Alex paused for a moment before adding, "I guess I should have checked my own air tank."

"So, Alex," David raised a questioning brow. "You think you'll be drinking any more tequila while you're here?"

Alex put her hands on her stomach. "David, after last night, I don't want to see another bottle of tequila, let alone drink any. The stuff is POISON!"

"Yeah, but what you need to taste is real one hundred per cent *agave* tequila. Did you know that ninety-five per cent of all the tequila in the world is made near here? There's a little town, four hours from Puerto Vallarta, called Tequila. All of the factories are there. They can't make the stuff here because they don't have the right soil or weather."

"Have you ever seen a tequila plant?" Pat asked.

Alex shook her head. "No, I don't believe I have."

"Well, they kind of look like a big cactus, but instead of the leaves growing straight up, they spread out from the middle. Sort of like an aloe plant," Pat added.

"The plant actually has a blue tint," David told Alex. "They call it the blue *agave* plant. It takes eight years to mature. When the plant's ready, a big flower grows up very tall from the center. That's what tells the farmers it's time to harvest. They uproot the plant and cut off the leaves. What's left looks like a root, but it isn't. They call it the *heart* or 'pineapple'. The real root is still in the ground and it produces more plants."

"The *heart* is full of sugar and starch. Sometimes, it can weigh up to eight pounds." Pat poked her husband in the arm. "David, tell Alex how they make the tequila."

David leaned back in his chair. "Well, they cook this heart for two-whole days. Then, they put it into round cement troughs and use a horse to pull a stone grinding wheel in circle to grind out all the juice."

"The large commercial tequila companies don't do it like that anymore," Pat stated, "but the small ones still do."

"That's right, Alex. In fact, the small companies are very proud of their tequila, because they still make it the old-fashioned way. They make it, by hand."

Alex was fascinated. "This is amazing. Where did you and Pat learn so much about tequila?"

David held his hand to the corner of his mouth and whispered, "Well, just between you and me, my brother has a small stake in a tequila farm."

"Wow, this is really interesting." Alex turned to Pat. "I'm learning a lot. I'll be so smart when I get home!"

"Well, when all of the juice is out of the plant," David continued, "they store it in oak barrels for three days to let it ferment. That's how they get *mescal*."

Alex screwed up her face. "Isn't that the one that has the worm in the bottom?"

"It sure is," David chuckled. "The worm-thing actually came from the farmers. They find the worm in the tequila plant and eat it for protein."

Alex's stomach heaved and she was glad now that she'd settled on black coffee for her morning meal.

"There are three types of tequila," David told Alex. "There is the *blanco* or white tequila for shots. There is the *resposado*, at least I think that's how you say it. It means that the tequila is rested for three to eleven months in oak barrels. That's the kind of tequila they use in margaritas and tequila sunrises. Now if you want really good tequila, the sipping kind..."

"There's such a thing as sipping tequila?" Alex interrupted.

"Oh, yes. They have tequilas that are as smooth as well-aged cognac. I think its pronounced *en-ha-doe,* but don't ask me to spell it. This stuff is top of the line; the best of the best. You sure don't want to use it to make a margarita," David chuckled. "There are over 1500 brands of tequila made in Jalisco, and that's not including the pirates."

"Pirates?"

"Sure," David grinned. "You've heard of the 'Pirates of the Caribbean', well in Mexico, they have 'Pirates of the Tequila'. They make it, put it in special bottles and try to sell it. Fifty-five years ago, Japan came to Mexico and purchased a bunch of tequila. They took it back to Japan and re-bottled it." David rolled his eyes. "Can you imagine buying tequila that says it was made in Japan? The Mexicans had a minor disagreement with the Japanese and made a law that tequila could only be produced in Jalisco. They can grow the blue agava plant in different states, but most of it ends up at the distilleries in Jalisco."

Pat glanced at her watch. "Oh, my, look at the time. We better get going or we'll miss the orientation."

The dance floor of the *Las Tropicales* disco was covered with rows of white plastic chairs. David guided the two women to the front row. When the crowd settled, an attractive Latin woman, with beautiful brown eyes, long brown hair and a brilliant white smile walked to the middle of the stage.

"*Buenos dias.* Thank you for coming this morning. My name is Carmen Sanchez. I am the manager of guest services here at *Las Tropicales*. If you have any questions about anything while you are here, please you come to see us. Myself, and my assistants," Carmen pointed to the side of the stage and motioned for the two employees standing in the doorway. "Ricardo and Karina are always there in the *Tropical* lobby and in the *Cocos* lobby during the daytime, and I can always be contacted by them."

The two employees smiled at the audience. "*Buenos dias*," they said in unison.

"*Buenos dias*," the crowd replied.

Carmen nodded to her assistants and they left the stage. "Now, there are some things at the desk where we are located that tells you about the hotel, about tours and about phone calls. Most important, it tells you when your flight leaves to go home." Carmen frowned at her audience. "You just arrived here in Mexico, and we are already talking about going home. Please come and check your flights while you are here. For example, one-day prior to departure, you come, and look on the board and there is your flight number.

"Please remember that twelve-thirty p.m. is always the check-out time. If your plane does not leave until later, we are going to give you a hospitality room. We are going to give you one-half hour per person so that you may take a shower before you are going to the airport. If you check out at noon, but you don't say for example, leave the hotel until six, you keep your bracelet and your card for the beach towel until you board the bus. For those peoples who are staying in the blocks one and two, you will do the check-out in the *Tropical* lobby. For those guests who are in *eh* the blocks three and four, you will do the check-out in the *Cocos* lobby."

Carmen clapped her hands together. "Now, let's talk about Mexico, and about the resort. Everyone who comes here to Mexico, they always talk about the water! The water here at the resort is purified, so you don't have to worry. If for example, you get the glass of water at the bar, or in a restaurant, or here in the disco. Even the ice cubes. Everywhere the water is one hundred per cent purified. In your room each day, you will get bottled water and these bottles can be filled up at the restaurant or at the bars.

"In your room, you can have a shower and brush your teeth with the water that comes from the tap, but just don't drink this water, please." Carmen screwed up her face and held her stomach. "We don't want you to get the *Montezuma's* revenge while you are here on vacation." Laugher erupted from the audience. "Do you all know about the *Montezuma's* revenge? Do you want me to tell you a story about this?"

"Yes," David loudly replied. He gave Alex a poke in the arm. "You're going to love this."

"The *Montezuma's* revenge it is a seed. The original *Montezuma's* revenge and it works very well," Carmen smiled. "*Montezuma*, he sent a message to the people that they use this seed for feeding the Spanish after the Conquest. The Mexican peoples, they were cooking for the Spanish and *Montezuma* said to do the revenge on the Spanish and the peoples they put this seed in the food. Soon ... the Spanish ... they all start to get the terrible diarrhea, and this could kill them sometimes in a week or ten days. That is how there came to be the *Montezuma's* revenge."

"I just love that story," David grinned.

"Okay, let us keep talking about the resort," Carmen continued. "We have here at *Las Tropicales,* three buffet-style restaurants. In these restaurants we serve *desayuno*, breakfast. We serve *almuerzo*, which is lunch and we serve *cena*, which is dinner. There are no reservations needed for these restaurants. They are open in the morning from seven-thirty a.m. until eleven a.m. for breakfast. They are open for lunch from noon until three, and open for dinner from six p.m. until nine-thirty. Each night there is a different buffet. Sometimes it is a Mediterranean cuisine and sometimes it is the French, but it is different every night.

"We have also a snack bar that is open from noon until five. We have *eh* four a la carte restaurants here at *Las Tropicales*. We have the Mexican seafood restaurant. We have the Piccolo, our Italian restaurant, we got the Steakhouse and we have the Kyoto, our Japanese restaurant. For these restaurants, please come to our desk at the *Tropical* lobby or the *Cocos* lobby in the morning to make the reservations. We have two seating times in all the restaurants. They are six-thirty p.m. and eight-thirty p.m. In our Piccolo, we have four seating; six, six-thirty, eight and eight-thirty."

"Can we make reservations the night before?" someone asked from the audience.

Carmen shook her head. "No. You must make reservations the morning that you want to go for dinner. We also have a midnight buffet that is open from eleven p.m. until two in the morning. Now, I would like to introduce for you Juanita, she is in charge of our animation team. We have one of the best animation teams in Puerto Vallarta. Please, welcome her to the stage."

The crowd applauded as Juanita walked to the microphone. "*Buenos dias.*"

"*Buenos dias,*" the audience replied.

"I am Juanita and I am in charge of the activities. We have activities all day here at the resort and it all happens by the pool number *uno*. That is pool number one. If you want to have quiet time, the left side of the resort is the place to be. If you want to have some fun, each day starting at eleven in the morning, we have things going on. Also in the *Tropical* and the *Cocos* lobby you will find a board. On that board you will find a list of activities we have here at *Las Tropicales*."

Juanita smiled at the audience. "Do you want to learn how to speak the Spanish? We can teach you how to speak Spanish. Do you want to play beach volleyball? We have that for you too. Peoples, do you want to learn how to dance the Latin beat?" Juanita clapped her hands and Roberto, the young man Alex had met earlier, appeared on the stage. Music started to play and Roberto and Juanita broke into the tango. When they were finished, the crowd stood and cheered.

When the room quieted, Juanita waved her hand in front of her face. "Wow...that was fun. You too can learn how to dance like this. Or, maybe you want to play tennis. We have *eh* the tennis court right next door. You just sign up your name and give your room number. We have bicycles there also. Again, just give your name and your room number.

"If you want to go on the water, down on the beach you will find the staff with the kayaks and the boogie boards. Remember, please to watch for the flags. Green means it is okay to go into the water, but if the red flag is up please stay out of the ocean."

"Are there any stingrays?" someone asked.

"Yes, there are stingrays, but you don't have to worry there are no sharks." Juanita gave the audience a devious smile. "Only the two-legged sharks that follow you down the beach!"

"Has anyone ever been bitten by a stingray?" the same guest inquired.

"*Si*, but it happens very rarely," Juanita told him. "And if something should happen, we have a doctor here also who will look after you. Thank you and please enjoy your stay." Juanita left the stage to a round of applause.

"Something Juanita didn't tell you," Carmen smiled, "is that her team of professional dancers put on a great show each night in our open-air theater, located directly behind us. The evening show starts at ten o'clock and each night the show is different. On Friday, Juanita and our animation team will be performing their Fantasy Show, which follows the Cirque de Soleil. On Thursday, we have our Mexican Fiesta night and there is a great show for you in the theater where you will learn about the Mexican culture. Each night after the evening show, we have also our disco from eleven at night until three in the morning.

"Now, let me talk to you about money. Right now the Canadian, and American dollar at par. When you change this money to *pesos,* you will get eleven cents on each dollar. You can exchange your money everyday of the week at the cashiers in both the *Tropical* and the *Cocos* lobby from seven in the morning until eleven at night. There also, is, the money exchange just on the road outside the front gate of the resort. Or, you can walk about fifteen minutes to the bank. If you go to the bank to exchange the money, please make sure that you have *eh,* the passport with you. The banks are open everyday, *Lunes,* Monday to *Viernes,* Friday from nine in the morning, until four in the afternoon.

"In Puerto Vallarta, every corner you have a bank, or there is a money exchange. The most important thing is that you have the *pesos.* That is the national money of Mexico. If you want to buy something it is best. If you have American money, they give you the worst exchange rate you can imagine. Visa and MasterCard are also accepted, but not, the American Express. You can also use an ATM machine and this will give you the best exchange rate.

"Now, we are going to talk about, the phone calls. We suggest that you do not call from your hotel room because you will see a charge on your bill when you check out of the resort. There are two ways for you to call back to Canada and the United States. For example, you have the direct service, if you want to call collect. You just dial and the operator is going to talk to you. Or, you can call with a credit card, but the cheapest way to call is to buy a phone card. The card it is for 100 *pesos* and it will give you twenty-eight minutes to talk to your people at home. There is no connection fee. There are three payphones you can use. One is, in the front of the *Tropical* lobby. The second is in front of the *Cocos* lobby and the third one is across the street from the hotel, beside the money exchange."

Alex did a mental calculation of the phone calls she'd made from her room to Sarah and Peter. *Oh well,* she thought. *It's only money and you can't take it with you.*

"Now, we talk about going outside the resort. You are going to feel very safe here at *Las Tropicales.* If you want to go outside the resort and you want to see Puerto Vallarta, and you should go see Puerto Vallarta. It is a beautiful place, and it is also very safe. There are two ways you can go to Puerto Vallarta." Carmen held up one finger. "First, you can go by taxi. Just go to the front gate of the resort and have *eh*, the bellman call the taxi. You are forty-five minutes from downtown and it will cost you *dos zero*, twenty American dollars. That is 200 *pesos*. Taxis are available twenty-four hours a day in front of the hotel and on every street corner in Puerto Vallarta.

"If you want to do it the Mexican way, you just walk to the highway and wait for a city bus. It will cost you ten *pesos*." Carmen held up ten fingers "That is one American dollar. You just wait at the entrance on the main highway. The bus will stop. The first bus it stops at six in the morning and the last bus, it stops at nine at night. You take the bus that says *Bucerias* going to Puerto Vallarta. When you step in the bus, pay your ten *pesos*, and ask that the driver let you off at Wal-Mart."

Laughter erupted in the audience and someone asked: "There's a Wal-Mart in Puerto Vallarta?"

"*Si*," Carmen smiled. "We have a Wal-Mart and because NAFTA, we have in Puerto Vallarta; a McDonald's, Kentucky Fried Chicken, Pizza Hut, Dominos Pizza, Carl's Junior, Outback Steak House, Starbucks. Then, there is *eh*, Woolworths, and Sam's Club and the Home Depot just opened. We have the Hard Rock Café and of course, we have Hooters. We have all these places and other things. The only one we don't accept here in Mexico is the Taco Bell.

"So now, to go downtown," Carmen continued. "At the Wal-Mart you pass across the street and you take the *blanco* bus, the white bus that says *Centro*. That means to the downtown. This bus will drop you at the centre of the *Malecon*. From this place, you have a beautiful walk along the seawall. You have the restaurants and the flea markets. There is a cigar store. What you see there, is cigars made by the local people of Jalisco. The seeds for the cigars, they come from Cuba, but the leaves are grown in Mexico in Veracruz. This is another state of the Gulf of Mexico. They have the same weather in that part of Mexico as they experience in Cuba, so the quality is just like a Cuban cigar, but it cost you half the price. If you are going to go to the United States, you will not have a problem with these Mexican cigars. They are legal in your country."

Carmen picked up a folder from the floor of the stage and held it above her head. "In the welcoming folders that are in your room, there is a map of Puerto Vallarta. It will show you everything downtown including the flea market. Remember, there is no tax when you leave Mexico so you can spend all of your *pesos*."

"Good!" a woman yelled.

"At this time of the season, the flea market is open from ten o'clock in the morning until ten o'clock at night. Everyday is a good day to shopping except, for Sunday. On Sunday, forget it, everything is closed. If you want to shop on Sunday, Bucerias is the place. You are in Bucerias and the main part of this small fishing village is just a fifteen-minute walk from the resort. Here at the hotel we are on Puerto Vallarta time, because that is the time of the airport, but the rest of Bucerias is one-hour difference. Right now, it is ten in the morning Bucerias time.

"There are two ways to go to downtown Bucerias. You can take a taxi ... it will cost you forty *pesos*. That is four American dollars. Or, you can walk, either along the beach or by the road in front of the hotel. Now," Carmen clapped her hands together. "Please remember, if you go to Bucerias on the road outside the hotel, you are going to see, the timeshare people. They will tell you free this and free that. They will tell you about two-for-one tours." Carmen's expression turned serious. "Guys, there is nothing for free in that world. If you sign up with those people, you have to attend an information briefing for two hours. At this briefing, they will try to sell you some condominiums. If you sign up with Pedro, or I don't know who, to take a tour in exchange for two hours of your vacation time, you will lose. You give them a deposit and you will never, never see your money again. It is always the same. You get to the tour and you have no confirmation number. So, please always book your tours through the resort. Now, to tell you about some of the tours we offer here at *Las Tropicales*, please I would like to introduce to you, our head dive instructor, Hans Zimmerman."

The tall, attractive German gentleman Alex had seen giving a diving lesson stepped onto the stage. "Good morning, everybody," he smiled. "Welcome to *Las Tropicales*." He rubbed his hands together. "So how many of you want to have some adventure?" A number of the recent arrivals raised their hands. "Well, we have all kinds of tours offered here at *Las Tropicales*. There is something for everyone. If it is your first time here in Mexico and you want to do a city tour, we recommend that you go by a tour guide. They work for these companies for ten years. You will be very happy with information they will give you. There is a tour that goes from in front of the hotel every day from nine o'clock in the morning until four o'clock in the afternoon.

"That tour will take you to Marina Vallarta and to the Church of *Lady Guadalupe*. You will see a tequila factory where you can sample the tequila. And you will go to the place where they filmed that movie, *The Night of the Iguana* with Richard Burton. Does anyone know of this movie?" Hans asked. "The movie was filmed here in Mexico in 1964. It is an old movie but that movie was very important for the history. That movie, helped to develop Puerto Vallarta as a tourist town.

"At the end of the tour, the tour guide will bring you to the jungle and you will have lunch and sample the Mexican food. There, you will see many birds. Does anyone know which is the national bird of Mexico?" Hans scanned the audience. "It is also an eagle, the royal eagle. Does anyone know, what is the national stone? It is the most precious stone. The most precious stone in Mexico; they call it the hummingbird stone. When you see that stone you are going to find out that it has another name. Does anyone know what this hummingbird stone is?"

"It's an opal," David yelled out."

"*Si*", Hans smiled. "The national stone of Mexico is an opal, and you are going to see these precious stones when you are on this Puerto Vallarta tour. If you want to see the ocean," Hans continued, "there is a national park that is protected by the Mexican government. We take you to that park on a boat. You are there for the day and you can snorkel.

"If you want to spend the day in paradise, Las Caletas is the place to go. Does anyone know the American film director, John Huston? Well, this was John Huston's home for many years. It is one and one-half hours from the Nuevo Vallarta marina. You go there by the catamarans to this beautiful place. When you are there you will spend the day. There is snorkeling, kayaking, yoga and even cooking lessons. If you like, you can go to the top of the mountain and have a massage. There is also scuba diving available. If you don't have equipment, you can rent it there on the island."

For the second time today, Alex was reminded about scuba diving. Maybe, instead of booking a dive with this Carlos person that Brian had suggested, she'd go to Las Caletas. It sounded beautiful and getting a massage in a tropical setting would be like a small piece of heaven.

"For those of you who are more adventurous," Hans smiled, "there is our Canopy Adventure."

Alex turned to Pat. "My daughter told me about that."

"You should try it," Pat smiled. "David and I did it last year and it was an absolute blast!"

"The one tour for me is the Sierra Madre tour," Hans grinned. "In one day you will see nature, culture and have a lot of fun. This tour is for people who like adventure because it is very rough to get there. You go in Mercedes Benz ATV's. You go off the beaten path to the Mexican outback. There are twelve people and one tour guide per vehicle. There is a nature walk and you will see not only some beautiful scenery, you will also see a true Mexican village. At the end of the tour, there is a big barbecue on the beach. On the way back, they show you twenty-one different ways to drink tequila!"

The word itself made Alex's stomach turn. Pat and David had asked her to go shopping with them. Perhaps after the orientation, she would just set up her dive and go back to her room for a nap.

"I am sure you are all anxious to get to the beach," Hans said, "so I am going to turn it back to Carmen. Please, in your folders in your room, you have a list of all the tours offered by the hotel. There is much to see and do here in Mexico, but please book your tours early. Most of all have fun, and enjoy this beautiful country of Mexico with its warm, friendly people."

The crowd applauded, and Carmen thanked Hans as he left the stage. "Now, just a few more things before we let you go to enjoy your vacation. Some people have asked me about tipping. There are a lot of people who ask me this question. You are on an all-inclusive package and tipping is at your discretion. For example, if you have good service and you would like to leave a tip, please always leave *pesos* or American money. Do not leave Canadian change. The staff has no way to exchange that money.

"If you want to leave something for the maid, you can just leave it on the pillow. There is a safe in each of your rooms. This safe is free and we advise that you always use the safe to place your valuables. Okay, we are finished with our orientation. Tonight, we invite you to attend our manager's cocktail party at pool number three, at six o'clock. Please, if anyone has any questions, you may come see me in the *Tropical* lobby. Enjoy your stay!"

"Are you are going to the cocktail party tonight?" Pat asked

"Yes," Alex smiled. "I wouldn't miss it for the world."

10

ALEX WAS GLAD NOW, that she'd let the Lawrences talk her into going to Bucerias for the afternoon. They'd had lunch at Claudio's, a quaint Mexican restaurant right on the ocean, and the grilled jumbo shrimp were the best she'd ever eaten. Afterwards, the three amigos shopped in the market and David gave Alex a lesson on purchasing silver.

"Did you know that Mexico is the largest silver producer in the world, Alex? You have to watch some of the guys in the flea market. They tell you, and show you, that the silver is stamped '925', and then offer you three or four bracelets for thirty or forty *pesos*. It sounds like a good deal, but the real McCoy is always more expensive. If you want real silver, you want to go to a jewelry store."

Alex had taken David's advice and purchased T-shirts, two ceramic Mexican Aztec masks, and a pair of leather sandals. She was here for another five days. On one of them, she'd take the tour to Puerto Vallarta and purchase her silver in town.

It had been a brutally hot day and when Alex stepped into her room, the air conditioning felt refreshing. She put her trinkets on the bed and noticed the message light blinking on the telephone. "I wonder what that's all about." She picked up the receiver and dialed the hotel operator.

"Front desk," a pleasant female voice answered.

"*Hola*. I'm just calling to see if there's a message for room 4211?"

"*Si Señora*, your husband, he called, to see about the diving."

"He's certainly being persistent," Alex remarked. "Thank you."

"*De nada*," the desk clerk replied.

Hanging up the phone, Alex decided there was no time like the present. She rummaged through her purse until she found the diving brochure Brian had given her and dialed the number.

"*Buenas tardes*. Good afternoon. This is Dive Dreams," a male voice answered.

"*Hola*, may I speak with Carlos?"

"*Si*, this is Carlos."

"Hello, Carlos, my name is Alex Granger. My husband, Brian Williams, made arrangements for me to go on a dive with your company."

"*Si, Señora*. I have been waiting for your call. Your dive is booked for*, Jueves*. That's Thursday."

"I was looking through your brochure. On Thursday you go to El Morro, correct?"

"*Si*. El Morro. There Ms. Granger, you will see, the marine life. We have the mantas and we have, the turtles and the dolphins."

"What about the sharks?" Alex chuckled.

"You don't worry about the sharks, Ms. Granger," Carlos reassured her.

"Your brochure says that it's an all-day dive."

"*Si*. We will leave from the marina in Nuevo Vallarta at eight-thirty in the morning and we are gone all day."

Alex didn't want to go on a full day's dive, not yet anyway. "Well, maybe I'll cancel then," she told Carlos "I haven't been diving in years and I don't think I could put in a full day. I was only planning on going for a few hours."

"No worry, *Señora*. If you, only want to dive for a few hours, this can be arranged. We will dive in the caves."

"Caves?" Alex hesitated. "I don't know about diving in caves. I haven't been diving in years."

"How is it they say in your country?" Carlos chuckled. "Oh yes, it is *eh*, like riding a bicycle. You never forget."

"That may be true, but caves!"

"*Si, Señora*, you leave your life with Carlos. I promised your husband that I would take care of you."

"Well, if you think so, let's go ahead with Thursday then."

"*Bueno*. You come to my place at three o'clock, on Thursday and we will go see the caves at El Morro."

"Do I need to confirm my reservation with the dive shop at the resort?"

"No, *Señora*, your reservation for diving, it is confirmed. It is not through the hotel. There is no need that you go to the dive shop."

Alex thanked him and told him she would see him on Thursday. She hung up the phone, opened the drawer of the night table and pulled out the ticket she needed to retrieve her diving gear. Staring down at it, Alex was reminded of the night her husband had given her the new equipment.

Brian had asked her to join him. He had something special he wanted to give her. He made arrangements for the two of them to have a romantic candlelight dinner on the terrace, something they hadn't done in years. Alex hated to admit it, but she'd actually had a good time. Brian was charming and sharply dressed in his black Armani suit. After dinner, he took her hands in his and gazed into her eyes. "Alex, I know that I haven't been the best husband over the years. I've blown a lot of money gambling and I know that sometimes I drink too much, but can you forgive me? There was a time when we were really good together. Remember when you first learned to dive and the great adventures we had? Do you remember how afterwards, when we were alone on the boat, we always made love?"

Brian walked to the corner of the terrace then, and retrieved a large cardboard box. "I want to rekindle the spark we once had. I have something that I hope brings back some of those good memories. Happy Birthday, Alex." He opened the box and pulled out a bright-yellow air tank, a new wet suit, flippers and mask. "I know how much you used to love diving. There's some great diving in Mexico." He handed her an envelope. "Here's the information from the dive company. It's all arranged."

A knocking sound brought Alex back to reality. She stood up, and made her way across the suite. When she opened the door, she was greeted with a beautiful bouquet of her favorite flowers: ivory roses and white calla lilies. "Oh, my," her face lit up in a smile. "These are beautiful." Alex took the flowers from the young man, positive that Sarah had sent them; after all, today was her birthday! She reached for the card and read it to herself: *Favorite flowers, for a favorite guest.* "Do you know who these are from?" she asked. "The card isn't signed."

"They are from the owner of the resort, *Señora.*"

"Oh! How thoughtful." Alex wondered how the owner could possibly know that these were her favorite flowers, but nonetheless, she was pleased. "If you'll just give me a minute, I'd like to write a thank you note."

"There is no need, *Señora.* Mr. B. said that, you can thank him in person at the manager's cocktail party in one hour."

"I'll be sure to do that."

When the young man was gone, Alex put the bouquet of flowers on the small table in her room and examined the card. "Why does everyone call you Mr. B.?" She closed her eyes and imagined what the man looked like. She assumed the resort's owner was somewhat of an eccentric ... only using an initial and not his full name. She envisioned him to be a portly, bald man in his late sixties, wearing a white linen suit and a straw derby. Alex was sure he'd be smoking a Cuban cigar. In fact, she was pretty sure he'd look just like old man Sanderson.

The image of Moe Sanderson suddenly brought back memories of his daughter, and Alex couldn't help but wonder whatever happened to Grace after Sam's death.

11

ANGELINA SPENT THE DAY preparing for the manager's cocktail party. It would be the first one they'd had at *Las Tropicales*, but something she'd been bugging Sam about for months. She arranged for a string quartet to play Mozart. Sam thought a mariachi band would be more appropriate but Angelina convinced him that a cocktail party required classical music.

In the garden beside pool number three, Angelina set up twenty small round tables and covered them with white linen tablecloths. In the center of each table, she placed a crystal vase filled with tropical flowers and hung a *Serape*, a colorful Mexican blanket common to the country, on the backs of two of the four chairs surrounding each table.

A portable bar was set up in the corner of the garden. Its main focal point; a champagne fountain surrounded by long-stemmed crystal flutes. Beside the bar, a second table displaying several brands of tequilas that guests would be invited to sample. Everything looked perfect and Angelina was sure Sam would be pleased.

At five-thirty p.m. the first of the sixty invited guests began arriving in the garden. Angelina recognized the blonde woman and the man on her arm. Yesterday, the woman had fallen by the pool causing a nasty gash above her right eye. Angelina had escorted the couple to the doctor's office, where the doctor advised the guest that her injury required stitches and an injection. The woman refused treatment and stormed out of the office with her boyfriend hot on her heals. When they returned, five minutes later, she apologized for her rude behavior and allowed the doctor to dress her wound. Afterward, the doctor suggested his patient go and lie down. Instead, the woman returned to the bar.

An hour later, while Angelina was on her way to the office, she saw the young man struggling to get his drunken girlfriend back to their room. He was having a terrible time and she'd called the front desk to have a porter give him a hand.

"Ms. Rodriguez." The young man approached Angelina and stuck out his hand. "I'd like to thank you again for having those guys help me with Jill yesterday."

"Oh, it was nothing." Angelina motioned toward the woman who was already standing at the bar. "I see your friend is feeling better."

The young man's face turned red with embarrassment. "I've learned that you shouldn't go on a vacation with someone you haven't lived with. I had no idea Jill drank this much. She's been loaded every day since we got here."

Angelina offered him a sympathetic smile. "I'm sure everything will be fine when you get home. She's on vacation. She's not the only person who has ended up with the tequila headache!"

"Thanks again. You've been great. This whole place is great. I'm definitely going to recommend it to my friends."

"*Gracias*" Angelina smiled. "Now if you will excuse me, there are some people I need to speak with."

If Angelina had learned anything the year she worked for Grace Bennett, it was how to work a room. She'd been witness to several of the Bennetts' private dinner parties. Grace was always dressed to perfection in the latest designer gown and she looked stunning as she circulated through the room. Grace would spend just enough time with each guest to make them feel welcome before moving on to the next. Angelina had mastered the same talent.

Thinking of Grace Bennett now, reminded Angelina that in four days, it would be the one-year anniversary of her death.

She made a mental note to go to the cemetery and put flowers on the grave before leaving for the Dominican Republic.

"Angelina, dear, there you are, I have been looking everywhere for you." Eveline Pritchard, the seventy- something widow who'd been coming to *Las Tropicales* three times a year since her husband died, threw her arms around Angelina and gave her a big hug. "I've finally decided what to do with Martin's ashes. I've been carrying him around in the trunk of my car since he died two and a half years ago. I didn't know where I should scatter him but yesterday, on the plane, it dawned on me. He always loved Mexico. What better place than here! Do you think we could get together tomorrow and work out the arrangements? I don't have him with me, but I could come back, let's say, in November. Don't the Mexican people have some type of a celebration in November to honor the dead?"

"Yes. On November second. *El dia de los muertos. The Day of the Dead*. If you like, I can have our guest services manager make all of the arrangements with you."

"Thank you Angelina. That would be great."

"I will talk to Carmen tonight," Angelina smiled. "You can call her from your room in the morning, or go to her office. It is right beside the front desk. She will make the appointment. Now if you will excuse me."

On the other side of the garden, Alex and Pat were admiring the surroundings. "What a beautiful setting for a cocktail party," Alex remarked. "I love those brightly colored Mexican blankets. I should get one to take home."

"You can buy them in the gift shop," Pat smiled. "Or, from the vendors that walk the beach."

"I've noticed the beach vendors here don't bother you as much as I've seen in other places."

"That's because they're on a contract with the hotel," Pat informed Alex. "They can only go out for a certain length of time, during specific times of the day. I think they get ten or fifteen minutes on the beach and then they have to wait an hour. There can only be so many of them out at any given time. If they show their wares and the hotel guest isn't interested, they must walk away."

"That's actually a very good idea," Alex nodded.

"I wondered where you girls got to." David gave Pat and Alex a beaming smile and handed them each a glass of champagne. "You see that guy standing over there by the bar," David pointed, "the short muscular guy with the great tan and the shoulder length blonde hair?"

"Yes." Pat replied.

"Apparently, he has a thong bathing suit for every day of the week!" David let out a hearty chuckle. "The one he was wearing today was fire engine red with a big yellow lightening bolt across the front."

Pat raised a questioning eyebrow. "And you know this how?" she asked.

"Well, I didn't see it personally," David frowned, "but I was just talking to the couple from England that we had cocktails with yesterday. Gary was telling me the guy has been giving hotel guests quite a show parading around between the three pools."

"And we missed it?" Pat exclaimed. She clutched Alex's arm. "We better hang out by the pool tomorrow instead of the beach so we can check out the action!"

"*Buenas noches,*" Angelina smiled as she approached Pat and David Lawrence, and the woman she'd put to bed last night. "How are you enjoying yourselves?"

"This is great," Pat replied. "There's never been a cocktail party any of the other times we've been here."

"No. This is the first one," Angelina smiled. "If it is successful, we will have one every week for the new people arriving."

"Well, young lady," David put his arm around Angelina's shoulder. "I suppose you were the one to come up with the idea and it's a damn fine one!" He turned to Alex. "Our Angel here has been working at *Las Tropicales* since the place opened.

She started out with the entertainment staff and has worked herself all the way up to assistant manager."

Angelina blushed at the compliment. "Well *Señor*, I love my job here and the boss is a pretty great guy to work for."

"Speaking of the boss," David scanned the garden, "I haven't seen his wife this trip. Where's she hiding? She's usually good for an hour or so of entertainment!"

"Is she a dancer?" Alex asked.

"Hell no," David laughed, "Not unless you call being an exhibitionist dancing." David leaned closer to Alex. "You know, it's really something. The guy who owns this place is great. He's one of the nicest men you'd ever want to meet, but his wife is a real piece of work. Every afternoon around three, they have a game of water polo at pool number one. It's usually the guests against the staff. When Pat and I were here last year, the guests were whipping the staff something awful. So what does the boss's wife do? She drops her bathing suit top and starts parading around the swimming pool to distract the winning team!" David turned to Angelina. "What's she going to do tonight, a striptease on top of the piano?"

Angelina's expression turned somber. "*Señor* Lawrence, I'm afraid to tell you that the *Señora* is dead."

The color drained from David's face. "Oh, I'm so sorry, how rude of me. What happened," he asked. "Was she sick?"

"No." Angelina replied. "It was the drugs that killed her."

"We always figured there was something strange about her," Pat remarked, "but we never though she had a drug problem."

"*Si*. It was very bad. I asked her many times to stop, but she would not listen. Now she is dead and the boss is alone. He should not be alone. He is too good a man to be alone for the rest of his life."

Pat shook her head. "We had no idea. When we had lunch with him, he didn't say a thing."

"The boss is a very private person," Angelina confessed. "He does not talk much about his private life."

David gave Angelina a fatherly smile. "Well, you two make a terrific looking couple. Maybe you should ask him to marry you. Then he wouldn't be a lonely old widower."

"Oh, no *Señor*," Angelina blushed. "This is not something a woman asks a man."

Alex had never lost a spouse so she had no idea what it felt like. She'd lost both of her parents, but her uncle Harvey, who'd been in the funeral industry for thirty-five years told her that grieving for a spouse was much different than grieving for a parent.

The closest Alex had come to experiencing a loss of that kind was when she lost Sam. He broke her heart when he left her standing at the altar. Five years later when she learned of the circumstances surrounding his and Grace's marriage, she forgave him and told him she still loved him. Neither of them was happy in their marriages; they talked about divorcing their spouses and spending the rest of their lives together. A week later, Sam was killed in a plane crash.

David gave Alex a gentle nudge. "What do you think about that?"

"Think about what?"

"What do you think about a woman asking a man to marry her? I don't care if it's improper or not." David gave Angelina a squeeze. "I think you and the boss make a great couple."

"Yes, he's such a wonderful man," Pat told Alex. "Every Christmas Eve, he and Angelina host a party for the kids from the orphanage. In the summer, depending on how well the children do on their exams, the boss sends them to a special summer camp."

"He sounds very nice," Alex smiled.

David pointed his index finger at Alex. "Oh, that's right. You probably haven't officially met him. I'm sure he's around here somewhere. I'll go find him and bring him right over."

When David vanished into the crowd, Angelina excused herself and left Pat and Alex standing alone. "She really is a lovely girl," Pat smiled. "Sam should marry her."

"Sam?"

"Yes, the owner of *Las Tropicales*."

Alex's mind suddenly flashed back to the airport and the man who looked like Sam. Last night, she dreamt that Sam carried her down a moonlit beach. This morning, David told her the owner had helped her back to her room. Everyone referred to this man as Mr. B. Could the 'B', stand for Bennett? "Pat, may I ask you a question?"

"Of course."

"What's the owner's last name?"

"I'll let him tell you himself." Pat pointed over Alex's shoulder. "Here they come now."

Alex took a deep breath and stood up tall. She straightened the front of her sundress and ran her fingers through her hair. She couldn't help but chuckle to herself thinking of the vision she'd created in her head earlier. She felt a hand on her shoulder and slowly turned around.

"Alex, I'd like you to meet Sam Bennett," David smiled. "He's the owner of *Las Tropicales*."

12

ANGELINA KNOCKED ON SAM'S office door and didn't wait for a reply before entering. He was sitting behind his desk. The tequila bottle in front of him was empty. "What was that all about?" she asked as she marched across the room. "That woman should be evicted from the property. She has a problem, *Señor!*" Angelina planted her hands firmly on her hips. "I had to help you with that woman last night because she was drunk, and now this. I had no idea she was so rude. To throw a drink in your face, that is just ..."

Angelina's words were a blur. The only words Sam could hear now were the ones Alex had shouted at him half an hour ago: "As far as I am concerned Sam Bennett, you can stay dead, and consider me dead too!" Sam could understand her immediate reaction at seeing him, but he was sure the note would have calmed the waters. Obviously it hadn't.

Sam flung his arms across the desk, knocking over a stack of files. It was then when he saw the ivory-colored envelope. "Shit! That explains it!"

"Explains what?" Angelina asked.

Sam didn't answer. Instead, he picked up the phone and dialed the front desk.

"*Hola.*"

"Is Luciano there?" Sam asked.

"No, *Señor* Bennett. He has left for the day."

"Is he in tomorrow?"

"*Si.* At seven in the morning."

"Tell the night manager I want Luciano in my office the minute he arrives!"

"*Si, Señor* Bennett. I will leave a note."

"No! Don't leave a note!" Sam grabbed the envelope and waved in the air. "Apparently, notes don't get delivered at this resort!"

"*Si Señor*, I will tell the night manager directly."

"*Gracias.*" Sam hung up the phone and reached into the bottom drawer of his desk for another bottle of tequila. He unscrewed the cap and took three big swigs. He would have finished the whole bottle if Angelina hadn't taken it from his lips.

"What is going on with you, *Señor*? You pulled a disappearing act yesterday. This morning you left in the middle of a meeting, and now I find you in your office keeping company with Jose Quarevo. Are you upset about what happened with that woman? What did she say to you? I can't imagine any woman could upset you like this."

Sam lowered his head. "She isn't any woman."

"Who is she?" Angelina asked. "Do you know her? Have you ever seen her before you helped her to her room last night?"

"Yes," Sam confessed, looking up at his assistant manager. "You've met my best friend, Michael Granger?"

"*Si*, Angelina nodded. "He was here two years ago."

"Well, the spitfire who just ripped me a new asshole is Michael's baby sister."

Angelina stomped her foot on the floor. "Well, if she is the sister of your best friend, how dare she be so rude?"

Sam let out a deep sigh. "She had every reason to do what she did."

"What reason would a person have to throw a drink in the face of another?"

"A person, who thinks the person they're looking at, is dead!"

Angelina shook her head in confusion. "You make no sense, *Señor*."

"Alex thinks I'm dead. In fact she thinks I've been dead for the past twenty years."

"I don't understand. How is that possible?"

"Have you got an hour?" Sam grunted.

"I always have time for you, Sam." Angelina pulled out a chair and sat down. "Please, *Señor,* tell me this story."

Sam ran his hands through his hair and took a deep breath. "I met Alex for the first time when she was in her late teens. She was a tomboy and I really didn't give her a second look. We were reintroduced five years later. She took my breath away. I fell head over heels in love with her." He reached across the desk and took Angelina's hand. "Have you ever been in love? I mean really in love?"

The color rose in her cheeks. "Yes, Sam. I have been in love."

"Then you know how a person can get under your skin. I've never felt for another woman what I felt for Alex."

"But you were married for almost twenty-five years to another woman. Why did you not marry Ms. Granger?"

Sam let go of her hand and leaned back in his chair. "When I met Alex for the second time, I was engaged to Grace. In fact, the wedding was scheduled for the following month. I'd been having second thoughts about marrying her. I wasn't thrilled with the little cocaine habit she was developing."

"So, *Señor,* tell me something?" Angelina folded her arms and leaned forward on the desk. "Why did you not leave Mrs. Bennett and marry this other woman?"

"Actually, that's what I planned to do. I spent a week with Alex at her uncle's fishing lodge. I couldn't bring myself to tell her that I was engaged, and I couldn't lose her, so I asked her to marry me. She accepted. We were supposed to go to Bermuda and be married on the beach."

"How could you ask this woman to marry you when you were already spoken for?"

"I was going to break it off with Grace."

"But you didn't," Angelina frowned. "Why not?"

"The morning I was leaving for Bermuda, I told Grace I was calling off the wedding. She took it better than I expected. Later at the airport, I discovered the reason why. Customs went through my luggage and found several grams of cocaine. The whole drug-thing was orchestrated by Grace's father. He told me, if I forgot about Alex, he'd make the drug charges go away. I didn't care about a black mark beside my name, but Grace's old man told me that if I didn't marry his daughter, he'd ruin my father's career. My dad was a United States senator at the time. I couldn't let that happen."

"How did you break the news to the Granger woman that you could not marry her?"

Sam's face turned red with embarrassment. "I didn't. I'm sure she found out the way most people did. My wedding picture was on the front page of the New York Times."

Angelina raised a questioning brow. "I still don't understand why you would have the Granger woman believe that you were dead."

"The death-thing happened five years after Grace and I got married. Michael convinced me to go to the Calgary Stampede with him."

"What is this Calgary Stampede?"

"It's a big rodeo they have in Calgary, Alberta, Canada, every year."

"And you went to this rodeo?"

"Yes," Sam nodded. "I wasn't going to go because I had a shit-load of legal work on my desk, but when Michael told me that Alex would be there, I knew I had to go. I had to see her and apologize for leaving her standing at the altar. I don't think Michael knew anything about my marriage proposal to his sister. I figured that if I just showed up, Alex would go ballistic. I told Michael he should let her know I was coming along, but he wanted the visit to be a surprise."

"Did you surprise her?" Angelina asked.

"Oh, we surprised her all right." Sam reached up and pulled down the corner of his lower lip. "I've still got the scar to prove it." Angelina flashed him a puzzled look. "It's a long story," he smiled, "let's just say, I got what I deserved."

"But I still don't understand why you have let this woman believe that you were dead all these years."

"When I got back to New York, I called Alex several times, but she wouldn't take my calls. I'd all but given up hope when I got a note from her. It was inside the invitation to Michael's wedding. Alex told me that after seeing me again, she realized she still loved me. The note said she'd forgiven me for marrying Grace, and if nothing else, she hoped we could still be friends.

"She asked me to meet her at her father's ranch the day before her brother's wedding. The wedding wasn't for another two months and I couldn't wait, so I started calling her on a regular basis. Grace overheard one of our conversations and threatened to commit suicide if I went to the wedding, but I didn't care. Alex said she loved me and I had to see her. So I went, without my wife, and I had a great time."

"I am very confused, *Señor*. You said you loved this woman and she loved you, so why then did you stay married to Grace, and why does this Alex woman think you are dead?"

"At Michael's wedding, Alex and I spent a lot of time together. She told me that she wasn't happy in her marriage. I told her I wasn't happy in mine either and we agreed to divorce our spouses. The day I told Grace it was over, for good, she presented me with this." Sam reached into the top desk drawer and pulled out a five-by-seven framed photo. He passed it across the desk.

Angelina looked down at the picture ... whose ripped pieces had been put back together like a jigsaw puzzle. "This is you and Ms. Granger, correct?" Sam nodded his head. "Who is the little girl?" she asked.

"Alex's, daughter."

Angelina handed back the picture. "I still don't understand. Please explain."

"Grace had one of her father's goons follow me to Michael's wedding. For three days, he took pictures of my every move. He also took hundreds of pictures of Alex's daughter. There were pictures of the little girl in her bedroom. There were pictures of her playing on the swings in her back yard; pictures of her coming out of school, pictures of her everywhere. Grace told me that if I ever went near Alex again, she'd kill Alex's child."

Angelina was in shock. She knew Grace Sanderson Bennett had been a cruel, vicious woman, but to say she would actually kill a child was unimaginable. "Why didn't you go to the police?"

Sam leaned forward and rested his head in his hands. "I wanted to, but the Sandersons had their hooks into me. I couldn't let Alex down, not again, and I couldn't let anything happen to her daughter. So, I figured the best way to handle it was to kill myself off. I called Michael and told him what was going on. I didn't tell him how deeply in love I was with his sister. I told him Grace was just crazy enough to go through with her threat.

"I told Michael the only way Alex's daughter would ever be safe, was if Alex thought I was dead. Michael didn't understand my request, but he did it. He called his sister and told her I'd been killed in a plane crash. Shortly thereafter, Grace's father bought a villa in Puerto Vallarta and I moved to Mexico. I've been here ever since."

Angelina reached across the desk and took Sam's hands in hers. "That is the most beautiful thing I have ever heard. You gave up your life and your love, to protect a child that wasn't yours. I knew your wife was evil, but I had no idea. Perhaps it is best that she is out of your life. Now you can go on. This woman is here, you must talk to her. She must forgive you. You have sacrificed so much for her. Go to her Sam, make her speak with you."

Sam shook his head. "Nice try, Angel, but Alex said she never wanted to see me again."

"But she doesn't know this beautiful story. You must share this with her. If you don't, I will!"

13

AFTER THROWING HER DRINK in Sam's face, and telling him to consider her *dead*, Alex stormed back to her room to pack. She was getting out of here tonight! There was a gentle tap on the door and Alex was sure that it would be Ricardo from guest services with information about her flight back to Denver. She was wrong.

"May I come in?" Angelina asked.

Alex backed way from the door. "Suit yourself."

The first thing Angelina noticed when she entered the room was the open suitcase on the bed. "Are you planning on going somewhere, *Señora*?" she asked.

"Yes. I'm leaving. I'm going back to the States."

"I am afraid not, *Señora*," Angelina frowned, "there are no more flights to your home this evening."

"Fine, then. I'll leave in the morning." Alex abruptly turned on her heels and stomped across the room to the open French doors. She didn't want to go home. The resort was beautiful and she'd met some very nice people but with Sam here, she knew she couldn't stay.

Angelina followed Alex across the room. "I know that you are very angry with *Señor* Bennett. Please *Señora*, this is not his fault."

Alex spun around. Her face was red with anger. "I suppose he sent you here?"

"No, *Señora*. He did not send me here. I have spoken to him and he told me the reason for his actions. You must not blame the *Señor*."

"What do you mean, I mustn't blame the *Señor*?" Anger rose in Alex's voice. "For twenty years, I have been led to believe that the *Señor*... was dead!"

"*Si Señora*," Angelina frowned, "but this was for your own protection and the protection of your child."

"Bullshit! What does my child have to do with this? Sam doesn't care about my child. He doesn't even know my child! He pulled this little disappearing act for no one but himself. Now, if you will excuse me, I'd like to be alone."

"As you wish." Angelina turned and slowly walked to the door. She stopped, and looked over her shoulder. "If you would like to go home tomorrow, I can make these arrangements, but I think it would be best if you talked to *Señor* Bennett first."

"I have nothing to say to *Señor* Bennett."

When Angelina was gone, Alex changed into her jeans and left the property. She didn't want to sit in her room tonight and she certainly couldn't walk around the resort. She'd made a complete ass of herself at the cocktail party. If no one knew her before ... they certainly knew her now.

Alex took a cab to Bucerias and asked the driver to drop her at Claudio's, the beachfront restaurant where she'd had lunch with the Lawrences. She wasn't hungry, but she was sure she wouldn't have a problem consuming a bucket of *Coronas*. "How many *pesos*, *Señor*?" she asked when the cab pulled into the courtyard.

"Twenty *pesos*, *Amiga*."

Alex dug into her jeans and pulled out a fifty *peso* bill. "Keep the change."

"*Gracias, Señora*," the driver smiled. "When you are ready to go back to *Las Tropicales*, they will call me and I will come for you."

Alex thanked the driver and got out of the cab. She walked up the ramp to the entrance of the restaurant and was greeted by a handsome Mexican gentleman.

"*Buenas noches, Señora*," he smiled. "Are you just one?"

"*Si*." Alex looked around the restaurant and spotted a vacant table in the corner by the open window. "May I sit there?" she pointed.

"Yes, please come." The man took a menu from a wooden stand and led her across the sand floor to the table of her choice. "The sun will be setting soon, *Señora*." He pulled out a chair facing the ocean and handed Alex a menu. "You sit *por favor*. What may I bring you to drink?"

"I'll have a Corona and a shot of tequila. Make it the best you've got."

"Ah, *si Señora*," the waiter smiled.

"What's your name?" Alex asked.

"Victor, my name is Victor."

She extended her hand. "*Hola*, Victor. My name is Alexandra." They shook. "I'm going to be here for awhile, so we might as well be on a first-name basis."

"*Si*. I will be back with your drinks."

When Victor was gone, Alex stared blankly at the ocean. She still couldn't believe that Sam was alive. He'd been alive the entire twenty years she'd been grieving him. "I've wasted half my life grieving for you, Sam Bennett," she whispered under her breath. "That stops right now."

After Sam's death, Alex cried herself to sleep for months. She wished she could talk to someone about her grief because she knew it would help, but no one in her family knew of her relationship with Sam. No one knew he was Sarah's real father.

Unable to grieve openly, Alex hid her pain behind a heart that had turned to stone. Once, she even tried to rekindle her relationship with Brian, hoping it would help her forget Sam, but soon realized there was nothing to rekindle. She only married Brian because she was pregnant. She liked him okay, and learned to respect him when he went to work for her father. That all changed the day he started blackmailing her. In hindsight, Alex wished now that she would have confronted her father with Brian's accusations of an affair, instead of paying him his *hush* money.

Years later, when Alex discovered that Brian was snorting coke and cheating on her, she moved his things into the guest room. She told her daughter the reason was his snoring, but the problems in their marriage ran much deeper than that. From then on, Alex spent very little time with her husband unless they were attending a family gathering, or a social function. On those occasions, they were the perfect married couple. They laughed and joked, and openly showed affection. When they got home, they went their separate ways.

"Your *cerveza Señora,* and *eh* the tequila."

"You know something, Victor," Alex looked up and gave him a courageous smile. "This morning, I told myself that I was never going to touch another drop of tequila as long as I lived."

"And why is that, *Señora*?" Victor asked when he put down the tequila, a Corona, a salt shaker and a bowl of sliced limes.

"Because," Alex frowned, "last night, I drank too much tequila! My throat is still burning!"

"*Señora*, to avoid this, you must learn to drink tequila like the Mexicans." Victor gave her a proud smile. "First, you take the tequila in one hand." He demonstrated with an imaginary glass. "Next, you take the lime. Then, *Señora*, and this is *eh* very important, you must take a deep breath." Victor inhaled. "Then, you must exhale that big breath." He exhaled. "When your head is out of air, you take the tequila in, the lime in, and without breathing, you swallow. After you swallow, you take again the breath. This way you no taste the tequila."

Alex picked up the shot glass and a piece of lime. She took a deep breath and exhaled before pouring the white liquid into her mouth, biting the lime and swallowing. When she inhaled again, a broad smile danced across her face. "You're right, Victor. My throat isn't burning, neither is my stomach and I can't taste a thing!"

"*Si*," he grinned. "Now, when you drink the tequila, you drink like a Mexican!"

"That was so good I think I'll have another."

"*Si Señora.*"

For over an hour, Alex sat and drank while contemplating her life. She had a beautiful, intelligent daughter. She owned a lucrative business and had numerous friends, some better than others, but ... had she truly been happy? Brian had been a good father to Sarah, but a poor excuse for a husband. If she hadn't been pregnant, she never would have married him. Thinking of Sarah, Alex was reminded of how much her daughter looked like Sam. She was sure if they were ever in the same room together, it would be obvious to everyone that they were related.

"Do you mind if I sit down?"

Alex looked up, Angelina was standing over her. "Be my guest." She motioned toward a vacant chair. "Would you like to join me for a drink?"

"*Si.*"

Alex called for Victor to bring another glass and he poured them each a shot. "Cheers," Alex smiled

Angelina watched with interest as Alex drank first. "I'm impressed, *Señora*," she smiled. "Most people make such a sour face with the tequila."

"I used to be one of those people," Alex slurred, "but Victor here taught me how to drink tequila like a Mexican. Are you Mexican?" Alex asked. "You're sure beautiful."

"No," Angelina blushed. "I am not from Mexico. I was born in Cuba."

"Cuba!" Alex let out a deep sigh. "I've always wanted to go to Cuba. Did you know that Jack Nicholson went to Cuba? He even had his picture taken with Fidel. I hear they have beautiful beaches in Cuba. When you stand in the water up to your shoulders and look down," Alex dropped her head, "you can still see your feet."

"Yes, that is true," Angelina replied. "The water in Cuba is very clear."

Alex offered Angelina a drunken smile. "Did you know that they don't let Americans into Cuba? Oh, of course you know that." She waved a limp wrist in Angelina direction, "you're from Cuba!" Alex put her elbows on the table and rested her head in her hands. "I guess a person could go to Cuba if you went from Canada or from Bermuda. Have you ever been to Canada, Angelina? Canada is a wonderful place. My uncle has a fishing lodge in Campbell River. That's in British Columbia. Do you know where British Columbia is?"

"No, *Señora*," Angelina shook her head. "I have never been to British Columbia. Perhaps some day I will go there."

"Have you ever been to Bermuda?" Alex asked. "I was in Bermuda once," she slurred. "I was supposed to meet your boss there. You know what he did Angelina? He never showed up." Alex reached for the tequila bottle and poured them another drink. When she slid a glass across the table, Angelina declined.

"No *gracias* I can have no more to drink," she smiled. "I am on a mission."

"What kind of a mission?" Alex drunkenly asked. "Did that bastard send you here to find me?"

"*Si Señora*. He is very worried about you."

"Like hell he is," Alex spat. "He wasn't worried about me twenty-five years ago when he left me standing at the altar, and when I was stupid enough to let him back into my life, what does he do? I'll tell you what he does, he fakes his own death."

Angelina leaned across the table. "Please, I ask you to listen to me. *Señor* Bennett had his reasons for pretending he was dead. You must let me tell you this story."

"Why should I? Sam Bennett has lied to me for the last time. Besides, I'm not interested in his reasons. They don't matter anymore." Alex poured another shot. "In fact, let's drink to his death." This time, the white liquid burned as it slid down her throat and her body shivered. "Aren't you going to drink with me?"

Angelina declined. "No, *Señora*. As I have said, I am on a mission to take you back to *Las Tropicales*."

"Well, I'll give you a mission." Alex sat up in her chair and teetered from side-to-side. "You can march right back there and tell him to go to hell!"

"I cannot do that, *Señora*. I promised him that I would find you and bring you back safely. It is my responsibility."

"Oh, poop." Alex leaned forward and waved a disapproving finger in Angelina's directions. "You don't need to be responsible for me," she hiccuped, "I'm as old as dirt. I'm responsible for me." Alex turned and stared out the window into the darkness. "Now, go back to Sam Bennett and tell him to go to hell. I have no desire to see him again as long as I live!"

Angelina reached into her pocket and pulled out a photo. "I want you to look at something, *por favor*."

"What?"

"It is a picture. Look at it *Señora*, then I will explain."

Alex grabbed the picture from Angelina's hand. It took her a few seconds to focus and when she did, her drunken expression instantly turned sober. There, staring back at her were three familiar faces; Sam's, Sarah's and hers. "Where did you get this?" she demanded

"I took it from *Señor* Bennett's office. You remember this occasion?" Angelina asked.

Alex nodded her head. "Yes. This picture was taken at my brother's first wedding, but what does it have to do with Sam pretending to be dead?"

"When *Señora* Bennett found this picture, she accused *Señor* Bennett of having an affair with you. She threatened that if he ever went near you again, she would kill your child. For this reason, *Señor* Bennett made arrangements for you to believe he was dead. He knew this was the only way he could keep himself from being at your side. He knew if he was to ever go near you again, it could mean the life of your child."

14

LAST NIGHT ALEX HATED Sam but this morning, after remembering her conversation with Angelina, she couldn't wait to find him and apologize for her behavior. Sam had staged his own death to protect the life of a child he didn't know was his. If that wasn't love, nothing was.

"Excuse me." Alex smiled at the woman behind the reception desk. "Could you please tell me where I might find *Señor* Bennett?"

"*Si Amiga. Señor* Bennett, he is in his office." The woman pointed to the east side of the open-air lobby. "Down that way, *Señora*. Follow the path and you will see *eh* where they are doing the new construction. *Señor* Bennett's office is by that building."

When Alex reached Sam's office, she gently tapped on the door. "Come in," a male voice replied. She took a deep breath and slowly opened the door. Sam was sitting behind his desk, the telephone receiver tucked between his ear and his shoulder. His face lit up when he saw her and he motioned for her to come in. Trembling legs carried her across the room and she took a seat in front of his desk.

Sam held his hand over the mouthpiece of the telephone. "I'll just be a few minutes." He pointed to the carafe on the wet bar. "Would you like a coffee?"

Alex's mouth was bone dry and she would have loved a coffee, but she knew her trembling legs wouldn't carry her across the room and back, so she declined. Sam never took his eyes off her the entire time he carried on his Spanish telephone conversation. It was making her nervous. When her hands started shaking, she clutched the sides of the chair.

"I'm sorry," Sam apologized as he hung up the phone. "You've probably noticed that we're in the middle of construction. We decided to try a different supplier for our furniture and I just got word that all of it has termite holes. It's going to have to be reordered ..."

Alex couldn't control herself any longer and she interrupted Sam in mid-sentence. "Please forgive me for the horrible things I said to you yesterday. It's just that when I saw you standing in front of me, I thought I was in a bad dream."

"Bad dream?" Sam frowned. "Thanks a lot."

"You know what I mean," Alex blushed. "I thought you were dead and there you were larger than life. I was in shock."

Sam offered her an apologetic smile. "I'm sorry about that. It was a lousy way to be reintroduced. Had I known you were the person David Lawrence was dying for me to meet I may have planned a different strategy." He paused for a moment before adding, "I did write you a note yesterday morning, explaining the reason for my deception. I wanted to give you a heads up before the cocktail party."

"I didn't get a note."

"Yes. I know." Sam opened the desk drawer, pulled out the ivory-colored envelope and held it in the air. "I tried to explain everything."

Alex reached across the desk and took Sam's hand. "I had a chat with Angelina last night. She told me all about Grace, and the reason you planned your own death. I can't believe what you've sacrificed over the years to protect our daughter."

"Our daughter?" Sam asked.

Realizing what she'd said, Alex quickly covered up. "You know what I mean, Brian's and my daughter."

Sam squeezed her hand. "Alex, I did what I had to do, to protect you and your child."

"I realize that, and I will be forever grateful, but you also gave up your relationship with my brother. The two of you were best friends and you've had to live without that friendship for the past twenty years."

"Michael knows I'm alive."

Alex's body stiffened. "What do you mean Michael knows you're alive?"

"In order for you to believe that I was actually dead, I needed your brother's help."

"Did you tell him about our short-lived relationship?"

"No. Michael didn't know about us. I didn't say anything to him about what happened in Campbell River, or about the time we spent together after his wedding. I told him what Grace had threatened to do to your daughter and that she was just crazy enough to do it."

"Michael showed me the obituary from the paper, and a picture of the hearse carrying your body to the cemetery."

"That was all staged for your benefit, Alex. I had a friend at the New York Times. He did up my obituary and took the cemetery pictures. I had to make you believe that I was really dead." Sam squeezed her hand tighter. "The last time we were together we made plans. I just couldn't let you think that I'd walked out on you again." He looked at her with pleading eyes. "Alex, I'm so sorry that I did this to you, but Grace left me no choice. After what happened when we were supposed to meet in Bermuda, I had to believe that she'd go through with her threat if I ever went near you again. So, I died in a plane crash and moved to Mexico."

Tears filled Alex's eyes. "Oh, Sam, please forgive me for all the hurtful things I said to you yesterday. I don't wish you were dead at all. I'm very glad that you're alive."

Sam stood up and walked around the desk. He smiled down at Alex, and wiped away the single tear rolling down her cheek. "I'll forgive you for calling me names," he winked, "if you forgive me for lying to you. How about we start over?"

"Okay," she sniffed.

"Hello," he extended his hand. "My name is Sam Bennett."

Alex stood up and put her hand in his. "Hello, Sam. My name is Alex Granger."

"I'm pleased to meet you, Alex," Sam smiled.

"The pleasure is all mine," she smiled back.

"Is this your first time to Mexico?" he asked.

"Yes, it is."

"Well then, if that's the case, I think you should let me take you on a tour of Puerto Vallarta!"

"Right now?"

"Yes, right now."

Alex raised a questioning brow. "Don't you have a hotel to run?"

"*Si, Señora.*" he grinned, "but that's why I have an assistant manager. What do you say?"

Alex gave him a beaming smile. "I can't think of anyone I'd rather have show me the sights."

"Great. Have you had breakfast?"

"No."

"Well, we need to take care of that." Sam put his arm around Alex's waist and led her to the door. "You can't go sightseeing on an empty stomach," he grinned, "and I just happen to know a place that makes a great omelet."

They left the office and made their way through the tropical gardens to the Royal restaurant. On route, guest after guest stopped Sam, shook his hand, and told him how much they were enjoying their stay at the hotel.

"You're pretty popular." Alex remarked.

"It's not me," Sam confessed. "It's my staff. They make every guest feel like they're part of the family."

"How many staff members do you have?"

"I have 650 at the moment. It sounds like a lot but this place is small compared to some resorts. Have you ever heard of the Bahia Principe chain?"

"Yes," Alex nodded. "I was at the Bahia Principe Punta Cana in the Dominican Republic with my sister-in-law three years ago. It's a beautiful property. Everything about it is first class and I've never seen such beautiful beaches."

"Well, their resort in the Mayan Rivera, the Gran Bahia Principe Riviera Maya, is three separate resorts in one. They started with the Tulum section in 1998. Tulum has 858 rooms. At full occupancy they can accommodate 1814 guests. They opened the Akumal section in 2000. That's where I stayed," Sam smiled. "Akumal has 640 rooms. At full occupancy they can accommodate about 2500 people. In 2005, they opened the Coba section. It has 1080 rooms. Full occupancy is around 4000. So the property, with three resorts in one, can have from 8500 to 9000 guests, depending on how many people are in each room."

Alex rolled her eyes. "I don't think I'd want to stay in a place that big. There are far too many people for my liking."

"I didn't find it that way at all," Sam replied. "The place is huge and when I was there, they were ninety-five per cent occupied. I never had a problem in any of the restaurants or the bars. You could always find a spot at the pool or on the beach. And the beauty of it all, no matter which location you stay at Tulum, Akumal or Coba, you can use the services of all three."

"If the property is that large, how do people get from one place to the other?" Alex asked.

"They have a shuttle service."

"They had one of those when I was in the Dominican Republic," Alex smiled. "It went between the lobby and the beach."

"The system in the Mayan is much bigger and it runs like a well-oiled machine. There are three levels in front of each lobby. If you're at the Akumal for example, and you want to go to the Tulum side, you take the shuttle on the middle level. All three lobbies are the same. Top level shuttle takes you to Akumal. The middle takes you to Tulum and the bottom level takes you to Coba. It's great, you never get lost.

"The lobby in each section of the resort is laid out the same. The reception, the lobby bar and the theater are on the right. The buffet and the shops are on the left. Speaking of buffets," they came to a stop in front of the Royal Restaurant, "here we are."

"*Buenos dias, Señor* Bennett," Armando smiled. "*Como esta?*"

"*Bien gracias,*" Sam answered back. "How are the omelets this morning, Armando?"

"Ah, *Señor*," Armando kissed the tips of his fingers. "As always, they are *bueno.*"

Sam's face lit up in a proud smile. "See, I told you I knew where we could get a great omelet. Let's go sit down." He escorted Alex to a small table in a back corner that provided a view of the entire restaurant. In the middle of the table there was a sign that read: *Reserved for Señor Bennett.*

"This is nice," Alex remarked, accepting the chair Sam had pulled out for her. "You have your own private table. I guess it pays to be the boss."

"My staff calls this the table of doom!"

Alex raised a questioning brow. "And, why would they call it that?"

Sam walked around the table and sat down. "They call it the table of doom because any staff member who sits here is usually in deep shit," he chuckled. "Knowing that prevents them from bugging me when I'm sitting here contemplating life."

"You do that too?" Alex grinned.

Sam's expression turned serious. "Alex, every day since I opened this joint, I have sat at this table and contemplated what my life would have been like with you in it." He reached across the table for her hand. "Don't say anything. Not yet. Just know that not a day has gone by in the past twenty years when I haven't thought about you." Alex opened her mouth to speak and Sam covered her lips with his fingers. "We'll talk about this later. Right now, I need to get you fed and watered so we can be on our way."

Sam helped Alex from her chair and led her to the grill. "Good morning, Rosa." He smiled down at the chubby, middle-aged Mexican woman wearing a white apron and a chef's hat. "I have someone here who's traveled all the way from Denver, Colorado, just to taste one of your fabulous omelets!"

"Oh no, *Señor*," Rosa giggled. "You are how you say in English, pulling my leg." She turned to Alex. "What may I make for you this morning, *Señora*?"

Alex examined the items at the side of the grill. "Well, I'll have one of your famous omelets, with ham, mushrooms, green peppers, onions and cheese, *por favor*."

"I'll have the same Rosa," Sam added. He looked over Alex's shoulder and saw Angelina engaged in a conversation with a table of guests. "Will you excuse me for a minute? I need to talk to Angelina."

"Oh, sure," Alex smiled. "I'll just take our food back to the table when it's ready."

Sam leaned over and kissed her on the cheek. "Thanks, I'll only be a few minutes." He made his way to the other side of the restaurant and waited until Angelina had concluded her conversation, then motioned for her to join him. "I need you to take care of things today."

"Like what?" Angelina smiled.

"I'm going to Puerto Vallarta for the day."

Angelina's cheerful expression changed instantly. "What? You can't. That reporter from the travel magazine is expecting to have lunch with you today."

Sam put his arm around her waist and gave her a squeeze. "Come on, Angel, you probably know this place better than I do! Just give her the grand tour. Feed her lobster for lunch and send her on her way."

"She's staying here for five days," Angelina frowned.

"That's nice," Sam casually replied waving over Angelina's shoulder in Alex's direction.

Angelina removed Sam's arm from around her waist. "I don't have time for this today. I am very busy with other things. The furniture problem needs to be dealt with, and ..."

"Let me take care of the furniture and if you don't want to entertain the *travel lady*, send her over to Juanita and let her watch the animation team rehearse the show." Sam stared down at Angelina with his big puppy-dog eyes. "What do you say? How often do I ask for a day off? This is really important to me. I need to spend some time with Alex. If I didn't think you were capable of handling this place alone, I wouldn't have asked."

Angelina motioned across the room toward Alex. "Does this mean that you and Ms. Granger have kissed and made up?"

Sam's face turned red. "Well, we haven't kissed, but the making-up seems to have gotten off to a good start."

15

"WELCOME TO MEXICO. I'LL be your tour guide on to-day's adventure." Sam smiled proudly at Alex and put the jeep in gear. As they pulled onto the highway, he went over their itinerary. "First, I'm going to take you to the marina in Marina Vallarta. With any luck, we may catch a cruise ship in port."

"How often do ships come to Puerto Vallarta?" Alex asked.

"Puerto Vallarta gets over 300 visits by different cruise lines every year. We have Carnival, Royal Viking, Royal Caribbean, Holland America, Celebrity, Disney, they all stop here. The ships usually stay for about twelve hours."

"I've never been on a cruise," Alex confessed.

"As I recall," Sam turned his attention from the road and gave Alex a sheepish grin. "Twenty-five years ago, you hadn't been diving either! Did you ever fulfill that fantasy?"

"Yes, actually I did," Alex smiled.

Sam pointed to his right. "There's the army base. In Mexico, it's mandatory to go into the military."

"Really," Alex remarked observing the passing buildings.

"Here, it's not a case of whether or not you want to go into the military," Sam explained. "At eighteen, you're in the army for a year whether you like it or not. When you're finished, they give you a certificate. No certificate, no job and it's harder to get a passport."

Alex pointed out the window. "That's the airport, right?"

"Yup, it was built in 1970," Sam informed her. "In fact, it was thanks to Richard Nixon's visit that it was actually finished. Before Nixon's trip, there wasn't even a road to Puerto

Vallarta. The renovations are really coming along. The new departures' terminal is open and all of the new jet-ways should be up and running in a in a couple of weeks."

"My daughter has been here a couple of times. She said the airport could really use a face-lift."

"How is your daughter?" Sam asked. "She must be what, in her mid-twenties by now?"

Alex felt her stomach churn. She wanted to blurt out that Sarah was his daughter too, but she knew she couldn't, not yet. "My daughter is fine."

"What does she do for a living?" Sam asked.

"You'd be very proud of her, Sam." Alex's face broke into a beaming grin. "She's a doctor." *Why, would I say he'd be proud of her,* Alex thought. *He doesn't even know her.*

"Wow, that's great! What's her specialty?"

"She just graduated in May. I don't think she's made up her mind, but I believe she's leaning towards pediatrics. She's working in emergency for the next six months." Alex let out a disappointed sigh. "She was supposed to come with me, but she got called back to the hospital at the eleventh hour to help cover shifts."

"You said your daughter has been here before?"

"Actually," Alex grinned, "she's been here twice and both times she stayed at *Las Tropicales.*"

"You're kidding? That's unbelievable. What did she think of the place?"

"Oh, she just loved it! She said the property was beautiful, and the staff friendly. In fact, she's the one who booked this trip for us. It was supposed to be a family vacation to celebrate my fiftieth."

"When's your birthday?" Sam asked.

Alex lowered her eyes. "It was yesterday."

"Yesterday! And your birthday celebration was our little blow-up? Well, we need to do something about that." Sam picked up his cell phone and hit the speed dial. "This is

Señor Bennett. *Yo quiero preparar una cena cumpleanos. Gracias.*"

"What was that all about?" Alex asked when Sam disconnected the call.

"Well, you can't turn fifty and not have a party, right? So tonight, we'll celebrate." He gave Alex a shy smile. "By the way, you look great!"

"Thank you," Alex blushed. "You seem to speak the language very well. How long have you lived here?"

"Since I died ... twenty years ago."

Sam pulled into the marina and searched for a parking spot. "I was hoping we could take a walk around, but I can see that parking is at a premium. You usually can't find a parking spot in Puerto Vallarta either. Even the tour buses drop off the sightseers and find another place to wait." Sam pulled back onto the main highway and headed towards the city. "I've got a buddy who owns a resort on the strip. We'll park there and take a cab to the plaza."

Twenty minutes later, Sam and Alex were standing in the main square. "Welcome to Puerto Vallarta," he smiled. The name used to be much longer. It was originally called *Puerto Las Penas eh Santa Maria eh Guadalupe*. Broken down, that means the Port of Las Penas, the Island of Santa Maria and the Virgin Mary of Guadalupe."

Sam slowly turned Alex in a circle. "The main plaza is very important in the Mexican culture. It's where everyone comes to meet, especially the young people. They come here to find a boyfriend or a girlfriend. They walk around the plaza until someone catches their eye. In some of the small outlying towns, Sunday is the best day to meet a new love interest."

"The people in this country are very beautiful," Alex commented as she watched a group of young people strolling by.

"The people in Mexico are mostly half-Spanish and half-Mexican, or Aztec and Spanish. Some people look more Spanish and some, more native. If you look at the vendors on the beach, they have a big eagle nose, big brown eyes, big lips and dark straight hair. They are more Aztec. We have white people in Mexico, too."

"People moving here from other countries?" Alex asked.

Sam shook his head. "No. White people who were born here. My friend, Mario has a white mother with brown eyes, a white father with grey eyes and he's dark. In Mexico, it's not uncommon to have a white mother and father and be dark, or the opposite, dark parents and the kid is white. It usually happens in the third generation."

"Everyone here seems to be so young," Alex remarked.

"They are," Sam agreed. "Sixty-five per cent of the population of Mexico is younger than twenty-eight, and most families have three to five kids." He turned and pointed over her shoulder towards the Pacific "In that area, by the water, usually on Saturday and Sunday evenings, they have a big festival. There are singers and musicians and local artists who display their work. Some Puerto Vallarta galleries display art valued in the tens of thousands of dollars."

Sam turned Alex to the right. "That's city hall. It's built like a *hacienda*. Can you see," he pointed, "that it's kind of a square with a courtyard in the center?"

"Yes," Alex answered.

"Years ago, the horses and the staff occupied the bottom floor of the *hacienda*. There was a stable and bedrooms for the servants and usually a kitchen. The owner and his family lived on the floors above. Before the revolution, on November 20th, 1910, the rich people owned whatever they could see around them. After the revolution, the land was given to the people who worked it. My buddy Mario for example, his great-grandfather got eighty hectares, that's about two hundred acres. You want to go for a little walk, and then we'll find some place to have a *cerveza*?"

"That sounds good to me!"

Sam took Alex's hand in his and they walked up the street to the Church of *Lady Guadalupe*. On the front steps, he gave Alex a history lesson. "When a man by the name of Guadalupe

Sanchez arrived in Puerto Vallarta, the first thing he did was build an altar for *Lady Guadalupe*. In 1810, a priest took *Lady Guadalupe* as a symbol of the independence of Mexico. *Lady Guadalupe* is important in Mexican history," Sam explained. "Not just for religious reasons, but also for cultural reasons. Before the Spanish arrived the Aztec people believed in human sacrifice. They believed in five-human generations, meaning four lives before this one. They believed the soul was in the heart, so instead of just offering gifts to the Gods' of gold and silver and semi-precious stones ... which they believed didn't have enough value to be considered a good omen, they offered up a human heart."

Alex held her hand over her eyes to block the sun and looked up at the church steeple. "How old is this building?"

"They started building it in 1810 and finished it in 1903. There were 6000 people in Puerto Vallarta back then. Would you like to go inside?" he asked.

The historic church had a stark white interior with beautifully stained-glass windows and a magnificent altar bordered in gold. "I can't even imagine what the upkeep must be on this place." Alex remarked in awe.

"There's a special association called Vallarta's Friends that keep the place looking immaculate. The electricity alone costs a grand a month and they just remodeled the main altar. That cost, twenty grand."

"This may sound morbid," Alex leaned closer to Sam, "but this would be a great place for a funeral."

"Or a wedding," he whispered back.

Alex was taken aback by Sam's words. Did he say this would be a great place for a wedding, or was she jumping to conclusions?

"I'm ready for that beer now, how about you?" Sam took Alex by the hand and they walked back to the main square. "Would you like to know how names are pronounced in Spanish?" he asked.

"Sure," Alex smiled.

"Well, Frank in Spanish is Francisco or Paco. Joseph is Jose or Pepe. Janice, Joan and Janet are Juanita. Marilyn in Spanish is Marialina. Dolores is Lolita."

"What is Edwardo in Spanish?" Alex asked.

"Edwardo?" Sam laughed. "You actually know someone named Edwardo?"

"*Si, Señor.*" Alex nodded.

"Well, the next time you see him you can say, *hola* Lalo."

They stopped at an open doorway across the street from the square. "Here we are." Sam escorted Alex up the stairs and across the terrace to a corner table. He pulled out a chair and invited her to sit down. "Did you know that Elizabeth Taylor and Richard Burton used to sit at this very table?"

"Really?"

"Really."

"*Hola Señor, eh Señora.* What can I bring for you today?" the waiter asked.

"Are you hungry, Alex?"

"Actually, I'm still full from the omelet, but I've heard the guacamole in Mexico is to die for!"

"Excellent choice!" Sam looked up at the waiter. "We'll have two Coronas, taco chips and guacamole, *por favor.*"

"*Si.*"

When the waiter was gone, Alex folded her arms on the table and leaned closer to Sam. "So, tell me about Liz and Richard."

"Well, they were traveling together promoting the movie *Cleopatra* and they fell in love. The only problem, Liz was married to someone else so they started having a secret romance. Richard gave Liz an engagement ring right under this table. Their affair was a big scandal, but the gossip was actually very good for Puerto Vallarta and the tourist industry in 1964. When they married, they bought a house here. They called it *Casa* Kimberly. After they divorced, Richard came back to Puerto Vallarta and built a house across the street from the one he'd shared with Liz. When they remarried, he built a bridge connecting the two properties."

When the waiter returned, he put a Corona in front of Alex, one in front of Sam and the chips and guacamole in the middle of the table. Alex stared down at the chunky green paste. "I've never seen guacamole with feta cheese on top."

"*Si Señora,*" the waiter smiled. "That's how they always serve it in Mexico." He turned to Sam. "Will there be anything else?"

"No, I think we're good for the moment," Sam smiled. "*Gracias.*"

Alex took a taco chip from the bowl and dug in. "Umm, this is delicious." When she'd savored the flavor, she delicately wiped her mouth with her napkin and placed it back in her lap. "So, tell me more about Liz and Richard."

"They used to come here every morning for cocktails."

Alex screwed up her face. "Cocktails for breakfast?"

Sam shrugged his shoulders. "Who knows about the life of the rich and famous? The house is only about six or seven blocks behind the church. It's a nice twelve-bedroom shack. They divorced again, and Liz sold the house in 1988, for around $350,000. Today, it's for sale for a million and a half."

"Can we go see it?" Alex asked.

"Actually," Sam frowned. "I had other plans."

"You're the tour guide!"

Sam smiled to himself as he watched Alex enthusiastically dive into the chips and guacamole. He still couldn't believe that she was here ... in Mexico ... with him. For years, he'd dreamt that somehow Alex would come back into his life. Now that he'd found her again, he was never letting her go.

"Will there be anything else, *Señor*?" the waiter asked.

"No. *La cuenta por favor.*"

"*Si,*"

"What did you just say?" Alex asked.

"You don't speak Spanish?"

Alex shook her head. "Not much."

"I asked for the bill."

They took a cab back to where Sam had parked the jeep and drove south out of the city. "This is the road that goes all the way to Acapulco," Sam told Alex. "It's about an eighteen-hour drive. Manzanillo is six hours. I don't know what they are building for houses in Denver these days, but you're going to see some pretty nice shacks along this road. The average selling price is $700,000 American."

Alex admired the homes that followed the shoreline and the ocean view accompanying them. "This bay is gorgeous," she remarked.

"Banderas Bay is one of the largest bays in the Pacific. It's twenty miles north to south, and twenty-six miles from east to west and in some places, hundreds of feet deep."

Half an hour later; after admiring the view and chatting like old friends, Sam pulled off the highway and parked the jeep. "Come on. I want to show you something." He helped Alex from the vehicle, took her hand, and led her to the protective railing at the edge of the cliff. He put his arm around her shoulder and pointed toward the boulders erupting from the turquoise water of the bay. "That's Las Arcos."

"Yes," Alex smiled. "Your diving instructor, Hans, mentioned it during the orientation. He said it was a fantastic place to dive."

"It is. There are shallow waters and a very impressive drop-off. Angelina and I try to get out there once a week."

"She's a very nice lady. How long has she worked for you?"

"She's been here since the day I took it over. She started with the animation team."

"How long has she been your assistant manager?" Alex asked.

"Almost a year. I originally gave her the position because of what Grace had done to her, but she's really proven herself. In fact, I'm thinking of buying a place in the Dominican Republic and I want Angelina to run it."

Alex turned from the view she'd been admiring and looked at Sam. Her face was serious. "It's probably none of my business, but what did Grace do to Angelina that would cause you to give her a big promotion?"

"Angelina was Grace's private assistant, but I'd have called it more like a personal slave. Grace treated her like shit, but I don't want to talk about Angelina. I want to talk about us." Sam put his hands on Alex's shoulders and looked deeply into her eyes. "You know, my dad always said that the Lord worked in mysterious ways."

"What do you mean?"

"All I have done for the past twenty-five years is wish and pray for the day that somehow you and I would be together again, and here you are." Sam couldn't control himself any longer. All he'd wanted to do since he first saw Alex was take her in his arms and kiss her. There was no time like the present. He leaned down towards her inviting mouth and there was no objection when his lips touched hers.

The kiss sent a tingling sensation throughout Alex's body. In her fifty years on earth, she'd never known anyone who kissed the way Sam Bennett kissed. His lips were full and soft and his tongue seductive as it gently explored her mouth. Her legs were shaking and her pulse raced. She'd packed her heart in ice years ago. Now, it was melting faster than the witch in 'The Wizard of Oz'.

A gentle breeze danced across Alex's lips and she opened her eyes. Sam was smiling at her. "Wow," he said.

"Wow," she replied.

Grinning from ear to ear, Sam turned Alex to the left and pointed to the distant shoreline. "I don't know if you can see it or not, but that's Mismaloya. That's where they filmed *The Night of the Iguana*, with Richard Burton, Ava Gardner and Deborah Kerr. Have you seen the movie?" Sam asked.

"Yes," Alex nodded. "As I recall, Richard is a renegade priest. The church sends him away to find himself. He ends up operating a religious ladies' tour group and is troubled by three women. The first one's chasing him. The second one's remembering how things were before he became a priest, and the third one is making him feel guilty for the pleasures of the first two."

"That's basically it. Three women ...one man ... one night; *The Night of the Iguana*." Sam let out a chuckle. "My father told me ... that's what the marquee outside the theater read when the movie first came out."

"When I was at the orientation, Hans mentioned that the movie brought a lot of tourism to Puerto Vallarta."

"Yes it did," Sam nodded. "Do you like old movies?"

"I love them," Alex smiled. "We get Turner Classic Movies back home. There's nothing I like better than to curl up in front of the fireplace on a cold-winter day and watch the classics."

"Me too, but I don't get much of a chance to do that here." He gave Alex a goofy grin. "Not much use for a fireplace in this climate. So, how do you feel about reptiles?" Sam asked out of the blue.

"Why?"

"You'll find out."

Sam took Alex's hand and enthusiastically led her down the path towards the souvenir stand. A teenage Mexican boy approached them. Sam and the boy exchanged words in Spanish. Then, the boy walked to a nearby tree and took something from a lower branch.

Alex's eyes widened and she took a step back as the boy approached. "Oh my God! That thing is huge!" she exclaimed.

Sam gave her a friendly poke. "You're not afraid of a little old lizard are you?"

The boy held the iguana out to Alex like an offering to the Gods. "What does he want me to do?" she asked.

"Put it around your neck and let me take a picture," Sam grinned.

Alex felt her skin crawl. She'd never been fond of reptiles, but at least this wasn't a snake. "Okay," she cringed, "if you say so." Her body stiffened when she felt the reptile on her shoulders. She was sure it weighed close to ten pounds, but it wasn't slimy like she thought it would be. The creature was warm and soft.

"Say cheese!" Sam snapped the picture and gave the boy twenty *pesos*. "You handled that very well," he smiled, taking the iguana from Alex's shoulders.

"I can't wait to get the picture developed!" Alex beamed. "I hate snakes and I've never been too fond of lizards! Sarah is going to have a fit when she sees this!"

Sam gave the iguana back to its owner and escorted Alex up the hill to the jeep. It had been a great day and he was positive it would only get better. He was about to help Alex into the vehicle when his cell phone rang. "I knew I should have shut this thing off. Will you excuse me?"

For five minutes, Sam carried on a conversation in Spanish. Alex couldn't understand a thing he was saying, but the tone of his voice told her he was upset. His face filled with disappointment when he hung up the phone. "I'm afraid we're going to have to cut our tour short. Something's come up. I need to get back to the resort."

16

SAM DROPPED ALEX AT the front lobby of *Las Tropicales* and told her he'd pick her up at six p.m. sharp. He had something special planned. It was only noon and she had no idea how she was going to occupy the remainder of the day until she ran into Pat Lawrence. Pat invited her to take a Spanish lesson.

"*Hola*, ladies and gentlemen, my name is Migel. I am with the recreation services department." The handsome Mexican man gave his students a friendly smile. "Here at *Las Tropicales*, we want you to feel like our family. Our family speaks Spanish! You too can speak this beautiful language. It is very easy. Some of you may already speak Spanish. How many people here know how to say hello?" All but one of the students held up their hand. "It is very easy. Hello is *Hola*." Migel motioned to the class. "Now, everyone say hello."

"*Hola*," the class responded.

"Now, I am going to say some words and I want you to repeat them. Good morning, in Spanish you say *buenos dias*." The class repeated the greeting. "Good afternoon, in Spanish you say *buenas tardes*." Migel smiled at the class and they repeated the greeting. "Good, now, it is at night and you are going to our fabulous Picollo restaurant for dinner and you want to greet the waiter. What would you say?" He pointed at Alex.

"You would say *buenas noches*."

"Very good," Migel clapped. "Okay, you are here at the resort and you want to go outside the property. Once outside you want to know things, *si*? That means yes, by the way!" he

grinned. "You are outside the resort and say, you want a restaurant. You would say *Yo quiero ir a un restaurante.*" Migel
wrote the sentence on the whiteboard. "If you look at this sentence," he pointed to the first word. "*Yo* in Spanish is I, but we
often don't use this.

"*Quiero* is want, so *quiero* is, I want. For the words ... to
go ...in Spanish, you say *ir.*" Migel reached up and tugged at
his earlobe. "Sounds like ear, but is not spelled that way. Now
we have this sentence. I want to go. Where, do we want to go?"
He pointed to the whiteboard. "We want to go to a restaurant,
a *un restaurante.* So we have, I want to go to a restaurant.
Quiero ir a un restaurante. Please repeat." The class repeated
the sentence, some with very little difficulty.

"Okay, now you want to go to the bank. Does anyone know
how you say bank in Spanish?" Pat held up her hand. "*Si
Señora,*" Migel smiled.

"Bank in Spanish is *banco,*" Pat replied.

"*Si*, yes, that is very good. Now that you know this can
you tell me how you would tell someone I want to go to the
bank?"

Pat cleared her throat. "You would say, *quiero ir al banco.*"

"Very good," Migel clapped. "Okay, now we will go through
the list I have given you. If you want to go somewhere, you will
know how to ask. First if you want to go to the movies, you say,
quiero ir al cine. Cine means the movies. We already know the
bank and the restaurant. What if you wanted to go to the post
office? You would say *quiero ir al correo.* If you were looking
for a beautiful park, you would say, *quiero ir al parque.* For
the store you would say, *quiero ir a la tienda.* How about the
pool? Can anyone tell me how you would ask for this?"

Pat held up her hand and Migel nodded for her to answer.
"You would say, *quiero ir a la piscina.*"

"Yes that is correct. See how easy it is! Now, to say ... I
need ... in Spanish you say *necesito.* Let us take for example I
need to go to the office. In Spanish you would say, *necesito ir*

a al oficina. I need to go to the office. We will go through the list and when we are finished you will be able to communicate some with the Mexican people."

After class, Pat and Alex took a walk down the beach to check out a new condominium complex being built nearby. When they returned to the resort, Alex had cocktails with the Lawrences before going to her room to get ready for her date with Sam. He was picking her up six p.m. sharp. She was ready at five forty-five.

At seven o'clock, the phone rang. "Hello?" Alex answered.

"Hi. I'm really sorry," Sam apologized. "I got tied up with something. Are we still on for our date?"

"You bet!"

"Dress casual. I'll be right there."

Alex changed from the sundress she selected to a linen tank top and clam diggers and had just finished touching up her make-up, when there was a knock at the door. She rushed to answer it.

"You look great," Sam smiled. "I thought I'd give you the ten-cent tour of the place before we have dinner."

"I'd like that." Alex hooked her arm in his. "I'd like that very much."

They walked down the open-air hallway, greeting guests who were emerging from their rooms to partake of the evening meal. Their first stop on the tour was the *Cocos* lobby so Sam could check his messages. There were two from Angelina.

Next, Sam took Alex to the site of the resort's newest building. "I know it may be hard to visualize right now, but when this area is finished, it will have a huge pool and beautiful gardens." A proud smile danced across his face. "It took us a few years, but we finally figured out that what we needed was a place for families to go with their kids'."

Sam put his arm around Alex's shoulder and pointed. "The big hole will be the swimming pool. More than half of it is a wading pool. It's only two-feet deep. The lobby is right behind it." He turned Alex to the left. "All of the rooms on the left side of the building will be adjoining rooms." He turned Alex to the right. "In that wing, the bottom floor will be one-bedroom suites and the second floor, two-bedroom suites. At each end of the third floor, there's a three-bedroom penthouse. In the middle a kids' play area with a sand box, swings and a slide." Sam let out a deep sigh. "I always wanted kids. I guess this is the closest I'll ever get to having any."

Alex's heart beat faster. She wanted to tell Sam that he had a beautiful daughter, but she couldn't. Not until her divorce was final. The moment she got home, she'd go directly to Peter Bailey's office and sign the papers. She'd have Brian removed from any involvement with her companies. She'd have his things removed from the ranch and the condo in town. When Brian was out of her life ... she'd tell Sam about Sarah.

From the construction site, Sam took Alex to his favorite spot at the resort. "This is our Picollo restaurant." He raised his fingers to his lips, "*Muy bueno.* I just love this place. It's first class all the way. Angelina came up with the idea after a big Italian family celebrated their reunion here. In fact, some of the recipes came right from the grandmother. Shall we go in and have a drink?"

Inside, Sam and Alex were escorted to a table for two that provided a beautiful view of the garden. They were no more than seated when Sergio, the head waiter, appeared carrying a bottle of champagne. "What's this?" Alex asked.

Sam raised an eyebrow. "Wasn't yesterday your birthday?"

"*Si,*" she blushed.

"Well, now we're going to start celebrating."

While they enjoyed the champagne, they talked about *Las Tropicales.* Alex was curious about Sam's little holiday destination and asked question after question. "How long has your resort been open?"

"The resort has been here for ten years," Sam told her. "I've owned it for eight."

"It must take a lot of different departments to run something like this?"

"Yes, it does," Sam nodded. "We have the general managers, housekeeping, reception, entertainment, laundry, security, tourist services, grounds maintenance, pool maintenance, general maintenance, food and beverage, sales and marketing department, quality control and guest services."

"I have another question."

"What's that?" Sam smiled.

"How do you determine how much food you need? What do you base it on? I assume it has something to do with the number of guests."

"It would seem to be challenging," Sam smiled, "but my guys have it down to a fine science. At any given time, there could be 1200 people having breakfast, lunch or dinner at the same time. We have our set menus for each restaurant, so the head chef knows how many pounds of fish or how much beef, rice and chicken we need. When we first opened, we only served bacon on certain days. People started to complain, so now we serve it every morning."

From the Italian restaurant, Sam and Alex walked hand in hand through the gardens to the *Tropical* lobby. Again, Sam checked his messages. This time, there were three from Angelina.

"If you'll excuse me for a minute, I just need to take care of something." Sam unclipped the radio from his belt, turned it on and said something in Spanish. A moment later, Angelina's voice replied in Spanish and Sam said, "I'll be right there." He hung the radio back on his belt and stared down at Alex. When he spoke, his voice was filled with disappointment. "I'm really sorry to have to do this to you, but Angelina needs me to take care of something. I'm afraid I won't be able to join you for dinner. I made reservations at Karen's Place's."

"Karen's Place?"

"Yeah," Sam smiled. "It's a little restaurant on the beach about five minutes from here. The owner's a friend of mine.

She's originally from England but moved here sixteen years ago. She was working at one of the local restaurants waiting tables when we met. She always told me someday she'd be waiting tables in her own place. Now she is!"

"Sam, we don't have to do dinner tonight. I'll just go to one of the buffets. We can always get together later."

Sam shook his head. "No. I insist you have dinner at Karen's."

"Insisting now, are we?"

Sam pulled Alex into his arms and looked down at her with wanting eyes. "The only thing I insist on is that we spend the rest of our lives together."

"We will. I promise," Alex whispered.

"Okay, so it's all settled then? Cesar will take you to Karen's. Trust me, you'll thank me. The food is fantastic and the atmosphere isn't bad either. Comfy chairs, candlelight, soft music." Sam winked at Alex. "Maybe it will put you in the mood for all the things I hope you'll do to me later."

"If it's that romantic, I may just run off with Cesar!"

"No fear of that," Sam grinned, "he's a happily married man." Sam looked at his watch. "I'm hoping this won't take long. I should be there before desert. Afterward, we have a date for a special screening of *The Night of the Iguana*."

Alex felt her heart melt. Somewhere between the time they'd left the resort this morning, and the issues Sam had to deal with when they got back from their tour, he'd managed to make arrangements for them to spend a special evening together.

"I'm going to have Cesar take you to the restaurant now. He'll stay and keep you company. If I'm not there by the time you've finished, he'll take you to my little private screening room and I'll meet you there."

At eleven p.m. when the movie was over, Alex and Cesar finished the remainder of their popcorn, hailed a cab and went back to *Las Tropicales*.

17

ANGELINA WAS FURIOUS WITH Sam. She hadn't been able to spend more than fifteen minutes with him in the past three days; Alex Granger was occupying all of his time. The happy couple had been to Puerto Vallarta. They'd spent a day on Las Caletas, and now, they were touring somewhere in the Sierra Madre Mountains. At least the other night, Sam had managed to tear himself away from the woman long enough to help her entertain two wealthy hotel guests, who insisted they dine with management.

Never before had Angelina seen anyone eat like these two women. On their first trip to the salad bar, they filled their plates with every fruit and vegetable available. At the buffet, they each took enough food to feed a small village, and stopped for a variety of desserts before returning to the table. The more rotund of the two was like an eating machine. She hadn't finished chewing and swallowing what was in her mouth before she was shoveling in more food. It was a very interesting experience.

At the first available opportunity, Sam thanked the women for the pleasure of their company, excused himself and left. Angelina was positive he was going to meet the Granger woman. She could understand his need to make up for lost time, but since her arrival, Sam had completely neglected his duties at the resort. There were hardly enough hours in the day to take care of her own duties, let alone take care of Sam's and she still hadn't completed her notes or packed for her trip to the Dominican Republic.

Angelina swallowed her last mouthful of coffee and glanced at her watch. It was ten a.m., time to begin the first of the five new-employee orientation sessions she would carry out today, thanks to Sam's absence. Somewhere in between, she had to help the sales department prepare a presentation for a new tour operator, and meet with two new suppliers. She'd handled everything somehow, but when her boss returned from his little adventure in Mountains, she was going to give him an earful!

Angelina left her office and headed to the smallest of the resort's three meeting rooms. A long boardroom table had been set up in the center of the room. Sitting around it were fifteen women ranging in age from eighteen to thirty. "*Buenas dias*. My name is Angelina Rodriguez. I am the assistant manager of *Las Tropicales*. Welcome aboard."

She made her way to the head of the table. "In front of you, you have an orientation folder that contains a lot of information. We are going to go through the folder but first, let me tell you a little about our property. This resort has been here for ten years. At that time there was only block one, located right on the beach and block two, located behind the main reception. There was one pool and two restaurants.

"Eight years ago, *Señor* Bennett purchased the property and changed the name to *Las Tropicales*. From that time on, his focus has been on providing quality service to each guest. Rarely are we below ninety-nine per cent occupancy. Our reputation over the years has allowed us to increase in size. We now have four blocks, three pools, six restaurants and a workout and spa facility. Our newest addition to the property is block five, which is scheduled to open in December.

"This block will be unique to the resort and cater to families. There will be one-and two-bedroom suites as well as adjoining rooms. Block five will have its own pool, with a large childrens' play area, an internet café, a bar, a snack bar, a restaurant and a separate check-in. This is the building that you ladies will be working in."

Angelina smiled at the new employees. "If you will open your folders, we will go through the information. First we have a map of the resort, showing where the buildings are located and what services they provide. At this moment, the laundry is located behind block three, but that will change when block five is opened. We are building a new laundry facility behind that building.

"The next page of the information package contains the names of each manager and their assistant from each department. We have a very open-door policy here at *Las Tropicales,* so please feel free to talk to us if you have questions, or if there is ever a problem. The resort is successful because the people who work here … work as a team. Welcome to the team!"

Angelina removed the Quality Control Program information and set it on the table. "Before we talk about the standard procedures that you will be involved in while doing your housekeeping duties, I would like to take a minute to explain our Quality Control Program. If you would please, remove this item from the folder."

She held up the stapled pages. "What is the Quality Control Program, you ask. The Quality Control Program was designed to provide ongoing improvements in each of our departments. These procedures are applied and followed in order to achieve the high standard set by *Señor* Bennett and this resort. As a result of these high standards, we are able to provide optimum service to both our internal clients as well as our external ones."

Angelina looked around the table at the smiling faces. "Can anyone tell me who an internal client would be?"

A young attractive American woman sitting at the end of the table held up her hand. "*Ellos son la gente que se queda internamente en el hotel.*"

"Your Spanish is very good," Angelina smiled. "Where are you from?"

"Chicago," the girl blushed.

"Our internal clients are not, as you have suggested, the people who stay internally at the hotel, but the people who work here. We are people committed to the company and very proud of our jobs. We are people who smile, and put aside obstacles to make the job and the environment we work in a nicer place. We are people who take pride in details to ensure that we exceed the expectation of our guests. We could not survive without guests. They are the pillar of our work and they make our hotel come alive. They deserve our best. We believe the Quality Control Program helps us achieve that goal."

Angelina flipped open the first page. "What is quality? Quality is something we can apply to everything we do. It's a smile and a warm greeting. It's our beautiful gardens and clean, tidy beach. Quality is well-maintained restaurants that provide our guests with great food and friendly service. Quality is about everything we do. The Quality Control Program allows us to ensure the continued satisfaction of our guests.

"Through the Quality Control Program," Angelina continued, "we are able to establish channels of communication and analyze the satisfaction of not only the people who stay here, but the people who work here. The program allows us to improve our products and services by helping determine the needs of our guests. The program allows us to identify a problem and find a solution."

Angelina put down her notes and smiled warmly at the new employees. "Our Quality Control Program is useless without the support of our staff. Why, because it is the staff who deal with the guests each and every day. You ladies in particular, will be cleaning their rooms and trust me, I speak from experience when I say there will be days when you will hate your job and the people you clean up after, just like the guest services department dislikes spring-break when teenagers sometimes cause problems with other guests. When you come by those days, remember that you are an important spoke in the wheel that drives our team.

"We invite you to make suggestions on things you feel could be improved. If your suggestion is put into practice and proves to be a valuable asset to our high standards, you will receive a check for 5000 *pesos*. On top of this, each month we recognize the employee of the month from each department at the resort. That person, who is chosen, will have one day off with pay. On this day, *Señor* Bennett will fill your position.

"We also give a reward for the employee of the year. This person will win a one-week vacation for two at the all-inclusive Gran Bahia Principe Bavaro in the Dominican Republic." Angelina closed her binder. "We are going to take a ten-minute break and then we will be joined by Marta Santo, who is our head of housekeeping. Marta will explain our standard room cleaning procedure."

Back at her office, Angelina checked her voice mail. There was a message from Sam: "Hi Angel. Hope your day is going well. I'm sure you're pissed at me for sticking you with the orientations today, but it was for a good cause. Alex and I are having a great time. I forgot how beautiful it is up here. Listen, kid, I promise tomorrow you'll have my undivided attention. Alex and I were going to go diving but Walter called, apparently there's another problem with the new furniture. We need to go and see him tomorrow just after ten. I hate to leave Alex high and dry, so could you do me a huge favor? Can you call Randy at Vallarta Adventures and make arrangements for Alex to go on the ten a.m. dolphin swim tomorrow. I have to go, the jeep's leaving. Thanks. I love yah."

Angelina erased the message, booked Alex's dolphin swim and returned several e-mails before heading back to the meeting room. When she arrived, Marta had already begun explaining the proper procedures for cleaning a room.

"We have the procedures when we clean the rooms. *Uno*, we must first knock the door and say, *Buenos dias,* good morning, housekeeping. Wait for an answer from inside and check also the door for the sign, *por favor arreglar la habitacion*, please clean the room, or the sign, *no molestar*, do not disturb. Next, *dos*," Marta held up two fingers, "we open the door, enter the room, and open the curtains and the window.

"*Tres*, number three, take out the trash and remove the sheets and blankets from the bed. Remove the dirty laundry and bring in the clean bed coverings and towels. *Cuatro*, number four, brush the room including the bathroom and the terrace. *Cinco*, number five is to wash the bathroom beginning with the water closet and apply cleanser to the bowl. While the product is acting, you pass to the sink area followed by the shower. Then you must finish the cleaning of the water closet and dry the bathroom. Supply then the toilet paper and the towels, including the bathmat, bath towels, hand towels and the cloth for the faces. Also you must replace the *agua*, the water."

"*Cuantas botellas de agua se ponen en cada habitacion?*" one of the new employees asked.

"The number of bottles of water each room will get depends on the people in the room," Marta explained. "Their numbers will show on your list. If there are three people you leave three *aguas. Numero seis*, number six, the next thing to do when inside the room will be making of the beds. Then you must wipe down the furniture inside and also on the terrace. Also you will wipe please the railing and make clean the windows and wash the floor of the terrace. When you pass back inside, see that, the chairs, pictures and lamps are in good position. Number *siete*, seven is for final, spray the air fresh, mop the floor before you pass out of the room. Lock ..."

A knock at the door, momentarily halted Marta's presentation. A young woman entered the room. "Excuse me Angelina, you are needed at, the guest services."

18

THE CHEERFUL EXCHANGE OF Spanish coming from outside her room woke Alex from a sound restful sleep, the first one she'd had in months. She reached over for the warmth of Sam's body, but the spot beside her was vacant. She panicked for a moment, thinking all of this had been a dream, until she remembered that Sam had a breakfast meeting. They would meet at ten a.m. and spend another glorious day together.

Alex looked at the clock on the bedside table. It was only nine ... she still had an hour. She closed her eyes and a beaming smile lit up her face. She was happier than she'd been in years and she had Sam to thank for it. If she died tomorrow, she'd die happy.

Sam may have stood her up the night he arranged for the two of them to have dinner at "Karen's Place" and watch *The Night of the Iguana*, but since then, he'd more than made up for it. They toured the Sierra Madre Mountains and Alex learned that the Mexican mountain range was part of the longest rock formation in the world, beginning in Argentina, and ending in Canada.

They spent a day on Las Caletas. Once the home of film director John Huston, the tropical sanctuary was Mexico's own Garden of Eden. Sam arranged for them to have a massage in the hillside spa and it was fabulous.

Afterward, while Sam attended to hotel business on his cell phone, Alex took a cooking lesson and learned how to make paella. After lunch, they went on a guided nature walk then spent the afternoon lying in hammocks strung between towering palms.

Alex told Sam of Brian's blackmail after learning that her father was having an affair. She told him she'd thought about taking the information to her mother, but she knew her mother would be devastated. Instead, she kept her mouth shut and paid Brian his hush money. Alex told Sam that her marriage had been a joke. She told him that Brian had been a lousy husband, but he'd made up for it by being a decent father to Sarah.

Alex had always known that Sam was her soul mate. Spending the past four days with him had reconfirmed it. Now, after years of separation, some cosmic force had brought them back into each others' arms. Last night when they made love, for the first time in so very many years, they found the passion they had both so desperately craved. They promised each other that they would never be apart again.

When Alex pulled back the covers to get out of bed a shiny object caught her eye. She raised her left arm and watched in amazement as a beautiful diamond bracelet slid down from her wrist. When she sat up, she saw a note on the pillow where Sam's head had been the night before. "What's this?" She picked it up and read it:

> *My darling Alex,*
>
> *I am so glad we have found each other again. This time, I'll never let you go. They say the third time's a charm!*
>
> *I wanted to give you this bracelet as a wedding present twenty-five years ago ... better late than never.*
>
> *We will be married my love, on the beach just as I promised the first time. I have always loved you. I will love you forever. Our life begins today!*
>
> *Sam*

Alex held the note to her heart and smiled. Her life had definitely taken a turn for the better since arriving in Mexico. She realized now that the man she'd seen in the parking lot at the airport had been Sam. The woman he was embracing, Angelina. Alex made a mental note to find Angelina today and thank her for being an important part of their reunion. She couldn't remember the last time she'd been this happy.

She didn't want to go home in two days, but she knew she had to. There were a million things that needed to be done. First, she'd go to Peter's office and sign her divorce papers. She was positive the divorce would come as quite a shock to Brian, especially after he'd done such an admirable job of wining and dining her prior to her departure for Mexico. Brian pleaded his case well, but Alex knew it was all an act. He hadn't changed, he would never change. The only thing she could give him credit for was the fact that this year, he'd actually remembered her birthday.

Twenty minutes later, Alex was standing at the entrance to the Royal restaurant. She scanned the room searching for Sam and spotted him sitting with four staff members. The group was engrossed in conversation.

"*Buenos dias*" a female voice called out.

Alex turned, and smiled warmly at Angelina. "*Buenos dias Señorita.*"

"Are you looking for Sam?"

Alex pointed towards the table at the opposite end of the restaurant. "I found him, but I can see he's busy."

"That's nothing new," Angelina chuckled. "He's always engaged in something." She gave Alex a sheepish grin. "Although ... lately, that *something* seems to be you, *Señora.*"

"I know," Alex blushed, "and I have you to thank for it. If you wouldn't have found me the other night and talked some sense into me, I may have left Mexico never knowing that Sam staged his own death to protect my daughter." Alex's smile turned serious. "Do you have a minute, Angelina? There's something I'd like to talk to you about."

"*Si.*" Angelina led Alex to a vacant table at the opposite side of the restaurant. When they sat down, she noticed the diamond bracelet hanging from Alex's wrist. "What a beautiful bracelet."

"Thank you." Alex blushed. "Sam gave it to me."

Angelina reached out and touched the sparkling gems. "*Si, it is very beautiful.*"

"Speaking of Sam," Alex leaned forward and rested her arms on the table. "You've known him for a long time and David Lawrence mentioned at the cocktail party the other night that you worked for his wife."

"*Si.*" Angelina nodded her head. "I worked for *Señora* Bennett."

"May I ask what happened with her death? Sam told me she had a drug problem, but he thought she kicked the habit."

"*Si, Señora,* it was very bad. Mrs. Bennett had been to drug rehab and after she returned, *Señor* Bennett took her on a second honeymoon. When they got back, *Señor* Bennett gave his wife a job in the guest services department." Angelina stared into her coffee cup. "I must say, at first I did not like the idea of working with Mrs. Bennett, but when she was not taking the drugs, she could be a very nice woman."

Concern filled Alex's eyes. "I tried to talk to Sam about Grace last night, but he cut me off. Do you have any idea what that's all about?"

"*Si, Señora.* Tomorrow is the one-year anniversary of *Señora* Bennett's death."

A gasp escaped from Alex's throat. "Oh, Angelina, I had no idea."

"He does not want to talk about it. I have tried."

"I hope you don't mind me asking, but what happened?"

A sad smile found its way to Angelina's face. "It's funny. After two months working together, *Señora* Bennett and I became friends. Several times she asked me to sit with her when she had an urge to do the drugs. One night she took me with her to a party in Puerto Vallarta. There were some people there. *Señora* Bennett told me that she knew these people from the United States. They offered her cocaine and I talked her out of it. When we got back to *Las Tropicales*, I went to her suite and we had a glass of wine. I told her how proud I was that she had not taken the drugs. I told her that her husband would be proud of her too. I left then, and she seemed to be in good spirits. On the way back to my room, I realized that I had forgotten my sweater. When I got back to *Señora* Bennett's suite, she was dead."

"Oh, Angelina, that must have been awful."

"Yes," Angelina hung her head. "It is something that I will never forget. There was a small mirror on the coffee table. It had remnants of white powder. There was also a razor blade, and a rolled up one hundred dollar bill. *Señora* Bennett was lying on the floor. I checked for a pulse but couldn't find it. I called the resort's doctor and he came immediately, but it was too late. *Señora* Bennett was dead."

"Did she overdose on the cocaine?" Alex asked.

"It was the cocaine, *si*, but it was not the cocaine which killed her."

Alex shook her head. "I don't understand."

"How do I explain?" Angelina thought for a moment. "*Eh,* the cocaine which the *Señora* took, it had cyanide in it."

"Cyanide!"

"*Si, Señora.* I know nothing about this drug. I have never done the cocaine, but from what I understand, when a person first puts this drug up their nose, the nose it begins to tingle. This too would have happened with *Señora* Bennett. She would not have known that there was this cyanide mixed in with the cocaine. *Señora* Bennett would have felt this numbness and believed that the cocaine was good."

"I'm sure it must have been devastating for Sam, especially when it sounds like their marriage was starting to go well."

"Yes, it was very sad for him, but I helped him with the grief."

Alex gave Angelina a warm, motherly smile. "You are

a wonderful woman, Angelina. Sam speaks very highly of you."

"*Gracias*," Angelina blushed. She glanced at her watch. "Oh, I must go. I have many things to do before I leave."

"Where are you going?" Alex asked

"I am flying to the Dominican Republic tonight. There is a hotel property there that *Señor* Bennett is thinking of purchasing."

"Sam told me about that," Alex smiled. "He said there was no doubt in his mind that you would do a marvelous job of running the Dominican resort."

"Yes she will," Sam announced as he approached the table. "Angie is my girl in the field." He leaned over and kissed the top of his assistant manager's head. "Good morning, ladies," he smile. "Isn't it a beautiful day?" He moved to Alex's side and kissed her on the cheek. "What do you think of the bracelet?"

Alex's eyes sparkled like the diamonds on her wrist. "Oh Sam, I love it, it's beautiful!" she beamed.

Sam turned to Angelina and smiled proudly. "Did Alex tell you that we're getting married?"

"Married? No, the *Señora* did not tell me this new."

Alex's face turned crimson. "Sam, we haven't really talked about this. Don't you think we should wait?"

"We will talk about it," Sam smiled, "and I can't wait!" He took Alex by the arm and helped her from the chair. "Come on, we have to go."

"Where are we going?" Alex asked.

"We're not going anywhere, you are." Sam turned and winked at Angelina. "Thanks for setting this up."

"*De nada*," Angelina replied with a grin.

Sam led Alex from the restaurant, through the lobby and to the taxi stand at the front of the resort. "I still feel terrible about standing you up for our *movie* date the other night."

"Sam, you've more than made up for it. These past days have been wonderful," Alex smiled.

"Well," he grinned. "I may have made up for the movie by showing you the countryside, but this will make up for missing your birthday. You're going to have a great time."

Alex raised a curious brow. "Where are you sending me?"

"I'm sending you on an adventure that you'll never forget." Sam kissed her on the cheek, opened the door of the cab and helped her inside. "I'll see you when you get back. Have fun."

The highway to Puerto Vallarta was busy with morning commuters heading into the city. The posted speed limit was sixty but as the little white Toyota zipped in and out of traffic, Alex was sure they were going much faster.

Fifteen minutes later, the vehicle came to a stop in front of a small yellow building. The sign out front read: *Vallarta Adventures.* "You are here, *Señora,*" the driver announced

"How many *pesos, Señor*?" Alex asked

"It is paid for, *Señora,*" the driver smiled. "I will pass by at twelve noon to pick you up and take you back to the hotel." He handed her an envelope. "Go inside and give this to the *Señorita.* She will take care of you. *Adios.*"

Alex thanked the driver and got out of the cab. She followed the signs down the cobblestone path until she reached the reception centre. "Good morning," she smiled as she approached the desk. "I'm supposed to give you this." Alex passed the envelope across the counter.

"*Gracias.*" The young girl opened the envelope and examined the contents then looked up at Alex. "*Buenos dias, Señora* Granger. We have been expecting you."

"*Buenos dias, Señorita,*" Alex smiled back.

The receptionist picked up a walkie-talkie, said something in Spanish then smiled at Alex. "You are going to have a great time. Randy will be here in one minute to get you."

Alex leaned closer to the counter. "I don't mean to sound foolish, but what exactly am I going to be having a great time at?"

"Ah *Señora*, you are going to be swimming with the dolphins."

Alex's face lit up like a child's on Christmas morning. "That's amazing! Swimming with dolphins is something I've always wanted to do." Excitement rose in her voice. "When I was a kid, I told my dad that I wanted to move to the West Coast so I could have a pet dolphin like Flipper!"

"*Señora* Granger?"

Alex turned and looked up at the handsome, six-foot-two, blonde haired, blue eyed American. "Yes. I'm Alex Granger."

He extended his hand. "I'm Randy Kipp. I'm the head trainer at Dolphin Adventures. Today, I'm going to teach you a little bit about dolphins and then you're going to get the opportunity to swim with them. How does that sound?"

"It sounds great!"

Alex was taken by boat to Vallarta Adventures' second dolphin tank where she met up with a group of fifty people who were all anxiously anticipating their adventure. "Good morning," Randy smiled. "My name is Randy Kipp and I am the head dolphin trainer here at Dolphin Adventures. Dolphins are considered the masters of the ocean and they have fascinated humans for centuries. Dolphins are considered to be very intelligent, but for a long time we didn't think they could feel pain or grief. We know now that's not true. Dolphins do show emotion. For instance; they demonstrate anger, joy, sadness, jealousy, anxiety, remorse and certainly affection.

"The Dolphin Adventure project was developed eight years ago to help us understand these beautiful animals. When the program began, we had five dolphins. Now," Randy smiled, "we have twenty dolphins. Seven of them were born at the facility. Humans take nine months to give birth, dolphins take eleven to twelve. They are born under water and helped to the surface to take their first breath by their mother or another female from the pod that's assisting with the birth. Almost like a midwife."

Randy pointed to the tank behind him. "These dolphins are not here to do tricks or perform. They're here to interact with people and participate in a genuine attempt at interspecies communication. Dolphins are very social animals. As I mentioned, they travel in pods like one big happy family. Dolphins love to be touched and we encourage you to pet them while you are in swimming with them, but they have very sensitive skin and we don't want you to injure them. So, we ask that you take off all your jewelry; rings, watches, bracelets, and with your bracelets from the hotel, put the black clasp on top and flip it backwards on your forearm. Is everybody ready?" he asked. "Okay, let's go have some fun."

Two hours later; on the cab ride back to *Las Tropicales*, Alex's face was still etched in a smile. Swimming with the dolphins had been the most incredible thing she'd ever experienced and she couldn't wait to tell Sam all about it.

Alex went to his office the minute she got back to the resort, but he wasn't there. After checking the restaurants she went to the guest services office. Cesar advised her that Sam and Angelina hadn't returned from their morning meeting, but he'd left a note. Reading it Alex discovered that Sam would be tied up all day. She was to meet him in the lobby bar at six p.m. for cocktails. Afterwards, he had a special dinner planned to celebrate their engagement.

Alex decided to spend the afternoon catching up on her tan and went to her room to change. The message light was blinking on the telephone and she called the front desk. "Hello, this is room 4211. You have a message for me?"

"*Si, Señora*. It is a reminder about the diving this afternoon."

Alex had planned on canceling her diving trip but now, with Sam tied up all day, perhaps she'd go. "Thank you very much." She hung up the phone and opened the drawer of her night table. "Yes, Brian," she announced as she pulled the ticket from its resting place. "I'll use the diving gear you gave me for my birthday, and then you can have it back. I hope you kept the receipt," she laughed, "because it's the only thing you're going to get in the divorce settlement!"

19

"OH, SAM, I JUST heard the awful news!" Angelina rushed across the office to his side. There were tears in his eyes and she stopped his hand as he tried to wipe them away. "Let it out, Sam," she told him in her warm, caring tone. "There's nothing wrong with a grown man crying."

Sam started sobbing then and Angelina held him in her arms while he cried like a baby. As he wept, she was reminded that he hadn't been this upset when Grace died. When his body stopped shaking, she unhooked her arms from his waist and led him to the sofa. "Sit down. I'll get us a drink."

"Make mine a double." He flopped onto the sofa and ran his hands through his thick grey hair. In his mind, his life was over ... Alex was dead. Twice on his way from the coroner's office after identifying her body, or what was left of it, he'd thought about killing himself ... there was nothing left to live for. The only woman he'd ever loved was gone, just when they'd found each other again. Then, he remembered Alex's daughter ... Sarah, and he knew he had to tell her in person how much her mother had meant to him. A sad smile found its way to his face remembering the day he first met the little girl.

***

The moment Sam landed in Denver he went directly to the Granger ranch. He wanted to let Michael know he'd arrived, at least that's the reason he'd given himself. Secretly, he hoped he'd run into Alex. She'd forgiven him for marrying Grace. She wanted to talk to him ... there was something she needed to say. In her last letter, Alex asked him to meet her at the ranch on Friday. That was tomorrow and he couldn't wait.

Finding no one at the main house, Sam headed to the barn. It was there, where he first caught sight of the little girl. She was standing in the middle of the corral dressed in a western shirt, Wrangler jeans, and cowboy boots. "Come here, Bucky," she called out, dangling a carrot in front of her. The Welch pony trotted to the little girl's side and she kissed it on the muzzle. "I picked 'em for yah this morning, right out of Ted's garden." She held the orange vegetable in front of her and the pony accepted it with a whinny.

"Good morning," Sam called out. The little girl looked up and gave him a beaming smile. He couldn't help but notice that she was missing her two front teeth.

"Good morning Mr.," she lisped. She pulled something from her back pocket. "Would you like to give Bucky a horse crunchy?"

"Sure," Sam smiled. Brunette ringlets bounced off the child's shoulders as she merrily skipped toward the fence and Sam couldn't help but notice there was something very famil-iar about the girl. She reminded him of his niece.

"Here you go, Mr." The little girl opened the clenched fist of her left hand and turned over a hard, dog biscuit shaped, horse treat . "My name is Sam," she smiled.

"Well, isn't that a coincidence," he chuckled, "so is mine." Sam extended his hand and the little girl's disappeared into it. "Is Sam short for Samantha," he asked.

"Nope, it's short for Sarah Alexandra Marie. I was named after a friend of my mom's. She's dead now. I think her name was Sarah, or something. My mom doesn't talk about her much." She looked up at him with her big blue eyes. "Well, I have to go. The *Big Bri Guy* will be looking for me. He's taking me out for breakfast.

"Is the *Big Bri Guy* your brother?" Sam asked.

"No, he's my dad. That's the nickname my nanny gave him. She calls him that when my mom's not around. His real name is Brian."

Sam could only imagine what else the nanny called the little girl's father when her mother wasn't around. That evening, at Michael's wedding rehearsal party, Sam discovered the little ray of sunshine he'd met earlier, was Alex's daughter. The *Big Bri Guy* ... Alex's cheating husband.

The sound of a sweet Spanish accent interrupted Sam's daydream. "Here's your drink." Angelina handed him the glass and sat beside him on the sofa. "Are you okay? You looked just now, like you were a million miles away."

"I was thinking about Alex's daughter. I haven't seen her since she was a little kid." He raised the glass to his lips, downed the tequila in one big gulp, and passed the glass back to Angelina. "I'll have another, *por favor*"

"Sam, you don't have to finish the whole bottle in five minutes."

"Angelina, just get me a goddamn drink!" Sam snapped. Hearing the harshness of his own voice, he quickly apologized. "I'm sorry, Angel. I don't mean to snap at you. None of this is your fault."

"It's okay, Sam. I can understand why you're so upset. From what Cesar told me, you've had a very trying evening."

Sam gave her a puzzled look. "Speaking of which, what are you doing here? You're supposed to be at the airport to catch your flight to the Dominican Republic."

Angelina took his hand in hers. "I was just about to turn off my cell phone and board my plane when Cesar called. He told me that Ms. Granger was missing and that you were frantic. He said you had people looking for her everywhere, but no one had found her. Naturally, I immediately came back to the resort to help in the search."

Sam leaned over and gave her a peck on the cheek. "Thank you, Angelina. Somehow, you're always here for me when there's a crisis. You were there for me when Grace died, thanks for being here for me now."

She offered him a caring smile. "I'll always be here for you, Sam. Is there anything I can do? Would you like me to call Ms. Granger's family and tell them of this news?"

Angelina's words brought back a vision of the shredded body Sam had just identified in the morgue. The shark attack was brutal, ripping through Alex's wet suit and chewing the flesh to the bone. The skin on her face was peeled back like a banana. The bones of her cheeks were crushed. Her right arm was missing at the shoulder. On her left, a wristband from *Las Tropicales* and the diamond bracelet he'd given her the night before.

Sam forced the image from his mind. "Thanks, Angel, but that's a phone call I need to make myself." He dug into his pocket and pulled out a small white piece of paper. "I had Cesar take Alex's home address and phone number from the computer." Staring down at the information, Sam knew this was going to be the hardest call he'd ever made and the sooner he got it over with, the better. He forced his legs to carry him to the telephone. With trembling hands, he punched in the thirteen digit number. It rang five times.

"Hello," a pleasant female voice answered.

"Hello, would Brian Williams be there please?"

"I'm sorry, my father isn't here."

Sam's pulse started racing. He was speaking to Alex's daughter. He swallowed the lump in his throat. "When will he be home?"

"I'm afraid he's out of town on business. I'm not expecting him back for several days. This is his daughter, Sarah. May I take a message? Or, is there something I can help you with?"

Sam knew he couldn't tell Alex's daughter the news like this. Not on the telephone. "No, that's fine," he answered. "I'll call back." He disconnected the call and immediately dialed Michael Granger's home.

"Hello," a deep male voice answered.

"Hey, Mike, it's Sam."

"Sam, how the hell are yah buddy?"

"I'm fine, thanks."

"Are you at the airport? I'll pick you up. Sharon took Eleanor and went to her mother's for a couple of days, so I'm all by myself in this great big house!"

Sam took a deep breath. "Michael, I'm not calling from the airport. I'm calling from the resort."

"Hey, my niece tells me that Alex is staying there. Have you seen her yet?" Excitement rose in Michael's voice. "Doesn't she look great... for an old broad ... that is? I bet it surprised the shit out of her when she found out you haven't been dead all these years, just unavailable! Is she with you? Let me talk to her!"

"You can't. Alex isn't here."

"So how come you're calling?" There was a pause before Michael let out a hearty chuckle. "Wait, I know. Alex finally decided to dump that lowlife she's been married to for twenty-five years and hook up with you! No offence to the dead, Sam, but I never could figure out what you saw in Grace Sanderson. Besides ..."

Sam cut Michael off in mid-sentence. "I don't know how to tell you this, other than to just come right out and tell you."

"Tell me what?"

"Michael, there's been an accident."

"What type of an accident? Did Alex wipe out parasailing? Is she hurt?"

"No, Michael." Sam took a deep breath and slowly exhaled. "Alex is dead."

When Michael spoke, his voice was filled with denial. "What do you mean, she's dead? What are you talking about?"

For the next twenty minutes, Sam went over the detail of Alex's disappearance. He told Michael that he and Alex had met for breakfast. They were planning on spending the day together until he was called to an emergency meeting. Alex had spent the morning swimming with the dolphins. They were going to meet for lunch, but he was called off the property. He left her a note telling her to meet him at the bar at six, so they could watch the sunset. When Alex hadn't shown up by seven, Sam checked her room ... she wasn't there.

He searched the resort, but Alex was nowhere to be found. He tracked down the Lawrences, a couple she'd befriended during her stay. They told him they saw her just after lunch. She mentioned she was going diving. When he checked with the resort's dive instructor, he learned that Alex had taken her diving gear and left the property shortly after two.

By eight o'clock, Sam had members of his staff calling every dive operator in a thirty-mile radius. No one could find her. He was about to call the police when they called him. Two fishermen had found a body. There was an identification bracelet from *Las Tropicales* around the victim's wrist.

Michael's voice was barely a whisper when he spoke. "Are you telling me that the body these two fishermen found is Alex's?"

"Yes, Michael, I'm afraid so."

"You're sure it was Alex?" His voice grew anxious. "You saw her face?"

Sam swallowed hard to force the foul taste of bile back from where it had come. It was bad enough telling Michael that his sister was dead, how could he tell him that she'd been mangled almost beyond recognition. "No, Michael, I didn't see Alex's face."

"What do you mean you didn't see her face?"

"There was a shark attack."

"What are you telling me, Sam, that my sister was fish food?" Anger rose in Michael's voice. "If you didn't see her face, then how the hell do you know it was Alex? Maybe she just decided to go off somewhere on her own. I'm sure she'll be back."

"Michael, I know it was Alex."

"How do you know?" Michael demanded.

"When they took off her wet suit, she was wearing the diamond bracelet I gave her."

There was a long silence. When Michael spoke again, his voice was calm and in control. "Have you called anyone yet?" he asked. "Does Sarah know about this?"

"I called Alex's place just before I called you. Your niece answered. I asked for Alex's husband, but apparently he's out of town on business."

"Monkey business, no doubt," Michael bitterly stated. "Did you say anything to her?"

"No."

"Good. I'll find Brian and tell him what happened. Do you know if Alex has talked to Sarah in the past few days?"

"I don't know. She did mention something yesterday about calling her tomorrow."

Michael took a deep breath and slowly exhaled. "I'll fly to Denver to tell Sarah. My uncle Harvey owns a funeral home there. I'll call him to make the necessary arrangements and get him to call you. Can you bring Alex home?"

"Yes, Michael. I'll bring her home."

"Thanks, Sam. I'll call you when I have more details. Goodbye."

Tears stung Sam's eyes. He hung up the telephone and headed to the liquor cabinet for another bottle of tequila. He unscrewed the cap and took a long swig. The alcohol burned as it slid from his throat to his stomach. He turned to Angelina and held up the bottle. "I'm sorry. Do you care to join me?"

"*Si.*" She patted the vacant spot on the sofa. "Why don't you come and sit down."

"Do you want a glass?"

"Of course not, *Señor.*" Angelina took the bottle from his hand. "I don't need a glass."

Sam couldn't help but smile as he watched her drink. Angelina could keep up with the best of them. At his birthday party last month, she'd challenged two of the entertainment staff to a drinking contest: "Tequila poppers, shot for shot," she'd told them. Eight times, Angelina put her hand over the shot glass, slammed it on the bar, and poured it down her throat. She walked home ...the two staff members had to be carried.

"That's what I love about you, Angelina," Sam put his arm around her shoulder and gave her a squeeze, "you can sure hold your liquor!"

Together, they drank until the tequila was gone. When the bottle was empty, Sam rested his head in his hands and started to cry. "God, what am I going to do? Just when I found Alex again, she's gone."

Angelina pulled him closer and held him while he sobbed. "It's okay," she whispered, "I'm here. I helped you get through Grace's death and I will help you get through Alex's."

Sam leaned back and looked into her hypnotic brown eyes. "Thank you, Angel." She smiled then and kissed him on the lips. When her mouth lingered a moment too long, he felt an urgent need to fill his emptiness. He took her face in his hands and kissed her hard, his tongue exploring deep into her throat.

Sam stood up then, scooped Angelina off the sofa, and carried her to the bedroom. He threw her on the bed and fell on top of her, pinning her arms at her side. He quickly undid the buttons on her blouse and there was no objection, only a soft moan, as his mouth explored its way from her ear to her throat and down her chest to the bare skin at her waist.

Like a madman, Sam ripped off her beige skirt and the thong underwear beneath it. Angelina screamed out his name when his tongue found the moisture between her legs. For hours, Sam took her again and again, the years of frustration being released on the firm-warm body lying under him. When his anger was gone, and his body spent, he passed out.

20

A BEEP ON HIS mike phone drew Harvey Ingles' attention from the elderly woman he was preparing for a ten o'clock viewing. "I'm sorry to bother you, Harvey, but there's a Michael Granger on line three. He said he's calling from the airport."

"Well, I'll be damned!" Harvey put down the pallet of face make-up. His nephew was on the line; Mrs. Hamilton would have to wait.

Long lanky legs quickly carried Harvey across the room. He took off his surgical gloves, opened the back door of the visitation suite and stepped into the hallway. He dropped his gloves into the trash receptacle then disinfected his hands with a squirt of waterless hand sterilizer before picking up the telephone. "Michael, how the hell are you, boy? My secretary tells me that you're at the airport. I'll send a limo to get you. Or would you prefer a funeral coach?" he chuckled. "I hope you'll have dinner with Jean and me tonight. I've already invited Sarah to join us. Brian is out of town on business and your sister is living it up in Puerto Vallarta!"

"I'm not at the airport in Denver," Michael quietly replied. "I'm in Boston."

"Well, then, to what do I owe the pleasure of hearing your voice?"

"I'm afraid this isn't a social call. I have some very bad news."

The smile disappeared from Harvey's face. "What is it, Michael? What's wrong?"

"Alex is dead." There it was cut and dried ... he'd said it. Michael had finally admitted that he would never see his sister again.

Harvey's legs buckled and he grabbed the wall for support. "Michael, what do you mean Alex is dead?"

"There was an accident."

"What kind of an accident?"

"She had a diving accident, Harvey."

"A diving accident? Was there something wrong with her equipment?"

"I don't think the equipment had anything to do with it." Michael calmly told his uncle. "Alex was attacked by a shark. Two fishermen found her a mile up the coast from the resort she was staying at."

"Who identified the body? Are you sure it was Alex?"

"Yes, Harvey, it's Alex. I got the phone call from a buddy of mine, Sam Bennett. He owns the resort Alex was staying at. Sam identified her."

"So, the attack wasn't that bad?"

Michael's voice quivered when he spoke. "From what I understand, it's not good. Sam didn't go into great detail, but it doesn't sound good, Harvey. It doesn't sound good at all. I don't think her face is recognizable, and she's missing her right arm at the shoulder." There was a long pause. "Harvey, can you take care of this for me? I'll give you Sam's phone number and you can call him directly. You said you're having dinner with Sarah tonight?"

"Yes, that's right. We're expecting her for cocktails at six."

"Good. I have to make a stop in Chicago on my way to Denver, but I should be on the ground by seven. I'll come right to the house."

"Would you like me to send a car for you?" Harvey asked.

"No." Michael replied. "I'll grab a cab at the airport. Can you make arrangements to get Alex back?"

"Of course, I'll take care of everything, but I do have a few questions I have to ask. Can you just hold for a minute? I have to go to my office. I'm upstairs."

Harvey put Michael on hold and dialed the front office. "Helen, will you have Tom finish Mrs. Hamilton, and get me the phone number for the U.S. Embassy in Puerto Vallarta, Mexico. I'll be in my office."

"Don't hang up yet," Helen said. "The Widows' Thompson, Sherri, Mary and Kerry are scheduled to meet with Leslie at three this afternoon, but they refuse to deal with anyone but you."

"Don't I have the Peterson service at three?"

"Yes. Would you like me to have the ladies come in just after lunch?"

Harvey checked his watch. It was eight forty-five a.m. Making arrangements to get Alex back to Denver was going to take most of the day. This wasn't the first time he'd retrieved a body from a foreign country. If he greased a few palms, he could probably expedite the process. He would have to find a translator at the embassy and have them get in touch with the funeral home that was holding Alex's body. Law stated that a body transferred by common carrier required embalming, but Harvey didn't want anyone touching his niece. He'd have Alex's remains shipped back in a hermetically sealed container.

"Harvey, are you still there?" Helen asked. "What do you want me to tell the three Thompson wives?"

"Leave the appointment as is. I'll handle it."

Harvey hung up the phone and hurried back to his office. He pulled a *First Call* sheet from his desk drawer. His hands shook as he filled in the date, the time, his name, and Alex's name. He picked up the phone and pressed line three. "Michael, are you still there," he asked.

"Yes, Harvey."

"I just have a few questions. When did Alex die?"

"Last night."

Harvey filled in the appropriate blank. "Place of passing?" he asked.

"Nuevo Vallarta, Mexico," Michael answered.

"What's the doctor's name?"

"Hector Fernandez."

Harvey completed the next three items on the form with Michael's name and his relationship to Alex. He put Brian Williams down as her next of kin. When he was finished, he took Sam Bennett's telephone number and reassured Michael once again that he would take care of everything. "I'll give Sam a call and see if he can put a fire under the Mexicans, but I just want you to know that sometimes it can take up to three weeks to get a body back from another country."

"Isn't there anything we can do to speed up the process?"

"Yes," Harvey replied, "you can bring Alex back on a private jet."

"We can do that?"

"As long as you have all the paperwork together, and you have access to one, there's no reason why not."

"Thanks, Harvey. We'll talk more about this tonight. I'll see you at the house."

Tears stung Harvey's eyes as he hung up the telephone. He'd been in the mortuary business for thirty-five years, during which time he'd restored hundreds of mangled bodies, but the thought of his niece lying on the prep-room table made him feel ill.

He flipped open the calendar on his desk. The coroner would do an autopsy, although a shark attack was the obvious cause of death, and that could take up to three days. Using a common carrier to get Alex home could take up to eighteen days. Michael had mentioned a private jet. If he could get his hands on one, Alex could be home by Sunday. There were a million things that needed to be done, but the first priority was to call his wife and tell her the news. Jean would be devastated.

21

SHARON GRANGER THREW HER hands up in frustration. "I've had just about as much of you as I can stand for one day, young lady!" Last night her daughter had refused to pack. Today, she'd thrown a fit on the flight from New York, and now this. "What's gotten into you? Apologize to your great-aunt Jean for destroying this beautiful flower arrangement."

Eleven-year-old Eleanor Elizabeth Granger opened her hand and dropped the only remaining white rose from the bouquet her great-aunt had just brought to the house for her uncle Brian and cousin Sarah. "I'm sorry Auntie Jean," the child apologized through tear-filled eyes.

Sharon pointed towards the stairs, "Now, go to your room and don't come out until you can start behaving yourself." When Eleanor was gone, Sharon bent to pick up what was left of the floral arrangement. "Jean, I'm so sorry," she apologized. "I don't know what's come over that child. I haven't talked about what was going to happen with Alex's funeral and every time Michael called, I made sure that I took the phone in the office so Eleanor wouldn't hear us discussing the arrangements."

"Oh, no dear, that's the worst thing you can do," Jean Ingles told her nephew's wife. "You can't be afraid to talk to Eleanor about Alex's death."

"No one talked to me about any of the deaths in my family when I was her age."

"They should have," Jean smiled. "You need to talk to children about death. Your daughter is a bright girl, Sharon. She knows things have changed. She's lost something too. Eleanor has spent every summer at the ranch with Alex since she was six, correct?" Sharon nodded her head. "Well, she'll never be able to do that again. Oh, she can come here with you and Michael, but her summers with Alex were special and now they're gone."

"I suppose you're right." Sharon agreed.

"Come on." Jean reached down and took Sharon by the arm. "Let's go have a chat."

"I can't leave this mess on the floor! You know what a neat-freak Brian is. He'll go ballistic if he sees this."

"You don't have to worry about Brian. He isn't here."

"Where is he?" Sharon asked. "Did he go to the funeral home with Michael?"

"No. He's out of town."

"What do you mean, he's out of town? I would think he'd be here. His wife just died for goodness sake!"

"You'd think so, but he's on business in the Bahamas. According to Harvey, he's not due back until Saturday afternoon."

"But that's three days from now. Doesn't he care about his daughter? He should be here for Sarah."

Jean rolled her eyes. "Apparently, his *business trip* has something to do with a quarter-horse breeding program Alex was working on before she left for Mexico. Brian is meeting with a big wig from the government. He told Harvey he couldn't change the appointment."

"Not even to help make his wife's funeral arrangements? That's ridiculous!"

"Brian doesn't need to be here to make funeral arrangements," Jean replied. "Alex made her own arrangements a few years ago. Michael called Brian last night and read him the riot act. He suggested it would be a good idea if he was here, but Brian told Michael that the project had been important to Alex and she would have wanted him to stay."

"But certainly he can postpone the meeting under these circumstances?"

"Let's change the subject, shall we? Discussing Brian Williams gives me indigestion." Jean put her arm around Sharon's shoulder. "Besides, your daughter is more important right now. Come on."

Jean led Sharon from the living room, through the foyer and down the hall to the library. When she stepped across the threshold, her breath caught in her throat and tears stung her eyes. She hadn't been in this room since Alex moved her collection of trophies and ribbons from the observation deck of the indoor riding arena. The hunter green walls were covered with mementoes of her niece's career as a horsewoman. It was a reminder of a lady who had touched the lives of so many people and now ... she was gone.

Jean motioned towards the sofa. "Let's sit, shall we?"

"Oh, Jean, I'm so sorry about the flowers," Sharon apologized again. "It was such a beautiful arrangement. I'll pay you for it."

"Don't be silly, the flowers aren't important. What's important is your daughter's strange behavior." Jean sat beside Sharon and took her hand. "Harvey and I have been in the funeral business for thirty-five years, dear. Children react differently towards death than we do. When they're small, they see death as something that's temporary. If they believe in magical thoughts, sometimes they think they caused the death and they can bring the person back if they wish for it hard enough.

"As they grow, they see death as being something final, but they think it only happens when you're old. Children, Eleanor's age are just starting to realize that death is final. They also realize it could happen to them, not just someone else. You mentioned in the living room that you haven't shown Eleanor any of your emotions."

"Yes, and it's been very difficult keeping everything inside," Sharon confessed.

"Children mimic what they see around them. Grieving in front of Eleanor will teach her that she can cry, and laugh, and just be herself when she's sad. You need to maintain as much of a routine as you can ... under the circumstances. Keep showing Eleanor affection and reassuring her that everyone loves her.

"You need to encourage your daughter to share her feelings, and you need to accept her responses unconditionally. And, when you talk to her about Alex's death, don't tell her that Alex has passed away, or that she went to sleep. Tell her that Alex died. Yes, it was a terrible accident, but nonetheless it was an accident and people do die from accidents."

Sharon rested her head on Jean's shoulder. "I feel so terrible. I never even thought about what Eleanor was going through. I was only concerned with how Michael was feeling. I've been a monster to my daughter these past few days. No wonder she's acting up. When she's wanted to spend time with me, I've told her to find something to keep herself occupied because I was too busy."

"Well, let's change all that, shall we?" Jean smiled.

Sharon looked pleadingly at the older, wiser, woman. "But how?"

"Would you like me to go and talk to her?"

"Oh, would you?"

"What are great-aunts for?" Jean winked. "Why don't you go to the kitchen and have something to eat. I hear Angelina has whipped up some interesting Cuban dishes."

"She's very nice, isn't she?" Sharon smiled.

"Yes ... and beautiful too!" Jean smiled back.

"She cares for Sam. You can tell by the way she dotes on him. Michael told me that he was married to a real witch who kept him on a pretty short leash. Some of the stories about the woman were unbelievable. Apparently, she had quite a drug habit."

"Just like Brian," Jean snidely remarked.

"Brian has a drug problem?"

"Several years ago, Alex came to me and told me that he was using drugs."

Sharon was shocked. "Do you think he's doing drugs again?"

"I don't know for sure, but let's just say its intuition."

The two women stood up and shared a warm embrace. "Oh, Jean, what are we going to do without Alex? She was like a sister to me."

"We're all going to miss her, dear, but you know very well that she wouldn't appreciate us moping around like this. Alex was too full of life to have us filled with sorrow at her death." Jean offered Sharon a motherly smile, "Now go and get some dinner." She glanced at her watch. "It's eight-thirty, Harvey, Michael and Sam should be back from the funeral home soon, and you know what our men are like around food. If you don't eat now," Jean chuckled, "you may not get the chance. I'll go and have a talk with Eleanor."

"Thank you."

When Sharon was gone, Jean noticed something protruding from between the sofa cushions where the two women had been sitting. She reached down and pulled the envelope from its hiding place. She turned it over and recognized Alex's handwriting immediately.

IF THIS ENVELOPE DOES NOT GO TO MY GRAVE WITH ME ... UNOPENED, I'LL COME BACK TO HAUNT WHOEVER DIS-OBEYED MY FINAL REQUEST.

A cold chill ran up Jean's spine. She felt the top and the sides of the package, curious as to what was hidden inside. *What could be so important that Alex would take it to her grave,* she wondered.

For a moment, Jean thought about giving the envelope directly to Harvey to make sure Alex's wishes were obeyed, but the proper thing to do was to give it to Brian. Whether she trusted him or not, he was still Alex's husband. She walked to the desk, pulled a sticky note from the pad, and wrote:

> *Brian, I found this between the sofa cush-*
> *ions. Please bring it to the funeral home and*
> *Harvey will make sure that it goes in Alex's*
> *casket.*

Jean attached the note to the envelope and tucked it under the corner of the desk blotter. "Now, I need to take care of my great-niece."

She opened the top drawer of the desk and took out the package of pastels, and the pad of sketch paper Alex had always kept there for Eleanor. She'd take the art supplies upstairs. If she could get Eleanor to draw something, it would give the child an outlet for her emotions. Leaving the library, Jean made a detour through the kitchen to get a glass of milk and three chocolate chip cookies for Eleanor.

When she opened the door of the brightly painted bedroom; Eleanor called her own when she stayed at the ranch, the child was sitting cross-legged on the bed clutching the plush, stuffed toy dog that Alex had given her when she was four.

"Hello, little Miss. I brought you a snack." Jean walked to the bed and put her offering on the night table. "Are you hungry?" Eleanor didn't answer. "You know, just in case you think I'm mad about the flowers, I'm not."

"You're not?" Eleanor sniffed.

"No, I'm not, sweetheart." Jean gave her great niece a reassuring smile and sat down on the bed. "Do you feel like having a talk about Aunt Alex?"

"No," Eleanor whispered.

Jean put her arm around the child's shoulder and pulled her closer. "I think you'd feel better if we talked about it."

"I don't know if I want to talk about it."

"Why?" Jean asked.

"Because, because ... I'm mad!"

When Eleanor Granger stubbornly folded her arms across her chest and kicked the edge of the bed with her heel, Jean was reminded of how much the child was like Alex at that age. In fact, now that she thought about it, Eleanor was more like Alex than Alex's own daughter. Sarah had grown into a beautiful, intelligent woman but her mannerisms had never been like Alex's. They weren't even like Brian's. There was something about Sarah that was different.

"Tell me what you're mad about?" Jean asked.

"It's not what. It's who."

"Are you mad at your mom because she yelled at you?"

"No."

"Are you mad at your dad because he missed your father-and-daughter banquet?"

"No."

"Then who are you mad at?" Jean asked.

"I'm mad at Aunt Alex. Why did she have to go scuba diving? She didn't like scuba diving."

"Aunt Alex liked scuba diving," Jean reassured the child, "you've seen her diving pictures."

"Yeah, Aunt Alex used to go scuba diving ... a long time ago, but I asked her once if she'd take me diving and she said she wouldn't because she was afraid to go scuba diving, just like I'm afraid to go into the coral with Spider."

Jean raised a questioning brow. "Your aunt Alex wasn't afraid of scuba diving, dear."

"Yes she was, since four years ago, when Uncle Brian tried to drown her."

Jean couldn't believe her ears. She knew Eleanor was upset about losing her aunt, but now she was blaming Alex's death on someone else. "Your uncle Brian never tried to drown your aunt Alex. Why would you say something like that?"

"Because ... it's true!" Eleanor stated. "Don't you believe me?"

Jean took Eleanor's hand and looked into the child's pleading eyes. "Why, yes, of course I believe you, but where would you ever hear such a thing?"

"Aunt Alex told me," Eleanor sniffled. "I bugged her to take me diving last year. I bugged her so much that she got mad at me and told me that she was afraid to go diving 'cause the last time she went, Uncle Brian pulled her mask off and she thought she was going to drown."

"Oh honey, I'm sure that Uncle Brian didn't mean to pull off Aunt Alex's mask. It was just an accident. Just like your aunt's death was an accident."

"But it didn't have to happen," Eleanor sniffled. "Why did Aunt Alex go diving when she was afraid?"

"Maybe, she wanted to overcome her fear. Didn't you get back on your horse after he dumped you off last spring and you broke your leg?"

"Yes."

"And don't you love to ride?"

"Yes."

"Well, maybe if you wouldn't have gotten back in the saddle, and conquered your fear, you never would have ridden again."

"But if Aunt Alex wanted to get over her fear, why did she have to do it in the ocean with sharks," Eleanor sobbed. "Why couldn't she just use the pool in her back yard? Now she's dead and she promised me before she left on her trip to Mexico that she was going to enter me in the All-American Quarter Horse Congress. She told me I could even ride Pride. She told me that we were going to go to all kinds of horse shows and now we're not. She lied to me!"

"Oh, honey, your aunt didn't lie to you." Jean pulled the whimpering child into her arms. "Come on now, don't cry. Aunt Alex didn't do this on purpose just so she wouldn't have to take you to the horse shows. It was an accident. Accidents happen. You'll still be able to go to horse shows. I know she would want you to. Aunt Alex was very proud of you."

Eleanor wiped her nose with the back of her sleeve. "She was?"

"Oh yes," Jean smiled. "She used to brag about you all the time."

"She did?"

"Yes she did. Do you know how many times she told me the story about your first horse show when you won all of your classes?"

Eleanor's eyes lit up. "I won the high-point all-around trophy," she beamed.

"Yes, I know."

An excited smile brightened Eleanor's face. "Would you like to see the photo album Aunt Alex made for me?"

"Yes dear. I think that would be great."

22

AFTER MEETING SAM'S PLANE and putting Alex's body in the funeral coach, Harvey took Michael and Sam to the funeral home and the three men proceeded to get pissed. When they'd finished their first bottle of Scotch, Harvey suggested they move their party to a more comfortable spot and the trio ended up in the smaller of the two casket selection rooms at Ingles and Hawthorne Funeral Home.

"These things are pretty comfy." Sam announced as he rolled back and forth in the $10,000 mahogany casket he was laying in.

"Yup," Harvey grinned. "That's the Cadillac of caskets all right. Real bed springs and satin lined. It's pretty popular with the Asians."

Sam sat up. "So, tell me something ... Harvey? What kind of a person becomes a funeral director?"

"A person with heart," Harvey stated. "I believe that funeral directing is something that comes from the heart. Oh, you've got the guys who are in it for the money, but the richest funeral directors I know, are rich because their career is very rewarding. They aren't interested in the money. They do, what they do, because they care about the people they serve. I have a buddy I went through mortuary school with. He's doing the seminar circuit now and I want to share one of his stories. Then you'll understand."

Harvey sat up in the oak casket he was occupying and his expression turned serious. "In a small Midwestern town, there lived a crazy old kook who was shunned by all and feared by many. The old boy had been a resident of the town since he was born and lived in a one-room shack. He never married and had no family. His greatest satisfaction came from tormenting town residents and scaring small children.

"The old guy didn't work, in fact," Harvey grinned, "he seldom bathed. The town's people wondered how he survived, but no one was brave enough to ask him. One day, a concerned neighbor noticed that he'd been absent from his porch for a few days so she called the local sheriff. They found him dead on the floor. Having no family, his affairs were left up to the public trustee.

"While removing the contents of the one-room shack, the trustee found an envelope containing the man's final wishes. He wanted to be buried at three in the morning. It was an odd request, and in order to fulfill the decedent's wishes, the trustee needed to find a funeral director, a grave digger, and a cemetery owner who would agree to perform a service in the middle of the night."

"Isn't three in the morning a strange time for a funeral?" Sam asked.

"Yes it is," Harvey replied. "The trustee called four funeral homes and was turned down by all of them. The fifth funeral home belonged to a young man who'd just graduated from mortuary school. When he was told of the circumstances and advised that he probably wouldn't get paid, the enthusiastic young man agreed to do the service anyway. He said he was a funeral director and burying people was his job."

Harvey took two big gulps of Scotch before continuing his story. "Having secured a funeral home, the trustee's next challenge was finding someone to dig the grave. Three grave diggers turned him down before he found one who agreed to dig it, and fill it in immediately following the three a.m. burial. Now that the trustee had a funeral director and a grave digger, he needed a cemetery. Cemeteries usually have fences around them. They open at sunup and close at sundown. Twelve cemeteries turned the trustee down before he found one who agreed to open their gates in the middle of the night. And so, the old boy's final wishes were carried out.

"Several weeks later, the funeral director, the grave digger and the owner of the cemetery were summoned to an attorney's office two counties away. With the men gathered, the lawyer explained that the deceased had only two final requests. First, he wanted to be buried at three in the morning just to make life miserable for everyone involved. And second, he wanted to reward anyone who was willing to get up in the middle of the night to pay their respects. Then the lawyer handed each man an envelope containing a check for one million dollars."

"A million bucks!" Michael exclaimed.

"That's right." Harvey nodded.

"But where did the old guy get the money?"

"Apparently, he was worth a fortune. He invested in Shell when the company first started." Harvey looked across at Sam. "Do you see what I mean, now? Those three guys weren't in the funeral business for the cash. They were in the business because the business came from their heart."

For hours, Harvey, Michael and Sam passed around the booze and told stories. Most of them ... about Alex. "I remember once," Michael began, "when Alex was supervising the Denver youth team at the All-American Quarter Horse Congress. One of the kids on the team was tied for high-point all-around youth. The day before the kid's horsemanship class ... the one that would win him the trophy, the boy's horse had an unfortunate accident."

"What happened?" Sam asked.

"Someone poured acid across the horse's back. I can't believe what lengths some people will go too, to win," Michael grunted. "Alex was livid. She had a good idea who'd done it, but she couldn't prove it ... nobody saw a thing. Anyway, she flew her mare from Denver to Ohio so the kid would have a horse to ride and he ended up winning the over-all high-point trophy." Michael looked down at the bottle of Scotch he was holding. The amber liquid was helping ease the gut-wrenching pain of his sister's death, and it was almost gone. He passed the bottle to Harvey. "I'm going for more booze."

"That was our Alex," Harvey slurred, "always taking care of the underdog. I remember once, she took a young Native-American fellow that worked for her to the country club to play a round of golf. When they wouldn't let him play, because they didn't allow *his type* on the course, Alex bought the kid a golf membership. It cost her twenty-five grand." Harvey took a swig of Scotch and wiped his mouth with the back of his hand before passing the bottle to Sam. "Boy, did that ever piss off Moe Sanderson!"

"Yah, my father-in-law was quite a piece of work," Sam hiccupped.

"Your father-in-law?"

"I was married to Moe's daughter, Grace."

"You're shittin' me?"

Sam downed the last of the Scotch and passed the empty bottle back to Harvey. "Nope, it's the truth. It's as true ... as sure as I'm sitting here," he slurred.

"If you don't mind me asking," Harvey raised a questioning brow. "Whatever happened to Grace? I heard she died about a year ago. She was always such a healthy nut. I figured she'd outlive her old man."

"Cocaine," Sam hiccupped. "She fried her brains with the white stuff. Only problem was, the white stuff she snorted that night wasn't pure cocaine. It was cut with cyanide. It killed her in seconds."

The door opened and Michael stumbled into the selection room. "We better make this bottle last, 'cause I think I cleaned out your liquor cabinet, Harv." He closed the door behind him and walked to the casket carriage that held the plywood cremation container they were now using as a portable bar. He held the fresh bottle of Scotch in the air. "Who's up for another drink?"

"Us!" Harvey answered.

Michael filled three glasses, set them on the plywood box, and wheeled it between the display caskets like a tea cart. He handed them each a drink and took one for himself. "Tell Sam about some of the interesting things you've seen over the years, Uncle Harvey."

"Let me think." Harvey scratched his chin and a broad smile lit up his face. "You'd be amazed at the things I've seen, but I think the best one was thirty years ago, when I was working for a funeral home in Los Angeles. I was on a service for some hot-shot Hollywood producer. It was a big funeral. There were probably five hundred people there.

"Sitting in the front row, was the old boy's current wife. In the row behind her, his ex-wife and in the last row the twenty-something starlet he was doing. It was an open-casket service, and it had no more than started when the beautiful blonde bombshell at the back of the church ran up the center aisle and threw herself into the casket. If that wasn't bad enough, she proceeded to tell the producer how much she was going to miss his *looooove machine*! To put it politely," Harvey winked.

The three men broke into laugher and Harvey had to compose himself before he could continue. "Well, the wife jumped up in hysterics and started clawing and scratching at the blonde. Two pallbearers got in on the act. They tried to break up the cat fight and pull the blonde off the corpse. She had such a death grip on the old boy that when they pulled her away, he came out of the wooden box right along with her. It was quite a sight," Harvey laughed, "the wife, the girlfriend and the corpse rolling around on the floor in front of the casket. You know, for a minute, I think I actually saw the old boy smile!"

Sam sat up in the casket, tears streamed down his cheeks. "Stop it, you're killing me." He doubled over and pounded on the side of the mahogany box. "But, at least I'm in the right place!" he laughed.

"I've got one for you," Michael announced through glazed eyes. "Last year, Sharon's parents were at their condo in the Mayan Riviera. They were lying out by the pool one afternoon when word spread that one of the tenants in the complex had died." Michael's drunken grin got bigger. "Apparently, the dead guy was huge. The four Mayans they sent up to his suite to get him were just tiny little guys." Michael held his hand at chest level. "You know, short. Well, there was no way they could carry him, so they decided to strap him to a board and lower him over the balcony. Well, they'd only lowered the guy about two floors ... in the four-story building, when the ropes broke!"

When Jean Ingles opened the door to the Ingles and Hawthorne selection room, her husband, her nephew, and Sam Bennett were laughing hysterically. "Harvey Ingles, what in God's name are you doing?" She stepped into the room and shut the door behind her. "Look at you boys, you're all drunk!"

"You bet we are," Harvey giggled. "Now come here and give your old man a big wet kiss." Jean let out a disgusted sigh and marched to the casket. "Are you mad?" Harvey asked, through drunken lips.

"Yes, I'm mad," Jean scolded. "You were supposed to be home hours ago. Do you have any idea what time it is? You scared the cleaning staff half to death when they heard the noise coming from up here."

"Oh honey, now don't be mad." Harvey pulled his wife closer and kissed her on the cheek. "We were just having a few drinks. That's all."

"Did you have to do it in here? Leslie has Mayor Patterson coming in first thing in the morning to make the arrangements for his mother. She's going to have a fit. Georgia is going to have to vacuum again, wipe down the caskets and air this place out." Jean pinched her nose with her thumb and index finger. "It smells like a distillery and a Cuban cigar factory in here. You should be ashamed of yourselves."

Michael staggered to his aunt's side and threw his arm around her shoulder. "Now, don't be mad Auntie Jean. We were just taking the merchandise for a test drive. You wouldn't buy a car without taking it for a spin. I was thinking that maybe I should purchase one of these babies." Michael slapped his hand on the casket Harvey was sitting in. "I could be gone tomorrow ... just like Alex."

The comment put a damper on the cheerful mood and Sam slowly pulled himself from the casket he'd been occupying. "I'm sorry Mrs. Ingles," he apologized. "We started talking about Alex and one thing lead to another."

Jean gave him a warm motherly smile. "Well, Sam, I don't know how well you knew my niece, but Alex had a wonderful sense of humor." She pointed skyward. "In fact, she's probably up there right now, laughing her ass off."

"Jean Ingles, you swore!" Harvey mumbled."

"Yes I did, and I'm going to swear a lot more if you don't get your carcass out of that box!" She grabbed her husband's legs and swung them over the edge of the full-couch oak casket. "Come on, boys. The party is over."

23

WHEN JEAN REACHED THE top of the driveway at the Granger ranch, the front porch lights were on and Brian's car was parked near the garage. "I see you changed your mind and decided to come home." She parked in front of the house and had no more than turned off the ignition when Sharon and Angelina appeared on the front porch.

"Hello, ladies," Jean called out as she exited the vehicle. "Can you give me a hand? These three are bombed."

Sharon rushed to the car and opened the back door. "Michael, where have you been? I've been worried sick that you were in a car accident!"

"We were at the funeral home having a little wake for my sister," Michael slurred. "Now I need to go to bed." He reached up for Sharon's arm and she pulled him from the car.

On the opposite side of the Chrysler 300 Hemi, Sam was making an attempt to exit the back seat. "*Buenas noches, Señor.* I see you've had a few too many," Angelina scolded. "Come on, I think we need to get you to bed." She helped Sam up from the back seat. "Are you ready?" she asked.

"Ready for what?" he drunkenly asked. "Are we going somewhere?"

"*Necesito meterte dentro de la casa,*" Angelina said. "We need to get you in inside. *Por favor.*"

It took all the strength Angelina had to get Sam from the car to the house. Once inside, going up the stairs became even more challenging. Encouraging Sam to place one foot in front of the other, she was reminded of a scene from the first John Wayne movie the two of them had ever watched.

Maureen O'Hara and Yvonne De Carlo were attempting to get the drunken acting legend up the stairs. When the trio was nearing the top they tumbled over backward.

Angelina was exhausted by the time they reached Sam's room. She pushed him onto the bed and leaned over to undo his tie. He grabbed her around the waist and pulled her to his chest. Before she could object, they were locked in a passionate kiss.

Angelina had denied her feelings for Sam. Then, the night of Alex's death, he'd taken her with a raw passion. The next morning, he apologized and told her it would never happen again. Sam hadn't touched her since.

She pulled back and looked into his eyes. "Please don't do this unless you mean it."

"I want you, Angelina," he whispered. "I need you. Maybe I always have."

***

Across the hall, Jean Ingles was trying to have a serious conversation with her husband. "Harvey, are you listening to me?" She stuck out her finger and poked him in the shoulder. "I talked to Eleanor earlier tonight and she said something that's been bothering me ever since."

"What is it, dear?" Harvey mumbled into his pillow.

"Harvey, look at me." Jean poked him again and he let out a grunt.

"Can't this wait till morning?"

"No it can't."

"Okay dear, if it's that important, you have my undivided attention." He rolled over, propped himself up on one arm and gazed at his wife. Her eyes were filled with concern.

"Eleanor is having a hard time with Alex's death. She doesn't believe that Alex would have ever gone scuba diving."

"Why would she say that?"

"She told me Alex was afraid to dive."

"Well, that's just silly," Harvey yawned. "Alex used to go diving all the time."

"Yes, I know, but according to Eleanor, the last time Alex and Brian were diving, Brian pulled Alex's mask off and it scared her so badly that she vowed never to dive again."

"Now, why would Brian do something like that, and how would Eleanor know?"

Jean's eyes grew larger. "Alex told her!"

"Alex?"

"Yes. Eleanor asked Alex to take her diving last year, and Alex refused. When Eleanor asked her why, Alex told her about the incident with Brian and said she hadn't been diving since."

"I think Eleanor is blowing this way out of proportion because she's having a difficult time dealing with Alex's death."

"Well, I thought so too, at first, but Eleanor insisted it was true." Jean rested her head on Harvey's shoulder. "Something else is bothering me."

"What's that dear?"

"I got a phone call from Leslie just after six. She told me that Sarah showed up at the funeral home to see Alex's body."

"What's so unusual about that? Sarah is Alex's daughter."

"Leslie didn't think it was strange that Sarah showed up at the funeral home. What she thought strange, was that after viewing Alex's body, Sarah insisted it wasn't her mother."

Jean now had Harvey's full attention. "What are you telling me? That the mangled body lying on the prep-table isn't my niece, because Eleanor said Alex would never go diving? There was an autopsy. Of course, it's Alex!" Harvey insisted.

"Actually, they didn't perform an autopsy. Apparently, Sam was so upset when the coroner in Mexico said they would have to keep Alex for a week in order to do an autopsy that, Angelina went over the coroner's head. Evidently, she has close friends in the Mexican government."

***

In the library, Brian Williams was finishing his fourth brandy. He'd heard the commotion when his uninvited house guests returned home an hour ago, but he wasn't interested in talking to anyone, so he didn't bother to greet them. He hadn't wanted to come back from the Bahamas; he was having far too much fun, but after the conversation with his brother-in-law yesterday, he decided it was best. Besides, in ten days, Peter Bailey would read Alex's *Last Will and Testament* and he would be a rich man. Then he'd go back to the islands.

Brian's plan to get rid of Alex was perfect and this time it hadn't failed. He glued the needle of the pressure gauge on her air tank to read full, when in actual fact, she only had ten minutes of air. He made arrangements for Carlos, the diving guide he'd hired, to take Alex into the underwater caves. Once Carlos was sure Alex was dead, all he had to do was open the pressure gauge and free the needle. For his effort, he would receive 50,000 American dollars.

Brian hadn't been to the funeral home to see Alex, he'd come directly to the ranch from the airport. Tomorrow, he'd go have a look. He'd request an open casket so people would weep for his loss. At just the right moment, he'd throw himself on the wooden box and sob uncontrollably for his dear-departed wife. Friends would rush to his side and offer their support in his time of grief.

A satisfied smile found its way to Brian's face and he reached across the desk for his brandy. Picking up the bottle, he noticed an envelope protruding from under the desk blotter. He grabbed at the corner. "What's this?" Examining it, Brian remembered seeing the envelope the day he took Alex's necklace from the wall safe. He read the note attached to the front and without hesitation ripped open the sealed package. Inside was a leather-bound journal. "Well, well. What do we have here? What dirty little secrets were you hiding, Alex?"

Brian poured himself another drink, then tucked the journal under his arm and made himself comfortable in a wingback chair in front of the fireplace. "This should make for some interesting reading." He rested the journal in his lap and opened the cover. Inside, Alex had written her name and the date 1983. He turned the page and read:

> *Dear Diary, Tonight I gave birth to the most precious little girl. She looks just like her father.*

Brian's face broke into a proud smile remembering how beautiful his daughter had been when the nurse put her in his arms. He read on.

> *It wasn't a difficult birth, after nine months and two days, Sarah Alexandra Marie was ready to greet the world. She looks just like her father; with a full head of thick dark brown hair, and piercing blue eyes.*

"Wait a minute." Brian body stiffened. "I don't have brown hair, or blue eyes." His interest grew and he read on.

> *If he could only see her, he would be so proud.*

Brian shook his head. "What are you talking about, Alex? I did see her. I've seen her almost every day for the past twenty-five years."

The next line of the journal gave him a start.

> *I miss Sam, more than I ever thought I would and I know that some day, he'll miss his daughter too.*

"His daughter, what the fuck is she talking about?" Brian turned the page and began examining his wife's diary like a legal document, reading every word. For five years, Alex wrote to a man named Sam. Never once did she mention his last name. She told this man all about Sarah, how she looked and acted more and more like him everyday. Alex told him about the first time Sarah fell off her pony and the day she learned to swim. She told him ... she was sure ... Sarah would be a doctor, just like his sister. She told him, about each and every one of Sarah's birthday parties, and every outing to the zoo. The final entry in the journal was dated September 6, 1988 it read:

Today I received a phone call. Sam is dead.

Brian was fuming. All these years Alex had led him to believe that Sarah was his daughter. His mind suddenly flashed back to the last line of Alex's will. Now, it made sense:

The remainder of my estate goes to Sarah's biological father.

"That fucking bitch!" Brian glared down at the leather book. It didn't matter that Sarah wasn't his biological kid. The only two people who know the truth were Alex and this Sam person, and they were both dead. As far as the family was concerned, he *was* Sarah's father and that's the way it's going to stay."

He stood up and opened the screen to the fireplace then held the diary to his lips and kissed the cover. "Farewell, Alex. Your secret is safe with me, but your money won't be!" With one quick flick of his wrist, the journal was in the flames.

24

FUNERAL DIRECTOR LESLIE MCPHERSON had been in the business for fourteen years. She loved her job and it gave her a great feeling of satisfaction helping families through the troubled waters. Last week, she'd been working late when the Watson family came in to drop off personal items and pictures for Robert Watson's memorial service the following day.

The widow was putting on a brave front, but Leslie could tell that she was devastated by her husband's sudden death. "I knew he'd go some day ... but I just didn't think it would be this soon." Mrs. Watson pulled a handkerchief from her pocket. "Robbie was out cutting the lawn and just like that," she snapped her fingers, "he was gone." She reached inside her handbag and pulled out a package of Winston cigarettes. "Robbie always said to bury him with a Coke and a smoke. Here are the smokes." She offered Leslie an apologetic smile, "but I'm afraid I forgot the Coke."

"Why don't you let us worry about that?" Leslie smiled. "We'll take care of everything." The company pop machine only carried Pepsi, but when the Watson's were gone, Leslie would run across the street and grab a can of Coke from the corner store.

For the next two hours, Leslie helped the Watson family set up nesting tables at the front of the chapel, where Robert Watson's urn would rest during his funeral service. She made chocolate chip cookies for the widow's grandson, to keep him occupied while Mrs. Watson and her family rearranged pictures and mementos that told the story of Robert Watson's life. Listening to the family speak of the deceased, Leslie knew she would have liked Robert Watson. The stories portrayed a kind caring man, who loved his family and showed them often ... just how much.

Looking after the dead had never been a career choice of Leslie McPherson's. She wanted to be a doctor, just like her father. As a child, her summer holiday was consumed with medicine. She opened a clinic in the gazebo in her back yard and used lounge chairs as examining tables. The hours of operation were Monday to Friday nine to five.

Leslie bandaged knees and dressed scraped elbows in sterile white bandages. She prescribed pretend medications and cough syrup on the personalized prescription pads her father had printed for her and was proud to wear the white lab coat, her mother had monogrammed to read: *Doctor Leslie McPherson.*

At fourteen, when most young girls were interested in boys, Leslie was interested in medical journals and anatomy books. Twice a week, she volunteered at the hospital as a candy striper. She made beds, took urine samples to the lab, and delivered patients to and from the operating theaters and the X-ray department. On Friday nights, when her girlfriends were out on dates, Leslie helped in the emergency department at the hospital. On Saturdays, she accompanied her father on rounds.

Leslie graduated from medical school with honors but her proud parents, Robert and Katherine McPherson, never saw their daughter accept her diploma. Noticeably absent from the ceremony, it wasn't until halfway through dinner when Leslie discovered the reason why. A uniformed officer escorted her from the banquet hall to the foyer. He told her there had been a horrific traffic accident. He asked her to come with him to identify the bodies.

Having been in the morgue hundreds of times, Leslie knew what twisted metal could do to the human form but nothing could have prepared her for what she was about to see. Her father had been decapitated and lost both legs at the knees.

Leslie's mother had no visible signs of trauma, but her body was crushed from the shoulders down.

From the hospital, Leslie was escorted to Ingles and Hawthorne Funeral Home where she first met Harvey Ingles and his wife, Jean. Harvey was a soft spoken man with compassion in his eyes. Jean had held her in her arms while she cried. By the end of their three hour meeting, Leslie knew her parents would be treated with dignity and respect and she'd been right. The Ingles and Hawthorne staff took care of everything from the visitations, to the service, the interment, and the reception. She knew she wouldn't have made it through without them.

A week after the funeral, Leslie made a decision. "I've given this a great deal of thought," she told Harvey and Jean Ingles, "and I've decided I want to be a funeral director." When she graduated from mortuary school, Harvey offered her a job and she hadn't looked back since.

Today, Leslie wasn't only the manager of the company, she was part of Ingles' family. Harvey and Jean had taken Leslie under their wings and included her in every family holiday celebration. She knew Michael and Sharon Granger and their daughter, Eleanor. She'd been to BBQ's at Alex and Brian Williams' ranch. Four months ago, she accompanied Alex to Sarah's graduation from medical school.

A knock at the door drew Leslie's attention from the staff schedule she was reviewing. She looked up and smiled at Linda Goddard. "What can I do for you this morning?" she asked.

"I think you'd better come with me. There's something I need to show you in the selection room."

Leslie shook her head and grinned. "Don't tell me that Bart broke something else? He's only been here for six weeks, and he's already had two car accidents."

"Two!" Linda exclaimed.

"Yes. He backed a funeral coach into a tree, and drove a limo into Kate's car."

"Bart had nothing to do with this." Linda motioned toward Leslie with her finger. "Come on. I'll show you."

When the two women reached the door of the selection room, Linda stopped and turned around. "Be prepared," she warned. "You're not going to be happy." She pushed open the door.

Leslie's nose was immediately insulted by the odor of stale booze and cigars. "My God, it stinks in here." She waved her hand in front of her face and her eyes anxiously darted back and forth as she walked around the room surveying the damage. Potato chips were ground into the emerald green carpet. Three of the caskets looked as if they'd been slept in. A cremation container was covered with empty booze bottles. "What in God's name happened here?" Leslie threw her hands up in frustration. "No, wait ... don't tell me, Bradley was in here with his buddies, wasn't he? I swear I've had it with that kid. This is the last time Bradley Hawthorne is going to hold a poker tournament in this funeral home! Where's Tim? That boy's ass is out of here, today!" She spun around and marched to the door.

"Bradley had nothing to do with this," Linda called after her. "It was Harvey who had the party last night and it looks like it was a good one too!"

Leslie stopped dead in her tracks. "Harvey wouldn't do this!" She turned and stared at Linda in disbelief.

A huge grin erupted on Linda's face. "Well, he did. Harvey, Michael, and that cute guy they came in with him yesterday. I just got off the phone with Jean. They spent the night at Alex's place and she's taking Harvey home. He won't be in today ... he has a head the size of Texas!"

Leslie glanced at her watch. "We have to get this place cleaned up. It's quarter after eight. The mayor is coming at nine to select his mother's casket."

"Actually, he won't be. He left a message with the answering service. He'll be here sometime tomorrow."

"Do we have any other arrangements scheduled for today?" Leslie asked. "I haven't even looked at the arrangement schedule."

"No. It's pretty quiet. We only have one service. It's at 'Our Lady of Perpetual Hope'. The interment is at 'Our Lady of Peace Cemetery'."

"Who's running the service?" Leslie asked.

"Brent is the director in charge. Charles and Leanne are helping usher. Brent's driving the lead car to the cemetery. Leanne is driving coach, and Bart is on family limo."

Leslie's eyes widened. "Did you say Bart is driving the family limo?"

"Yeah, Randy called in sick."

"Do you know what happened the last time Bart drove a family?"

"No what?"

Leslie couldn't help but grin as she shared the story with her co-worker. "They were at the cemetery and it started to rain. Brent suggested that Bart take the grandmother's back to the limo."

"So, what's unusual about that?"

"He took them back to the limo, and then drove them home. When the graveside service was finished, the family was left standing in the rain with no vehicle to get them to the reception."

"I feel sorry for him," Linda frowned. "He really wants to be in this business, but he's all thumbs. While you were away, Harvey asked him to take flowers to a graveside and get it set up. He was really excited and set the grave up beautifully. Then, he stood there like a proud employee waiting for the funeral procession to arrive. Well ... when they did ... they drove right past him. Bart had put the flowers on the wrong grave."

Leslie shook her head. "I'm surprised Harvey didn't fire him on the spot."

"Well, he thought about it, but Jean talked him out of it."

"That's our Jean, the HR specialist." Leslie let out a deep sigh. "We better get this room cleaned up. Brian and Sarah are supposed to come in this afternoon to go over Alex's funeral arrangements."

"How's the reconstruction going?" Linda asked.

"Not great," Leslie admitted. "I've put shotgun victims back together and made them look like they were sleeping, but Alex just isn't working. Harvey told me that Brian wants to have an open casket, but I'm thinking closed would be much better for everyone."

"Has Brian seen Alex?"

"No. Sarah has, and when she did, she claimed it wasn't her mother."

"She's just upset."

"I thought so too ... at first, but yesterday I looked at the clothes Jean sent over with Harvey. They look way too big."

"Alex had lost weight."

"She may have lost weight, but I don't think she shrunk."

25

"IT'S NICE TO SEE you again, Brian." Leslie extended her hand. "I'm so sorry it has to be under these circumstances." As they shook, she couldn't help but notice how red and puffy his eyes were. It looked as if he'd been crying for hours. "Please, have a seat."

"Is this going to take long?" Brian asked as he plopped himself in a wing-back. "I have some stuff I need to do."

"Not long," Leslie smiled, "Alex made her own funeral arrangements a few years ago."

"Well, then, let's get on with it shall we?"

Leslie glanced at her watch. "Shouldn't we wait for Sarah?"

"Sarah won't be joining us. A doctor at the hospital gave her a sedative and she's at the ranch sleeping." Brian rolled his eyes and let out a chuckle. "Sarah has this stupid notion that the person in your prep-room isn't Alex. She's been a basket-case since she was here yesterday. The grief counselor at the hospital told me it was a normal reaction. He said she just can't accept the fact that her mother is dead, and she's come up with this cock-and-bull idea that the body belongs to someone else. I'm sure she'll get over it once the funeral is finished and the estate has been settled."

That's a strange comment, Leslie thought. What did Alex's estate have to do with the fact that his daughter was having a difficult time dealing with her mother's death? Leslie knew that Alex was worth a small fortune, but surely Brian wasn't concerned about the money at a time like this.

Brian shifted nervously in his chair. "Let's speed this up. I need to get going."

"Certainly," Leslie smiled. "As I mentioned, Alex has pre-arranged her funeral. She requested a mahogany Marcella casket with a memory drawer."

"A memory drawer, what the hell is a memory drawer?"

"It's a drawer inside the casket where you can place pictures or memorabilia. Anything you like. Eleanor and Alex were always very close. You can tell Eleanor ... if she likes ... she can draw a picture for Alex and we can place it in the drawer."

Listening to Leslie, Brian was reminded of the diary he tossed in the fireplace last night. That was one item that wouldn't be going into the memory drawer of his wife's casket. He offered Leslie a false smile. "I'll make sure I tell the kid."

"Alex has requested a church-type service," Leslie continued, "but without the minister. The service will be held in our chapel and I'll make arrangements for a funeral celebrant."

"What's a funeral celebrant?"

"It's a person who conducts secular funeral services." Leslie reached for her business card file. "I'll call Pam Evans. Alex met her once at a Christmas function Harvey had for the staff. She really liked her."

Brian raised a questioning brow. "So what does this celebrant do?"

"First, she'll meet with you and Sarah and basically help plan the service, although by making prearrangements, Alex pretty much has everything covered."

"So what do we need this celebrant for?"

"Well, the celebrant not only helps plan the service, but conducts it just as a minister would. When you sit down with Pam, she'll ask you questions about Alex's life, and then design a service to go along with it. Alex picked her own music, but Pam will help you with the tributes and the eulogy."

"So, how does the service work?"

"Alex has asked that her casket be placed at the front of the chapel prior to the funeral service, and ..."

"The casket will be open, right?" Brian interrupted. "I think it's important that Alex's friends be able to see her."

Leslie folded her arms and leaned forward on the desk. "Brian, I know you want an open casket, but considering the circumstances surrounding Alex's death, perhaps a closed casket would be a better idea."

"Why?"

"Alex's face is damaged."

"So?" Brian shrugged his shoulders. "I'm sure you can fix it. You did a great job on the sister of that Indian kid who works for Alex when she stuck a shotgun in her mouth."

"Yes, Brian, that's true, but Alex's situation is different."

"How bad can it be? She died because she ran out of air when she was diving. What? Is her body all bloated or something?"

The color drained from Leslie's face. "Brian, hasn't anyone told you that Alex was killed by a shark?"

"What?" This time Brian's face turned white. "When Michael called me in the Bahamas, all he said was the Alex was found in the ocean."

"I'm sorry, Brian." Leslie apologized. "I just assumed that you knew. I can make arrangements for you to see Alex, and then you can decide about an open casket."

"So when we're finished with this paperwork stuff, you're going to take me into the prep-room?" Brian rubbed his hands together. "I've always wanted to see the inside of that place. It must be creepy with all those dead bodies."

"Actually, I won't be taking you into the prep-room. We don't allow anyone but staff into that area of the facility. It's a very sacred place."

Brian waved off Leslie's comment. "Well, then just put her in one of those visitation rooms. I don't care, whatever works." He glanced at his watch. "Can we just get on with this? Like I said, I have another appointment."

"Yes, by all means." Leslie pulled her reading glasses from her pocket and perched them on the end of her nose. "I'll just go over the information with you and then you can be on your way. Alex has requested that her service take place at six o'clock in the evening."

"Six! Whoever heard of a funeral taking place at six at night?" Brian leaned back in his chair and hooked his thumbs into the front pockets of his jeans. "My old pappy always said that in the little drink-ass town he grew up in, the Catholics went to see God at ten in the morning and everyone else went at three! Why should this funeral be any different?"

"Most funerals do take place during the day," Leslie told Brian, "but Alex was special and she wanted her funeral at a special time. She asked that the service be held by candlelight. We'll place two hundred vanilla scented candles around the chapel and light them fifteen minutes prior to the service.

"The service will start at six p.m. sharp and we'll play the first piece of music. Alex selected the Nora Jones' song, *Come Away with Me*. While the song is playing, we will project a picture of Alex on the projection screen. I need you to go through your photo albums as soon as possible and bring in pictures of Alex so we can select some and burn them onto a disk for the video tribute."

"What kind of pictures?" Brian asked.

"Pictures of Alex from the time she was born. The horse shows she participated in, birthday parties, family gatherings ... that type of thing." Leslie stared at Brian's blank expression. "Maybe you should write this down?" She pushed a pad of paper across the desk.

"It's okay. I have one." Brian reached into his pocket and when he pulled out his day-timer, the joint he'd rolled before leaving the ranch fell out onto the floor. "Don't mind me." He leaned over, picked it up and put it back in his pocket. "I just need something to get me through this," he grinned

"Whatever it takes, Brian." Leslie turned her attention back to Alex's funeral arrangements. "As I was saying, the service will start with the song *Come Away with Me*, by Nora Jones. Once the song is finished, the procession will begin. Pam and I will walk in together, followed by the pallbearers and the family.

"Alex has asked that the service open with a reading of *The Lord's Prayer*. After the reading, Pam will speak. When she's finished there will be another piece of music and we will show the video tribute. When that's finished, Michael will give the eulogy. When he's finished, Sarah will read the prayer, *Now I Lay Me Down to Sleep*.

"To end the service, Alex has requested that we play chamber music. We will leave the chapel the same way we came in. Pam and I followed by the pallbearers, then the casket, the family and the mourners. Once Alex's casket is in the funeral coach, we will proceed to the Granger cemetery."

Brian's voice was sarcastic. "This sounds like a goddamn theater production, not a funeral!"

Leslie paid no attention to his remark. "Alex also requested that there be two visitations the day before the funeral. The first one will be open to the public and take place from one o'clock in the afternoon until four. At seven p.m. there will be a second visitation; a champagne reception for family and close friends only."

"A champagne reception? Is she nuts?" How much is all of this going to cost me?"

Leslie looked through the folder for the invoice. "I believe the total cost for everything Alex has requested including the flowers, her casket, the burial vault, both visitations and the reception at the ranch after the interment is around thirty thousand."

Brian shot out of his chair. "Thirty grand! She's got to be out of her fucking mind?"

"Brian, the funeral ..."

"I'm not paying thirty grand to bury my wife," Brian interrupted. "Her uncle owns the damn funeral home. You'd think he'd give me a discount for christsake." He pulled a cigarette from his pocket and stuck it between his lips.

"There's no smoking in here," Leslie firmly stated.

Brian flashed her a sarcastic glare. "What are you going to do, have me arrested? If I'm paying thirty grand for my wife's funeral, I'll damn well smoke anywhere I want."

"Fine, Brian." Leslie stood up and made her way around the desk. "If you must smoke, I'll get you an ashtray, but I'd appreciate it if you'd sit down so you don't drop ashes on the carpet."

Leslie left the room and when she returned a few minutes later, Brian was still pacing the floor. "Would you sit down, please? Here's your ashtray and I brought you some water. You seem agitated."

Brian flopped into a chair. "You're goddamn right I'm agitated. Who the hell ever heard of paying thirty grand for a funeral? It's a damn good thing we don't have to pay to put her in the ground!" He grabbed the ashtray from Leslie's hand and butted out his cigarette.

"Brian, you really need to quit worrying about money. Alex's funeral is completely paid for, including the refreshments for the gathering during her evening visitation and the reception following the funeral."

"So this money doesn't get paid by the estate?"

Leslie shook her head. "No."

"Thank God for that!" Brian gave Leslie a pleased smile. "You know what, Alex planned this whole thing and told you guys what to do, so just do it." He stood up. "I need to get going. Just call the house, and let me know what time the limo will be there to pick us up for the visitation thing."

Leslie called after him as he headed for the door, "I thought you wanted to see Alex so we can make a decision about the casket."

Brian stopped in his tracks remembering what Leslie had said earlier about the state of Alex's body. He took a deep breath and forced his eyes to water before turning around. "I don't think I can handle seeing Alex if she's as bad as you say." He buried his face in his hands and started to sob.

Leslie went to Brian's side to offer comfort. She put her arm around his shoulder. "It's okay Brian. This is very difficult for all of us."

Brian's body stiffened. As quickly as he turned on his tears of grief, he turned them off. "She's been identified, right?"

"Yes, of course. Alex was identified in Mexico by Sam Bennett."

"Who?"

"Sam Bennett, the man who owns the resort she was staying at. He and his assistant manager brought Alex's body back."

Brian raised a questioning brow. "Why would the owner of the resort bring back my wife's body?"

"Sam is a good friend of Michael's. He and Angelina, that's his assistant, are staying at the ranch. Haven't you met them?"

Brian shook his head. "No. I didn't get in till late last night. I was beat when I got home and went right to bed. There was nobody around when I got up this morning."

For the second time during his conversation with Leslie, Brian's mind was taken back to Alex's diary. Was this Sam Bennett person ... the Sam Alex had written to? She'd never mentioned the last name of Sarah's real father. "It can't be the same guy," Brian mumbled under his breath, "he's dead."

"Did you say something," Leslie asked

"You say this Sam character is a friend of Michael's?"

"Yes."

"Did Alex know him?

"Oh, I don't think so. I believe they just met for the first time at his resort last week."

"But why would he go to all the trouble of bringing Alex home if he didn't know her?"

"He's friends with Michael. I'm sure that if a friend of yours lost his sister in a foreign country and you were in a position to help, you would."

"Yeah, I guess you're right," Brian agreed. "And this guy identified Alex's body in Mexico?"

"Yes, that's right."

"So all the nonsense Sarah is spouting off about the body not being her mother's and wanting an autopsy is ridiculous?"

"I think so. The minute you see Alex, you'll know it's her."

"You said she was killed by a shark? How bad was it?"

Leslie looked into his eyes. "It's bad Brian. Alex's face is unrecognizable and her right arm is gone at the shoulder. That's why I highly recommend that you have a closed casket for both the visitation and the funeral. I could make a prosthetic arm to replace the one she's missing, but her face is quite badly damaged. I can reconstruct it, but there is a great deal of trauma and she isn't going to look like she did when she left for Mexico."

Brian felt his stomach heave. "If she's that gross, I don't think I want to see her."

"You don't have to look at Alex's face to identify her. Look at her left hand. You'll know it's Alex." She gave him a compassionate smile. "Seeing the deceased is the first step on the road to dealing with your grief."

Brian thought for a moment. "Okay, I'll see her."

Leslie picked up the telephone and punched out three numbers. "Could you please bring Alex up to the Rosemount room?" She thanked the person on the other end and hung up the phone. "It will take a few minutes to get things set up. Would you like more water?"

"No, I'm good."

Ten minutes later, Leslie and Brian were standing outside the Rosemount visitation suite. "I want you to know that the casket Alex is in isn't the casket she'll be in for the funeral. I just didn't want you to see her in an identification container.

Her face has been covered so just look at her hand." Leslie squeezed Brian's arm. "Are you ready?"

"As ready as I'm going to be." When the door to the visitation room opened, the familiar funeral home aroma filled Brian's nostrils. He held his breath and stepped across the threshold. "I think I'd like to be alone with my wife, if you don't mind."

"Of course, I'll just be out here if you need me."

Brian closed the door and stood for a moment staring at the oak casket. It was finally over; Alex was gone ... at last. He walked to the wooden box and looked down at his wife. Her face was covered with a white terry-cloth hand towel. She was wearing a blue hospital gown. Her left hand was resting on her stomach. There was a pillow where her right arm used to be.

Brian debated looking under the towel and when his curiosity got the best of him, he pulled it from Alex's face. The sight was grotesque. The bits of skin left on her face had been peeled down to her neck and up over her forehead. Cotton was packed in her right eye socket. Having submerged the urge to throw up, Brian couldn't stop himself from reaching down and poking at what was left of his wife's face. The exposed muscles were cold and as hard as a rock. "You look like something out of a freak show," he laughed. He threw the towel over the corpse's face and let out a satisfied sigh. His financial problems were finally over.

Brian had big plans for the estimated millions he'd get from his wife's death. It would have been more, if she hadn't been so generous with her family members. Alex left the ranch to Sarah, and Michael ... which was understandable considering it had been in the Granger family for years, but Brian was sure his wife had other reasons.

Sarah was also left the contents of the house and twelve million dollars ... two million of which was to be placed into a separate account for the children she would have some day. Alex left her brother three million; to be given to the charity of his choice, and made arrangements for Michael and his wife to take a three-month, six-destination Caribbean vacation. Alex put one million into an account for her niece, Eleanor, and gave the kid her two favorite horses. Alex signed her shares of the quarter horse breeding operation over to her ranch foreman, Ted Nelson, but Brian was sure with enough booze, he could convince the old man to sign the shares over to him ... then, he'd liquidate them.

Brian's eyes traveled down Alex's body, stopping when they reached her left hand. He stared at it for several minutes before reaching into the casket and picking up the left arm it was attached to. Something wasn't right. He examined the cold flesh like a CSI examines a crime scene. Leslie said he would recognize Alex's hand, but this hand was unfamiliar to him. There was no evidence of the horseshoe-shaped scar that had been left by Don Barkwell's fondue incident. He dropped the embalmed arm and jumped back from the casket.

"Holy shit! What if Sarah was right? What if this isn't Alex?" Brian's mind started racing. If this wasn't his wife ... then who the hell was it, and what had Carlos done with Alex? He'd gambled on a lot of things over the years but he wasn't prepared to gamble on this. If someone at the funeral noticed the absence of the scar, they may start to ask questions. Questions lead to investigations.

Brian abruptly turned on his heels and marched across the visitation room. When he opened the door, Leslie was waiting for him. "I've made a decision," he stated. "I've decided on a closed casket. Can you seal it now?"

"Brian, I told you the casket Alex is in, isn't the one she'll be buried in."

"Is her casket here?"

"Yes."

"Well put her in it and seal it. I can't bear the thought of anyone else seeing what that fish did to my wife!"

Leslie called after Brian as he walked away. "Jean told me that she left a package on your desk in the library at your house. She said you were going to bring it to the funeral home so it could be placed in the memory drawer of Alex's casket. You don't happen to have it, do you?"

"No," Brain replied over his shoulder. "I'll bring it in tomorrow."

26

SARAH DISMOUNTED, THREW THE reins over her shoulder and walked into the barn, followed by the jet-black quarter horse mare she'd been riding. It had been a while since she'd been in a saddle. The last time was with her mother on Mother's Day; a tradition the two of them had shared for as long as Sarah could remember.

Getting out in the fresh air had done her a world of good. She'd been thinking of nothing but her mother's body since it arrived from Mexico. Sam Bennett told the family that although it was impossible to make a positive facial identification, the numbered armband on her mother's wrist matched the one on record at the hotel.

Sarah knew better, but she just couldn't bring herself to believe that it was actually her mother lying in the morgue at Ingles and Hawthorne. She was so positive, in fact, that for the past two days she'd done everything she could to convince her father they should do an autopsy, but he wouldn't hear of it.

"Don't you think your mother has suffered enough? You're a doctor. You know what they do to a body in an autopsy. Face it, Sarah, your mother is gone and you need to forget this ridiculous idea."

Last night, Sarah had a long talk with Angelina. She too had lost her mother. Angelina told Sarah that it was normal to believe the body at the funeral home belonged to someone else. It was a way of denying the death to prevent the grief.

"I will tell you something," Angelina smiled, "then, perhaps you will look at death differently. In Mexico, there is a tradition. It is called *The Day of the Dead. El dia de los muer-*

tos. It is celebrated each year on the second day of November. This is a day when the Mexican people feel that their dead loved ones come back to visit."

Sarah eyes widened. "That's certainly different than here."

"*Si,* it is very different. Here, I find that all of the people are so sad. The Mexican people, they too are sad when a loved one dies, but on *The Day of the Dead*, it is like a big celebration."

"What do they do?" Sarah asked.

"The family put out candles and food, and the drink that was the favorite of the deceased. Sometimes, it is tequila," Angelina winked. "The family, they put out the favorite clothes of the dead person because they believe on that night, the dead will come back to visit. The people don't believe they will actually see the dead person," Angelina explained, "but that night, their spirit will come. The people, they stay all night in the cemetery and they feel the dead person is there with them.

"The celebration takes place over two days. One day is for the adults and one day is for the children. In all of Mexico, it is the same. Before the cemetery, the people go to church and say many things for the dead person."

"It sounds like the Mexican culture believes when you're dead you go on to another life," Sarah smiled.

"*Si,* that is correct. The Mexican people think it is good when they are still alive, but if you are dead, that is even better."

"Do they have parties on the street and everybody celebrates?"

"Not all of the people, not anymore. Now, it is about half-and-half. In the big city it is more difficult because of the cemeteries. It's different than in the small towns."

"Maybe the Mexican people have the right idea. Here, once the funeral is over, most people try to put the death out of their mind as soon as possible. I sure can't imagine anyone in this country spending the night in a cemetery!"

"There is a little town, not far from *Las Tropicales*. There is a lake there. In the middle of the lake, there is a little island. It is small, but very nice. People take their boats and go there with things like candles, and food, and all the favorite things of the dead person."

Sarah gave Angelina a warm smile. "It's interesting that the Mexican people feel that way about death. The Hindu religion believes in reincarnation."

"The Mexican people, they think that death is not really bad. In their customs and traditions, they believe that death is another step to life."

"Am I interrupting anything?"

The sound of a deep male voice brought Sarah back from the conversation she'd had last night with Angelina. She looked up, Sam was standing in the doorway of the barn and she motioned for him to come in. "You're not interrupting at all," she smiled. "Please, come in."

"This is a beautiful animal," he remarked as he ran his hands across the horse's slick jet-black coat.

"Jingles Midnight Pride, she's my mom's horse. Or should I say, she was my mom's horse." Sarah fought to hold back tears as she undid the saddle girth and took the bridle off Pride's head. "Do you ride, Sam?" she asked.

"I used to do a little riding with your uncle Mike, when we were in college, but I can't remember the last time I was in a saddle."

"I've been riding since before I could walk and I've always wanted to ride bareback down a white sandy beach."

"Well," Sam smiled, "You'll have to come back to the resort some time and we'll make sure we go for a ride." When Sarah reached for the saddle, Sam stepped in to help. "Here, let me take that for you." He lifted the saddle from the horse's back and the mare shook her body in appreciation. "Where would you like this?"

"The tack room is three stalls down on the left," Sarah pointed. "Any empty saddle rack will do." She gave the mare a slap on the rump. "Go on, old girl. It's time for a bath." Pride let out a soft whinny and clip-clopped along the cement barn floor, turning right when she reached the wash rack.

"She seems to know where she's going," Sam chuckled as he stepped from the tack room.

"That she does. It's time for her bath." Sarah took Sam by the arm and led him down the alleyway of the barn. "Come on, I want to show you something."

As the words came out of her mouth, Sam was reminded that he'd heard the same words from Alex when they were in Campbell River twenty-five years ago. He wished now that he would have ignored Moe Sanderson's cocaine threat and run off with Alex like they'd planned. If he had, maybe this beautiful young woman would be his daughter and Alex would still be alive.

When Sarah and Sam reached the end of the barn, the mare; who obviously had a personality of her own, was stomping her hoof on the rubber floor mat. "Now, there's a woman who knows her own mind," Sam laughed.

"Watch this." Sarah looked into the horse's eyes. "Do you want a drink, Pride?" The mare curled her upper lip and bobbed her head up and down in reply.

Sarah turned on the tap and for several minutes the horse slurped and sucked at the end of the hose as if it were a water fountain. "She's sure enjoying that," Sam smiled.

"This horse loves water. My mom always said she was worse than a kid. If there's a puddle anywhere in the pasture, Pride is sure to find it. When she does, she comes in from the field covered in mud." Sarah gave the mare a friendly pat on the neck. "Had enough?" she asked. The mare let out a snort and moved her mouth away from the end of the hose.

Sam shook his head in amazement. "It's almost like that horse knows exactly what you're talking about."

"I'm sure she does." Sarah adjusted the water temperature and covered the horse's body with lukewarm water. "My mom always said this horse was the reincarnation of a human. She loves eating Fig Newton cookies and she drinks Pepsi."

"Really?"

"Oh yeah," Sarah eyes lit up "from the time Mom first started showing her. At every horse show, as soon as the classes were finished, Mom gave Pride two Fig Newtons and a bottle of Pepsi."

"Wouldn't that be bad for her?"

"It apparently hasn't done her any harm," Sarah smiled. "Pride is eighteen-years-old." She handed Sam a bottle of shampoo. "Run a line from between her ears, down her mane, down the middle of her back and over her rump to the tip of her tail."

Sam followed Sarah's instructions and squeezed the blue liquid from its container. When he reached the horse's withers, the mare's head spun around and she took a nip at his pant leg. He quickly jumped back to avoid the animal's teeth. "I don't think she likes me."

"Oh, sure she does," Sarah reassured him. "She's just checking you out. She probably wonders why Mom isn't here doing this, or you may have touched her side. She's pretty sensitive."

"Ticklish?"

"No, injured. When she was a three-year-old, my dad was having a party and one of his buddies turned her out in the pasture with some horses that were being boarded here for a week. Two of the geldings took after her and ran her through a barbed wire fence. It took the vet three hours and over nine hundred stitches to put her back together."

Sam examined the scar that ran the length of the horse's barrel between her shoulder and flank. He gently laid his hand on the mare's side and the horse gave a soft whinny. "It's okay, girl. I'm not going to hurt you." Sam looked over at Sarah. "How long has your mom had the mare?"

"All of her life." Sarah wet a sponge and gently scrubbed the horse's coat. "Pride is the daughter of the first quarter horse my mom ever owned. I wasn't here the night Pride was born, but my grandfather talked about it all the time. Mom spent every night sleeping in the barn waiting for Pride's mother to foal. During the day, she checked the stall every half an hour.

"She'd promised my grandpa that she'd deliver a stallion to a ranch in Tennessee. Mom put her trip off as long as she could ... waiting for the mare to foal. When she couldn't wait any longer, she loaded the stallion in the trailer and hit the road." A broad smile danced across Sarah's face. "My grandfather said that my mom hadn't been gone an hour when Pride's mother lay down and gave birth. Mom was furious that she'd missed the whole thing.

"Four days later, when she got back from her trip, she walked into the stall and this crazy horse bit her." Sarah put her arms around Pride's neck and kissed the horse's velvety soft muzzle. "Mom bit her back. The two of them have been best friends ever since."

When Pride was squeaky clean, Sarah rinsed her off and wiped away the excess water with a sweat scraper. She took a wool horse blanket from the hook on the wall and threw it over Pride's back. "You always did look good in blue," Sarah smiled, pulling the light weight wool blanket towards Pride's ears. She tucked the white, braided-cotton cord under Pride's halter, tied the two front neck straps, then slid her hand down the mare's neck and pulled the wool blanket over the horse's back and rump. "You know Pride, of all the coolers your mother won over the years, this one meant the most to my mother."

Sam read the words on the blue blanket out loud. "1974 All–American Quarter Horse Congress. High Point Youth Champion." He looked at Sarah. "How come this blanket was so important?"

"Mom didn't start showing on the quarter horse circuit until she was in her late teens. She never had time because she was always too busy helping my grandfather with the ranch. She worked really hard all year to make it onto the youth team.

Some of the stuck-up rich bitches didn't think she should be there because it was her first year of showing, but according to the rules of our Quarter Horse Association, Mom had earned enough points to travel to Columbus, Ohio, that year with the team."

Sarah gave Sam a proud smile. "If it wouldn't have been for my mom, the team wouldn't have won the trophy. Pride's mother and my mother placed first in horsemanship. There were one hundred and fifty entries in the class. They won both the Western, and English pleasure classes. Mom won the showmanship class, placed second in the trail class and second in the reining. They won the Western riding and placed fourth in the jumping."

"That's quite an accomplishment."

"Yes it is. My mother was a very accomplished horse-woman." Sarah moved to the mare's hindquarters and pulled Prides silky black tail through the rear blanket strap. "There you go old girl. All ready for your trip into town."

"A trip to town?"

"Yes," Sarah nodded, "Pride is going to Mom's visitation tonight."

"Excuse me?" Sam flashed Sarah a puzzled look.

"Tonight, family and close friends are going to the funeral home to pay their last respects to my mother. Pride was one of Mom's close companions. When I was talking to Angelina last night, she told me that in Mexico they have a celebration called *The Day of the Dead.*"

Sam nodded his head. "*Si. El dia de los muertos.*"

"When Angelina told me about the Mexican funeral custom, I figured I should quit being such an idiot. Mom wouldn't want me acting the way I have, especially towards my father. It seems that we haven't said a civil word to each other in days. I don't know what's come over him. He's been like a total stranger to me since he came home for Mom's funeral."

Sam walked around the horse and put his hands on Sarah's shoulders. He kissed the top of her forehead then gave her a

hug. "Don't take it personally. I'm sure your father is very upset about your mother's death. I understand that he was supposed to go along on the trip to Mexico."

Tears came quickly to Sarah's eyes. "So was I. If we had,
my mother would still be alive."

27

BRIAN STARED IN THE mirror at his reflection. "God, you're a handsome bugger!" He smiled proudly at himself and tightened the knot on his silk tie. Tonight, he would give the performance of his life. He realized when he got back from the funeral home the other day that he'd perhaps given Leslie McPherson the wrong impression about his feelings towards his wife. Tonight, that would all change.

He held his head in his hands and started to sob. "You were my whole life, Alex. How will I ever live without you?" Tears streamed down his face and his body heaved as he cried. He pulled a handkerchief from the breast pocket of his suit and wiped the tears from his cheeks, then looked back at himself in the mirror and smiled. "There. That ought to get the family and friends going." He stuffed the handkerchief back in his pocket and left the bedroom.

***

In the guest room at the end of the hall, Michael was sitting on the edge of the bed drinking his third Scotch since getting out of the shower. Alex was dead ... his family was dead. He was the only Granger left. The reality of his sister's death hadn't set in, but Michael was sure it would tonight, when he set foot into the visitation room at Ingles and Hawthorne.

"How are you doing, honey?" Sharon asked as she entered the room.

Michael shrugged his shoulders. "I'm fine, I guess."

Sharon crossed the room and sat on the bed at his side. "The limos are here. Everyone is downstairs. Are you coming?"

Michael gave her a sad smile. "I don't want to, but I guess I have no choice."

***

Downstairs in the library, Jean was having a conversation with Harvey about the envelope she'd found earlier in the week. "Harvey, did Brian give you the envelope for the memory drawer in Alex's casket?"

"What envelope?"

"The day Sharon and Eleanor arrived, I found an envelope tucked between the cushions of the sofa in the library. The envelope was Alex's. On the front she wrote a request that the envelope go to her grave unopened."

Harvey raised a questioning brow. "That's interesting."

"I thought so too, at first, but no matter what Alex's reason, she wanted it with her. Did it go into her casket?"

Harvey shook his head. "I never saw an envelope."

Jean pointed toward the desk, "I left it over there, with a note for Brian to deliver it to the funeral home." She walked to the desk and examined the contents of the papers scattered across it. "I don't see it. I'll check with Brian. Maybe he gave it to Leslie."

"Speaking of Brian, I had a chat with him about what Eleanor told you regarding Alex's little diving incident a few years ago."

"What did he say?"

"He told me he had to pull out Alex's regulator because she'd run out of air. The only way he could get her to the surface, was to have her breathe through his regulator."

Jean let out a sigh of relief. "That explains it. I don't trust Brian, but I didn't think he'd ever try to harm Alex."

***

In the kitchen, Angelina was feeding Sam his third Alka-Seltzer in as many hours. "Promise me, when we get back to Mexico, you will go and see the doctor about your stomach."

Sam downed the fizzy beverage and handed back the glass. "I will. I promise."

"I had a long talk with Sarah last night," Angelina casually remarked.

"Yes, I know."

"How do you know about this?"

"I ran into her down at the barn. When we were walking back to the house, she said that you've been very beneficial in helping her deal with her mother's death."

"She is a beautiful young lady," Angelina smiled. "I know what she is going through. It is very hard to lose your mother."

"Sarah told me that you convinced her to drop the idea that it wasn't Alex we brought home from Mexico."

"*Si*." Angelina nodded. "She is very upset at the death of her mother. I told her it is a natural thing to not accept this death. I told her it was also difficult for me to accept my mother's death."

"I thought you were only three when your mother died?"

"Yes, but I was older when I lost my grandmother. She was like my mother because she raised me."

Sam leaned over and kissed Angelina on the cheek. "Well, whatever you said to her appears to have helped."

***

In the living room, Brian downed the remainder of his martini and set the glass on the coffee table. "Well, I guess we should get this show on the road." He walked across the foyer and opened the leaded glass front door.

Parked on the circular driveway, waiting for the family, were three funeral vehicles from Ingles and Hawthorne. The first vanilla Chrysler 300 would carry Brian and Sarah. Following behind in the limo: Michael, Sharon and Eleanor, Jean and Harvey, Sam, Angelina and Ted Nelson; Alex's ranch foreman. Behind the limo; a vanilla Dodge Ram pulling the horse trailer that would transport Alex's mare, Jingles Midnight Pride, to the funeral home.

Ingles and Hawthorne employees stood at attention beside the driver's door of each vehicle. They were sharply dressed in black suits, white shirts and sage and black striped ties. Their shoes were polished to a brilliant shine. Harvey gave them a nod as the family exited the house and the drivers' opened their vehicle doors in unison.

With everyone in place, the funeral procession slowly made its way down the driveway; passing the Granger family cemetery before turning onto the highway and heading for town.

28

SAM LEANED BACK ON his heels and tipped his head slightly to the right to eavesdrop on a conversation taking place behind him.

"My, my, Brian must have really loved Alex," a woman said. "My friend Val is a grief counselor. She told me that people often show their love of a spouse by throwing an elaborate funeral. I've never been to a visitation like this before. There's champagne, imported cheese, canapés, and fresh fruit imported from Mexico. And did you see the coffin! It looks like solid mahogany. It must have cost Brian tens of thousands of dollars."

"Maybe this isn't to show how much Brian loved his wife," the gentleman standing with the woman replied, "but to make up for being such an asshole to her for the past twenty-five years. Alex was a wonderful person. I don't know how she put up with his extra-curricular activities."

"Extra-curricular activities, what are you talking about?"

"Brian has been screwing around on Alex for years."

"I don't believe that," the woman announced.

"Well, believe it. I know for a fact it's true."

Sam hadn't spent much time talking to Alex's husband in the days since his arrival, but Michael had filled him in on some of the comings and goings of the Widower Williams. Brian loved to gamble, and it was rumored that he had a very expensive cocaine habit.

Sam knew all about cocaine habits; Grace had one for years. Five months before she died, he told her he wanted a divorce ... he'd had enough. Grace promised she'd quit. She asked for his help, so he sent her to the Betty Ford Clinic for six weeks. When she came home, she was the same Grace he'd first met years ago. The Grace he once loved.

She told him she wanted to get more involved in his life and in the resort. She asked him if she could help out in guest services and against his better judgment, Sam gave her a chance. He was pleasantly surprised at the outcome.

When Grace had been clean and sober for two months, Sam was so impressed with her progress and the new ideas she'd come up with for the hotel that he took her to the Dominican Republic for a second honeymoon. They stayed at a five star, beach-front resort thirty-five minutes from the airport. Sam was concerned when they arrived and he discovered the place had a casino, but during their entire stay, Grace hadn't wanted to visit it once.

By eight each morning, they'd finished their breakfast. Afterwards, they took an hour-long walk down the beach and talked like they hadn't talked in years. They spent the remainder of the morning lying by the pool. After lunch, they went back to their room and made love. Sam saw a side of Grace he'd long since forgotten. For the first time in a long time, he felt like a husband who was proud of his wife. On the way back to Mexico, they talked about adopting children. Two weeks later, Grace was dead.

Sam stared across the room at Alex's daughter. Sarah didn't look like Alex. In fact, he didn't think she looked like Brian either, but the young woman certainly had her mother's charm and she was holding up very well under the circumstances.

"How are you doing?" Leslie asked him as she approached with two glasses of champagne.

"I'm good. How are you? Michael tells me that you and Alex were pretty close."

"We were," Leslie frowned. "When my parents died, the Ingles' sort of took me in. They've always treated me like part of the family. I guess you could say that Alex and I were like cousins. Were you close to her, Sam?"

Sam wanted to scream, *YES. I was close to Alex. We were going to spend the rest of our lives together.* Instead he casually answered, "Michael and I have been buddies since college. I first met Alex when she was in her late teens. I was reintroduced to her when she was twenty-five. I saw her again five years later at Michael's first wedding, and then, not until I discovered that she was in Mexico."

"Harvey tells me that you own a resort there."

"Yes," Sam smiled. "You'll have to come down for a visit sometime. All you need to do is get to Puerto Vallarta and I'll take care of everything else. I'll give you the best room in the joint!"

Leslie let out an exhausted sigh. "You have no idea how great that sounds, but sometimes getting a vacation in this business is like pulling teeth. Unfortunately, death has its own timetable. Last Monday, we had nothing on the board. By Wednesday, we were swamped and on Thursday, we did twelve funerals before noon."

Sam looked at her curiously. "How do you do this? How do you deal with death everyday?"

Leslie shrugged her shoulders. "Actually, I don't really think about it. I deal with families and help them get through the troubled waters. A funeral director is usually the first person the family sees after a death. The family is grieving and confused about what happens in the funeral home. My job is to walk with them through the process."

"It must be really hard on people when they go into the casket room." Sam's face turned red. "Speaking of the casket room, I'm sorry we made such a mess in yours the other night."

"Oh, don't worry about it," Leslie smiled. "It was nothing that couldn't be cleaned up."

"I noticed that there's quite a price variance."

"Yes."

"I've always been curious," Sam gave her a sheepish grin. "Do funeral directors guide people towards the more expensive merchandise?"

"I know funeral directors that do," Leslie frowned, "and they give the rest of us a bad name. I always tell people, before I take them into the selection room, that we are about to embark on a business transaction. I tell them they have to think about what the person would like, and then walk around until they find a casket that appeals to them not only in appearance, but also in price. By the time we go into the selection room, all of the funeral arrangements have been made. I review with the family how much they've spent so far, and tell them that when they walk out the front door, I want them to still have money in their pockets."

"How do they react?" Sam asked.

"People are quite pleased and often surprised."

"This is very interesting," Sam smiled. "I haven't had much to do with funerals in my family. When my dad died, the U.S. government took care of everything. Do you do more burials or cremations?" he asked.

"We still do a number of burials, but cremation is becoming more popular. We have a transient society. A lot of people don't spend their entire life in one place anymore. They may have been born in Texas and lived in as many as twelve states before they die."

"What do people do with the ashes?" Sam asked.

"Some people purchase a cemetery plot and bury the ashes, or have them placed in a columbarium."

"What's a columbarium?"

Leslie pointed over his shoulder. "Do you see that room over there?" Sam turned to look. "That's our columbarium, it's like ... a wall full of pigeon holes. Some of the compartments hold one urn, others hold two. And, if you want a *family plot*, we have niches that will hold up to twelve urns."

"So people store the urns there?"

"I guess you could say that. The room is quite comfortable and we invite family members to visit their loved one anytime they like. All we ask is that they call first to let us know they're coming."

"Can't they just go in there during your regular business hours?"

"Well, yes, they can," Leslie smiled. "The reason we ask them to call first is so that we can prepare the room."

"What do you mean prepare the room?"

"Well, when we're making funeral arrangements with a family, we ask a lot of questions about the deceased. We find out what kind of flowers they like, what their favorite cookie was and what kind of music they listened to. When the family arrives, we have all of those things ready for them. We put a bouquet of flowers in the room, pipe in music and provide coffee and cookies."

"That's amazing," Sam smiled. "I've never heard of a funeral home that goes to such lengths."

"Ingles and Hawthorne does more than that. Have you seen the little black book Harvey carries around?"

"Yes," Sam nodded.

"Well, when we make funeral arrangements for a family, Harvey always asks how many family members they have left. If they tell him that they're now alone, he puts their name, address, phone number and birthday in his book. On the person's birthday, Harvey sends them a bouquet of flowers. At Christmas, Harvey and Jean invite the people with no family to have Christmas dinner with them."

"Harvey sounds like an amazing man."

"He is." Leslie agreed.

"With the cremation thing, do you ever have people who want to take the ashes home and put them on the mantel?"

"Oh, yes. In fact, we did a service last week where the widow took her husband's ashes home. She said she was going to keep them beside his favorite chair. When she dies, she wants to be cremated and have her ashes put in with her husband's so they can be together again. The woman has pre-planned her funeral. She did it right after her husband died."

"Is that common?"

"Not really, but she said the service we did was so beautiful that she wanted hers to be the same."

"No offence," Sam frowned, "but how can a funeral be beautiful?"

"Well," Leslie smiled. "People are starting to get away from the traditional funeral that's conducted by a minister. There are a lot of people who aren't religious and they don't want any religious overtones in the service.

"My grandfather wasn't a religious man, but ten years ago when you went to a funeral home to make arrangements; it was just sort of an unwritten law that a man of the cloth did the service. If you didn't have a minister, the funeral home found one for you,"

Leslie let out a deep sigh. "While we were making the funeral arrangements for my grandfather's funeral, the funeral director asked my grandmother about a minister. She told him that my grandfather hadn't been a religious man. The funeral home said they would find a minister.

"The minister came to my aunt's house and from what I remember ... he only stayed about half an hour. He asked some of the pertinent questions, like when and where my grandfather was born. He asked when my grandparents were married and how many children they had, and that was about all.

"The day of the service, he stood at the podium and started talking about how *God* had always been an important part of my grandfather's life. That was the first surprise of the service. The second came a few minutes later. While talking about my grandfather, the minister called him by my uncle's name. It bothered me at first, but I figured what the heck, everyone who was there knew my grandfather's name."

The color rose in Leslie's face. "Then, the guy did something that really bothered me. He started talking about the poem *Footprints*, whose author is unknown. I'm sure you've heard it. It starts out with ...one night a man had a dream ... and goes on about how there were two sets of footprints in the sand until times started to get tough and then there was only one.

"Apparently, the minister knew the author. He started talking about how his friend never received any royalties from the poem and how it seems to be displayed everywhere. He went on, and on, and on about it to the point that I was actually embarrassed. His little sermon upset my family and left the mourners wondering if they were at the right funeral!"

"So, what do people do if they don't want to use a minister?" Sam asked.

"When a family doesn't want a minister, we suggest a funeral celebrant. They conduct non-religious services and focus on the life of the person, not religious readings. You'll see tomorrow. Alex's service will be conducted by a celebrant."

"Will Alex be buried at a cemetery here in town?" Sam asked.

"No, she's being buried at the ranch."

"At the ranch?"

"Yes, the Grangers have a family cemetery on the property. You would have driven past it on the way here."

Sam shook his head. "I didn't see it. I guess I had my mind on other things."

"Excuse me, Leslie."

Leslie turned and looked at Funeral Attendant Bart Bigalow. "Yes, Bart."

"Uh, the Greens are here to pick up their mother."

"And?" Leslie asked.

Bart shifted nervously from foot to foot. "Ah, I just thought that, ah you'd like to give them the ashes."

Leslie gave the young man an encouraging smile. "You can do it Bart. You've been with the family through their whole ordeal."

Bart's eyes lit up. "Gee, thanks, Leslie, this will be great. They're scattering the ashes up at the ski hill!" He gave her a quick smile, turned on his heels and disappeared in the crowd.

"He's certainly an anxious young man," Sam remarked.

"Yes he is. I can tell he really wants to be a funeral director, but God, is he a klutz!" Leslie shook her head. "It would be just Bart's luck that while he was running up the stairs to return Mrs. Green to her family, he'd trip and spill her all over the place!"

Sam couldn't help but laugh imagining the sight. "That's what I call *scattering* the ashes!"

Leslie rolled her eyes. "Trust me. It wouldn't be the first time."

Sam raised a curious brow. "I've heard that it's actually illegal to scatter someone's ashes."

"People do it, but we don't recommend they broadcast it. We also recommend that they don't get rid of all the ashes."

"Why?"

"Well, it has been our experience that when people scatter all of the ashes they often wish they wouldn't have, because they have no special place to go to remember their loved one. That's why we started our Memorial Park, as a memorial to the lives that have come and gone.

"When a family entrusts us to look after their loved one, we plant a tree in our forest to memorialize that person. It's great for the families. We have a tree planting ceremony every spring and the families we have served throughout the previous twelve months are given a tree to plant in memory of their loved one. If you're interested in this type of thing," Leslie smiled, "I'll gather up a few of the *American Funeral Director* magazines. You'll find some interesting reading."

"Sounds good," Sam smiled. "I hope you don't mind me picking your brain like this."

"Not at all," Leslie smiled.

"Do you get people who don't want to have a funeral? All they want is to have the person cremated and that's it?"

"Yes, but I won't let them do that." Sam gave her a strange look. "I'll give you an example. A few months ago, I had a family come in whose mother had been ill for quite sometime. The family had been anticipating the death for so long that when the woman finally died, they just wanted everything over and done with. They told me that they wanted their mother to be cremated but they didn't want a funeral service. I told them I couldn't do that."

"That must have surprised them," Sam replied.

"It did. I told them that we were a funeral home and what we did was funerals. I told them that we would be taking their mother to the crematorium at noon the next day. Beforehand, the staff and I would have a small service to say a few words about the woman.

"Well, the next day the family showed up just as we were putting their mother in the funeral coach. I asked them if they would like to spend a few minutes with her and they told me they would. A funeral attendant took the family to an arrangement office, and asked them if they would wait for a few minutes while we prepared things.

"We took the woman to the Rosewood room and set everything up as if we were preparing for a funeral. We put a casket spray on top of the cremation container and floral arrangements on flower stands at both ends. We found an appropriate piece of music and then brought the family in."

"Wow," Sam shook his head. "That must have really blown them away."

"It did," Leslie smiled. "The oldest daughter called me the next day to thank me. She told me the family went home and spent the remainder of the day sharing stories about their mother. She said that if Ingles and Hawthorne hadn't done what they had, her family would have some day regretted that they didn't have a service.

"We didn't charge the family anything. All they paid for was the cremation container and the cremation. The oldest daughter wanted to send us a check but I told her that we weren't interested in their money. All we were interested in was helping the family through this difficult time.

"People seem to think that they don't need to view the body, or they don't need a funeral to say goodbye, but those two things are actually a very big step in accepting the death and dealing with the first stages of grief. You need to physically see the person. That's why we always have a family member do the identification. Some people don't agree, but death is final and it needs to be accepted."

"Yes, death is final." Sam took a deep breath to fight back the tears. "I know why I'm here tonight, and why all these people are here, and I know it's Alex lying in that mahogany box, but I still can't believe it."

"Neither can I," Leslie sighed. She glanced at her watch. They'd been chatting for almost thirty minutes. "Oh, my, look at the time. I need to go make the rounds."

"Maybe I'll go talk to Eleanor." Sam pointed across the room where Alex's niece was sitting in a wing-back chair clutching a stuffed toy dog. Sam couldn't help but notice that she looked so lost in this world of death."

"Good idea," Leslie smiled. "We'll chat later."

Sam put down his champagne glass and walked to Eleanor. "Do you mind if I sit down?" he asked.

The child looked up at him with big, sad eyes. "No. It's okay."

Sam perched himself on the arm of the chair. "Where are your mom and dad?"

"My mom went to get me something to eat and my dad is in with my aunt Alex."

Sam felt a lump in his throat. Not knowing what to say, he reached over and touched the fake fur of the stuffed toy. "That's a pretty nice dog you have there. What's his name?"

Eleanor clutched the dog tighter. "His name is Bernard. My aunt Alex gave him to me when I was four." She turned in her chair and looked up at Sam. In a matter-of-fact tone, she said, "I was talking to Angelina yesterday and she told me that dogs are very important to the people in Mexico."

"Why, yes they are," he smiled. "People use dogs for companionship in Mexico, just like they do here."

"I know, but Angelina told me that a dog's most important mission in life was to be a companion when someone dies. She told me that in Mexico, people need to be buried with a dog because people can't see in the dark and a dog can. Angelina told me that the dog guides the dead person to the next life."

"That's right." Sam was very impressed with the eleven-year-old. She was direct and to the point, much like her father. "What's wrong?" he asked when noticed Eleanor's bottom lip started quiver.

"I wanted to put Bernard in the casket with Aunt Alex but Uncle Brian won't let me. He said it was a stupid idea."

Eleanor started to cry and Sam put his arm around her. "It's okay. Don't cry. I'll get Leslie to talk to your uncle Brian. I'm sure we can work something out." He pulled a handkerchief from his pocket and wiped the tears from the little girl's cheeks.

"You will?" she sniffed.

"Yes, I will."

"Do you really think that Leslie can get Uncle Brian to change his mind?"

Sam gave her an encouraging smile. "I'm sure she can." Eleanor handed him the stuffed animal and he handed it back. "Why don't you hold on to Bernard until I've had a chance to set things up with Leslie?"

"Okay." Eleanor sniffed "Maybe it would be better if I spend one more night with Bernard." She kissed the stuffed animal's head.

"I think he'd like that too." Sam agreed.

29

AT TWO IN THE morning, when Angelina couldn't sleep, she left her room and wandered downstairs to the library in search of reading material. She thumbed through a stack of *Western Rider* magazines and *American Quarter Horse Journals*, but nothing grabbed her attention until she saw the magazine with Harvey Ingles' picture on the front cover. "This doesn't look like a horse magazine." Angelina pulled it from the pile and examined it. "*American Funeral News*. This should be interesting."

Angelina made herself comfortable on the sofa and flipped through the glossy pages of the magazine. An article titled: '*Thanks for the Memories*', caught her eye and she started to read:

'My father's final wish before he died was to be taken from the hospital to the crematorium. He requested that his ashes be scattered in the lake near the house where he'd spent the past twenty years with my mother. His family obliged.

Like so many families who have chosen to release their loved ones to the four winds; there's no Graham family plot, no headstone and no place for my mother, or any of my siblings, to spend time and reflect on the life of a man who brought life to so many others.

Statistics show us that society is leaning towards cremation, rather than traditional burials. It also shows us that the funeral service has gone from a somber occasion, to a celebration of life. *Shall We Gather At the River,* has been replaced with *Fly Me to the Moon*, and instead of sipping coffee and tea, mourners are sipping Chardonnay.'

"You can say that again," Angelina chuckled, remembering the champagne that had been flowing at Alex's visitation.

At the age of thirty-five, Angelina had been to several funerals, but never anything like the American funeral visitation this evening. Alex's horse was brought in from the ranch and placed in a twenty-by-twenty portable corral at the front of the building. Beside the corral, display tables were covered with the ribbons and trophies that Alex and the beautiful jet-black horse had won over the years.

Inside the funeral home, several picture boards took mourners on a trip down memory lane. They told the story of Alex Granger's life from the time she was born ... until her death. There were pictures of Alex as a child frolicking in the snow. There were pictures of her at horse shows and on hayrides. There were family Christmas pictures and pictures of summer vacations. Alex's graduation and wedding pictures were there, as was the snapshot Sarah told Angelina had been taken at Alex's fiftieth birthday party three weeks ago.

Looking at the woman's life through snapshots saddened Angelina. She hadn't spent much time with Alex in Mexico, but the pictures portrayed the life of a kind, caring, giving soul. Angelina knew that Alex would be missed. Sam had been terribly upset by her sudden death. In fact, he'd taken the news harder than Alex's own husband.

There's an interesting character, Angelina thought. Brian Williams was extremely charming, but there was something about him that Angelina didn't trust. Perhaps he was too smooth. She turned her attention back to the article and continued to read:

'So the funeral is over and in the eyes of the family, and the *"Director"*, it was a huge success. You've followed Uncle Charlie's final wishes and he's now hovering somewhere off the coast of Mexico. But then, you think: "Did I make a mistake? Who will know, that Uncle Charlie was ever here?"

Fear not. You no longer need a headstone to memorialize the loss of a loved one. Today, there are options that give the living a place or a way in which to remember the dead. Ingles and Hawthorne Funeral Home opened their *Memorial Park* in 1990. That year, they planted 500 trees. Since then, over 20,000 trees have been planted as a memory of people who once walked the earth.

At the entrance to the park, granite tablets list the names of family and friends who are now remembered in death through the life of Mother Nature. On any given day, hundreds of people wander through the park giving thanks to the trees that provide shade from the beating sun and protection from a biting north wind. With the creation of Ingles and Hawthorne's *Memorial Park*, Harvey Ingles has ensured that loved ones are never forgotten, but grow stronger each year'.

Angelina wasn't surprised that Harvey Ingles would create such a place. If there was such a thing, as a funeral director's ... funeral director, she was sure Harvey would be it. He was a kind, compassionate, soft-spoken man and his wife Jean, was charming. They welcomed her into their lives like a long-lost relative and made her feel right at home. Alex was a lucky woman to have had the love of such a family.

Angelina closed the magazine, turned off the lamp and stretched out on the sofa. She couldn't understand why anyone would want to be in the funeral business, but after reading the article, she was glad there were people like Harvey Ingles to help families deal with their grief.

The sound of footsteps on the hardwood floor woke Angelina. She lifted her head and peered over the back of the sofa. Brian Williams was standing at the desk. He opened the drawer and pulling out a small black book. She watched as he flipped through the pages, stopping when he found what he was looking for.

Brian picked up the telephone and punched out an eleven digit number. Impatiently, he drummed his fingers on the desk while he waiting for someone to answer. "*Hola*," he said. "*Estas seguro que el cuerpo en la caja es Alex*?" There was a pause before he added, "*Muy buen trabajo Carlos. Le hare la transferencia a su cuenta por la manana.*" He hung up the phone, turned off the light and left the library.

Lying in the darkness, Angelina couldn't believe what she just heard. Had Brian Williams really asked the person on the other end of the telephone if they were sure the body in the box was Alex? Then, congratulate them on a job well done, and tell them he would transfer the money tomorrow?

30

AT FOUR FORTY-FIVE p.m. sharp, Bart Bigalow took his place at the front door of Ingles and Hawthorne Funeral Home. He would wait there until the family limo arrived and once he'd shown them inside, take his place in the parking lot as this evening's parking attendant.

Bart would rather have been stationed inside helping funeral guests into the chapel, but after dropping off the wrong body for a service at St. Mary's this morning, he'd been put on a month's probation and ordered to take two weeks off without pay. The only reason he hadn't been sent home immediately, was because of Alex Granger's funeral tonight. They were anticipating a crowd of over four hundred people and every employee would be working the service

Bart spent his entire lunch break locked in an arrangement office trying to figure out his finances. He'd never been one of those organized financial wizards who always had three months wages stashed in a savings account. Bart lived paycheck to paycheck. He was very grateful that Ingles and Hawthorne supplied his suit, tie, shirt and shoes and paid the dry cleaning bill, or he'd be screwed.

At work, Bart used a company vehicle, so he'd managed to save money on gas, but his roommate moved out a month ago and he was having trouble scraping up his rent money. Two weeks without pay would put him behind the eight ball. As a last resort, he could always ask his mother for a loan, but she was having a hard enough time as it was paying for her cancer treatments.

When Bart spotted the Ingles and Hawthorne vehicles coming up the driveway, he quickly walked to the curb and stood at attention until the cars came to a stop in front of the funeral home. He opened the back door of the first vehicle; a vanilla Chrysler 300 Hemi, and Brian and Sarah Williams stepped out. Bart moved to the limo and opened the door. The first person to emerge was the Latin woman he'd seen last night at Alex Granger's visitation. She was strikingly beautiful and reminded him of Catherine Zeta-Jones in Zorro. Behind her the distinguished grey haired gentleman who'd been speaking with Leslie last night. Next, were Michael and Sharon Granger and their daughter.

Bart took the group into the funeral home, and led them to the family room where the immediate family would gather with relatives prior to the service. "Please, help yourself to the sandwiches and beverages. I believe you've given Leslie a list of the people you've asked to join you prior to the service. We'll bring them in as they arrive. Leslie will be in to see you shortly to explain the processional procedures for tonight's service. If there is anything else you need," Bart walked to the door and pointed to the bell on the wall. "Just press the button."

As Bart turned to leave, Brian grabbed him by the arm. "Hey, kid, can you show me where the can is?"

"Yes, of course, sir." Bart led Brian down the hall and stopped in front of the door to the men's restroom. "There you go."

"Could you come in with me for a minute?" Brian asked. "I want to talk to you about something." Bart followed Brian into the restroom and they stood at the sinks. "Listen, kid, if anyone asks you about the envelope with my wife's diary, tell them you put it in the memory drawer in her casket."

Bart shook his head. "But I didn't. I haven't even seen the envelope."

"I know," Brian smiled, "but if anyone asks, tell them I gave it to you last night and you put it in my wife's casket." He reached into his pocket, pulled out his money clip and peeled off fifty one-hundred-dollar bills. "This should more than take care of your little white lie."

Bart stared down at the money and shook his head. "But I couldn't. I ..."

"Come on kid," Brian smiled. "I know you guys only make twelve bucks an hour. How long would you have to work to make five grand?"

"Five grand?"

"That's right, and it's all yours."

"But, I ..."

"Look kid," Brian interrupted, "the envelope has my wife's diary in it. I don't want it buried with her. I want to keep it close to my heart so I'll always have a piece of her with me." He stared at the funeral attendant with pleading eyes. "You can understand can't you?"

Bart nervously kicked at the ceramic floor with the toe of his polished shoe. "Well ... when you put it that way." He stared down at the money. It was like a gift from God. He could pay off his bills, take a trip to the Caribbean during his two-week suspension and still have money left to give his mother. So what if the envelope wasn't actually in the casket? No one would check. The casket was sealed before it was set up in the chapel. Bart looked at Brian. "Well, I guess it is more important that you keep your wife's diary."

"That 'a boy." Brian gave the young man a friendly pat on the back. "Let's just say the five grand is a gift from my wife."

31

IT HAD BEEN FOUR months since Sarah put her mother in the ground and she was still going through the grieving process. She'd lost one set of grandparents and she remembered being sad, but losing her mother was devastating. Several long chats with her uncle Harvey had helped, and her aunt Jean had given her a book by Michael R. Leming and George E. Dickinson titled: *Understanding Dying, Death and Bereavement.*

Sarah hadn't read the book from cover to cover, but she'd picked up enough information to know that grief was a process everyone handled differently. She learned that it manifested itself in strange behavior and unexplained feelings. The book told Sarah that grief often included shock and denial. She'd experienced the shock ... when she learned of her mother's death and the denial ... when she viewed the body.

The book told Sarah that other symptoms of grief included disorganization, volatile reactions, guilt, loss and loneliness. She experienced bouts of guilt almost every day. If she would have gone to Mexico instead of covering shifts at the hospital, her mother would still be alive.

She hadn't been disorganized, but she'd become the world's biggest procrastinator. Every Saturday since the funeral, she stood at her mother's bedroom door trying to muster up the courage to go inside and clean out the closet. It was only today after having a long chat with herself, and drinking a bottle of Chardonnay, that she finally decided it was time.

Sarah slowly opened the door and stepped across the threshold. The air still held the faint aroma of Clinique

Aromatics Elixir; her mother's favorite fragrance, and she took a deep breath. Trembling legs carried her across the room to the bay window. She sat on the window seat and a warm smile found its way to her face, remembering the nights she and her mother had sat in this very spot sharing hot chocolate and girl talk.

It was times like this when Sarah felt the loss and loneliness that accompanied grief. The book told her that going through the stages of grief would eventually lead her to reestablishment. When that happened, she would be able to move from a world with her mother in it ... to a world without her. She had no idea when that would happen, but she knew for some people it took years.

Sarah stood up and slowly walked to the dresser where she picked up her parents' wedding picture. Her mother was stunning in the white satin gown and her father dashing in his black tie and tails. Looking at the picture now, Sarah felt like an orphan. Her mother was gone and her father had become a stranger. They'd hardly spoken since the funeral and, in the past three months, he'd been away more than he'd been at home.

Last month a man came to the house looking for her father. She told the stranger that she hadn't seen her father in weeks, and she wasn't expecting him home anytime soon. The man represented the company that manufactured her mother's diving gear. He asked if he could take it with him to examine and Sarah willingly turned it over. When her father called the next day and she told him what happened, he went ballistic. They hadn't spoken to each other since.

Sarah put the picture back on the dresser and forced her unwilling legs to carry her to the walk-in closet. She would go through the items, keep a few things for herself, and give the rest to charity.

Deciding to work her way from the top down, Sarah pulled out the step ladder her mother always kept in the corner and set it up at the back of the closet. There were eight western hat boxes on the top shelf and she took them down one by one. Climbing the ladder for the last hat box, Sarah lost her balance and slipped. She grabbed at the shelf, to save herself and in the process knocked the box onto the floor. It landed upside down.

Sarah climbed down from the step ladder and flipped the box over. The lid popped off and the contents tumbled onto the carpet. "What's this?" She reached over and picked up a stack of five-by-seven envelopes. They were tied into a neat package with a pink ribbon. She sat down on the carpet, crossed her legs and put the package in her lap. Carefully, she untied the bow and took the first envelope from the pile. She opened the flap and pulled out the contents. The letter was in her mother's handwriting. It was dated March 15, 1983 ... the day she was born.

She read the first paragraph of the letter out loud. "Our daughter was born today and she is the most beautiful thing I have ever seen. She looks just like you. I can see your strength in her eyes and her smile could melt an iceberg. You would be so proud." A broad smile erupted on Sarah's face and she continued to read:

> *I got to the hospital about one this after-noon. An intern examined me and told me I would be lucky if I had this child by midnight. I told her I planned on having this kid and being back in my room in time for dinner!*
>
> *At five p.m. a nurse examined me and told me I was only four centimeters. I rang for the nurse fifteen minutes later and told her I was having this child right now. Of course, being a first time mom, the nurse didn't believe me, but at least she had the decency to appease me and she checked. She was shocked to discover that I had gone from four centimeters to eight in fifteen minutes*

> *They rushed me to the delivery room and*
> *at five thirty-five our daughter entered the*
> *world with a bang! It was a beautiful experi-*
> *ence. I just wish you could have been there to*
> *share it with me.*
>
> *Alex*

Sarah folded the letter, put it back in the envelope and set it on the floor beside her. The second letter was dated March 15, 1984.

> *Today Sarah turned one and she had quite*
> *a party. While my mom and I were out shop-*
> *ping, my dad put our daughter and a choco-*
> *late cake in the tub, and let her have-at-it!*

Going through the letters describing her second, third, fourth and fifth birthdays, Sarah couldn't help but notice that they'd been written as if her father was absent from the event, but she couldn't remember one birthday in the past twenty-five years when her father hadn't been present.

She put the thought from her mind and reached for the next letter in the pile. It was written on different paper and dated, September 6, 1988.

> *Today, I received a phone call from my*
> *brother. He told me you were dead. He told*
> *me you were killed in a plane crash. I couldn't*
> *believe my ears. It was only two weeks ago*
> *when you held me in your arms for the first*
> *time in so very many years. We made plans.*
> *We promised each other that we would be to-*
> *gether for the rest of our lives. We were go-*
> *ing to be a family and now you're gone. I only*

wish I would have told you when I saw you
that Sarah was your daughter ...

Sarah dropped the letter on the floor. The blood drained from her face and she felt light-headed. What was her mother taking about? What did she mean she wished she would have told this man that he was her father? Brian Williams was her father. His name was on her birth certificate.

It dawned on Sarah then that the birthday letters she just read hadn't been written to her father ... they'd been written to someone else. She re-examined them again and again. Why had her mother been lying to her all these years? Who was this man her mother had loved and lost? She had to find out.

Sarah jumped to her feet and raced across the room to the telephone. She picked up the receiver and quickly she punched out her uncle Michael's seven digit phone number.

"Hello." A familiar female voice answered.

"Hi, Aunt Sharon, it's Sarah. Is Uncle Michael home?"

"Yes, he is."

"May I speak to him please?"

Three months later

32

AT THE SOUND OF the bell, Michael Granger raced to the front door, pulled it open and gave his guest a welcoming hug. "I'm so glad you're here. Please, come in." Michael took Sam's bag, set it in the foyer and led him down the hall to the library. "How was your flight?"

"Long," Sam yawned.

"I'll get us a drink. What's your pleasure?"

"A Scotch on the rocks would be great," Sam remarked over his shoulder.

"I'm sorry that I had to drag you all the way up here," Michael apologized as he handed Sam his drink, "but I needed to tell you this in person."

Michael had piqued Sam's curiosity when he called the resort yesterday and told him he needed to see him right away. He hadn't told Sam the reason, all he said was it concerned Sarah and Alex.

"Nice little shack you've got here in the Hamptons." Sam remarked admiring his surroundings.

"That's right. You haven't been here have you?"

Sam shook his head. "No. Grace and I were supposed to come for your housewarming three years ago, but I think we were detained by the Betty Ford Clinic!" He turned to Michael. "So, what's so important that you couldn't tell me over the phone?

"Let's sit down, shall we." Michael motioned to the wingbacks and the two men made themselves comfortable. "You're well aware from our conversation at Alex's funeral that I don't have much use for my brother-in-law. I never have, but my sister married him and he was a good father to Sarah, so I let a lot of things slide."

"What do you mean, he *was* a good father?" Sam asked. "Did something happen to him?"

"Oh, something happened to him all right. Yesterday, Brian was convicted of Alex's murder."

"Murder!" The color drained from Sam's face. "What do you mean he was convicted for Alex's murder? Alex died from a shark attack. We all know that."

"I thought so too," Michael agreed, "but after you told me about the conversation Angelina overheard Brian having the night before the funeral, I started having my suspicions. On the flight home a few days later, Eleanor and I were talking about Alex. She said she couldn't understand why her aunt would have gone diving, because she was afraid to dive. I asked her where she would come up with such a crazy idea because Alex loved to dive." Michael's eyes widened. "Then I remembered a conversation I had with Alex four years ago. She'd just come back from a dive with Brian to the Great Barrier Reef. She told me that they were down thirty feet when she ran out of air. She said she'd checked her tank not three minutes earlier and she had lots of air. She told me Brian had filled her tanks.

"As soon as we got home, I called a PI buddy of mine and asked him to do some snooping around. He went to the ranch and posed as a sales rep from the company that manufactured Alex's diving gear. Brian wasn't home, but Sarah willingly turned over the equipment. When he checked it out, he discovered that the needle on her air gauge had been glued into place. Taking into consideration what Alex told me about her little diving mishap with Brian, something about her death didn't sit right."

"But what about the shark attack?" Sam asked.

"When Greg examined Alex's wet suit, he found a lot of small rips and tears from the waist down. He figured she might have gotten caught in the caves where she was diving. That's when the shark got her.

"Caves?"

"Yeah, the company Alex went diving with that day took her to the caves at Las Marietas."

Sam shook his head. "I don't understand the connection."

"Brian gave Alex the diving gear for a birthday present, and made arrangements for her dive.

"Are you saying that Brian rigged Alex's air tank?"

"The district attorney and the jury seemed to think so."

"What I don't understand, if Alex was so afraid of diving, why did she go in the first place?"

"My sister always taught Sarah, and my daughter, to face their fears. Maybe Alex decided it was time she face her own."

"Daddy, Daddy," a voice called from the front door.

Michael's face lit up in a proud smile. "It sounds like my girls are home. Sharon took Eleanor shopping for new riding boots."

"And she must be wearing them!" Sam grinned as he listened to a clip-clopping running down the hardwood floor. For a moment, he was envious of Michael and his beautiful family. It had always been his dream to have a big house filled with the laughter of children.

Michael set his glass on the end table and stood up. "We'll finish this later."

At the entrance to the library, Eleanor Granger took a leap, by-passing the two steps leading from the hallway and raced across the room, into her father's open arms. "I missed you today, Dad. You should a come with us. It was a blast!"

"You should *have* come with us," her mother corrected. "Your grammar is atrocious young lady!" Sharon dropped her packages on the floor and gracefully walked across the room to greet Sam. "It's good to see you again," she smiled.

Sam rose to his feet and they embraced in a warm hug. "You have a beautiful home."

"Thank you, Sharon blushed. "We like it, don't we dear?"

"Yeah, it's great," Michael agreed.

"Hello Mr. Bennett," Eleanor released her arms from her father's waist. "Did Dad tell you that I have some questions about Mexican burial customs and dogs?"

"No, I'm afraid he didn't."

Eleanor planted her hands firmly on her hips and stared up at her father. "You promised."

"I'm sorry pumpkin," Michael apologized. "Mr. Bennett and I have been gabbing like old women since he got here."

Eleanor turned and smiled at Sam. "Mr. Bennett, about the dogs ..."

"Not now, Eleanor," Sharon interrupted. "You can ask your questions later." She motioned to the packages on the floor. "Be a dear and take these to your room. Then you can help me set the table."

Sam took a deep breath and his nostrils filled with the pleasant aroma of home cooking. "Something sure smells good."

"What are we having, Mom?" Eleanor asked.

"Rack of lamb; with a nice rosemary-mint sauce, rice pilaf and fresh asparagus. For dessert, a lovely glazed Grand Marnier cheesecake."

Sam's eyes lit up. "Wow ... that sounds great. Rack of lamb is one of my favorites."

"I know," Sharon winked. "Angelina told me. Now if you gentlemen will excuse me, I need to tend to dinner." She motioned to her daughter. "Come on Eleanor. Let's leave Dad and Mr. Bennett to talk."

When the women of the house were gone, Michael poured each of them another drink and their conversation picked up where it had left off. "I was telling you about Brian," Michael began. "Well, when my buddy discovered the gauge on Alex's tank had been glued, he started digging deeper. He asked me about Alex's money so I got in touch with Peter Bailey, Alex's lawyer. I think you met him at the funeral. Anyway, Peter told me that Brian was going through Alex's estate like it was water. He bought a jet and a condo in the Bahamas. Greg started following the paper trail and it led him to gambling, drugs and a hooker named Trixie."

Sam rolled his eyes, and let out a chuckle. "Trixie! That's an appropriate name for a *lady of the night.*"

"Anyway, this broad told Greg that she was with Brian the day Alex left for Mexico. He told her he didn't have any money to pay her but in two weeks, he'd give her ten times her going rate. When she jokingly asked him if he was planning on winning the power ball lottery, he told her he was planning on inheriting the family farm.

"Peter found a transaction that showed Brian deposited fifty grand into a bank account in the Cayman Islands. I gave the information to Greg and he discovered that the account belonged to a guy in Puerto Vallarta, who worked for the dive company Alex went diving with."

Michael took a deep breath and slowly exhaled. "Apparently, Brian planned the whole thing before Alex even left for Mexico. He made arrangements for this Carlos guy to take her diving. That, and the fact that Alex's air tanks had been messed with, plus a statement from the hooker, led the police to believe that my sister's death wasn't accidental."

"So, let me get this straight, Brian gave Alex the diving gear for her birthday and booked her dive with the sole intention of killing her? But why?" Sam asked.

"Alex told me, not long before she left for her Mexican vacation, that she was fed up with Brian's bullshit. When I was at Peter's office he told me she'd filed for a divorce. He drew up the papers before she left for Mexico, but she didn't sign them. According to Peter, she was going to take care of it when she got home. Alex threatened Brian lots of times with divorce. I think the only reason she didn't leave him was because of Sarah. Maybe my brother-in-law got wind of her plans. Alex was worth a lot of coin. If she divorced him he'd get jack-shit. Now, he won't get anything. He's upstate doing twenty-five to life."

"What ever happened to this Carlos person?" Sam asked.

"He's in jail in Mexico."

Sam stood up and paced the room. "God, Michael. This is crazy. Alex and I talked about her husband when she was at the resort. He sounded like a real jackass, but to murder her, that's unbelievable. Her daughter must be devastated."

"Not as much as you'd think. Sarah came upon some information while she was cleaning out Alex's closet three months ago. That's helped her get through it."

"Dinner," Sharon's sweet voice called out from the formal dining room.

An hour later, having enjoyed a feast fit for a king, and enchanting conversation; most of it provided by Eleanor, Sam felt more relaxed than he had in months.

"Sam, may I interest you in coffee and dessert?"

"Coffee sounds great, Sharon, but I think I'll pass on dessert. Dinner was fantastic and I'm stuffed."

"Mom, can I talk to Mr. Bennett now about the dog?" Eleanor asked.

"Yes, Eleanor," Sharon smiled, "as long as Mr. Bennett doesn't mind."

Sam leaned across the table towards the charming young child. "How about we drop the Mr. Why don't you just call me uncle Sam?"

"Okay, Uncle Sam," Eleanor beamed. She folded her arms on the dining room table and her expression turned serious. "Do you remember when we were talking at my aunt Alex's funeral and you asked me about my dog, Bernard?"

"Yes."

"And do you remember talking about what Angelina told me that a dog is very important in the Mexican culture?"

"Yes."

"And that a dog goes with a dead person to give them eyes to see into the next life?"

"Yes," Sam smiled. "I remember talking about that. You were going to put Bernard, in the casket with your ..." Sam stopped in mid-sentence. "Oh, I'm sorry," he apologized.

"Oh, it's okay," Eleanor reassured him. "We can talk about my aunt Alex's death. It's good to talk about it. It helps us move from a world with our loved one in it, to a world without them."

Sam was astonished by the young girl's maturity. He turned and grinned at Michael. "Are you sure Eleanor isn't a vertically challenged thirty-year-old?"

"Sometimes I wonder," Michael laughed.

Sam turned his attention back to the child. "Yes, you told me that you wanted to put Bernard in the casket with your aunt Alex. I believe Leslie was going to do that for you. She was going to talk to your uncle Brian."

"She did talk to my uncle Brian but he wouldn't let her open the casket once it was closed."

"So you didn't get to send Bernard with your aunt?"

"Well, I kind of did." Eleanor's face turned red and she flashed Sam a sheepish grin. "After the funeral, after they put Aunt Alex into the ground, and everybody was back at the house, I put Bernard in a box and went back to the cemetery and I put him in the grave with Aunt Alex. Do you think he'll still be able to guide her even if he isn't right beside her?"

"I'm positive," Sam smiled.

Eleanor jumped at the sound of the telephone. "I'll get it. It's probably Bradley Carlton," She pushed herself away from the table. "Can you imagine anyone naming their child after a soap opera character," she giggled, as she dashed from the room.

"Who's Bradley Carlton?" Sam asked.

"Eleanor's, first crush. She'll be twelve next month, so she figures she should have a boyfriend. Her mother and I don't agree, but Bradley is the son of a colleague and he's a nice, polite kid."

"Here we go, gentlemen." Sharon gave them each a steaming cup of coffee. "Are you sure I can't talk you into dessert, Sam?"

"Oh, no thank you, Sharon. I couldn't eat another thing."

"Well, if you change your mind, I'll leave it in the fridge. Just help yourself. *Mi casa su casa* or something like that," she winked. "Now, if you'll excuse me I have to make some phone calls for the Parent-Teachers' Association. If I don't see you later, Sam, have a good evening and we'll chat at breakfast."

"I'm going to have to leave here pretty early to get to the airport," Sam frowned, "so I probably won't see you."

"Trust me, Sam," Sharon grinned, "I'll be seeing you in the morning."

When Sharon was gone, Michael opened the bottom drawer of the china cabinet and pulled out a bottle of Cognac. "My dad's brother-in-law, Harvey, gave him this the day I was born. As tradition goes," Michael set the bottle on the table. "I was supposed to give it to my brother-in-law the day his first child was born. I didn't, because I thought Brian was an asshole."

A smile came to Michael's face. "They say that everything happens for a reason. I guess the reason he didn't get it was because he wasn't supposed to have it."

Michael had no idea how Sam was going to take the bombshell he was about to drop. He could only hope for the best. He took a deep breath and slowly exhaled. "Do you remember me telling you before dinner that Sarah found something that helped her deal with the fact that her father murdered her mother?"

"Yes." Sam nodded.

"When Sarah finally got up the nerve to clean out Alex's closet she found a box of letters."

"Letters?"

"Yes," Michael smiled. "They were letters to Sarah's father, a man Alex loved very much. There were twenty-five of them, one for every year of Sarah's life."

"Alex told me she didn't love Brian. She told me she was planning on getting a divorce."

"I didn't say the letters were for Brian," Michael smiled. "I said they were for Sarah's father."

Sam shook his head. "Now, I'm really confused."

"The letters weren't written to Brian. They were written to you ... Sam."

"Me? What makes you think they were written to me? I'm not Sarah's father."

"But that's just it. You are her father."

Sam stood up and paced around the dining room table. "Michael, that's impossible. How could I be Sarah's father?"

"One of the letters Sarah found was about the night she was conceived in Campbell River. I couldn't recall Alex and Brian every going to Campbell River, and I sure as hell never went fishing with him, so I figured the person Alex was talking about had to be you."

Sam stopped dead in his tracks. "Campbell River. Alex got pregnant when we were in Campbell River." He pulled out a dining room chair and sat down. His expression was blank. *Why didn't you tell me, Alex?* Sam thought. *Things would have been so different if you would have only told me.* Sam stared across the table at his best friend. "I've kept this from you for years. I guess it's time to spill my guts. Alex and I made plans in Campbell River to get married. I talked to her three weeks later. It was the night before I was leaving for Bermuda. I remember that conversation as if it happened only yesterday. She told me how much she loved me and how happy our lives would be together. She never mentioned anything about being pregnant. Surely she would have known. If she would have told me I wouldn't have caved at Moe Sanderson's threat."

"What threat?" Michael asked.

"The night I was leaving for Bermuda to get everything ready for Alex's and my wedding, I got pulled over by customs. They found cocaine in my briefcase. Grace's father as much as admitted he planted it there. He told me that if I didn't go through with my marriage to his daughter, he'd call the cops."

Michael shook his head and grinned. "You know, I always wondered why that grand wedding of yours was cancelled in favor of a private family function."

"Moe told me he'd harm Alex if I ever went near her again. I couldn't call and tell her I was backing out of my proposal ... to marry Grace. I hadn't even told Alex that I was engaged. Moe made sure that our wedding picture was on the front page of every paper in the country. I knew when Alex saw it, she'd hate me and I was right."

Michael poured them each another drink. "I always wondered why Alex married Brian. Now that I think about it, their wedding wasn't too long after yours. When Sarah was born, Alex told everyone that she was premature."

For twenty-five years, Sam had kept his secret love of Alex locked deep in his heart. They'd found each other again ... when she was in Mexico and now she was dead, killed at the hands of her own husband, a man Alex had lied to about a child ... his child. "Michael, I don't know what to say."

"You don't have to say anything," Michael re-assured him. "I know how much my sister meant to you. Sarah left the letters here. I'll give them to you to read."

"Speaking of Sarah, she must be completely beside herself over all this, learning that her father killed her mother and then discovering that Brian isn't her father at all." Sam put his elbows on the table and rested his head in his hands. "Who does she have for a father? Some dumb-ass jerk, who disappeared on her mother before she was even born?"

Michael reached over and squeezed Sam's shoulder. "Don't go beating yourself up. Sarah was upset at first. In fact, the day she phoned me and told me about the letters she was frantic. I flew to Denver and we had a long chat. I told her about your so-called death and I told her you did it to protect her and her mother. I told her that Grace had threatened her life. After that, she started looking at things a bit differently."

"What should I do Michael? Should I call her?"

"No. She said you were charming and she could understand how her mother had fallen in love with you." Michael gave Sam an encouraging smile. "I'm sure you're as curious about her as she is about you. If you like, I have Alex's collection of home movies. There's a VCR in the guest room."

The chimes from the grandfather clock rang out ten times. Sam needed to call the airport and cancel his flight. Wedding or no wedding, he couldn't go home now. "I know I said I was only staying the night, but would you mind if I hung out for a few days. This is a lot to digest."

"I figured you'd want to do that," Michael smiled. "Sarah is staying in the city with friends. She was here for Brian's trial. I've made arrangements for the three of us to have lunch on Saturday."

33

BEFORE SETTLING DOWN TO watch the home movies Michael had given him, Sam knew he had to call Angelina and he wasn't looking forward to the reaction she'd have when he told her he wasn't coming home tomorrow. He couldn't leave now ... not after learning that Sarah was his own flesh and blood. He flipped open his cell phone and punched out the resort's phone number.

"*Buenas noches, Las Tropicales.* How may I direct your call?"

"*Hola,* it's Sam. Who's this?"

"Ah *Señor* Bennett. This is Juanita. What may I help you with this evening? Would you like to talk to your bride? She is very anxious for the wedding on Saturday!"

"Yes. Is she in the office?"

"*Si, Señor.*"

"Put me through, please."

The phone rang three times before the familiar voice answered. "*Buenas noches.* This is Angelina Rodriguez."

"Hi. It's Sam."

There was excitement in Angelina's voice when she spoke. "Sam! I wasn't expecting to hear from you tonight. Did your flight time get changed? Let me get a pen and write it down. Hang on a minute."

"Wait, Angelina. You don't have to write anything down. My flight times didn't get changed."

"So you will be home at three tomorrow afternoon. You've only been gone since this morning and I miss you already!"

"Angelina, I won't be coming home tomorrow." There was dead air only seconds before the explosion.

"What do you mean you won't be coming home tomorrow? We're getting married on Saturday. There are still many last minute things that need to be taken care of, and ..."

"Angie, about the wedding," Sam interrupted. "I'm afraid that something's come up and we're going to have to put it off for a week or so."

Angelina's anger turned to sorrow and she started to cry. "Why are you doing this to me?" she sobbed. "Don't you love me? Has this all been a sick joke?"

"Angelina, please let me explain."

"What is there to explain? You asked me to marry you and now you're backing out?"

"Angie, I'm not backing out. It's just that ..."

"You are backing out," Angelina sobbed. "You're going to leave me standing at the altar ... just like you left Alex!"

"Angelina, please stop crying. I'm not going to leave you standing at the altar. I love you. I just need to postpone the wedding for a few days, that's all."

"But why?" she asked in a whisper. "Everything has been arranged. What could be more important than our wedding day?"

What was more important right now was Sarah ... the daughter Sam never knew existed. "Angelina, I do want to marry you," he reassured his bride-to-be. "I love you. Please don't cry."

"But, Sam, you promised."

"I know, and I'll keep my promise. We'll get married, just not on Saturday."

"But, why?" Angelina pleaded.

"I just found out from Michael that Alex's husband has been convicted of her murder."

"Convicted of her murder? How is this possible?"

For the next five minutes, Sam told Angelina of the investigation leading up to Brian's arrest and conviction. He told her if she hadn't overhead Brian's telephone conversation the night before Alex's funeral, he might have gotten away with it.

"But why do you have to be in New York for Alex's daughter?" Angelina asked. "Her aunt and uncle are there."

"Angelina, you know how much I love you. If I didn't love you, I never would have asked you to marry me. I loved Alex too. I just think I need to be there right now for her daughter." Sam's voice was soft and compassionate. "You do understand, don't you?

When Angelina spoke again, her voice was calm and warm. "If Alex's daughter needs your support, then you must be there for her. You were close with her mother and I think I understand why you must do this. I know you love me, Sam. I love you with all my heart. We will be together for the rest of our lives, so I guess one more week won't make a difference. I'll contact our guests and let them know that there has been a change in plans."

Sam let out a sigh of relief. "Thank you, Angelina. Your kind heart and compassion for other people is only one of the many reasons I love you like I do."

"How long will Sarah be in New York?" Angelina asked.

"I don't know. Michael didn't say. Two or three days I guess. I'm having lunch with her on Saturday."

"I have an idea," Angelina announced.

"What's that?" he asked.

"Why don't you bring Sarah to *Las Tropicales*? I'm sure it would help get her mind off this terrible tragedy."

"You wouldn't mind?"

"Of course not."

Sam's voice filled with excitement. "I think that's a great idea. I'll call the airline in the morning and make the arrangements. I love you Angelina. Thanks for understanding and I promise I'll make this up to you when I get home."

"Call me when you have made your flight arranged and I'll have a room prepared for Sarah."

"Thanks for understanding. I love you."
"I love you too."

34

SARAH HAD SPENT PRACTICALLY every waking hour with Sam since their arrival at *Las Tropicales* a week ago. Their meeting in New York had only touched the tip of the iceberg and Sarah had an urgency to learn all she could about her real father. When Sam suggested she return to Mexico with him she couldn't refuse.

Yesterday, Sarah and Angelina had gone for a long walk down the beach. They talked about Sam and his first wife, Grace. A woman Sarah didn't know existed until she found the letters in her mother's closet. Listening to Angelina, Sarah could tell that the beautiful Cuban woman was in love with Sam and she knew she would make him a fine wife.

When they talked about Brian and the details surrounding his arrest, Angelina told Sarah that she could only imagine how difficult it was to learn that her father had been responsible for her mother's death. Sarah wanted to tell her that Brian wasn't her father, but Sam had made her promise to keep that *'family secret'* to herself for the time being. He said he would break the news to Angelina when the time was right.

Sarah felt a hand on her shoulder and she turned around. Sam was standing behind her; his face lit up in a proud smile. "You ready to go?" he asked.

She smiled and kissed him on the cheek. "I really appreciate you doing all of this for me. I've always believed that things happen for a reason. You gave up your life once to protect me. Maybe Mom's life was taken to bring us together. If this wouldn't have happened, I may never have known that you existed, and that would have been a terrible loss." She threw her arms around him and gave him a warm hug. "I just know that the last days of my mother's life were the happiest because she was with you."

Sam wiped a tear from Sarah's cheek and gave her a proud fatherly smile. "Thank you for saying that. It really means a lot." He kissed her on the forehead. "Well, we've taken all but one of the tours I was on with your mother. You went swimming with the dolphins. Yesterday we were in Las Caletas, the day before Puerto Vallarta and today, we're going on a Sierra Madre expedition."

Fifteen minutes later, Sam and Sarah were at Vallarta Adventures being briefed on their day "*Hola,* my name is Raoul. How is everyone doing this morning?" The group of fifty erupted in cheers. "This tour is about energy and motivation, so our staff has to be motivated." He pointed to the gentlemen standing to his left. "A way to motivate the staff, and prove your energy, is by saying, *buenos dias.*" The group repeated the Mexican greeting and the staff members booed.

"Okay," Raoul frowned, "we are going to give you one more chance to say *buenos dias.* If it is not good this time," he waved his hand and turned his back on his audience, "we send all of you back to your hotels! Okay, so let's hear it."

"*Buenos dias,*" the tour group replied.

A beaming smile danced across his face. "Now that's what I'm talking about." He pointed to the men on his right. "These six-sexy boys right here, they are the drivers. They are going to take care of you and whatever they want, you give it to them, like your wallet, your sunglasses, your necklace, even your wife." Laughter rumbled through the group. "Now you have to keep these guys happy all day, and always motivated, because your life ... and my life ... it is in their hands. So what about a nice applause for our drivers?"

Raoul pointed to the door. "Outside we have the rock stars. They are our tour guides." He waved his arm. "Come in rock stars." Six Mexican men ranging in age from twenty to thirty entered the staging area. "Whatever you want to know about

Mexico, if they know the answer, they will tell you. If they don't know, they will make it up," Raoul laughed. "You also have to keep your guides happy and working hard, so give them a hard time with you questions and make them cry!" The guides rubbed their eyes with their knuckles. "If you make them cry, we give you a bottle of tequila! So what about a nice applause for our guides?"

When the group quieted, Raoul went on to explain the tour procedure. "First of all, we are going to jump into our open-air limousines. Everyone has seen these big yellow vehicles parked out front? They are Mercedes Benz all-terrain vehicles. Each jeep will hold twelve people." He patted his backside. "Not to worry, the place where you sit, it is padded, and you have also the holy-shit handle."

"What's that?" a woman asked.

"You will find out, when you are going on the bumpy road and you reach for the handle and say, HOLY SHIT!" He clapped his hands. "Okay let me tell you about this day. First we are going to start driving inside the area and we are going to stop in a little town and we are going to show you what real Mexico looks like. We are going to walk around a little plaza and go to the church in that village. You will have ten minutes to walk around and take pictures."

The tour guide's smile turned serious. "Now, this is very important. You must use the toilet in that town because you will not have another chance. When we leave this town, we are going to drive inside the valley area and we are going to show you most of the crops we have. Then we have another stop in a little house and we are going to show you how real Mexican people live down here. Then, we will have a stop in the forest and we are going to do a nature walk. We are going to walk in the forest for about forty-five minutes to an hour. If you survive," he smiled, "we will give you a *cerveza*. Then we will drive towards the beach where lunch is waiting for us."

One of the guides leaned over and whispered something in Raoul's ear. "Okay guys, we just had news that the chef, he didn't show up today. He got divorced about a week ago. Good for him," Raoul chuckled, "and he is still on the fiesta so the guides are also going to provide us with lunch. Roadside service," his expression turned serious, "road kill, anything that comes in the way. Donkey ... pelican ... iguana!" He clapped his hands. "Okay, guys, next to the grill, we have an open bar..."

Sam leaned closer to Sarah. "These tours go from *Las Tropicales* during high season and most participants are loaded by the time they get back at four."

"Do people really drink that much during lunch?" Sarah asked.

"Yes," Sam smiled, "and they don't stop drinking all the way back to the resort. We had one guest who was so loaded he fell out of the jeep at the resort and broke his leg."

Sarah shook her head. "You know, I never could understand the concept of spending your whole vacation blasted! When I was down here the first time with friends from school, two of them were drunk the entire week." She gave Sam a shy grin. "You probably don't remember, but I met you the first time I stayed at the resort."

Sam raised a questioning brow. "You did?"

"Yes." Her face turned red. "You actually checked us in when we arrived. My girlfriends thought you were pretty HOT!"

"Well, you probably don't remember, but we met long before that."

"We did?"

"Yes," Sam smiled. "I think you were about five or six. It was two days before your uncle's wedding. You were in the corral, feeding carrots to your pony."

"That was you?"

"It was me!"

Sarah hooked her arm in Sam's. "Who'd have thought then, that someday we'd be together like this? It's amazing, where the road of life takes you." They smiled at each other then and turned their attention back to front of the staging area.

"We are going to stay on the beach for one and a half hours," Raoul advised his eager audience. "Eat lunch, have a few drinks and enjoy the ocean. The only problem with the ocean is guys, it is the open sea, so be aware of the shoreline. If there are two red flags, don't swim. When we leave the beach we are going to drive you back to your hotels. It takes an hour more or less to get home and we are going to have a bottle of tequila during this time." Raoul looked at his watch. "You will be back at your hotels by five-thirty and the tour will be done. "Is everybody ready?" he asked. "Okay, let's go!"

Sarah and Sam were placed in a jeep with a family of three from Great Britain, and two Texas gentlemen accompanied by their sons. "*Hola Señor y Señoritas.* My name is Pablo," the tour guide announced. "We are going to see lots of things today," he smiled, "but first you must buckle yourself in your seat. This will be a bumpy ride and we don't want to lose anyone." He pointed to the leather straps hanging from the roof of the vehicle. "Those are the holy-shit handles Raoul was telling you about. Trust me," he grinned, "before the day is over, you will be using these handles"

Pablo gave his group a smile. "Today for you guys, it is going to be a very long day. This is a very educational tour. All of the different things you are going to hear about today is about the conditions in Mexico and the trees, plants and animals. My mission is to make sure that you become Mexican, so we are going to be like a Mexican family. I am going to put a Mexican name to this family. Today, you are going to be the *Frijoles* family. So, when we are walking around today in the villages and you hear me yell *Frijoles* you will know that I am talking about you. This way, we can all stay together and no one will get lost or left behind."

When everyone was strapped in, Pablo said something to the driver in Spanish and the Mercedes jeep pulled out of the lot and onto the highway. "As we travel, I will tell you about my Mexico. Mexico City is the most populated city. There, we have *eh* thirty-two million people." He turned and looked at one of the young boys from Texas. "That is a lot of people, *si*?"

"*Si*," the young boy blushed.

"In Canada for example," Pablo smiled, "there are only thirty million people in the whole country. So, I will give you some advice. If you ever get a chance to go to Mexico City," he shook his index finger in the air. "Don't go!"

Pablo looked over his shoulder and pointed. "Bay of the Flags is the name of this bay right here. It is in the middle of two states. The State of *Nayarit* to the north and *Jalisco* to the south. In the middle of the bay we have a river and that river divides the two states and also divides the two time zones. When you cross that river, you are one hour younger."

As the convoy proceeded up the highway, Pablo talked about the weather. "Right here we have only two seasons, the dry season and the rainy season. The rainy season starts in June and at this time, it is going to rain for three or four months. It is going to rain all the time and at night it comes with a lot of thunder and lightening. We have eighty inches of rain right here and this is what it's going to be for three to four months ..."

Sarah leaned closer to Sam. "You know, I was really upset when I found Mom's letters and discovered that Brian wasn't my father. When he was arrested for her murder, I was devastated." She dropped her head. "Mom and Dad, I mean, Brian, had their problems over the years but I still can't believe that he killed her."

Sam put his arm around Sarah's shoulder. "According to what the detectives uncovered, Brian had some major gambling debts and when he found out that your mom was going to divorce him, he knew he'd be screwed."

Sarah let out a sigh. "A lot of good the money is doing him now, and besides, he wouldn't have gotten it anyway, not the way Mom's will read."

"No one knew that Brian wasn't your biological father. People may have questioned the wording of your mother's will, but that's probably as far as it would have gone."

"Sometimes I get really mad at Mom. If she would have divulged this *family secret*, she may still be here."

"Your mom wouldn't have had any reason to tell you. She thought I was dead." Sam pulled her closer. "She may not be here anymore, but I am. I'll always be here for you, Sarah."

When the jeep came to a stop, Pablo stood up and clapped his hands. "Okay, we are here in the first village. The name of this village is *San Jose*." A goofy grin broke out on his face. "So guys, today I have already shown you the way to *San Jose*!"

Pablo climbed out of the jeep and the group followed him across the street to the plaza. "One thing that is very important that you will always find here in the plaza in the Mexican villages ... there is a cathedral, the main square, a school and the government office. Please follow me."

He led his tour group up the steps and into the plaza's gazebo. "This is like a bandstand in America, yes? Every town has one of these." He moved to the centre of the structure. "If you stay right here, in the middle, you are going to hear an echo sound. That is why it is designed this way. When you stand in the middle and talk your voice echoes so the villagers who are standing around can hear." He pointed around the square. "This is a very unique town. First of all, everyone knows Mexico was conquered by the Spanish, but who conquered the Spanish?" Pablo pointed to Sarah. "Do you know the answer to this question *Señorita*?"

Sarah shook her head. "I'm sorry to say, I don't."

"I will tell you. The Moorish conquered Spain and that is why you will see a lot of arches and even domes on the tops of houses. That is a Moorish tradition and so is the combination of colors." Pablo pointed to the homes on the street. "Do you notice that all the houses are painted two colors? I will tell you the reason for this. Back in the revolution the government didn't give the school to the people, so the people didn't know how to read. So, how do they shop? The people recognize several places where they have to buy food, tortillas, milk, and to recognize these places they paint the shop in a combination of colors. Everybody knows the color of *cerveza*, right?"

"*Si Amigo,*" one of the men from Texas piped up. "The colors are blue, yellow and white."

"*Si Señor,*" Pablo smiled, "this is correct. Okay, you are always going to put the dark color on the bottom of the shop because it is easier to clean." Again, he pointed to the buildings surrounding the square. "Check it out, like that house over there. Remember the street used to be full of dirt so when a car was driving by, the dirt on the street would be on the building. So, for the people, it was easier to clean."

Pablo rubbed his chin with the tips of his fingers. "We are called the people of the corn. Years ago there was a God and the people actually believed they were made out of corn. We eat a lot of corn. Every single Mexican eats tortillas three times a day. We are made out of corn ... we eat corn ... we are very corny people," he laughed. "People of the corn, what can I tell you about these things. We have more than fifty species of corn. All the colors of the rainbow we got it from the corn. The original corn, it was from Mexico. We have thirty-five species of cactus and we can eat this cactus. We cook it, boil it and even eat it raw." Pablo clapped his hands. "Okay, I am going to let you have ten minutes to walk around and then we will be back in the jeep and on our way."

Their next stop on the tour was a Mexican graveyard. Listening to Pablo speak reiterated the Mexican belief that there is life after this one. "Did I tell you that I used to work in a funeral home?" Pablo smiled. "I am not from here. I am from California. Before coming here to this place I used to be in charge of a big funeral home in Baja, California. So, when I came here I was really surprised to see how people celebrate November second, *The Day of the Dead*. Have you ever heard about this?" he asked. "I was really impressed so I am going to tell you something else. In Mexico, eighty-five per cent of the people here are Catholic and very devoted to Saint Mary and the people have very strong family ties. These people care for the family, even the people who are dead. I was very surprised when I went to the State of *Jalisco* because that is a very traditional state from Mexico. It is where the tequila was born and also the mariachi music."

Pablo's smile got bigger. "So, when I went over there what I saw in the graveyard was on November second a big fiesta. A big fiesta and everyone was having a great time. They were drinking tequila and they were eating food and dancing. Everything was filled with flowers. I am going to make an example," he smiled. "Let's say my father dies. My father used to love tequila and tamales. Do you know tamales? You got to try tamales," Pablo grinned "Tamales are a very traditional food right here. It is made with dough and put the dough with vegetables, chicken or pork and wrapped in leafs to cook."

Pablo clapped his hands. "Okay, so here we are at the cemetery. So, on November second I would come to the graveyard and I will drink a couple of shots of tequila and eat tamales Then, I will leave a couple of tamales on the gravestone. In Mexico, and this is an Aztec tradition also, we believe that our people are going to come from the dead so they can eat these things and continue to travel to the other world."

Sarah turned to Sam. "You know, things would be so much easier if people in the States looked at death the way the Mexicans do. Mom would have thought a celebration was a great idea. Maybe next year, we can do something for her on November second."

"We will," Sam smiled.

When the twelve-passenger jeep pulled back onto the main road, Pablo opened the cooler at his feet and offered his passengers a *cerveza* "Okay, now we are going to have refreshments."

"But it's only ten in the morning," the woman from Britain remarked.

"*Si*," Pablo replied, "but it is cocktail hour somewhere in the world!"

Sarah turned to Sam. "I'm sure Mom didn't partake of a beverage this early in the morning."

"Actually, she did," Sam chuckled. "When she turned down the beer, our guide offered her tequila. She said no to that too, but our guide told her he'd make her something special."

"What was that?" Sarah asked.

"I'll get you one."

Sam said something to Pablo in Spanish and the Mexican tour guide's face lit up in a big smile. "*Si, Señor.*" He took a white Styrofoam cup from inside his cooler and poured in tequila until the glass was one-third full. He added Pacifico beer and filled the remaining third of the cup with lemon-lime soda.

Sarah screwed up her face. "You've got to be kidding, right?"

"Try it," Pablo encouraged. "You will enjoy it. Trust me." He handed Sarah the cup. "Fold it like a taco then it is easier to drink."

Sarah followed Pablo's instructions and held the cup to her lips. She took a drink and her face lit up. "You're right. This is very refreshing. I can't even taste the tequila!" She passed her cup to Anna, the British woman sitting beside her. "Here, try it."

Anna took a sip. "Yes, this is very good," she smiled. "I'll have one as well, please."

The next stop on their tour was a small Mexican farm that Sarah thought was located in the middle of nowhere. In the front yard, Pablo showed them lime trees and explained that lime had many uses. Some of which Sarah would never have though of. "Okay, here in Mexico," Pablo smiled, "when you don't have time to put the deodorant, you go to the market. You buy a lime, you cut it in half and you squeeze it in your armpits. I have seen people also put lime on their heads to make the hair flat."

Pablo took the group through the yard and told them about the trees and crops grown on the land. "This is not a thistle. It is a very thick root and we make a lot of salsa with this root. Do you remember me telling you about the jack fruit? You need to try this fruit. Go to the fruit stand and ask for *jacka* and you are going to try one of the sweetest fruits ever. This fruit can weigh up to forty pounds. Inside it looks like a little orange. The color is yellow with orange in the middle and that is what you are going to eat."

Sam leaned over and whispered in Sarah's ear. "There's a fruit stand not far from the resort. We can check it out tomorrow if you like."

"That sounds great," she smiled.

"Please follow me," Pablo said. He led the group across the yard to the small farm house. "Okay guys, let's go inside." The group followed him through the door. "In this house, this kitchen you see here to the right is the summer kitchen. It is made from adobe bricks. To make these bricks to build the houses you take a mixture of sandy clay, straw and water and then use the sunshine to dry it. The thing is," he smiled, "when the rainy season starts, it gets so hot inside the house that the cook has to come outside and cook right here. The *Señora*," Pablo pointed to the Mexican woman with the friendly smile, "is going to make you a taco from tortillas, the corn. Remember I said we are the people of the corn? Well, now you are going to taste a handmade tortilla with salsa that is handmade from the cactus, onion, tomatoes and chilies. And there is the guacamole. No taco is going to be more Mexican than that."

Pablo held up a small bag of flour. "Modern technology can give us corn flour and we only have to mix it with hot water and we got dough for tortillas. See the colors on the bag. Green and white, tortilla colors right here. This is one of the most famous corn flours in Mexico. Okay, everyone get your tortilla and we will meet back by the jeep in ten minutes."

The group's next stop was a nature hike through the rain forest. "First of all," Pablo began, "these kinds of conditions you see right here is not a jungle. Jungle means dense vegetation. This is a tropical forest. There are no jungles in America. Jungles you are going to find in India, Africa. In Mexico, this is called a *selva*, so let's walk through the *selva*. But first, you must put on the bug spray."

Forty minutes after learning about the vegetation and inhabitants of the tropical forest, Pablo loaded his group back into the jeep. On the way to the beach, where they would enjoy their barbecue, Pablo shared many stories of Mexico. "Over on the other side of Mexico, by Cancun, they call this the Yucatan Peninsula. The guy who went to the Mayan ruins, he asked to the people. What is the name of this place and the Mayan people answered, Yucatan. And he thought, wow, this is a beautiful place, this place is called Yucatan. Actually," Pablo smiled, "what the Mayan guy was saying is we don't understand your language!"

By the time the group arrived at the beach to meet up with the other forty people, who had been at the orientation, Sam was starving. He grabbed Sarah's arm and led her past the bar directly to the buffet table. They filled their plates and found a spot under the shade of a palm tree.

Sarah watched in amazement as Sam devoured the food on his plate. "You must be hungry," she chuckled. "You're an eating machine just like my uncle Michael."

"We used to have eating contests when we were in college." Sam wiped his mouth with his napkin and pushed his empty plate aside.

"You really shouldn't eat that fast, it's not good for you," Sarah scolded.

"Are you giving me daughterly advice?" Sam asked.

"Yes," she smiled, "I guess I am. You don't mind do you?"

"No. I don't mind at all."

"Speaking of our father-daughter relationship," Sarah leaned across the table, "when are you going to tell Angelina that she's inheriting a step-daughter? I've almost let it slip a couple of times this week."

Sam's expression turned serious. "I am doing the right thing, aren't I?"

"What do you mean?" Sarah asked.

"Marrying … Angelina. She's been a really good friend to me over the years and I trust her with my life, but it's only been seven months since your mom died and somehow I feel like I'm cheating on her."

Sarah reached out and took his hand. "Sam, I know that Mom loved you very much and I know that you loved her too, but she's gone. She would want you to be happy. Like I said this morning, the last days of her life were the happiest because you were in them. She'll always have a place in your heart and I know she wouldn't want you to spend the rest of your life alone."

"I'm not going to be alone," Sam smiled. "I have you."

"Yes, you do, but I can't stay here forever. I have to get back to the hospital to finish my internship."

"So, finish your intern thing and move to Mexico. You can have one of the management apartments and we can see each other every day."

"That sounds great," Sarah smiled, "but you've hardly spent any time with your soon-to-be bride since we arrived. If I moved here, she'd be asking for a divorce." Sarah raised a concerned brow. "Speaking of my step-mother, when do you plan on telling her about me?"

"I thought I'd do it tonight at dinner," Sam smiled. "I told her I had a big surprise for her."

Sarah rolled her eyes and let out a chuckle. "Oh, I'm sure she'll be surprised."

35

SAM STARED BLANKLY INTO his empty wine glass. *Twenty-five years,* he thought. *Twenty-five years and I didn't know until last week that I had a child.* His first reaction to Michael's news was shock. It was followed by anger. He was angry at Alex for keeping Sarah a secret. If he would have known the child Grace threatened to kill was his own, he would have killed her himself long before she ever overdosed on cocaine. For years, he'd lived with Grace when he should have been with Alex and their daughter. Now, Alex was gone and in two days, he would marry another woman.

Sam loved Angelina. She was a kind, caring, compassionate person and she would make a fine wife. He trusted her with his life. When Grace died, Angelina blamed herself, but Sam reassured her that Grace had always been headed for an overdose. He was only surprised it had taken so long.

The night Alex died Angelina postponed her trip to the Dominican Republic. She stepped in and took over when Sam found the tasks at hand more than he could handle. She acted as a liaison between Ingles and Hawthorne and the funeral home in Puerto Vallarta. She took care of the paperwork with the Mexican Government and the American Embassy. She'd even made arrangements for a private jet to speed up the process of getting Alex home.

Sam saw Sarah standing at the door to the restaurant and a proud fatherly smile lit up his face. She was stunningly beautiful in her buttercup yellow sundress. Her skin held a dark radiant tan from the days she'd spent on the beach. Her long, silky dark hair was done up in a French twist. As she walked toward him, he couldn't help but notice how much she resembled the pictures he'd seen of his mother at that age. Sam stood when Sarah reached the table. "You look great." He leaned over and kissed her on the cheek before she sat down. "The dress is very becoming."

"Thanks." Sarah blushed. "Angelina helped me pick it out."

"She's got great taste all right."

"Where is she, by the way?"

"She'll be here in a bit. She had to take care of something in her office." Sam motioned for a waiter and the young man hurried to the table with a bottle of champagne.

"What's this?" Sarah asked.

"We're celebrating."

"Shouldn't we wait for Angelina?"

"When she gets here, we'll order another bottle. This one is for us."

The waiter popped the cork and poured them each a glass. "Will there be anything else, *Señor*?"

"No, *gracias*," Sam smiled. "We're good for now."

Sam raised his glass in the air. "To Sarah, my beautiful daughter. All my life I've wanted a child and I couldn't be happier. I know that I've missed out on your first twenty-five years, but now that we've found each other, we have an opportunity to make up for lost time. Thank you for allowing me to share the rest of my life with you."

Tears filled Sarah's eyes and she picked up her glass. "Thank you, Sam."

"Cheers." When they had each drank, Sam put his glass on the table and smiled at Sarah. "Are you sure I can't convince you to leave Denver and move to Mexico?"

"The offer of being the resort's doctor is very appealing, but let me think about it for a bit."

"I don't mean to sound like a pleading parent," Sam apologized, "but it took me twenty years to find your mother. Now that I've found you, I don't want to let you out of my sight."

Sarah reached across the table for Sam's hand. "I promise you, when I get home, I'll e-mail you everyday." Her face turned crimson. "I always was better at expressing myself on paper. Not like Mom. When there was something on her mind, she just spit it out."

"Hello. I'm sorry I'm late," Angelina apologized as she approached the table. She leaned over and kissed Sam on the cheek, then smiled at Sarah. "Are the two of you enjoying yourselves?"

"Yes," Sam grinned. "Our trip today was great. Would you like a glass of champagne?" He held up the bottle.

Angelina nodded in reply, then sat down and turned her attention to Sarah. "Who was your tour guide today?"

"Pablo."

"*Si*, I know Pablo. He is much fun as a guide. Did you enjoy the barbecue on the beach?"

"Oh, it was fabulous," Sarah beamed. "There was tons of food." She gave Angelina a silly grin. "Your fiancée certainly has an appetite."

"Yes he does! It's a good thing that I don't have to cook for him," Angelina laughed.

For the next two hours, the three enjoyed a fabulous meal and chatted about everything from Sarah's childhood to Sam and Angelina's wedding. Sarah told them about some of the comical things she'd seen in the emergency department and Angelina shared colorful stories of guests who'd stayed at the resort.

When their dessert was finished and they were enjoying a Spanish coffee, Angelina leaned across the table toward Sarah. "I just want you to know that Sam and I feel terrible about your father. Not that he's in jail for what he has done ... he should be in jail, but to have done such a thing to your mother. How could a man do this to his wife? I will just never understand."

"He did it for the money," Sarah quietly answered. "My mother had a lot of it ... he wanted it."

Angelina tilted her head. "Your father, he will be in jail for a long, long time, *si*?"

"*Si*", Sarah replied, "and I hope he's there until the day he dies!"

Sam nervously rubbed his hands together. "Ladies, this conversation is getting depressing. Let's talk about something else, shall we?"

"But Sam, this poor child has no mother and now she has no father. This has to be a very difficult time. I cannot imagine going through such a thing."

Sarah's face turned red. "It's really not as hard as you may think."

That was Sam's cue and he decided there was no time like the present to tell Angelina the truth. He turned to his fiancée and took her hands. "Angelina, remember I told you that I had a surprise for you?"

"Oh, yes," she smiled. "I have been trying to imagine what it is. You told me when we postponed the wedding that you would make it up to me. What did you do," Angelina blushed, "book a beautiful honeymoon in France?"

"Actually, I did make arrangements for us to spend our honeymoon in France, but that's not what I ..."

Angelina's shriek of excitement filled the restaurant and she threw her arms around Sam's neck. "Oh this is wonderful. You're wonderful. I have always wanted to go to France and now I will be in Paris with the man I love." She gave him a devious grin. "Maybe we can start working on our family while we are in Europe?"

Sam unhooked Angelina's arms from around his neck and gently pushed her back into her seat. "Angel," he smiled. "We already have a family." He motioned across the table to Sarah.

"Yes I know. Sarah will be like a family member to us but we will have children of our own some day."

"Angelina, you don't understand. Sarah is our family. She's my daughter."

The color drained from Angelina's face and she was momentarily at a loss for words. "But how is this possible, Sam? Sarah is twenty-five. Until her mother arrived here for a vacation, you hadn't seen each other in years?"

"Do you remember after the cocktail party when Alex first saw me again, I told you that I'd met her when she was in her late teens and then saw her again on my Campbell River fishing trip?"

"Yes."

"Well," Sam hung his head in embarrassment. "What I didn't tell you is that we slept together. When Alex and I were making plans to run off to Bermuda and get married, she never told me she was pregnant." He turned to Sarah. "If I would have known I never would have married Grace."

"But ... what of Brian Williams?" Angelina asked.

"Angelina, Brian is the only father I have ever known. He raised me from the time I was born, but he is not my biological father ... Sam is."

"Alex kept Sarah a secret from everyone, including Brian," Sam explained. "Sarah discovered the truth purely by accident."

"While I was cleaning out my mother's closet, I found a box of letters. They explained everything."

"What kind of letters?" Angelina asked

"For the first six years of my life, including the day I was born, my Mom wrote a letter to my dad telling him of the festivities. I thought it was strange because my dad ... I mean Brian ... had been at every one of my birthday parties. The last letter was dated September 6, 1988. It said my mom had received a phone call from my uncle telling her that my father was dead.

Angelina shook her head in confusion. "I don't understand."

"The phone call Alex received from Michael that day ... was the one he made to tell her I was dead."

Sarah let out a deep sigh. "I was really confused when I read the letter, so I called my uncle. He told me about Sam and the threats his wife had made and why he staged his own death. My uncle was as surprised as I was to discover that Brian wasn't my real father."

"And you know this to be true?"

"Yes, Angelina," Sam answered. "Sarah and I had a paternity test done while we were in New York."

"Does Brian Williams know this news?"

"He does now," Sam answered.

For what seemed an eternity, Angelina sat in silence digesting the information she'd just been given. Slowly, the corners of her mouth curled and her face broke into a beaming smile. "This is wonderful news. You will not have to go through the rest of your life thinking that your father was responsible for your mother's death. You have a father that you can be proud of and a woman, who may not be your real mother, but someone who will always be your friend. Welcome to our family!"

36

WHEN THE LAST OF the guests had gone, Angelina poured another glass of champagne and returned to the terrace. The 2500 square-foot penthouse condo, with its breathtaking view of Puerto Vallarta and the Bay of Banderas, was an early wedding present from Sam. It was his way of apologizing to her for the delay in their nuptials.

Two weeks ago, when he called her from New York and told her they would have to postpone the wedding, Angelina was furious. Tonight, she was glad they'd waited. Sam promised he'd make it up to her and he'd certainly kept his word.

The intimate gathering of twenty ... originally taking place on the beach ... was now taking place in the church of *Lady Guadalupe* in Puerto Vallarta. With Sarah's help, Sam also planned a huge cocktail reception following the service and everyone staying at the resort had been invited to attend.

After the reception, there would be a formal sit-down dinner for wedding guests. The meal would be followed by speeches and pictures and an evening of dancing. Best of all ... at midnight ... a limousine would take the newlyweds to the airport where a private jet would whisk them off to Paris for a two-week honeymoon at the Ritz

Sam flew his mother, and his two sisters and their families in for the occasion. Tomorrow at noon, Michael and Sharon Granger and their daughter, Eleanor, would arrive. Harvey and Jean Ingles would be in at three p.m. and Leslie McPherson was scheduled to land at seven-twenty. Their wedding was turning into a real 'family affair' and Angelina couldn't have been happier.

She'd been nervous about meeting Sam's family, but the 'Bennett Clan' welcomed her with open arms. Yesterday, Sam's mother took her shopping and insisted that she buy Angelina a new dress: "Dear, my son tells me that you were going to be married on the beach and wear something simple. With the wedding now taking place in a church, I insist that you let me by you a formal wedding gown."

Angelina smile remembering the look on Mrs. Bennett's face when she stepped from the change room. There were tears of joy in the old woman's eyes when she said she'd never seen a more beautiful bride.

Tonight, Sam's sisters had thrown her a surprise bridal shower. The giggling group of women drank champagne and ate hors d'oeuvres and Angelina listened to stories of Sam's escapades as a child. She opened gifts of lotions and potions and sexy lingerie.

They played silly games and one of them ... using a needle and thread told her that she would someday be the mother of two. A devious grin curled the corners of her lips. She stopped taking the pill two weeks ago. With any luck, she'd be pregnant by the time she got home from her honeymoon.

Angelina walked to the edge of the terrace and stared out at the lights of Puerto Vallarta. Never in a million years would she have ever imagined that she would someday end up in a place like this ... about to marry Sam Bennett.

She knew she would be a much better wife to Sam then Grace had ever been. She would love him and cherish him and treat him the way he deserved to be treated. In return, he would do the same for her. He would love and cherish her and always protect her. Sam would be her savior. Just as she'd ... been his. It broke Angelina's heart to see how the rude obnoxious woman, with her abusive tongue and scandalous behavior, was destroying Sam's personal and professional life.

In the years Angelina had worked for Sam he'd always been kind to her, but their conversations were rarely of a person nature. It wasn't until after Grace's funeral that Sam opened up. He began to confide in her and they soon became good friends. When Angelina was promoted to assistant manager, she found herself spending sixteen to eighteen hours a day with Sam and as she learned about the man who had kept his private life secret ... she fell in love.

Angelina was sure their business relationship was about to move to a romantic level when Alex Granger arrived at *Las Tropicales*. The night of the cocktail party when Sam told her of his history with this woman, Angelina was afraid she might lose him. The morning she was leaving for the Dominican Republic and Sam announced his and Alex's engagement ... she knew she had.

***

Angelina left the table and hurried back to her room. How could this be happening? How could Sam propose to this woman that he hadn't seen in twenty years? She paced the floor of her apartment. There had to be someway to get Sam away from this woman. Then it hit her and she knew exactly what she had to do.

After seeing Alex hail a cab and leave the property, Angelina called security to find out where she was going. Marcos told her she was going diving. Next, she went to the front desk and took two numbered wristbands from the guest registration folder. From the front desk, she went to the reservations office and changed Alex's identification number in the computer so it would match the wristbands. Before leaving the property, Angelina called Dive Dreams to confirm that Ms. Granger had arrived.

Alex was surprised to see her at first, but when she explained that she'd missed her weekly dive and thought ... perhaps ... Alex would enjoy the company; the woman welcomed her with open arms.

While the ladies were changing into their wetsuits, Angelina noticed the diamond bracelet on Alex's wrist and suggested she take it off. "You don't want to lose that. Why don't you give it to me and I'll have Carlos put it in the safe." Alex willingly turned over the jewelry and they headed out to sea.

***

Eliminating Grace from the picture with tainted cocaine had been a breeze. Getting rid of Alex couldn't have turned out better if Angelina had planned the event months in advance. The corners of her mouth broke into a devious grin and she let out a contented sigh. How ironic it was now that Brian Williams was doing twenty-five to life for his wife's murder. Brian may have rigged Alex's air tank, but he wasn't the cause of her death ... Angelina had taken care of that.

The prostitute had been an added bonus and she'd come along at just the right time. The woman was a bit shorter then Alex, but their facial features were similar and Alex's wetsuit had fit her perfectly. So had the diamond bracelet and the armband from *Las Tropicales*.

Angelina made sure the Mexican coroner didn't perform an autopsy and she knew the prostitute wouldn't be missed. As far as the Granger family was concerned, their dear-departed mother, sister and friend, was six-feet under in the family plot.

At last, Angelina had Sam all to herself ... except for Sarah Granger. Sam had been spending a great deal of time with his new-found daughter since she'd arrived in Mexico, but if Sarah became a problem ... she'd get rid of her too!

THE END

ISBN 1425164133-7